国家级一流本科专业建设配套教材

英语成长小说教程

A COURSEBOOK ON ENGLISH BILDUNGSROMAN

王 卓 主编
李 慧 王秀香 任爱红 副主编

清华大学出版社
北京

内 容 简 介

本书通过对英语世界成长小说的历时梳理、理论阐释和文本解读，将成长小说美学和教育的双重属性融为一体，引领学生历经一场既浪漫又充满挑战的成长之旅。教程以英语成长小说类型为框架，按照经典英语成长小说、女性英语成长小说、族裔英语成长小说、殖民/后殖民英语成长小说四个部分设计，使整部教材覆盖主要英语成长小说史及主要类型。每个部分均设计有精彩导读，一方面梳理出英语成长小说的发展脉络，另一方面提炼出不同类型英语成长小说的美学特点、叙事特点、人物特点等。本书精选23部/篇英语成长小说代表作，聚焦其华彩章节，精心设计启发性问题，引领师生进行文本细读。

本书突出英语文学课程的多样性和多维能力指向，提升学生的文学鉴赏能力、文学批评能力、跨文化交际能力、批判性思维能力和价值判断能力；突出文学的思政育人功能，通过阅读成长小说启迪心智，引领学生思考人生，树立正确的价值观和人生观。

版权所有，侵权必究。举报：010-62782989，beiqinquan@tup.tsinghua.edu.cn。

图书在版编目（CIP）数据

英语成长小说教程/王卓主编.—北京：清华大学出版社，2023.4（2025.1重印）
国家级一流本科专业建设配套教材
ISBN 978-7-302-61996-3

Ⅰ.①英… Ⅱ.①王… Ⅲ.①英语文学–小说研究–世界–高等学校–教材
Ⅳ.①I106.4

中国版本图书馆 CIP 数据核字（2022）第 184088 号

责任编辑：曹诗悦
封面设计：李尘工作室
责任校对：王凤芝
责任印制：丛怀宇

出版发行：清华大学出版社
网　　址：https://www.tup.com.cn, https://www.wqxuetang.com
地　　址：北京清华大学学研大厦A座　　邮　编：100084
社 总 机：010-83470000　　邮　购：010-62786544
投稿与读者服务：010-62776969, c-service@tup.tsinghua.edu.cn
质 量 反 馈：010-62772015, zhiliang@tup.tsinghua.edu.cn

印 装 者：天津鑫丰华印务有限公司
经　　销：全国新华书店
开　　本：185mm×260mm　　印　张：20.75　　字　数：447千字
版　　次：2023年4月第1版　　印　次：2025年1月第2次印刷
定　　价：88.00元

产品编号：096170-01

前 言
PREFACE

教材定位

《英语成长小说教程》是一部为我国高校英语专业本科生、研究生以及英语文学爱好者编写的教材。这部教材对英语成长小说进行了历时梳理、理论阐释和文本解读，充分发挥成长小说独特的审美和教育的双重功能，集思想性、文学性、教育性、时代性于一体，以满足学生语言学习、文学品读、人格成熟、思想升华的多维发展需求。

《英语成长小说教程》以服务我国高等教育全面提高人才培养质量，促进人的全面发展和社会全面进步为宗旨，符合新时代我国高等教育价值引领和课程思政要求。教材聚焦青少年成长和教育问题，使得学生能够在文学和语言学习过程中体验人生、陶冶情操。此外，该教材也符合新时代我国英语专业人文性的专业属性定位。《普通高等学校本科专业类教学质量国家标准（外国语言文学类）》明确指出，英语专业是人文性专业，而英语专业回归人文性对高等学校文学类课程的设置提出了更高的要求。文学类课程要开满、开足、开出特色，让学生直接与原典对话，汲取英语作品中最有营养的精华，同时培养学生的跨文化交际和思辨能力。与通常意义上的英语成长小说教材不同，这部教材打破了以英美经典成长小说为主导的模式，融入了族裔英语成长小说、女性英语成长小说和殖民/后殖民英语成长小说，并以中国学者的视角对英语成长小说进行了全新导读。

教材理念

- 突出英语文学课程的多样性和多维能力指向，提升学生的文学鉴赏能力、文学

批评能力、跨文化交际能力、批判性思维能力和价值判断能力。

• 突出基于文学文本阅读和研读的文学教学，以文本为依托推进学生在文学知识、文学理论、文学鉴赏与批评等方面的学习和能力提升。

• 突出文学的思政育人功能，通过阅读成长小说启迪心智，让学生思考人生，树立正确的价值观和人生观。

教材特色

⊙ 选材丰富，经典性与时代性相结合

教材中成长小说作品的选择体现了以下四个原则：（1）经典性原则，首选广为认可的、兼具思想性和文学性的优秀文学作品；（2）代表性原则，作品能够反映一个作家的基本特征、一个时期的文学面貌，能够体现文学观念、样式、风格、艺术的变迁，能够代表文学史的关键节点；（3）可读性原则，所选作品语言优美，人物丰满，故事情节吸引人、感动人；（4）时代性原则，所选作品既有18世纪、19世纪的经典成长小说，也有当代的成长小说，体现人物成长的时代性特点，更为贴近学生的现实生活。

⊙ 精彩导读，文学史与文本阅读相结合

教材以英语成长小说类型为框架，按照经典英语成长小说、女性英语成长小说、族裔英语成长小说、殖民/后殖民英语成长小说四个部分设计，使整部教材覆盖主要英语成长小说史及其主要类型。每个部分均设计有精彩导读，一方面梳理出英语成长小说的发展脉络，另一方面提炼出不同类型英语成长小说的美学特点、叙事特点、人物特点等。教材精心遴选23部/篇英语成长小说代表作，聚焦其华彩章节，并精心设计启发性问题，引领师生进行文本细读和深入思考。

⊙ 问题导向，推动探究性文学学习

教材以文学作品选读为基本形式，围绕作家作品设计有关成长小说文学史、文学知识、文学批评理论与方法、文学批评实践的相关问题，以作品为基础，以问题为导向，引导学生通过探究学习和合作学习获取文学知识，提升文学鉴赏水平，培养文学批评能力，促进综合能力发展。

⊙ 线上线下，促进智慧学习

教材编写采用"纸质教材+线上教学视频+视听资源数据库"的融合模式。教材配有在线共享课，线上教学资源丰富；纸质教材与在线课程高度呼应，方便学生在线学习。视听资源数据库中主要包括作家信息、文学史、文学知识、与文学作品相关的拓展性知

识等，学生可以通过扫描教材中的二维码获取。

教材内容

本教材共四个部分，即经典英语成长小说、女性英语成长小说、族裔英语成长小说、殖民/后殖民英语成长小说，共 23 讲。每部分均包含导言和拓展性阅读；每讲按照作家小传、预习问题、文本阅读、文本认知、批判性阅读、学术阅读与写作、拓展活动等环节设计。教师可根据本校课时安排以及不同授课对象等具体情况，从教材提供的 23 讲中选择精讲内容，并依托线上教学资源，采用翻转课堂的方式，更为高效地使用本教材。

编写团队

本教材由山东省教学名师王卓教授带领的团队编写。该团队曾获省级课程思政示范课教学团队、校级优秀教学团队称号，团队主讲的"成长小说"是山东省在线共享课程。全书的设计、选篇，以及序言"作为教育媒介的成长小说"及各讲的导言由王卓负责。第一部分"经典英语成长小说"由李慧编写，第二部分"女性英语成长小说"由任爱红编写，第三部分"族裔英语成长小说"由王秀香编写，第四部分"殖民/后殖民英语成长小说"由王卓编写。此外，何亦可、宋婉宜、郭丹阳也承担了部分编写工作。

鉴于本教材为全新编写，难免有不足之处，欢迎专家、教师和同学在审读和使用的过程中提出宝贵意见，以使教材不断完善。

王 卓

2022 年 7 月

目 录
CONTENTS

序 言 作为教育媒介的成长小说 / XIII

01 第一部分
经典英语成长小说（Classic English Bildungsroman）

导 言 / 2

Lecture 1   Charles Dickens / 11

Profile of the Writer / 11

 I Preview Questions / 12
 II Literary Reading: *Great Expectations* (Chapter 1) / 12
 III Thinking, Talking and Writing About Literature / 16
 IV Further Activity / 18

Lecture 2   James Joyce / 19

Profile of the Writer / 19

 I Preview Questions / 20
 II Literary Reading: *A Portrait of the Artist as a Young Man* (Chapter 2) / 20
 III Thinking, Talking and Writing About Literature / 24
 IV Further Activity / 26

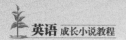

Lecture 3   Mark Twain / 27

Profile of the Writer / 27
- I   Preview Questions / 28
- II   Literary Reading: *The Adventures of Huckleberry Finn* (Chapter 1) / 28
- III Thinking, Talking and Writing About Literature / 31
- IV   Further Activity / 33

Lecture 4   Stephen Crane / 34

Profile of the Writer / 34
- I   Preview Questions / 35
- II   Literary Reading: *The Red Badge of Courage* (Chapter 3) / 36
- III Thinking, Talking and Writing About Literature / 42
- IV   Further Activity / 44

Lecture 5   Sherwood Anderson / 45

Profile of the Writer / 45
- I   Preview Questions / 46
- II   Literary Reading: The Egg / 46
- III Thinking, Talking and Writing About Literature / 54
- IV   Further Activity / 57

Lecture 6   William Golding / 58

Profile of the Writer / 58
- I   Preview Questions / 59
- II   Literary Reading: *Lord of the Flies* (Chapter 7) / 60
- III Thinking, Talking and Writing About Literature / 72
- IV   Further Activity / 74

02 第二部分
女性英语成长小说（Female English Bildungsroman）

导　言 / 76

- **Lecture 7　Jane Austen / 86**

  Profile of the Writer / 86
  - I　Preview Questions / 87
  - II　Literary Reading: *Pride and Prejudice* (Chapter 36) / 87
  - III　Thinking, Talking and Writing About Literature / 91
  - IV　Further Activity / 93

- **Lecture 8　Charlotte Brontë / 94**

  Profile of the Writer / 94
  - I　Preview Questions / 96
  - II　Literary Reading: *Jane Eyre* (Chapter 1) / 96
  - III　Thinking, Talking and Writing About Literature / 100
  - IV　Further Activity / 103

- **Lecture 9　George Eliot / 104**

  Profile of the Writer / 104
  - I　Preview Questions / 105
  - II　Literary Reading: *The Mill on the Floss* (Chapter 11) / 106
  - III　Thinking, Talking and Writing About Literature / 115
  - IV　Further Activity / 117

- **Lecture 10　Kate Chopin / 118**

  Profile of the Writer / 118
  - I　Preview Questions / 119
  - II　Literary Reading: *The Awakening* (Chapter 1) / 119
  - III　Thinking, Talking and Writing About Literature / 121
  - IV　Further Activity / 123

Lecture 11　Virginia Woolf / 124

Profile of the Writer / 124
- I　Preview Questions / 125
- II　Literary Reading: *Mrs. Dalloway* (Chapter 1) / 126
- III　Thinking, Talking and Writing About Literature / 133
- IV　Further Activity / 135

Lecture 12　Sylvia Plath / 136

Profile of the Writer / 136
- I　Preview Questions / 137
- II　Literary Reading: *The Bell Jar* (Chapter 1) / 137
- III　Thinking, Talking and Writing About Literature / 145
- IV　Further Activity / 147

03 / 第三部分
族裔英语成长小说（Ethnic English Bildungsroman）

导　言 / 150

Lecture 13　Ralph Ellison / 164

Profile of the Writer / 164
- I　Preview Questions / 165
- II　Literary Reading: *Invisible Man* (Chapter 1) / 166
- III　Thinking, Talking and Writing About Literature / 178
- IV　Further Activity / 179

Lecture 14　Zora Neale Hurston / 180

Profile of the Writer / 180
- I　Preview Questions / 181

  II Literary Reading: *Their Eyes Were Watching God* (Chapter 1) / 182

  III Thinking, Talking and Writing About Literature / 187

  IV Further Activity / 188

Lecture 15 Maya Angelou / 189

Profile of the Writer / 189

  I Preview Questions / 190

  II Literary Reading: *I Know Why the Caged Bird Sings* (Chapter 4) / 190

  III Thinking, Talking and Writing About Literature / 194

  IV Further Activity / 196

Lecture 16 Paule Marshall / 197

Profile of the Writer / 197

  I Preview Questions / 198

  II Literary Reading: *Brown Girl, Brownstones* (Chapter 1) / 198

  III Thinking, Talking and Writing About Literature / 208

  IV Further Activity / 210

Lecture 17 Toni Morrison / 211

Profile of the Writer / 211

  I Preview Questions / 212

  II Literary Reading: *The Bluest Eye* (Chapter11) / 212

  III Thinking, Talking and Writing About Literature / 223

  IV Further Activity / 224

Lecture 18 Sandra Cisneros / 225

Profile of the Writer / 225

  I Preview Questions / 226

  II Literary Reading: *The House on Mango Street* / 226

  III Thinking, Talking and Writing About Literature / 228
  IV Further Activity / 230

04 第四部分
殖民 / 后殖民英语成长小说（Colonial/Postcolonial English Bildungsroman）

导　言 / 232

- **Lecture 19 Olive Schreiner / 242**

  Profile of the Writer / 242
   I Preview Questions / 243
   II Literary Reading: *The Story of an African Farm* (Chapter 1) / 243
   III Thinking, Talking and Writing About Literature / 249
   IV Further Activity / 251

- **Lecture 20 Chinua Achebe / 252**

  Profile of the Writer / 252
   I Preview Questions / 253
   II Literary Reading: *Things Fall Apart* (Chapter 1) / 253
   III Thinking, Talking and Writing About Literature / 256
   IV Further Activity / 259

- **Lecture 21 Abdulrazak Gurnah / 260**

  Profile of the Writer / 260
   I Preview Questions / 261
   II Literary Reading: *Paradise* (Chapter 6) / 261
   III Thinking, Talking and Writing About Literature / 275
   IV Further Activity / 276

Lecture 22　Chimamanda Ngozi Adichie / 277

Profile of the Writer / 277
- I　Preview Questions / 278
- II　Literary Reading: *Half of a Yellow Sun* (Chapter 1) / 278
- III　Thinking, Talking and Writing About Literature / 297
- IV　Further Activity / 299

Lecture 23　Chigozie Obioma / 300

Profile of the Writer / 300
- I　Preview Questions / 301
- II　Literary Reading: *The Fishermen* (Chapter 1) / 301
- III　Thinking, Talking and Writing About Literature / 308
- IV　Further Activity / 310

序 言
作为教育媒介的成长小说

成长小说是一种独特的小说类型，有其特定的人物类型、叙述模式和语言风格。从18世纪歌德（Johann Wolfgang von Goethe，1749—1832）的《威廉·迈斯特的学习时代》（*Wilhelm Meister's Apprenticeship*）开始，成长小说经历了漫长的发展过程，其内涵和外延也随着时代的发展变得越来越丰富。成长问题是一个严肃的社会问题，然而当这一问题"成长"为一个文学主题的时候，却在作家的笔下幻化出各种风格迥异、变幻莫测的文学佳作，成长的模式也在这些作品的勾画下成为或痛苦，或浪漫，或曲折，或滑稽的人生之旅。在一次次富有戏剧性的冲突中，在人性的弱点被层层揭露的过程中，文学作品中的人物也以各自的方式完成了自我的成长。

作为能够成功地构建人性自我发展的小说文类，成长小说在文学史上占据着十分重要的地位，在世界文学的版图中，成长小说的发展一直悄然改变着整个文学发展的轨迹和格局。从某种程度上说，成长小说的发展过程也同时是小说的发展过程，更是小说研究视野的拓展过程。在英语文学史上，成长小说跨越了从18世纪到21世纪的漫长发展过程，成为一种成熟的文学类型，形成了完善的创作模式，具有特定的小说叙述结构、人物原型、叙事特征以及独特的文化审美视角。在西方悠久的文学史链条中，成长小说往往是其中起着承接作用的关键环节。事实上，我们所熟悉的很多英语小说，比如《大卫·科波菲尔》（*David Copperfield*）、《简·爱》（*Jane Eyre*）、《哈克贝利·芬历险记》（*The Adventures of Huckleberry Finn*）等都是经典的成长小说。几乎每一个历史时期都会随着时代的律动涌现出成长小说的经典作品，更为重要的是，这些作品不但反映人性的自我成长，也往往是那个时代成长的历史见证。成长小说不仅具有独特的美学特点，还有独特的人格教育功能。在不同时代的成长小说塑造的青少年形象以及他们的成长故事中，

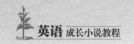

尽管主人公已然长大成人，但由于特殊的境遇而经历的心理或精神的顿悟，都为一代又一代读者提供了可资借鉴的成长模式、可以体味的人生经历和可以感受的精神力量。

莎拉·格雷厄姆（Sarah Graham）在其编著的《成长小说史》(A History of the Bildungsroman)"序言"中曾言，任何读小说的人最终都会遇到一部成长小说——一种关于青年人面对挑战的成长的小说，"因为它是文学史上最流行、最永恒的文类"[1]。成长小说也被称为教育小说或者教育成长小说，其主要原因在于成长小说具有独特的多维教育功能，包括情感教育、人生观教育、价值观教育、审美教育等，这些均蕴含在成长小说所描写的青少年成长历程之中。尼日利亚女作家奇昆耶·奥贡耶米（Chikwenye O. Ogunyemi）因此说，成长小说在讲述他人的教育故事时也起到了教育的功能，"因此，一个有趣的现象是，主人公和读者都从此教育中受益"[2]。从这一意义上来说，成长小说在形塑人的精神、素养、情操等方面具有其他类型的文学作品所不具备的重要价值。

西方成长小说在中国拥有大量读者，中国学界对其研究开展得也很充分。毫不夸张地说，很多中国读者的启蒙外国文学读物就是成长小说。西方成长小说进入中国的历史已逾百年。一般认为，1903年包天笑从日文转译的《三千里寻亲记》是最早译介到中国的国外成长小说，但如果把西方来华传教士的译介活动考虑在内的话，成长小说进入中国的时间至少还要提前50年。歌德的《威廉·迈斯特的学习时代》、托马斯·曼（Thomas Mann，1875—1955）的《魔山》(The Magic Mountain)、狄更斯（Charles Dickens，1812—1870）的《远大前程》(Great Expectations)和《大卫·科波菲尔》、奥斯丁（Jane Austen，1775—1817）的《傲慢与偏见》(Pride and Prejudice)、艾略特（George Eliot，1819—1880）的《弗洛斯河上的磨坊》(The Mill on the Floss)、夏洛蒂·勃朗特（Charlotte Brontë，1816—1855）的《简·爱》、乔伊斯（James Joyce，1882—1941）的《一个青年艺术家的肖像》(A Portrait of the Artist as a Young Man)、马克·吐温（Mark Twain，1835—1910）的《哈克贝利·芬历险记》、塞林格（J. D. Salinger，1919—2010）的《麦田里的守望者》(The Catcher in the Rye)等欧美经典成长小说陪伴了很多中国读者走过生命中最宝贵的青葱岁月，而中国读者对其喜爱的程度不亚于我们自己的文学。

欧美成长小说不仅成为广大中国读者的阅读文本，也走进中国的教育体系，成为教材或者推荐学生阅读的素材。还以狄更斯和他的成长小说为例。著名作家、翻译家谢六

---

[1] Graham, Sarah. "Introduction." *A History of the Bildungsroman*. New York: Cambridge University Press, 2019. 1.
[2] Ogunyemi, Chikwenye O. "Ralph Ellison's *Invisible Man* as a Novel of Growth." *Nigerian Journal of the Humanities* 4 (1980): 15.

逸[1]曾指出，狄更斯的作品在中国的学校很早就被当作文学读物和教材。商务印书馆1905年推出的《帝国英语读本》就收录了根据狄更斯作品改编的阅读文本，1910—1911年商务印书馆推出了"英文文学丛书"，1918年又推出了《英语模范短篇小说》和《英语模范读本》，这些选读都收录了根据狄更斯小说改编的故事。中华人民共和国成立以后，狄更斯的作品更是进入大学中文系、外文系的英美文学教材中，也走进了中学的语文教材。这些欧美成长小说对中国读者起到了知识拓展、跨文化交流、教育和启蒙的作用，其积极意义不可小觑。

成长小说具有"成长维度"和"教育维度"高度融合的特点。这种文学形式通常试图教会读者理解他们当下和过去的情感、成长和归属的过程；在传统意义上的经典成长小说中，教会读者成为"公民"的模式是小说文本的主要内核。成长小说中独特的教育、教诲目的以及蕴含其中的价值观传递和人格塑造功能，在任何其他类型的文学作品中都不具备或者难以凸显。成长小说的人格塑形功能可以从该词的构成清楚地显现出来。"Bildungsroman"中的"Bildung"一词从构词法的角度来看，"Bild"是"形象、图像"，既有"VorBild"，也就是"范本"之意，又有"NachBild"，也就是"摹本"之意。[2] 总体而言，这一词的含义就是按照范本进行摹写，按照某种既定的理想进行教化或陶冶，是主体主动地认识自己、塑造自己的过程。

成长小说还带有强大的社会文化塑形功能。成长小说在线性或者非线性地记录下主人公与自己的社会价值取得认同的过程中，还承担着与主人公成长其间的社会秩序和社会价值协商的使命。成长小说不仅涉及主人公的身体成长和情感成长，还深刻地触及自我与社会之间的协商、互动关系。正如阿莫科（Apollo Amoko）所言，成长小说聚焦于年轻的主人公在一个不确定的世界中的塑形，因此成长小说中的个人成长往往也是国族重构的隐喻，涉及个人成长与社会转型、现代化进程等复杂的互动关系。[3] 就像成长小说研究专家莫雷蒂（Franco Moretti）所言，成长小说"不仅在小说史中，而且在我们整个文化遗产中"都是至关重要的，因为随着我们阅读这些小说，它们"描写并重构了与社会整体的关系"。[4]

---

1 谢六逸，《西洋小说发达史》，《小说月报》，1922年第6期，第63-70页。
2 加达默尔，《真理与方法》，洪汉鼎译。上海：上海译文出版社，1999年，第22-25页。
3 Amoko, Apollo. "Autobiography and Bildungsroman in African Literature." *The Cambridge Companion to the African Novel*. Ed. Abiola Irele. Cambridge: Cambridge University Press, 2009. 200.
4 Moretti, Franco. *The Way of the World: The Bildungsroman in European Culture*. London & New York: Verso, 1987. 23.

成长小说的读者群体既有青少年，也有成年人。事实上，无论是狄更斯的《远大前程》还是塞林格的《麦田里的守望者》，抑或是戈尔丁（William Golding, 1911—1993）的《蝇王》（*Lord of the Flies*），都是很多成年读者的保留阅读书目。究其原因，成长小说的"大致轮廓"往往都涉及从童年到成年的转化，而叙事也往往是在童年和成年的双重视角下展开的。比如在狄更斯的《大卫·科波菲尔》《远大前程》、福楼拜（Gustave Flaubert, 1821—1880）的《情感教育》（*Sentimental Education*）中，主人公大卫（David）、皮普（Pip）、弗雷德里克（Frederic）都在成长过程中获得了某种社会角色：大卫成为令人尊重的作家和记者，皮普成了伦敦的绅士，弗雷德里克最后成为中产阶级中的一员。这种从少年到成年的转化过程对青少年和成年人均具有启发性，因此成长小说拥有庞大的阅读群体。

众所周知，关于成长小说的名称一直还没有出现一个统一而权威的声音，这是令许多成长小说研究者头痛的事情；然而从另一个角度考虑，这种现象却恰恰说明成长小说内涵的丰富性和审美的宽泛性，以及文类的可融性。这对成长小说来说实际上是一件幸事。

在成长小说的发源地德国，成长小说的命名就有数种，其中常见的有"Bildungsroman""Entwicklungsroman""Erziebungsroman""Kunstlerroman"等。冯至先生在《威廉·迈斯特的学习时代》的"译者序"中采用了"Bildungsroman"一词，因为他认为这一词强调的是小说中人物个性和人格的"内在塑造"，这一理解与中国人对成长的理解比较贴近。"Entwicklungsroman"的内涵比"Bildungsroman"更为宽泛，强调的是人物的"全面成长"；"Erziebungsroman"强调的是人物因受正规教育而得到的心智的发展，而"Kunstlerroman"强调的是"Kunstler"（艺术家）的成长。[1] 然而，不论这些命名强调的侧重点有何不同，关注人物身心成长历程的核心从来没有偏离过。

与德语中的四个基于对成长小说的不同侧重而出现的不同命名既相互呼应又有所发展，英美文学中的成长小说的命名也是五花八门，常见的有"Initiation story""Novel of initiation""Growing-up novel""Coming-of-age novel""Novel of adolescence"等。不过，"Bildungsroman"在英语中也已经成为一个专有名词而被文学研究界广泛使用。

除了命名，对于成长小说的界定也存在着各种表述上的差异和侧重点的不同。在文学研究领域，为数不少的评论家都曾经尝试对成长小说进行界定，其中比较权威的有巴赫金（M. M. Bakhtin）、莫迪凯·马科斯（Mordecai Marcus）、杰罗姆·巴克利（Jerome

---

[1] 关于德国成长小说的传统，详见芮渝萍，《美国成长小说研究》。北京：中国社会科学出版社，2004年，第39-47页。

Hamilton Buckley)、玛瑞安·赫什（Marianne Hirsch）等人的论述。巴赫金曾专门对教育小说进行过研究，并撰写了《教育小说及其在现实主义历史中的意义》一文，对成长小说的教育功能、人物类型和人物形象进行了界定：

> 大部分小说只掌握定型的主人公形象。除了这一占统治地位的、数量众多的小说类型外，还存在着另一种鲜为人知的小说类型，它塑造的是成长小说中的人物形象。这里，主人公的形象不是静态的统一体，而是动态的统一体。主人公本身的性格在这一小说的公式中成了变数，主人公本身的变化具有了情节意义。与此相关，小说的情节也从根本上得到了再认识，再构建，时间进入了人的内部，进入了人物形象本身，极大地改变了人物命运及生活中一切因素所具有的意义。这一小说类型从最普遍含义上说，可称为人的成长小说。[1]

从巴赫金的成长小说定义可以看出，他关注的是成长小说中人物成长的动态变化模式，以及这一模式赋予小说叙事的动态力量。换言之，他强调的是成长小说中人物从懵懂的状态进入成熟状态的动态过程。

莫迪凯·马科斯在《什么是成长小说》（"What Is an Initiation Story?"）一文中，对成长小说进行了全面的研究和界定，他认为：

> 成长小说展示的是年轻主人公经历了切肤之痛的事件后，或改变了原有的世界观，或改变了自己的性格，或两者兼而有之；这种改变使他摆脱了童年的天真，并最终把他引向了一个真实而复杂的成人世界。在成长小说中，仪式本身可有可无，但必须有证据表明这种变化对主人公会产生永久的影响。[2]

马科斯的定义比巴赫金的要宽泛一些，对叙事与人物的关系逐渐淡化，但马科斯有一点与巴赫金别无二致，那就是，他同样强调了人物的转变过程。马科斯对成长小说的贡献还在于他对这一小说文类所做的分类研究。他根据主人公的心理和行为的转变度，

---

[1] 巴赫金，《小说理论》，钱中文主编。石家庄：河北教育出版社，1998年，第230页。
[2] Marcus, Mordecai. "What Is an Initiation Story?" *The Young Man in American Literature: The Initiation Theme*. Ed. William Coyle. New York: The Odyssey Press, 1969. 32. 译文参阅了芮渝萍，《美国成长小说研究》。北京：中国社会科学出版社，2004年，第6页。略有改动。

把成长小说分为两个层次:第一个层次是主人公获得了性的体验,而这一新鲜的体验带来的对自我的重新认识引领他进入成熟之门;第二个层次是主人公在对人生的顿悟和自我的觉醒之后而迈出了人生中至关重要的一步。

玛瑞安·赫什在《作为文类的成长小说》("*The Novel of Formation as Genre: Between Great Expectations and Lost Illusions*")一文中,把成长小说定义为"在一个特定的社会秩序的环境中独立的个体的成长和发展的故事"。在这个较宽泛的定义的基础之上,他确立了成长小说的三个特点:其一,为了让角色开始他们的旅程,"某种形式的迷失或者不满一定要在早期阶段使他们与他们的家庭环境格格不入";其二,成长的过程是漫长的、艰辛的、渐进的,由主人公的需求和欲望与坚持目标的社会秩序强加的观念和判断之间的不断冲突所构成;其三,"社会秩序的精神和价值在主人公身上显现出来,于是主人公被接纳到社会当中"。[1] 赫什所界定的成长小说似乎更关注人物与社会之间的互动关系,并以主人公本人对自己在社会中的新位置的评价和认同作为判断人物成长的终极标准。

成长小说经历了从特定的18世纪晚期和19世纪早期的德国现象,到包括欧洲其他国家相似题材的演化,再到包括女性作家和少数族裔作家的作品的漫长演化过程。在长达三个多世纪的历史流变中,作为亚文类的成长小说显示出不同寻常的"适应性"和"多元性"。传统意义上的成长小说被视为青年白人,尤其是欧洲白人男性的小说。对于该亚文类的起源有两种比较典型的观点。一种观点是成长小说的唯一源头是德国特定时期的小说作品。秉持此观点的学者认为,歌德的多卷本小说《威廉·迈斯特的学习时代》是成长小说的典型例子和"原文本"(urtext)[2],是成长小说"原型"(prototype)[3]。另一种观点认为,在德国之外也有一个强大的成长小说传统。秉持此观点的学者们纷纷在法国小说、英国小说、俄国小说中探源成长小说的缘起。此两种观点在特定的语境下均有其道理。但无论其起源如何,毫无疑问,在历代小说家的不断创造中,成长小说已经拥有了枝繁叶茂的"成长小说家族树"[4],并由此产生了各种"变体"。成长小说的这种极强的适应性使得该文类不断发展壮大。

---

1 Hirsch, Marianne. "The Novel of Formation as Genre: Between *Great Expectations* and *Lost Illusions*." *Genre* 12.3 (1979): 294–295.

2 Graham, Sarah. "Introduction." *A History of the Bildungsroman*. New York: Cambridge University Press, 2019. 2.

3 Jost, François. "Variations of a Species: The Bildungsroman." *Symposium: A Quarterly Journal in Modern Literatures* 37.2 (1983): 125.

4 Jost, François. "Variations of a Species: The Bildungsroman." *Symposium: A Quarterly Journal in Modern Literatures* 37.2 (1983): 144.

可以说，成长小说这一文类本身随着时代发展和作者群体的变化而不断成长。阿贝尔（Elizabeth Abel）、玛丽安·赫希（Marianne Hirsch）、伊丽莎白·朗兰（Elizabeth Langland）等人高度概括了成长小说不断随着时代发展的变化轨迹：

> 拓展文类的观念已经成为成长小说批评的一个传统：首先超越德国的原型，然后超越历史范畴，现在超越成长作为男性的观念，并超越发展情节作为线性的、前景化的叙事结构的形式。这种重新阐释，通过把一种普遍认识的历史和理论文类转化为一种更为灵活的、其合法性依赖于其作为认知工具的有用性的类型，参与到一种批评传统之中。[1]

20世纪八九十年代女权主义、后殖民和少数族裔研究的兴起更是拓展了传统成长小说的定义。21世纪的成长小说研究的焦点已经转向少数族裔成长小说和后殖民成长小说。因此，本书不仅涉及传统意义上的经典成长小说，也遴选了优秀的女性成长小说，英美黑人作家、美国印第安作家等族裔作家的成长小说，以及后殖民视域下的非洲英语成长小说，以期完整地呈现出英语成长小说的全貌及其嬗变轨迹。

拓展阅读文献

Abel, Elizabeth, Hirsch, Marianne, and Langland, Elizabeth. *The Voyage In: Fictions of Female Development*. Hanover & London: University Press of New England, 1983.

Graham, Sarah. *A History of the Bildungsroman*. New York: Cambridge University Press, 2019.

Howe, Susanne. *Wilhelm Meister and His English Kinsmen: Apprentices to Life*. New York: Columbia University Press, 1930.

Song, Mingwei. *Young China: National Rejuvenation and the Bildungsroman, 1900—1959*. New York: Harvard University Asia Center, 2016.

孙胜忠，《西方成长小说史》。北京：商务印书馆，2020年。

王卓、任爱红、李慧，《成长小说》在线课程。智慧树平台。

---

[1] Abel, Elizabeth, Hirsch, Marianne, and Langland, Elizabeth. *The Voyage In: Fictions of Female Development*. Hanover & London: University Press of New England, 1983. 13–14.

01

第一部分
经典英语成长小说

Classic English
Bildungsroman

导 言

经典英语成长小说的主人公通常为中产阶级白人男性，其中的经典情节线索均聚焦于一位野心勃勃的男性主人公，他"在乡村的贫寒家庭成长，但被灌输了一种冒险精神，离开家寻找自己的命运，并实现他的雄心"[1]。成长小说研究专家杰罗姆·巴克利（Jerome Buckley）在《青春季节》（*Season of Youth*）中为"典型的（维多利亚时期）成长小说情节"提供了一种"大致轮廓"：一个敏感孩子在乡村或者偏远小城成长，在那里他发现社会和情感的藩篱限制了他的自由想象。他的家庭，尤其是他的父亲，对他的创造性的本能、想象和雄心十分反感，甚至憎恨，因此，他在青葱岁月就离开了那个压抑的家庭环境，去城市寻找独立的发展之路。在那里他的真正的"教育"开始了：他至少经历了两次恋情或者性行为，见证人情世故，学会生存本领，为未来的职业生涯做好准备，并开始重新评价自己的价值，于是他摆脱了幼稚的青春岁月，进入到成熟期。他的成长完成了，重回故园，展示自己的成功或者他的选择的明智[2]。此种情节框架在狄更斯的《大卫·科波菲尔》《远大前程》等经典英语成长小说中都清晰地呈现出来。可见，传统成长小说中主人公旅程的终点是与自我和社会达成和解，求得人生的和谐。传统的成长小说在线性地记录下主人公与自己的社会价值取得认同的过程中，充当着一种与可接受的社会秩序和价值求得一致的方案。

英国成长小说

在英国经典成长小说中，向社会上层流动是主人公成长的主要动因，也是成长的归

---

1 Al-Mousa, Nadal M. "The Arabic Bildungsroman: A Generic Appraisal." *International Journal of Middle East Studies* 25.2 (1993): 223.

2 Buckley, Jerome. *Season of Youth: The Bildungsroman from Dickens to Golding.* Cambridge: Harvard University Press, 1974. 17–18.

宿，带有明显的功利主义目的。英国经典成长小说大多反映的是资产阶级的人文主义观念，在新兴中产阶级中寻找到最为适合的生长土壤。帕特丽夏·奥尔登（Patricia Alden）在对英国成长小说中的社会流动性的专门研究中，有过这样的论述：

> 从一开始，英国小说就是新兴中产阶级的宠儿，他们回到如何使用这种形式更好地表达个体经验，并因此赋予其价值。日常事务，以及结婚、生子、死亡、遗产继承等人生大事，尤其是普通人得以规划自己人生轨迹的社会流动这种新体验，都成了小说的素材。关于普通男女价值的新思想以及社会流动的合法性于是就找到了一种文学表达方式——没有什么比成长小说更合适的了。[1]

这种对社会阶级跃层和对以财富积累为目的的个人价值实现的追求贯穿于整个英国经典成长小说发展历程之中。可以说，英国文学从18世纪的《鲁滨孙漂流记》（*Robinson Crusoe*）开始，就策动了一场男性漫长的自我成长的探求行动。《鲁滨孙漂流记》的作者丹尼尔·笛福（Daniel Defoe，1660—1731）曾明确提出把小说的创作对象确定为个体的人所经历的具体事件上，从而"让个体经验成为备受关注的焦点"[2]。《鲁滨孙漂流记》正是这样一场个体经验的体验和个人历练的成长之旅。继笛福之后，另一位伟大的现实主义作家亨利·菲尔丁（Henry Fielding，1707—1754）也厚描了一个"个体经验"的体验和成长过程。他的鸿篇巨制《汤姆·琼斯》（*The History of Tom Jones, A Foundling*）在主人公汤姆·琼斯的经历和人生体验中，为"读者上了一堂人生教育课"[3]。弃儿琼斯不受欢迎的出生，到被逐出养父沃尔华绥（Allworthy）的天堂府，他精神迷茫，道德沉降，到最后获得身份，悔过自新，重返家园，这一历程构建起了经典的男性成长的模式雏形。

英国19世纪探索男性成长问题的最重要的作家当数狄更斯。他的三部代表作——《雾都孤儿》（*Oliver Twist*）、《大卫·科波菲尔》和《远大前程》同时也是成长小说研究中公认的经典作品。这三部小说体现了传统成长小说的几乎全部内涵和模式。主人公均为出身卑贱的下层社会的孤儿或是苦儿，他们的成长充满了艰辛和磨难，在一次次偶然和必然的机缘下，他们经历了身心的震撼和顿悟，终究寻求到自我价值和社会位置。贯穿于

---

[1] Alden, Patricia. *Social Mobility in the English Bildungsroman: Gissing, Hardy, Bennett, and Lawrence.* Ann Arbor: UMI Research Press, 1986.
[2] 殷企平等，《英国小说批评史》。上海：上海外语教育出版社，2001年，第18页。
[3] 李赋宁，《菲尔丁》，《中国大百科全书·外国文学》。北京：中国大百科全书出版社，1982年，第303页。

男性主人公成长过程中的往往还有对于自身身世之谜的寻求和破解，这更使得他们的成长充满了家族传承的使命感。

20世纪上半期，英国文学中成长小说的代表作品是乔伊斯的《一个青年艺术家的肖像》。这部篇幅不长的小说的写作历时十年之久，可以说写作过程本身就是一个成长的过程。有评论家认为"在本世纪追溯年轻人内心历程的'成长小说'之中，《一个青年艺术家的肖像》可以说是最有深度的一部"[1]。这部小说细腻地刻画了主人公斯蒂芬·迪达勒斯（Stephan Dedalus）在性格形成和心智发展过程中所经历的不同阶段，展现了在维多利亚时代后期和爱德华时代初期的时代背景下，斯蒂芬如何克服了来自家庭、社会和教会的压力，最终在艺术的天地中寻找到了心灵的安居地。乔伊斯对成长小说最大的贡献在于他引入了成长中的"顿悟"观念。乔伊斯对"顿悟"曾经有过明确的论述：

> 首先我们认识到有关物体是一个整体，然后我们认识到它是一个有组织、有结构的复合体……最后，当各个部分之间的关系达到微妙的程度——各个部分都和某个特殊的点发生了联系时，我们认识到了它的实质。它的灵魂、它的本性冲破了它的外衣，跳入了我们的眼帘。当其结构如此调整之后，最普遍的物体的灵魂似乎在向我们灵光四射。此时的物体给我们带来了顿悟。[2]

经过乔伊斯的概括和文学实践，"顿悟说"已经成为一个成熟的小说创作理论，其核心就是主张"通过艺术对生活的细节进行加工，从而把读者引入精神感悟的境界，产生豁然开朗的效果"[3]。这一观念在其后的英美成长小说，如《小镇畸人》（*Winesburg, Ohio*）、《麦田里的守望者》中得到了继承和发展，并成为成长小说的特色和模式之一。乔伊斯对成长小说的另一个重要贡献在于他确立了一种成长小说的语言模式。在《一个青年艺术家的肖像》中，乔伊斯在人物成长的不同阶段运用了不同的语言风格，从而实现了人物成长与小说叙事风格的完美结合。小说的开端描写斯蒂芬幼年的经历，小说的语言显得天真而稚嫩，句式也以简单句为主；而随着主人公年龄的增长，小说的语言也逐渐发生了变化。由于斯蒂芬对文学和艺术的热爱，他的语言呈现出文雅、学究气等特点，句式变得复杂，用词开始咬文嚼字，叙事的风格也变得严肃，时而激情澎湃，时而沉静深邃，

---

[1] 袁德成，《詹姆斯·乔伊斯——现代尤利西斯》。成都：四川人民出版社，1999年，第188页。
[2] 殷企平等，《英国小说批评史》。上海：上海外语教育出版社，2001年，第18页。
[3] 芮渝萍，《美国成长小说研究》。北京：中国社会科学出版社，2004年，第36页。

总之，语言风格与人物的心智的成熟和成长结合得天衣无缝。乔伊斯所确立的成长小说对语言变化的关注深深地影响了其他英美作家。在《麦田里的守望者》等经典成长小说中，作家无一例外地关注了语言的运用问题。乔伊斯对成长问题也从来未曾放弃过尝试和书写，他的"天才之书"《尤利西斯》（Ulysses）事实上也是一部充满了成长的诱惑的作品。这部著作与荷马史诗《奥德修纪》之间结构框架和叙事模式的平行性无时无刻不在提醒着人们这部作品中蕴藏着的漂泊和求索的主题。《尤利西斯》在意识流叙事中构建的不仅仅是小说中人物的成长，更是现代社会的嬗变，是关于整个西方文明发展变化的一部成长小说。

1983年荣获诺贝尔文学奖的威廉姆·戈尔丁的《蝇王》是20世纪中期一部重要的成长小说。从小说的表层结构和含义来看，这是一部流行的"荒岛生存"小说。然而从深层结构和深层含义来看，《蝇王》却是对人性本质的深层解读和探索。在摆脱了社会规范限制的生存环境中，人性中邪恶的本原毫无顾忌地暴露出来。从某种角度来看，作为成长小说，《蝇王》在对人物的成长模式的描述上，已经与经典的成长小说发生了背离，甚至是背叛。流落到荒岛上的孩子们，逐渐分化成两派：以中产阶级家庭出身的孩子拉尔夫（Ralph）为首的有教养的一派和以出身低贱的杰克（Jack Merridew）为首的暴力派。两个孩子各自为政，不断发生冲突。拉尔夫希望孩子们能够文明地生活，互相团结；而杰克觉得过野人的生活充满刺激，不断鼓动其他孩子玩暴力游戏。结果以杰克为代表的"向恶派"逐渐成为主流，拉尔夫败下阵来。戈尔丁所勾画的人的成长轨迹迎合的是20世纪之初现代派的悲观和失望的情绪，以及现代派对人性和荒诞的现代社会的恐惧心理。同时，戈尔丁也告诉人们，成长的轨迹既可以是上升的，也可以是下降的，甚至可以是以毁灭收场的。

美国成长小说

作为新兴的民族，美国作家对青少年的成长问题表现出了异乎寻常的热情。在这种热情的感召下，美国的成长小说在美国文学中所占的比例和取得的成就也就可想而知了，以至于评论家莱斯利·费德莱尔（Leslie Fiedler）由衷地说："美国历代最著名的小说家中，只有亨利·詹姆斯一个人可以不算在儿童作家之列，即使是霍桑，虽然不同于马克·吐温和麦尔维尔,其声誉也建立在他那些以青年人为题材的儿童所喜爱的小说上。"[1] 费德莱尔尤其偏爱马克·吐温的《哈克贝利·芬历险记》和麦尔维尔(Herman Melville, 1819—1891)的《莫比·迪克》(*Moby Dick*)。当谈到这两本书时,他的赞美之情溢于言表:"美国人总是憧憬着童年。在我国文化遗产里为数不多的伟大著作中,有两本最令人神往的书,看见它们摆在儿童图书馆的书架上没有谁会感到吃惊。这里指的当然是《白鲸》(《莫比·迪克》)和《哈克贝利·芬历险记》。虽然在表现手法和使用的语言方面,两者迥然不同,但同样是儿童喜爱的书,说得确切一点,是男孩子喜爱的书。"[2]

费德莱尔对《哈克贝利·芬历险记》和《莫比·迪克》的高度评价折射出美国评论家偏爱的成长小说的两个特点。第一个特点就是在美国成长小说中,主人公似乎更加年轻,通常都是十几岁的孩子。费德莱尔对此的解释也颇有代表性,他认为:"仅仅是找到一种语言,学习在一个没有社交常规的地方说话,没有特殊的等级习语和不同等级的对话,没有一种连续的文学语言,这些就已经让美国作家精疲力竭了。他永远都在开始,第一次讲述(没有一个真正的传统就不会有第二次)独自一人面对自然的感受,或者在城市里感受到的可怕的孤独,就像独自在原始森林一样可怕。"[3] 费德莱尔所强调的是,作为新兴的民族,美国缺乏悠久的文学传统,美国作家的创作就像懵懂的少年艰难求索,因此,美国作家也最能够体验成长的酸甜苦辣。美国作家的这种独特的体验与美国民族成长的体验也不谋而合。因此,美国的成长小说往往带有个人和民族的双重成长,并在个人与民族成长的既相互支撑又互相冲突的互动中获得了一种独特的审美体验。对于个人成长与美国的民族成长之间的关系,不少富有真知灼见的美国评论家都曾经十分关注。菲利普·扬(Philip Young)在对海明威(Ernest Hemingway, 1899—1961)的"尼克系列小说"的研究中,就指出:"它[尼克系列小说]不只是建立在每一个人成长的经历之上,而且是建立在美利坚民族独特的历史经验之上。"[4] 对于菲利普·扬来说,年轻人成长的历程就是美国成长的历程,而年轻人成长的神话就是美国成长的神话:"这个出自美国人民经历的神话告诉我们的人民说,我们启程时,满面春风,对世界和所有伙伴抱着与

---

[1] 莱斯利·费德莱尔,《好哈克,再回到木筏上来吧!》,见叶舒宪选编《神话—原型批评》。西安:陕西师范大学出版社,1987年,第340-341页。

[2] 莱斯利·费德莱尔,《好哈克,再回到木筏上来吧!》,见叶舒宪选编《神话—原型批评》。西安:陕西师范大学出版社,1987年,第341页。

[3] 转引自芮渝萍,《美国成长小说研究》。北京:中国社会科学出版社,2004年,第18页。

[4] 菲利普·扬,《世界和一个美国神话》,见董衡巽选编《海明威研究》。北京:中国社会科学出版社,1985年,第407页。

人为善的态度。我们自己的形象就是这位天性善良、单纯、天真、满怀希望的少年。但是，我们一步入人生的历程，便被打翻在地，从此一蹶不振，没有任何灵丹妙药能够恢复我们的本来面目。"[1] 事实上，美国作家意识的深处对成长总有一种矛盾的情结：一方面是拒绝成长的情结，他们清楚地知道，成长是要付出代价的，因此他们本能地拒绝成长；另一方面，成长过程的新鲜感又充满着诱惑，因此他们又有一种不可遏制的渴望成长的情结。这种矛盾心理构成了美国成长小说中的成长的焦虑，也形成了美国成长小说的一个情节推进方式和叙事模式。第二个特点就是美国作家和评论家界定的成长小说依旧是"阳性中心"的思考模式。费德莱尔特别强调了《哈克贝利·芬历险记》和麦尔维尔的《莫比·迪克》是"男孩子喜爱的书"，而他对美国成长小说的研究与巴克利在《青春季节》一书中对成长小说的研究遵循了一个共同的模式，那就是，所有被他引为范例加以研究和讨论的，几乎都是男性作家书写男性成长经历的小说。费德莱尔在其成长小说研究的力作《美国小说中的爱情与死亡》（*Love and Death in the American Novel*）一书中，追溯了从华盛顿·欧文（Washington Irving, 1783—1859）的《瑞普·凡·温克尔》（"Rip Van Winkle"）到杰克·凯鲁亚克（Jack Kerouac, 1922—1969）《在路上》（*On the Road*）的美国成长小说的发展，并确立了美国成长小说的人物、叙事等模式。然而遗憾的是，这些结论均建立在对男性成长小说的研究基础之上。

无论是德国的教育小说，还是英美的成长小说，其主体和模式主要是着眼于男性的成长，呈现出一种"阳性中心"的思考模式。无论是在追寻美国梦中的成长、历险中的成长、战争中的成长还是顿悟中的成长，其成长环境均是传统的男性的成长空间，其中，历险游历和战争战场更是"让女人走开"的男人的空间。在传统成长小说建构模式中，除了作为成长主体的主人公，成长的引路人也是美国成长小说中一个关键因素，而这个引路人也往往是由男性角色扮演的。芮渝萍在《美国成长小说》中对引路人的原型进行了论证：

> 从人类文明发展历史来看，成长小说中的引路人原型可以追溯到神话中的神和童话中的国王或白马王子。在宗教统治时期，神作为至高无上的权威统领着世间万物。他或指引迷途的"羔羊"，或拯救受难的子民。希腊神话中的人的命运都操纵在诸神手里，个人的意志和选择是有限的。在格林童话《马利亚代养的孩子》中，拯

---

[1] 菲利普·扬，《世界和一个美国神话》，见董衡巽选编《海明威研究》。北京：中国社会科学出版社，1985年，第408页。

救金发女孩走出荒野的是国王，但最后的拯救者是圣母玛利亚。随着人类社会从宗教统治走向世俗王权统治时代，国王或王子代替了上帝，成为"拯救者"。例如，唤醒白雪公主的是白马王子，拯救灰姑娘的也是王子。到了现代民主社会，普通人取代了皇家权威，但他的功能和作用不再是"拯救者"，而变成了"引路人"，因为在现代民主社会中，人们普遍的理念是，个人的权威应该是有限的，人们的目光也从高向低投向普通人身上。[1]

从这段论述中不难看出成长小说引路人原型所呈现出来的男性中心主义的思维模式。尽管圣母玛利亚曾经充当过拯救者的角色，但其意义与其说反映了女性拯救的力量，不如说更体现了神性的伟大。另外，圣母玛利亚的原型体现的更多的是母系社会和文化中对"母权"的崇拜。成长小说引路人的原型衍变曲折，折射的恰恰是男性中心的思维模式：男性充当着女性的拯救者，充当着女性的引路人。因此，在传统成长小说中，这个关系不是互动的、双向的，而是单维的。对于以男性成长为主体的成长小说，其传统的模式也是男性充当领路人的角色。《莫比·迪克》中的正面引路人——"高尚的野蛮人"魁奎格（Queequeg）不但让伊什梅尔（Ishmael）认识到友谊和兄弟情谊的重要性，而且用自己的棺材为伊什梅尔充当了生命之舟；而艾哈伯（Ahab）船长则充当了反面引路人的角色，他的偏执和狭隘把全船人送上了不归路。《哈克贝里·芬历险记》中的吉姆（Jim）则是哈克的伙伴和引路人，他不但让哈克学会了在自然中求生的本领，而且彻底改变了哈克对黑人的错误认识，使哈克从一个调皮的孩童走上了解救朋友的成熟之路。

女性生活在"文化的边陲"，"被动依赖而且不成熟"的地位在传统男性成长小说中得到了文学实践的生动体现。在《莫比·迪克》和《哈克贝里·芬历险记》中，主人公的成长过程中女性是缺失的，看来麦尔维尔和马克·吐温似乎真的认为成长与女性无关。男性成长过程中女性的缺席在传统成长小说中并不是个别现象，在海明威的《老人与海》(The Old Man and the Sea) 中，女性也只是成了那片作为隐喻的大海而时隐时现。在斯蒂芬·克莱恩（Stephen Crane, 1871—1900）的《红色英勇勋章》(The Red Badge of Courage) 中，母亲反对弗莱明（Henry Fleming）上战场，因此弗莱明成长的起点是他试图挣脱母亲的束缚。在这里，母亲成了妨碍弗莱明走向成熟、走向被社会认同的男性价值的障碍。因此，弗莱明走向成熟的第一步是与母亲的较量，这与弗洛伊德（Sigmund

---

[1] 芮渝萍，《美国成长小说研究》。北京：中国社会科学出版社，2004 年，第 124 页。

Freud，1856—1939）和拉康（Jacques Lacan，1901—1981）的精神分析以及列维-施特劳斯（Claude Lévi-Strauss，1908—2009）的规范婚姻纽带和亲属关系的社会法则的语言结构是不谋而合的。在舍伍德·安德森（Sherwood Anderson，1876—1941）的《小镇畸人》中，母亲是一个让儿子乔治·威拉德（George Willard）感到尴尬的梦魇。母子之间彼此为对方的出现感到不安、尴尬和莫名的紧张。乔治热爱母亲，却无从表达，而母亲对他也暗暗关心，却对表达关爱羞于出口。母亲是社会和家庭的牺牲品，她在这个父辈留下来的小旅馆中耗尽了自己的青春、憧憬和生命；从一个年轻的美少女变成枯槁的怨妇的过程浓缩了女性在封闭的小镇中生命的无奈。在菲茨杰拉德（F. Scott Fitzgerald，1896—1940）的《了不起的盖茨比》（*The Great Gatsby*）中，女性成为男性梦魇的开始。盖茨比（Gatsby）的疯狂晚会是为了呼唤昔日的恋人黛西（Daisy），然而黛西的到来却带来了死神和幻灭。黛西天性贪图享受，浮华浪荡，她对任何男人都没有真正的感情，她爱的只有金钱和地位。小说中对黛西的几次描写很能说明问题。在第八章，尼克（Nick）转述了盖茨比对黛西的叙述：

> 黛西当年还很年轻，而且又生活在一种浮华的社会环境中，她的周围弥漫着兰花馥郁的香气，洋溢着显贵傲慢的欢乐气氛。管弦乐队演奏着当年流行的旋律，新的曲调反映出人生中的哀怨和彷徨。……
>
> 在这个繁星闪烁的宇宙中，黛西又开始追逐新的欢乐；她一反常态，每天都要与五六个男人约会，直到黎明的时候才昏昏沉沉地入睡，夜礼服的珠子和纱巾同凋谢的兰花乱七八糟地丢在窗边的地板上。她的内心一直渴望着做出一个抉择，她要立即安排自己的终身大事——这一抉择必须有某种力量才能促成——爱情、金钱和真正实用的东西——而这一切又都是非常容易实现的。[1]

同样，在这部小说中的另一位女性乔丹·贝克（Jordan Baker）不但无情无义，而且满嘴谎言。这些女性的负面形象使尼克对爱情和婚姻不由得退避三舍，他最终疏远了黛西，也斩钉截铁地掐断了与乔丹尚处于萌芽状态的爱情，远离了这些"美丽的小傻瓜"。在菲茨杰拉德的世界中，女性是男性成长中的毁灭性的因素。

在男性成长小说中，几乎没有一个女性人物真正经历了与男性共同的身体和心智的

---

[1] F.S. 菲茨杰拉德，《大人物盖茨比》，范乐译。沈阳：辽宁人民出版社，1983年，第203-204页。

成长，因为在男性的书写中，"女性成长的可能性被一一围堵"。可以说，传统的男性成长小说是一个"让女人走开"的文本空间。

拓展阅读文献

Alden, Patricia. *Social Mobility in the English Bildungsroman: Gissing, Hardy, Bennett and Lawrence*. Ann Arbor: UMI Research Press, 1986.

Buckley, Jerome. *Season of Youth: The Bildungsroman from Dickens to Golding*. Cambridge: Harvard University Press, 1974.

Emra, Bruce. *Coming of Age: Literature About Youth and Adolescence*. Lincolnwood: National Textbook Company, 1999.

芮渝萍，《美国成长小说研究》。北京：中国社会科学出版社，2004年。

Lecture 1
Charles Dickens

Profile of the Writer

Charles Dickens
(1812–1870)

Charles Dickens was born in Landport, Portsmouth, on February 7, 1812 and later his family settled down in a poor neighborhood in London. The defining moment of Dickens's life occurred in 1824 when his father was imprisoned in the Marshalsea debtor's prison. This forced the 12-year-old Dickens to leave school and work in a warehouse that handled "blacking" or shoe polish to help support the family. Though his father was released a few months later and he was allowed to go back to school, this experience left on Dickens profound psychological and sociological effects. He gained firsthand experience of poverty and became the most vigorous and influential voice of the working classes in his age.

At 15 Charles Dickens began to work as an office boy and then a reporter. In 1833 Dickens began to contribute short stories and essays to periodicals. His first book, a collection of stories titled *Sketches by Boz*, was published in 1836. In the same year he married Catherine Hogarth. Together they had ten children before they separated in 1858.

After the great success of *The Posthumous Papers of the Pickwick Club* (1836–1837), Dickens embarked on a full-time career as a novelist, producing work of increasing complexity: *Oliver Twist* (1837–1839), *Nicholas Nickleby* (1838–1839), *The Old Curiosity*

Shop and *Barnaby Rudge* as part of the *Master Humphrey's Clock* series (1840–1841).

From 1842 to 1846, Dickens ever travelled to the United States, Canada, Italy and Switzerland, and continued his success with five Christmas books. His later works include *Dombey and Son* (1848), the largely autobiographical *David Copperfield* (1849–1850), *Bleak House* (1852–1853), *Hard Times* (1854), *Little Dorrit* (1857), *A Tale of Two Cities* (1859), and *Great Expectations* (1861).

In 1858, Dickens began a series of paid readings, which became instantly popular. During his readings in 1869 he collapsed, showing symptoms of mild stroke and finally died at home on June 9, 1870 after suffering a stroke. Contrary to his wish to be buried in Rochester Cathedral, he was buried in the Poets' Corner of Westminster Abbey. The inscription on his tomb reads:

"He was a sympathizer to the poor, the suffering, and the oppressed; and by his death, one of England's greatest writers is lost to the world."

 Preview Questions

1. *Great Expectations* (1861) is one of the most famous and much-loved novels by Charles Dickens, the master of Victorian prose. How do you interpret the name of the book?

2. "In a word, I was too cowardly to do what I knew to be right, as I had been too cowardly to avoid doing what I knew to be wrong." This quote from the novel *Great Expectations* tells of cowardice. To what extent do you agree with the idea that growth is to overcome cowardice?

 Literary Reading: *Great Expectations* (Chapter 1)

My father's family name being Pirrip, and my Christian name Philip, my infant tongue could make of both names nothing longer or more explicit than Pip. So, I called myself Pip, and came to be called Pip.

I give Pirrip as my father's family name, on the authority of his tombstone and my sister, —Mrs. Joe Gargery, who married the blacksmith. As I never saw my father or my mother, and never saw any likeness of either of them (for their days were long before the days of photographs), my first fancies regarding what they were like were unreasonably derived from their tombstones. The shape of the letters on my father's, gave me an odd idea that he was a square, stout, dark man, with curly black hair. From the character and turn of the inscription, "Also Georgiana Wife of the Above", I drew a childish conclusion that my mother was freckled and sickly. To five little stone lozenges, each about a foot and a half long, which were arranged in a neat row beside their grave, and were sacred to the memory of five little brothers of mine, —who gave up trying to get a living, exceedingly early in that universal struggle, —I am indebted for a belief I religiously entertained that they had all been born on their backs with their hands in their trousers-pockets, and had never taken them out in this state of existence.

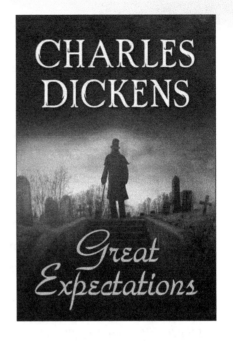

Ours was the marsh country, down by the river, within, as the river wound, twenty miles of the sea. My first most vivid and broad impression of the identity of things seems to me to have been gained on a memorable raw afternoon towards evening. At such a time I found out for certain that this bleak place overgrown with nettles was the churchyard; and that Philip Pirrip, late of this parish, and also Georgiana wife of the above, were dead and buried; and that Alexander, Bartholomew, Abraham, Tobias, and Roger, infant children of the aforesaid, were also dead and buried; and that the dark flat wilderness beyond the churchyard, intersected with dikes and mounds and gates, with scattered cattle feeding on it, was the marshes; and that the low leaden line beyond was the river; and that the distant savage lair from which the wind was rushing was the sea; and that the small bundle of shivers growing afraid of it all and beginning to cry, was Pip.

"Hold your noise!" cried a terrible voice, as a man started up from among the graves at the side of the church porch. "Keep still, you little devil, or I'll cut your throat!"

A fearful man, all in coarse gray, with a great iron on his leg. A man with no hat, and with broken shoes, and with an old rag tied round his head. A man who had been soaked in water, and smothered in mud, and lamed by stones, and cut by flints, and stung by nettles, and torn by briars; who limped, and shivered, and glared, and growled; and whose teeth chattered in his head as he seized me by the chin.

"Oh! Don't cut my throat, sir," I pleaded in terror. "Pray don't do it, sir."

"Tell us your name!" said the man. "Quick!"

"Pip, sir."

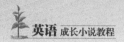

"Once more," said the man, staring at me. "Give it mouth!"

"Pip. Pip, sir."

"Show us where you live," said the man. "Pint out the place!"

I pointed to where our village lay, on the flat in-shore among the alder-trees and pollards, a mile or more from the church.

The man, after looking at me for a moment, turned me upside down, and emptied my pockets. There was nothing in them but a piece of bread. When the church came to itself, —for he was so sudden and strong that he made it go head over heels before me, and I saw the steeple under my feet, —when the church came to itself, I say, I was seated on a high tombstone, trembling while he ate the bread ravenously.

"You young dog," said the man, licking his lips, "what fat cheeks you ha' got."

I believe they were fat, though I was at that time undersized for my years, and not strong.

"Darn me if I couldn't eat em," said the man, with a threatening shake of his head, "and if I han't half a mind to't!"

I earnestly expressed my hope that he wouldn't, and held tighter to the tombstone on which he had put me; partly, to keep myself upon it; partly, to keep myself from crying.

"Now lookee here!" said the man. "Where's your mother?"

"There, sir!" said I.

He started, made a short run, and stopped and looked over his shoulder.

"There, sir!" I timidly explained. "Also Georgiana. That's my mother."

"Oh!" said he, coming back. "And is that your father alonger your mother?"

"Yes, sir," said I; "him too; late of this parish."

"Ha!" he muttered then, considering. "Who d'ye live with, —supposin' you're kindly let to live, which I han't made up my mind about?"

"My sister, sir, —Mrs. Joe Gargery, —wife of Joe Gargery, the blacksmith, sir."

"Blacksmith, eh?" said he. And looked down at his leg.

After darkly looking at his leg and me several times, he came closer to my tombstone, took me by both arms, and tilted me back as far as he could hold me; so that his eyes looked most powerfully down into mine, and mine looked most helplessly up into his.

"Now lookee here," he said, "the question being whether you're to be let to live. You know what a file is?"

"Yes, sir."

"And you know what wittles is?"

"Yes, sir."

After each question he tilted me over a little more, so as to give me a greater sense of helplessness and danger.

"You get me a file." He tilted me again. "And you get me wittles." He tilted me again. "You bring 'em both to me." He tilted me again. "Or I'll have your heart and liver out." He tilted me again.

I was dreadfully frightened, and so giddy that I clung to him with both hands, and said, "If you would kindly please to let me keep upright, sir, perhaps I shouldn't be sick, and perhaps I could attend more."

He gave me a most tremendous dip and roll, so that the church jumped over its own weathercock. Then, he held me by the arms, in an upright position on the top of the stone, and went on in these fearful terms: —

"You bring me, tomorrow morning early, that file and them wittles. You bring the lot to me, at that old Battery over yonder. You do it, and you never dare to say a word or dare to make a sign concerning your having seen such a person as me, or any person sumever, and you shall be let to live. You fail, or you go from my words in any partickler, no matter how small it is, and your heart and your liver shall be tore out, roasted, and ate. Now, I ain't alone, as you may think I am. There's a young man hid with me, in comparison with which young man I am a Angel. That young man hears the words I speak. That young man has a secret way pecooliar to himself, of getting at a boy, and at his heart, and at his liver. It is in wain for a boy to attempt to hide himself from that young man. A boy may lock his door, may be warm in bed, may tuck himself up, may draw the clothes over his head, may think himself comfortable and safe, but that young man will softly creep and creep his way to him and tear him open. I am a keeping that young man from harming of you at the present moment, with great difficulty. I find it wery hard to hold that young man off of your inside. Now, what do you say?"

I said that I would get him the file, and I would get him what broken bits of food I could, and I would come to him at the Battery, early in the morning.

"Say Lord strike you dead if you don't!" said the man.

I said so, and he took me down.

"Now," he pursued, "you remember what you've undertook, and you remember that young man, and you get home!"

"Goo-good night, sir," I faltered.

"Much of that!" said he, glancing about him over the cold wet flat. "I wish I was a frog. Or a eel!"

At the same time, he hugged his shuddering body in both his arms, —clasping himself, as if to hold himself together, —and limped towards the low church wall. As I saw him go, picking his way among the nettles, and among the brambles that bound the green mounds, he looked in my young eyes as if he were eluding the hands of the dead people, stretching up cautiously out of their graves, to get a twist upon his ankle and pull him in.

When he came to the low church wall, he got over it, like a man whose legs were numbed and stiff, and then turned round to look for me. When I saw him turning, I set my face towards home, and made the best use of my legs. But presently I looked over my shoulder, and saw him going on again towards the river, still hugging himself in both arms, and picking his way with his sore feet among the great stones dropped into the marshes here and there, for stepping-places when the rains were heavy or the tide was in.

The marshes were just a long black horizontal line then, as I stopped to look after him; and the river was just another horizontal line, not nearly so broad nor yet so black; and the sky was just a row of long angry red lines and dense black lines intermixed. On the edge of the river I could faintly make out the only two black things in all the prospect that seemed to be standing upright; one of these was the beacon by which the sailors steered, —like an unhooped cask upon a pole, —an ugly thing when you were near it; the other, a gibbet, with some chains hanging to it which had once held a pirate. The man was limping on towards this latter, as if he were the pirate come to life, and come down, and going back to hook himself up again. It gave me a terrible turn when I thought so; and as I saw the cattle lifting their heads to gaze after him, I wondered whether they thought so too. I looked all round for the horrible young man, and could see no signs of him. But now I was frightened again, and ran home without stopping.

Ⅲ Thinking, Talking and Writing About Literature

1 Textual Cognition

Make an introductory presentation on the following terms related to this literary work.

1) critical realism
2) the Victorian age

2 Textual Reading

Search for evidence in the text and answer the following questions.
1) How does Dickens use setting to convey the mood right at the opening?
2) Who does Pip meet in the graveyard and what does it foreshadow in the story?
3) What is Pip ordered to fetch under the threat of losing his heart and liver?

4) Can you explain how Pip and Joe were "brought up by hand"?

③ Critical Reading

Discuss in groups the following questions to further explore this literary work.

1) What narrative point of view does Charles Dickens adopt in the novel and what are its advantages in narration?

2) The novel *Great Expectations* chronicles the coming of age of the orphan Pip. What changes do his values and goals undergo in the novel? What events and experiences cause this transformation?

④ Writing About Literature

Read the following critical excerpt and then write an essay.

> Dutton, Richard. "The Critical Fortunes of *Great Expectations*."
> *Hyphen* 6.5 (1991): 209–210.

Recent criticism of *Great Expectations*, in short, is virtually unanimous in regarding it as a sombre and successful moral fable; there has been some occasional interest in the technical questions of the first-person narrative, periodical publication and the changed ending, but even these are generally measured in terms of their bearing on the overall moral tone/design of the novel. The revolution in taste that has taken place in the century or so since Dickens's death could hardly be more complete; it bears comparison with the shift in taste between Johnson—who looked to Shakespeare's comedies for the true artist—and Coleridge, who looked to the tragedies. Where Dickens's contemporaries looked for comedy, and apparently found it, we discover disturbing psychological concerns; where some of them—and later proponents of the "art" of the novel—decried the caricature-style of the characterization or rather feebly tried to defend it as "realistic", most of us now calmly accept it as part of his complex, symbolically pointed style; where they yearned for him to keep repeating his exuberant early triumphs, we seem to be rather pleased, in a way, that his later years were riddled with doubts and anxieties—as titles such as *The Melancholy Man: A Study of Dickens's Novels* (John Lucas, 1970, 1980) and *The Violent Effigy: A Study of Dickens's Imagination* (John Carey, 1973) testify. Like Shakespeare, Dickens seems to be sufficiently multi-faceted to have something significant to offer to each successive generation of critics. This may be one definition of greatness. It says something for Dickens's stature that so forceful a critic as F. R. Leavis, after all but dismissing him in *The*

Great Tradition, felt obliged to recant and, with his wife, Q. D. Leavis, produced a full-scale study of the novels: *Dickens the Novelist* (1970). (The chapter on *Great Expectations* is in the characteristic imperative mode of his later years: "How We Must Read *Great Expectations*".) The tradition of criticism of Dickens poses one question most acutely: How proper or useful is it to discuss individual texts in relation to a writer's other works or against the background of his supposed "imaginative career"? Dickens seems especially to attract such criticism, with all the dangers it runs of prejudging or distorting a text in order to make it fit some preconceived pattern. Once again, we should be aware that the popularity in the classroom of the text we have been considering is not entirely due to the qualities most frequently discussed in formal criticism. *Great Expectations* has the merit of being relatively short, unlike *Bleak House* (1852–1853) or *Little Dorrit* (1855–1857), the other masterpieces of Dickens's later career (which many critics would judge to be even finer works), and unlike Dickens's other fictional "autobiography", *David Copperfield* (1849–1850). It is also generally believed that young people find stories of growing up inherently interesting and "relevant" to themselves: hence the frequent appearance of such texts as *Great Expectations*, James Joyce's *A Portrait of the Artist as a Young Man*, D. H. Lawrence's *Sons and Lovers*, J. D. Salinger's *The Catcher in the Rye* and Laurie Lee's *Cider with Rosie* on school syllabuses.

Essay Writing

As mentioned in the above passage, *Great Expectations* is more than a moral fable and Dickens is multi-faceted and has something significant to offer to each successive generation of critics. Criticism of Dickens usually discusses individual texts in relation to his other works or against the background of his writing career. So can you compare *Great Expectations* with another autobiographical work of Dickens, *David Copperfield*, to see the differences and similarities of the two in terms of narrative art and thematic matters? Write an essay on the comparison of the two novels with no less than 500 words.

IV Further Activity

Scan the QR code and listen to the audio of Chapter 2 of *Great Expectations*.

Lecture 2
James Joyce

Profile of the Writer

James Joyce
(1882–1941)

One of the most influential and innovative writers of the 20th century, James Joyce was the author of the short story collection *Dubliners* (1914) and the novels *A Portrait of the Artist as a Young Man* (1916), *Ulysses* (1922), and *Finnegans Wake* (1939). His collections of poetry include *Chamber Music* (1907) and *Pomes Penyeach* (1927).

Joyce was born in a suburb of Dublin. He attended a Jesuit school until his parents could not afford the tuition, and then Belvedere College (where he was awarded tuition) and University College, Dublin. Upon graduation, Joyce moved to Paris and, after 1904, returned to Ireland only sporadically. He lived in Trieste with his partner and later wife, Nora Barnacle, and their children. During World War I the family lived in Zurich, moving to Paris after the war, and then to the south of France before the Nazi invasion. The family was living in Zurich when Joyce died.

Joyce's first published book was *Chamber Music*, a collection of 36 love poems. Despite his poetic success, Joyce is better known as a novelist, and by 1932 he had stopped writing poetry altogether. Joyce's novels, with their innovative language, use of dialogue, characteristic modernist forms, and social frankness, met with resistance when they first appeared in print. *Ulysses* was serialized in the United States and England before Sylvia Beach, legendary owner of the bookstore Shakespeare & Co. in Paris, published it as a complete book. It was banned in the United States from 1922 until 1933.

A Portrait of the Artist as a Young Man, an autobiographical novel by James Joyce, published serially in *The Egoist* in 1914–1915 and in book form in 1916, is considered by many the greatest Bildungsroman in the English language. The novel portrays the early years of Stephen Dedalus, who later reappeared as one of the main characters in Joyce's *Ulysses*.

Each of the novel's five sections is written in a third-person voice that reflects the age and emotional state of its protagonist, from the first childhood memories written in simple childlike language to Stephen's final decision to leave Dublin for Paris to devote his life to art, written in abstruse Latin-sprinkled stream-of-consciousness prose.

Preview Questions

1. What are the shared subject matters and thematic ideas of the Irish literature?

2. *A Portrait of the Artist as a Young Man* is the first semi-autobiographical novel by Irish writer James Joyce. It traces the religious and intellectual awakening of young Stephen Dedalus, a fictional alter ego of Joyce and an allusion to Dedalus, the consummate craftsman of Greek mythology. So what do you know about Dedalus?

Literary Reading: *A Portrait of the Artist as a Young Man* (Chapter 2)

Stephen's mother and his brother and one of his cousins waited at the corner of quiet Foster Place while he and his father went up the steps and along the colonnade where the Highland sentry was parading.

When they had passed into the great hall and stood at the counter Stephen drew forth his orders on the governor of the bank of Ireland for thirty and three pounds; and these sums, the moneys of his exhibition and essay prize, were paid over to him rapidly by the teller in notes and in coin respectively. He bestowed them in his pockets with feigned composure and suffered the friendly teller, to whom his father chatted, to take his hand across the broad counter and wish him a brilliant career in after life. He was impatient of their voices and could not keep his feet at rest.

But the teller still deferred the serving of others to say he was living in changed times and that there was nothing like giving a boy the best education that money could buy. Mr. Dedalus lingered in the hall gazing about him and up at the roof and telling Stephen, who urged him to come out, that they were standing in the house of commons of the old Irish parliament.

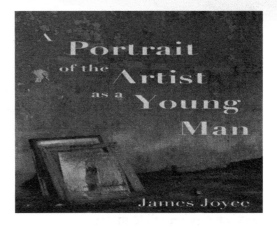

—God help us! he said piously, to think of the men of those times, Stephen, Hely Hutchinson and Flood and Henry Grattan and Charles Kendal Bushe, and the noblemen we have now, leaders of the Irish people at home and abroad. Why, by God, they wouldn't be seen dead in a ten-acre field with them. No, Stephen, old chap, I'm sorry to say that they are only as I roved out one fine May morning in the merry month of sweet July.

A keen October wind was blowing round the bank. The three figures standing at the edge of the muddy path had pinched cheeks and watery eyes. Stephen looked at his thinly clad mother and remembered that a few days before he had seen a mantle priced at twenty guineas in the windows of Barnardo's.

—Well that's done, said Mr. Dedalus.

—We had better go to dinner, said Stephen. Where?

—Dinner? said Mr. Dedalus. Well, I suppose we had better, what?

—Some place that's not too dear, said Mrs. Dedalus.

—Underdone's?

—Yes. Some quiet place.

—Come along, said Stephen quickly. It doesn't matter about the dearness.

He walked on before them with short nervous steps, smiling. They tried to keep up with him, smiling also at his eagerness.

—Take it easy like a good young fellow, said his father. We're hot out for the half mile, are we?

For a swift season of merrymaking the money of his prizes ran through Stephen's fingers. Great parcels of groceries and delicacies and dried fruits arrived from the city. Every day he drew up a bill of fare for the family and every night led a party of three or four to the theatre to see INGOMAR or THE LADY OF LYONS. In his coat pockets he carried squares of Vienna chocolate for his guests while his trousers' pocket bulged with masses of silver and copper coins. He bought presents for everyone, overhauled his room, wrote out resolutions, marshalled his books up and down their shelves, pored upon all kinds of price lists, drew up a form of commonwealth for the household by which every member of it held some office, opened a loan bank for his family and pressed loans on willing borrowers so that he might have the pleasure of making out receipts and reckoning the interests on the sums lent. When he could do no more he drove up and down the city in trams. Then the season of pleasure came to an end. The pot of pink enamel paint gave out and the wainscot of his bedroom remained with its unfinished and ill-plastered coat.

His household returned to its usual way of life. His mother had no further occasion to upbraid him for squandering his money. He too returned to his old life at school and all his novel enterprises fell to pieces.

The commonwealth fell, the loan bank closed its coffers and its books on a sensible loss, the rules of life which he had drawn about himself fell into desuetude. How foolish his aim had been! He had tried to build a break-water of order and elegance against the sordid tide of life without him and to dam up, by rules of conduct and active interest and new filial relations, the powerful recurrence of the tides within him. Useless. From without as from within the waters had flowed over his barriers: their tides began once more to jostle fiercely above the crumbled mole.

He saw clearly too his own futile isolation. He had not gone one step nearer the lives he had sought to approach nor bridged the restless shame and rancour that had divided him from mother and brother and sister. He felt that he was hardly of the one blood with them but stood to them rather in the mystical kinship of fosterage, fosterchild and fosterbrother.

He turned to appease the fierce longings of his heart before which everything else was idle and alien. He cared little that he was in mortal sin, that his life had grown to be a tissue of subterfuge and falsehood. Beside the savage desire within him to realize the enormities which he brooded on nothing was sacred. He bore cynically with the shameful details of his secret riots in which he exulted to defile with patience whatever image had attracted his eyes. By day and by night he moved among distorted images of the outer world. A figure that had seemed to him by day demure and innocent came towards him by night through the winding darkness of sleep, her face transfigured by a lecherous cunning, her eyes bright with brutish joy. Only the morning pained him with its dim memory of dark orgiastic riot, its keen and humiliating sense of transgression.

He returned to his wanderings. The veiled autumnal evenings led him from street to street as they had led him years before along the quiet avenues of Blackrock. But no vision of trim front gardens or of kindly lights in the windows poured a tender influence upon him now. Only at times, in the pauses of his desire, when the luxury that was wasting him gave room to a softer languor, the image of Mercedes traversed the background of his memory.

He saw again the small white house and the garden of rose-bushes on the road that led to the mountains and he remembered the sadly proud gesture of refusal which he was to make there, standing with her in the moonlit garden after years of estrangement and adventure. At those moments the soft speeches of Claude Melnotte rose to his lips and eased his unrest. A tender premonition touched him of the tryst he had then looked forward to and, in spite of the horrible reality which lay between his hope of then and now, of the holy encounter he had then imagined at which weakness and timidity and inexperience were to fall from him.

Such moments passed and the wasting fires of lust sprang up again. The verses passed from his lips and the inarticulate cries and the unspoken brutal words rushed forth from his brain to force a passage. His blood was in revolt. He wandered up and down the dark slimy streets peering into the gloom of lanes and doorways, listening eagerly for any sound. He moaned to himself like some baffled prowling beast. He wanted to sin with another of his kind, to force another being to sin with him and to exult with her in sin. He felt some dark presence moving irresistibly upon him from the darkness, a presence subtle and murmurous as a flood filling him wholly with itself. Its murmur besieged his ears like the murmur of some multitude in sleep; its subtle streams penetrated his being. His hands clenched convulsively and his teeth set together as he suffered the agony of its penetration. He stretched out his arms in the street to hold fast the frail swooning form that eluded him and incited him: and the cry that he had strangled for so long in his throat issued from his lips. It broke from him like a wail of despair from a hell of sufferers and died in a wail of furious entreaty, a cry for an iniquitous abandonment, a cry which was but the echo of an obscene scrawl which he had read on the oozing wall of a urinal.

He had wandered into a maze of narrow and dirty streets. From the foul laneways he heard bursts of hoarse riot and wrangling and the drawling of drunken singers. He walked onward, dismayed, wondering whether he had strayed into the quarter of the Jews. Women and girls dressed in long vivid gowns traversed the street from house to house. They were leisurely and perfumed. A trembling seized him and his eyes grew dim. The yellow gas-flames arose before his troubled vision against the vapoury sky, burning as if before an altar. Before the doors and in the lighted halls groups were gathered arrayed as for some rite. He was in another world: he had awakened from a slumber of centuries. He stood still in the middle of the roadway, his heart clamouring against his bosom in a tumult. A young woman dressed in a long pink gown laid her hand on his arm to detain him and gazed into his face. She said gaily:

—Good night, Willie dear!

Her room was warm and lightsome. A huge doll sat with her legs apart in the copious easy-chair beside the bed. He tried to bid his tongue speak that he might seem at ease, watching her as she undid her gown, noting the proud conscious movements of her perfumed head.

As he stood silent in the middle of the room she came over to him and embraced him gaily and gravely. Her round arms held him firmly to her and he, seeing her face lifted to him in serious calm and feeling the warm calm rise and fall of her breast, all but burst into hysterical weeping. Tears of joy and relief shone in his delighted eyes and his lips parted though they would not speak.

She passed her tinkling hand through his hair, calling him a little rascal.

—Give me a kiss, she said.

His lips would not bend to kiss her. He wanted to be held firmly in her arms, to be caressed slowly, slowly, slowly. In her arms he felt that he had suddenly become strong and fearless and sure of himself. But his lips would not bend to kiss her.

With a sudden movement she bowed his head and joined her lips to his and he read the meaning of her movements in her frank uplifted eyes. It was too much for him. He closed his eyes, surrendering himself to her, body and mind, conscious of nothing in the world but the dark pressure of her softly parting lips. They pressed upon his brain as upon his lips as though they were the vehicle of a vague speech; and between them he felt an unknown and timid pressure, darker than the swoon of sin, softer than sound or odour.

III Thinking, Talking and Writing About Literature

1 Textual Cognition

Make an introductory presentation on the following terms related to this literary work.

1) stream of consciousness

2) Künstlerroman

2 Textual Reading

Search for evidence in the text and answer the following questions.

1) How did Stephen spend his prize money?

2) Why did Stephen keep himself separate from his family each evening and walk by himself along the streets?

3) What do you think of Stephen's first sexual relationship?

4) What did the bank teller think of Stephen?

❸ Critical Reading

Discuss in groups the following questions to further explore this literary work.

1) While thinking about the title of Joyce's first novel, would you emphasize *A Portrait of the Artist* or would you emphasize *as a Young Man*? Do you think Joyce was justified in writing "portrait of the artist" rather than "portrait of an artist"?

2) The novel is highly autobiographical. So in what ways is the life of Stephen Dedalus the mirror to that of James Joyce?

❹ Writing About Literature

Read the following critical excerpt and then write an essay.

> Wells, H. G. *The New Republic*, 10 March, 1917: 158–160.

The interest of the book depends entirely upon its quintessential and unfailing reality. One believes in Stephen Dedalus as one believes in few characters in fiction. And the peculiar lie of the interest for the intelligent reader is the convincing revelation it makes of the limitations of a great mass of Irishmen. Mr. Joyce tells us unsparingly of the adolescence of this youngster under conditions that have passed almost altogether out of English life. There is an immense shyness, a profound secrecy, about matters of sex, with its inevitable accompaniment of nightmare revelations and furtive scribblings in unpleasant places, and there is a living belief in a real hell. The description of Stephen listening without a doubt to two fiery sermons on that tremendous theme, his agonies of fear, not disgust at dirtiness such as unorthodox children feel but just fear, his terror-inspired confession of his sins of impurity to a strange priest in a distant part of the city, is like nothing in any boy's experience who has been trained under modern conditions. Compare its stuffy horror with Conrad's account of how under analogous circumstances Lord Jim wept. And a second thing of immense significance is the fact that everyone in this Dublin story, every human being, accepts as a matter of course, as a thing in nature like the sky and the sea, that the English are to be hated. There is no discrimination in that hatred, there is no gleam of recognition that a considerable number of Englishmen have displayed a very earnest disposition to put matters right with Ireland, there is an absolute absence of any idea of a discussed settlement, any notion of helping the slow-witted Englishman in his three-cornered puzzle between North and South. It is just hate, a cant cultivated to the pitch of monomania, an ungenerous violent direction of the mind. That is the political atmosphere in which Stephen Dedalus grows up, and in which his essentially responsive mind orients itself. I am afraid it is only too true an account of the atmosphere in which a number of brilliant young Irishmen have grown up. What is the good of pretending that the extreme Irish "patriot" is an equivalent and parallel of the English or American liberal? He is narrower and intenser than any English Tory. He will be the natural ally of the Tory in delaying British social and economic reconstruction after the war. He will play into the hands of the Tories by threatening an outbreak and providing the excuse for a militarist reaction in England. It is time the American observer faced the truth of that. No reason in that why England should not do justice to Ireland, but excellent reason for bearing in mind that these bright-green young people across the Channel are something quite different from the liberal English in training and tradition, and absolutely set against helping them. No single book has ever shown how different they are, as completely as this most memorable novel.

Essay Writing

As said in the above selection, the political atmosphere in which Stephen Dedalus and a number of brilliant young Irishmen have grown up is hatred toward the Englishmen. What does Stephen think of the Irish society and culture and why does he decide to leave Ireland at the end of the novel? Write an essay about Stephen Dedalus's national complex with no less than 500 words.

Ⅳ Further Activity

Scan the QR code and listen to the audio of Chapter 2 of *A Portrait of the Artist as a Young Man*.

Lecture 3
Mark Twain

Profile of the Writer

Mark Twain
(1835–1910)

Mark Twain (a.k.a., Samuel Langhorne Clemens), one of America's first and foremost realists and humanists, was born in the little town of Florida, Missouri, on November 30, 1835. When he was about four, his family moved to Hannibal, a small town in Missouri.

Twain's father was a lawyer by profession but was only mildly successful. He was, however, highly intelligent and a stern disciplinarian. Twain's mother, a Southern belle in her youth, had a natural sense of humor, was emotional, and was known to be particularly fond of animals and unfortunate human beings. Although the family was not wealthy, Twain apparently had a happy and secure childhood.

Twain's father died when Twain was twelve years old and, for the next ten years, Twain was an apprentice printer and then a printer both in Hannibal and in New York City. Later on a riverboat to New Orleans, he met a famous riverboat pilot who promised to teach him the trade for five hundred dollars. After completing his training, Twain piloted riverboats along the Mississippi for four years. During this time, he became familiar with the towns along the mighty River and became acquainted with the characters who would later inhabit many of his novels, especially Tom Sawyer and Huckleberry Finn.

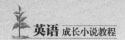

When the Civil War began, Twain's allegiance tended to be Southern due to his Southern heritage, and he briefly served in the Confederate militia. Twain's brother Orion convinced him to go west on an expedition, a trip which became the subject matter of a later work, *Roughing It* (1872).

Even though some of his letters and accounts of traveling had been published, Twain actually launched his literary career with the short story "The Celebrated Jumping Frog of Calaveras County", published in 1865. This story brought him national attention, and Twain devoted the major portion of the rest of his life to literary endeavors. In addition to *The Adventures of Tom Sawyer* and *The Adventures of Huckleberry Finn*, some of Twain's most popular works include novels such as *The Prince and the Pauper* (1881), *Life on the Mississippi* (1883), *A Connecticut Yankee in King Arthur's Court* (1889), and *Pudd'nhead Wilson* (1894), as well as collections of short stories and essays, such as *The 1,000,000 Bank-Note and Other Stories* (1893), *The Man That Corrupted Hadleyburg and Other Essays* (1900), and *What Is Man?* (1906).

I Preview Questions

1. What do you know about the Mississippi River as well as the state of Mississippi and people there?

2. What adventures did Tom Sawyer and Huckleberry Finn go through in the novel *The Adventures of Tom Sawyer*?

II Literary Reading: *The Adventures of Huckleberry Finn* (Chapter 1)

You don't know about me without you have read a book by the name of *The Adventures of Tom Sawyer*, but that ain't no matter. That book was made by Mr. Mark Twain, and he told the truth, mainly. There was things which he stretched, but mainly he told the truth. That is nothing. I never seen anybody but lied one time or another, without it was Aunt Polly, or the widow, or maybe Mary. Aunt Polly—Tom's Aunt Polly, she is—and Mary, and the Widow Douglas is all told about in that book, which is mostly a true book, with some stretchers, as I said before.

Now the way that the book winds up is this: Tom and me found the money that

the robbers hid in the cave, and it made us rich. We got six thousand dollars apiece—all gold. It was an awful sight of money when it was piled up. Well, Judge Thatcher he took it and put it out at interest, and it fetched us a dollar a day apiece all the year round—more than a body could tell what to do with. The Widow Douglas she took me for her son, and allowed she would civilize me; but it was rough living in the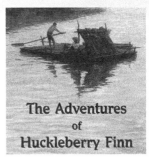
house all the time, considering how dismal regular and decent the widow was in all her ways; and so when I couldn't stand it no longer I lit out. I got into my old rags and my sugar-hogshead again, and was free and satisfied. But Tom Sawyer he hunted me up and said he was going to start a band of robbers, and I might join if I would go back to the widow and be respectable. So I went back.

The widow she cried over me, and called me a poor lost lamb, and she called me a lot of other names, too, but she never meant no harm by it. She put me in them new clothes again, and I couldn't do nothing but sweat and sweat, and feel all cramped up. Well, then, the old thing commenced again. The widow rung a bell for supper, and you had to come to time. When you got to the table you couldn't go right to eating, but you had to wait for the widow to tuck down her head and grumble a little over the victuals, though there warn't really anything the matter with them, —that is, nothing only everything was cooked by itself. In a barrel of odds and ends it is different; things get mixed up, and the juice kind of swaps around, and the things go better.

After supper she got out her book and learned me about Moses and the Bulrushers, and I was in a sweat to find out all about him; but by and by she let it out that Moses had been dead a considerable long time; so then I didn't care no more about him, because I don't take no stock in dead people.

Pretty soon I wanted to smoke, and asked the widow to let me. But she wouldn't. She said it was a mean practice and wasn't clean, and I must try to not do it any more. That is just the way with some people. They get down on a thing when they don't know nothing about it. Here she was a-bothering about Moses, which was no kin to her, and no use to anybody, being gone, you see, yet finding a power of fault with me for doing a thing that had some good in it. And she took snuff, too; of course that was all right, because she done it herself.

Her sister, Miss Watson, a tolerable slim old maid, with goggles on, had just come to live with her, and took a set at me now with a spelling-book. She worked me middling hard for about an hour, and then the widow made her ease up. I couldn't stood it much longer. Then for an hour it was deadly dull, and I was fidgety. Miss Watson would say, "Don't put your feet up there, Huckleberry"; and "Don't scrunch up like that, Huckleberry—set up straight"; and pretty soon she would say, "Don't gap and stretch like that, Huckleberry—why don't you try to behave"? Then she told me all about the bad place, and I said I wished I was there. She got mad then, but I didn't mean no harm. All I wanted was to go somewheres; all I wanted was a change, I warn't particular. She said it was wicked to say what I said; said she wouldn't say it for the whole world; she was going to live so as to go to the good place. Well, I couldn't see no advantage in going where she was going, so I made up my mind I wouldn't try for it. But I never said so, because it would only make trouble, and wouldn't do no good.

Now she had got a start, and she went on and told me all about the good place. She said all a body would have to do there was to go around all day long with a harp and sing, forever and ever. So I didn't think much of it. But I never said so. I asked her if she reckoned Tom Sawyer would go there, and she said not by a considerable sight. I was glad about that, because I wanted him and me to be together.

Miss Watson she kept pecking at me, and it got tiresome and lonesome. By and by they fetched the niggers in and had prayers, and then everybody was off to bed. I went up to my room with a piece of candle, and put it on the table. Then I sat down in a chair by the window and tried to think of something cheerful, but it warn't no use. I felt so lonesome I most wished I was dead. The stars were shining, and the leaves rustled in the woods ever so mournful; and I heard an owl, away off, who-whooing about somebody that was dead, and a whippowill and a dog crying about somebody that was going to die; and the wind was trying to whisper something to me, and I couldn't make out what it was, and so it made the cold shivers run over me. Then away out in the woods I heard that kind of a sound that a ghost makes when it wants to tell about something that's on its mind and can't make itself understood, and so can't rest easy in its grave, and has to go about that way every night grieving. I got so down-hearted and scared I did wish I had some company. Pretty soon a spider went crawling up my shoulder, and I flipped it off and it lit in the candle; and before I could budge it was all shriveled up. I didn't need anybody to tell me that that was an awful bad sign and would fetch me some bad luck, so I was scared and most shook the clothes off of me. I got up and turned around in my tracks three times and crossed my breast every time; and then I tied up a little lock of my hair with a thread to keep witches away. But I hadn't no confidence. You do that when you've lost a horseshoe that you've found, instead of nailing it up over the door, but I hadn't ever heard anybody say it was any way to keep off bad luck when you'd killed a spider.

I set down again, a-shaking all over, and got out my pipe for a smoke; for the house was all as still as death now, and so the widow wouldn't know. Well, after a long time I heard the clock away off in the town go boom—boom—boom—twelve licks; and all still again—stiller than ever. Pretty soon I heard a twig snap down in the dark amongst the trees—something was a stirring. I set still and listened. Directly I could just barely hear a "me-yow! me-yow!" down there. That was good! Says I, "me-yow! me-yow!" as soft as I could, and then I put out the light and scrambled out of the window on to the shed. Then I slipped down to the ground and crawled in among the trees, and, sure enough, there was Tom Sawyer waiting for me.

III Thinking, Talking and Writing About Literature

1 Textual Cognition

Make an introductory presentation on the following terms related to this literary work.

1) slave narrative
2) vernacularism

2 Textual Reading

Search for evidence in the text and answer the following questions.

1) How did Huck differ from the Widow Douglas and Miss Watson in terms of his idea of lying?
2) Why did Huck return to the Widow Douglas after running away?
3) How is Huck intuitively against any social norms?
4) What childish superstitions of Huck's are mentioned in the excerpt?

3 Critical Reading

Discuss in groups the following questions to further explore this literary work.

1) Critics have argued a lot about race and the ending of *The Adventures of Huckleberry Finn*. What ideas about racism and slavery do you find in the novel?
2) In the novel *The Adventures of Huckleberry Finn,* Huck's artless vernacular speech is adapted to detailed and poetic descriptions of scenes, vivid representations of characters, and narrative renditions that are both broadly comic and subtly ironic. Can you list some examples of vernacular expressions in scenery description and irony in the novel?

4 Writing About Literature

Read the following critical excerpt and then write an essay.

> Morrison, Toni. "Huck Finn in Context Coursepack." *The Oxford Mark Twain: Adventures of Huckleberry Finn*. Ed. Shelley Fisher Fishkin. Oxford: Oxford University Press, 2009. 153–160.

As an abused and homeless child running from a feral male parent, Huck cannot dwell on Jim's confession and regret about parental negligence without precipitating a crisis from which neither he nor the text could recover. Huck's desire for a father who is adviser and trustworthy companion is universal, but he also needs something more: a father whom, unlike his own, he can control. No white man can serve all three functions. If the runaway Huck discovered on the island had been a white convict with protective paternal instincts, none of this would work, for there could be no guarantee of control and no games-playing nonsense concerning his release at the end. Only a black male slave can deliver all Huck desires. Because Jim can be controlled, it becomes possible for Huck to feel responsible for and to him—but without the onerous burden of lifelong debt that a real father figure would demand. For Huck, Jim is a father-for-free. This delicate, covert and fractious problematic is thus hidden and exposed by litotes and speechlessness, both of which are dramatic ways of begging attention.

Concerning this matter of fatherhood, there are two other instances of silence—one remarkable for its warmth, the other for its glacial coldness. In the first, Jim keeps silent for practically four-fifths of the book about having seen Pap's corpse. There seems no reason for this withholding except his concern for Huck's emotional well-being. Although one could argue that knowing the menace of his father was over might relieve Huck enormously, it could also be argued that dissipating that threat would remove the principal element of the necessity for escape—Huck's escape, that is. In any case, silence on this point persists and we learn its true motive in the penultimate paragraph in the book. And right there is the other speech void—cold and shivery in its unsaying. Jim tells Huck that his money is safe because his father is dead.

Essay Writing

There is much critical controversy concerning race and the ending of *The Adventures of Huckleberry Finn*. Some critics believe that this is an anti-racist text, while others hold that Mark Twain is a racist. How does Toni Morrison reframe the debate? Write an essay about Morrison's criticism of *The Adventures of Huckleberry Finn* with no less than 500 words.

Ⅳ Further Activity

Scan the QR code and listen to the audio of Chapter 2 of *The Adventures of Huckleberry Finn*.

Lecture 4
Stephen Crane

Profile of the Writer

Stephen Crane
(1871–1900)

Born on November 1, 1871, in Newark, New Jersey, Crane was the 14th and last child of the family. The young Crane attended preparatory school at Claverack College and later studied at Lafayette College and Syracuse University.

Crane truly embarked upon a literary career in the early 1890s when he moved to New York and began freelancing as a writer, coming to work for the *New York Tribune*. Living a bohemian lifestyle among local artists, Crane gained firsthand familiarity with poverty and street life, focusing his writing efforts on New York's downtrodden tenement districts, especially Bowery.

Although Crane most likely had completed an early draft of his first book, the novella *Maggie: A Girl of the Streets* (1893), while studying at Syracuse, it wasn't until after moving to Bowery that he rewrote and finalized the piece. A compassionate story of an innocent and abused girl's descent into prostitution and her eventual suicide, *Maggie* was initially rejected by several publishers who feared that Crane's description of slum life would shock readers. Therefore, Crane ended up publishing the work himself in 1893 under the pseudonym Johnston Smith.

In 1895, Crane published *The Red Badge of Courage*, a work that followed an individual soldier's emotional experiences in the midst of a Civil War battle. *Courage* became renowned for its perceived authenticity and realistic depictions of violent conflict. He had in fact never been in military combat, but constructed scenes from research and what he referred to as skirmishes on the football field.

Due to Crane's new reputation as a war writer, as well as his curiosity and accuracy in depicting psychological states of combat, he undertook a new career: war correspondent. In 1897, Crane set sail for Cuba to report on the insurrection there. However, the ship on which he was traveling sank. Crane wrote his more-than-a-day drifting experience into one of the world's great short stories, "The Open Boat".

Unable to get to Cuba, in April 1898, Crane went to Greece to report on the Greco-Turkish War. After an armistice was signed between Greece and Turkey in May of that year, Crane left Greece for England. Crane continued to write, but mostly negative reviews of every novel since *Courage* caused his literary reputation to dwindle. Despite *Courage* being in its 14th printing, Crane was running out of money partially due to an ostentatious lifestyle.

On top of his mounting financial troubles, Crane's health had been deteriorating for a few years; he had contracted everything from malaria to yellow fever during his Bowery years and time as a war correspondent. In May 1900, Crane checked into a health spa in Germany. One month later, on June 5, 1900, Crane died of tuberculosis at the age of 28.

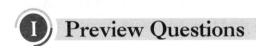
Preview Questions

1. Without any war experience, Stephen Crane realistically depicts the psychological complexities of battlefield emotion and makes *The Red Badge of Courage* a literary classic. Does that mean that experience does not count much in writing?

2. Stephen Crane is also known for authoring *Maggie: A Girl of the Streets*, and has been credited with establishing the foundations of modern American naturalism. What do you know about this novel?

II Literary Reading: *The Red Badge of Courage* (Chapter 3)

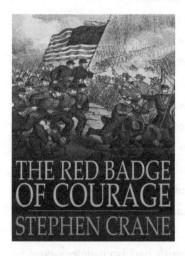

When another night came, the columns, changed to purple streaks, filed across two pontoon bridges. A glaring fire wine-tinted the waters of the river. Its rays, shining upon the moving masses of troops, brought forth here and there sudden gleams of silver or gold. Upon the other shore a dark and mysterious range of hills was curved against the sky. The insect voices of the night sang solemnly.

After this crossing the youth assured himself that at any moment they might be suddenly and fearfully assaulted from the caves of the lowering woods. He kept his eyes watchfully upon the darkness.

But his regiment went unmolested to a camping place, and its soldiers slept the brave sleep of wearied men. In the morning they were routed out with early energy, and hustled along a narrow road that led deep into the forest.

It was during this rapid march that the regiment lost many of the marks of a new command.

The men had begun to count the miles upon their fingers, and they grew tired. "Sore feet an' damned short rations, that's all," said the loud soldier. There was perspiration and grumblings. After a time they began to shed their knapsacks. Some tossed them unconcernedly down; others hid them carefully, asserting their plans to return for them at some convenient time. Men extricated themselves from thick shirts. Presently few carried anything but their necessary clothing, blankets, haversacks, canteens, and arms and ammunition. "You can now eat and shoot," said the tall soldier to the youth. "That's all you want to do."

There was sudden change from the ponderous infantry of theory to the light and speedy infantry of practice. The regiment, relieved of a burden, received a new impetus. But there was much loss of valuable knapsacks, and, on the whole, very good shirts.

But the regiment was not yet veteranlike in appearance. Veteran regiments in the army were likely to be very small aggregations of men. Once, when the command had first come to the field, some perambulating veterans, noting the length of their column, had accosted them thus: "Hey, fellers, what brigade is that?" And when the men had replied that they formed a regiment and not a brigade, the older soldiers had laughed, and said, "O Gawd!"

Also, there was too great a similarity in the hats. The hats of a regiment should properly represent the history of headgear for a period of years. And, moreover, there were no letters of faded gold speaking from the colors. They were new and beautiful, and the color bearer habitually oiled the pole.

Presently the army again sat down to think. The odor of the peaceful pines was in the men's nostrils. The sound of monotonous axe blows rang through the forest, and the insects, nodding upon their perches, crooned like old women. The youth returned to his theory of a blue demonstration.

One gray dawn, however, he was kicked in the leg by the tall soldier, and then, before he was entirely awake, he found himself running down a wood road in the midst of men who were panting from the first effects of speed. His canteen banged rhythmically upon his thigh, and his haversack bobbed softly. His musket bounced a trifle from his shoulder at each stride and made his cap feel uncertain upon his head.

He could hear the men whisper jerky sentences: "Say—what's all this—about?" "What th' thunder—we—skedaddlin' this way fer?" "Billie—keep off m' feet. Yeh run—like a cow." And the loud soldier's shrill voice could be heard: "What th'devil they in sich a hurry for?"

The youth thought the damp fog of early morning moved from the rush of a great body of troops. From the distance came a sudden spatter of firing.

He was bewildered. As he ran with his comrades he strenuously tried to think, but all he knew was that if he fell down those coming behind would tread upon him. All his faculties seemed to be needed to guide him over and past obstructions. He felt carried along by a mob.

The sun spread disclosing rays, and, one by one, regiments burst into view like armed men just born of the earth. The youth perceived that the time had come. He was about to be measured. For a moment he felt in the face of his great trial like a babe, and the flesh over his heart seemed very thin. He seized time to look about him calculatingly.

But he instantly saw that it would be impossible for him to escape from the regiment. It inclosed him. And there were iron laws of tradition and law on four sides. He was in a moving box.

As he perceived this fact it occurred to him that he had never wished to come to the war. He had not enlisted of his free will. He had been dragged by the merciless government. And now they were taking him out to be slaughtered.

The regiment slid down a bank and wallowed across a little stream. The mournful current moved slowly on, and from the water, shaded black, some white bubble eyes looked at the men.

As they climbed the hill on the farther side artillery began to boom. Here the youth forgot many things as he felt a sudden impulse of curiosity. He scrambled up the bank with a speed that could not be exceeded by a bloodthirsty man.

He expected a battle scene.

There were some little fields girted and squeezed by a forest. Spread over the grass and in among the tree trunks, he could see knots and waving lines of skirmishers who were running hither and thither and firing at the landscape. A dark battle line lay upon a sunstruck clearing that gleamed orange color. A flag fluttered.

Other regiments floundered up the bank. The brigade was formed in line of battle, and after a pause started slowly through the woods in the rear of the receding skirmishers, who were continually melting into the scene to appear again farther on. They were always busy as bees, deeply absorbed in their little combats.

The youth tried to observe everything. He did not use care to avoid trees and branches, and his forgotten feet were constantly knocking against stones or getting entangled in briers. He was aware that these battalions with their commotions were woven red and startling into the gentle fabric of softened greens and browns. It looked to be a wrong place for a battle field.

The skirmishers in advance fascinated him. Their shots into thickets and at distant and prominent trees spoke to him of tragedies—hidden, mysterious, solemn.

Once the line encountered the body of a dead soldier. He lay upon his back staring at the sky. He was dressed in an awkward suit of yellowish brown. The youth could see that the soles of his shoes had been worn to the thinness of writing paper, and from a great rent in one the dead foot projected piteously. And it was as if fate had betrayed the soldier. In death it exposed to his enemies that poverty which in life he had perhaps concealed from his friends.

The ranks opened covertly to avoid the corpse. The invulnerable dead man forced a way for himself. The youth looked keenly at the ashen face. The wind raised the tawny beard. It moved as if a hand were stroking it. He vaguely desired to walk around and around the body and stare; the impulse of the living to try to read in dead eyes the answer to the Question.

During the march the ardor which the youth had acquired when out of view of the field rapidly faded to nothing. His curiosity was quite easily satisfied. If an intense scene had caught him with its wild swing as he came to the top of the bank, he might have gone roaring on. This advance upon Nature was too calm. He had opportunity to reflect. He had time in which to wonder about himself and to attempt to probe his sensations.

Absurd ideas took hold upon him. He thought that he did not relish the landscape. It threatened him. A coldness swept over his back, and it is true that his trousers felt to him that they were no fit for his legs at all.

A house standing placidly in distant fields had to him an ominous look. The shadows of the woods were formidable. He was certain that in this vista there lurked fierce-eyed hosts. The swift thought came to him that the generals did not know what they were about. It was all a trap. Suddenly those close forests would bristle with rifle barrels. Ironlike brigades would appear in the rear. They were all going to be sacrificed. The generals were stupids. The enemy would presently swallow the whole command. He glared about him, expecting to see the stealthy approach of his death.

He thought that he must break from the ranks and harangue his comrades. They must not all be killed like pigs; and he was sure it would come to pass unless they were informed of these dangers. The generals were idiots to send them marching into a regular pen. There was but one pair of eyes in the corps. He would step forth and make a speech. Shrill and passionate words came to his lips.

The line, broken into moving fragments by the ground, went calmly on through fields and woods. The youth looked at the men nearest him, and saw, for the most part, expressions of deep interest, as if they were investigating something that had fascinated them. One or two stepped with overvaliant airs as if they were already plunged into war. Others walked as upon thin ice. The greater part of the untested men appeared quiet and absorbed. They were going to look at war, the red animal—war, the blood-swollen god. And they were deeply engrossed in this march.

As he looked the youth gripped his outcry at his throat. He saw that even if the men were tottering with fear they would laugh at his warning. They would jeer him, and, if practicable, pelt him with missiles. Admitting that he might be wrong, a frenzied declamation of the kind would turn him into a worm.

He assumed, then, the demeanor of one who knows that he is doomed alone to unwritten responsibilities. He lagged, with tragic glances at the sky.

He was surprised presently by the young lieutenant of his company, who began heartily to beat him with a sword, calling out in a loud and insolent voice: "Come, young man, get up into ranks there. No skulking 'll do here." He mended his pace with suitable haste. And he hated the lieutenant, who had no appreciation of fine minds. He was a mere brute.

After a time the brigade was halted in the cathedral light of a forest. The busy skirmishers were still popping. Through the aisles of the wood could be seen the floating smoke from their rifles. Sometimes it went up in little balls, white and compact.

During this halt many men in the regiment began erecting tiny hills in front of them. They used stones, sticks, earth, and anything they thought might turn a bullet. Some built comparatively large ones, while others seemed content with little ones.

This procedure caused a discussion among the men. Some wished to fight like duelists, believing it to be correct to stand erect and be, from their feet to their foreheads, a mark.

They said they scorned the devices of the cautious. But the others scoffed in reply, and pointed to the veterans on the flanks who were digging at the ground like terriers. In a short time there was quite a barricade along the regimental fronts. Directly, however, they were ordered to withdraw from that place.

This astounded the youth. He forgot his stewing over the advance movement. "Well, then, what did they march us out here for?" he demanded of the tall soldier. The latter with calm faith began a heavy explanation, although he had been compelled to leave a little protection of stones and dirt to which he had devoted much care and skill.

When the regiment was aligned in another position each man's regard for his safety caused another line of small intrenchments. They ate their noon meal behind a third one. They were moved from this one also. They were marched from place to place with apparent aimlessness.

The youth had been taught that a man became another thing in battle. He saw his salvation in such a change. Hence this waiting was an ordeal to him. He was in a fever of impatience. He considered that there was denoted a lack of purpose on the part of the generals. He began to complain to the tall soldier. "I can't stand this much longer," he cried. "I don't see what good it does to make us wear out our legs for nothin'." He wished to return to camp, knowing that this affair was a blue demonstration; or else to go into a battle and discover that he had been a fool in his doubts, and was, in truth, a man of traditional courage. The strain of present circumstances he felt to be intolerable.

The philosophical tall soldier measured a sandwich of cracker and pork and swallowed it in a nonchalant manner. "Oh, I suppose we must go reconnoitering around the country jest to keep 'em from getting too close, or to develop 'em, or something."

"Huh!" said the loud soldier.

"Well," cried the youth, still fidgeting, "I'd rather do anything 'most than go tramping 'round the country all day doing no good to nobody and jest tiring ourselves out."

"So would I," said the loud soldier. "It ain't right. I tell you if anybody with any sense was a-runnin' this army it—"

"Oh, shut up!" roared the tall private. "You little fool. You little damn' cuss. You ain't had that there coat and them pants on for six months, and yet you talk as if—"

"Well, I wanta do some fighting anyway," interrupted the other. "I didn't come here to walk. I could 'ave walked to home-'round an' 'round the barn, if I jest wanted to walk."

The tall one, red-faced, swallowed another sandwich as if taking poison in despair.

But gradually, as he chewed, his face became again quiet and contented. He could not rage in fierce argument in the presence of such sandwiches. During his meals he always wore an air of blissful contemplation of the food he had swallowed. His spirit seemed then to be communing with the viands.

He accepted new environment and circumstance with great coolness, eating from his haversack at every opportunity. On the march he went along with the stride of a hunter, objecting to neither gait nor distance. And he had not raised his voice when he had been ordered away from three little protective piles of earth and stone, each of which had been an engineering feat worthy of being made sacred to the name of his grandmother.

In the afternoon, the regiment went out over the same ground it had taken in the morning. The landscape then ceased to threaten the youth. He had been close to it and become familiar with it.

When, however, they began to pass into a new region, his old fears of stupidity and incompetence reassailed him, but this time he doggedly let them babble. He was occupied with his problem, and in his desperation he concluded that the stupidity did not greatly matter.

Once he thought he had concluded that it would be better to get killed directly and end his troubles. Regarding death thus out of the corner of his eye, he conceived it to be nothing but rest, and he was filled with a momentary astonishment that he should have made an extraordinary commotion over the mere matter of getting killed. He would die; he would go to some place where he would be understood. It was useless to expect appreciation of his profound and fine sense from such men as the lieutenant. He must look to the grave for comprehension.

The skirmish fire increased to a long clattering sound. With it was mingled far-away cheering. A battery spoke.

Directly the youth could see the skirmishers running. They were pursued by the sound of musketry fire. After a time the hot, dangerous flashes of the rifles were visible. Smoke clouds went slowly and insolently across the fields like observant phantoms. The din became crescendo, like the roar of an oncoming train.

A brigade ahead of them and on the right went into action with a rending roar. It was as if it had exploded. And thereafter it lay stretched in the distance behind a long gray wall, that one was obliged to look twice at to make sure that it was smoke.

The youth, forgetting his neat plan of getting killed, gazed spell bound. His eyes grew wide and busy with the action of the scene. His mouth was a little ways open.

Of a sudden he felt a heavy and sad hand laid upon his shoulder. Awakening from his trance of observation he turned and beheld the loud soldier.

"It's my first and last battle, old boy," said the latter, with intense gloom. He was quite pale and his girlish lip was trembling.

"Eh?" murmured the youth in great astonishment.

"It's my first and last battle, old boy," continued the loud soldier. "Something tells me—"

"What?"

"I'm a gone coon this first time and—and I w-want you to take these here things—to—my—folks." He ended in a quavering sob of pity for himself. He handed the youth a little packet done up in a yellow envelope.

"Why, what the devil—" began the youth again.

But the other gave him a glance as from the depths of a tomb, and raised his limp hand in a prophetic manner and turned away.

III Thinking, Talking and Writing About Literature

1 Textual Cognition

Make an introductory presentation on the following terms related to this literary work.

1) imagery
2) symbolism

2 Textual Reading

Search for evidence in the text and answer the following questions.

1) What was Henry's feeling toward the dead soldier who was described in great detail in the text?

2) Why did the loud soldier commit "a little packet done up in a yellow envelope" to Henry Fleming?

3) What effect does Henry Fleming's perception of himself have on his reactions to the war and on other soldiers?

3 Critical Reading

Discuss in groups the following questions to further explore this literary work.

1) Why does the author refer to Henry Fleming as "the youth", his friends "the tall soldier" and "the loud one", instead of Jim Conklin and Wilson?

2) The Civil War battlefields are nothing like Henry Fleming had imagined them to be. Henry's ideas about war changed during the march. Can you draw a map showing the gradual changes of Henry's mood and ideas on the way?

④ Writing About Literature

Read the following critical excerpt and then write an essay.

> Salerno, Patrick. *CliffsNotes on Crane's* The Red Badge of Courage. Foster City: IDG Books Worldwide, 2000. 81–83.

Stephen Crane consistently uses figurative language to create images that vividly describe all aspects of war. For example, in the passage, "The cold passed reluctantly from the earth, and the retiring fogs revealed an army stretched out on the hills, resting", an example of personification, the cold, the fog, and the army are described as persons with specific behaviors, feelings, and needs. In addition, Crane uses personification to create a personality for the combatants, both collectively and individually. The clauses, "brigades grinned" and "regiments laughed", are good examples. When Henry's voice is described "as bitter as dregs", this simile allows the reader to experience the voice of an individual soldier.

The imagery developed for an impending battle uses similar techniques. The battle is "the blaze" and "a monster"; the combatants are "serpents crawling from hill to hill"; Henry's regiment is a "blasting host" (a killing machine); "red eyes" (enemy campfires) watch across rivers. All these images contribute to an ominous mood of foreboding.

The regiment is sometimes identified as a person, sometimes a monster, and sometimes a reptile. These images cause the reader to lose sight of the fact that the regiment is really a unit of men—of individual soldiers. The continued use of personification draws the reader to a feeling that a battle is a battle of regimental monsters, not of individual men.

In Chapter 5, Crane continues the use of figurative language, including simile, personification, and metaphor, to paint images of war. For example, he writes that "A shell screaming like a storm banshee went over the huddled heads of the reserves", a simile, and "They could see a flag that tossed in the smoke angrily", a personification, and that "The composite monster which had caused the other troops to flee had not then appeared" a metaphor. The enemy is still not visible. The wait for that "composite monster", continues. Just as the troops experience the dreadful wait, the reader feels the same emotions that all the soldiers are feeling. Crane develops this fear by using figurative language to create monster imagery.

Crane employs similes and personification to draw pictures of soldiers and their weapons. For example, a soldier's "eyeballs were about to crack like hot stones"; "The man at the youth's elbow was babbling something soft and tender like the monologue of a babe"; "The guns squatted in a row like savage chiefs". Crane uses both personification and simile in the line, "The cannon with their noses poked slantingly at the ground grunted and grumbled like stout men, brave but with objections to hurry." This line makes the weapons appear to be living creatures. The use of personification in the line, "The sore joints of the regiment creaked as it painfully floundered into position", turns the regiment into one large, tired soldier. Crane's similes describe groups and individuals in these examples: the rebel forces were "running like pursued imps" and Henry, at first, "ran like a rabbit" and, later, "like a blind man".

Crane develops imagery, using metaphor and personification, to make it clear that Henry has lost all his rational powers and that he is in a total state of panic. For example, to Henry, the enemy soldiers are metaphorically "machines of steel", "redoubtable dragons", and "a red and green monster"; the men who were nearest the battle would make the "initial morsels for the dragons"; "the shells flying past him have rows of cruel teeth that grinned at him". These images clearly show Henry's fright of the enemy.

Essay Writing

Stephen Crane brings his readers back to the Civil War with *The Red Badge of Courage*, which is known for its "fascinatingly historical" quality. Different from earlier war literature, Crane's narration and his soldiers' talk are realistic and unsentimental, making his depiction real and believable. Write an essay to show how Crane used his modern sensibility and modern techniques to animate a historical period, making his soldiers convincingly alive. Your essay should not be shorter than 500 words.

IV Further Activity

Scan the QR code and listen to the audio of Chapter 3 of *The Red Badge of Courage*.

Lecture 5
Sherwood Anderson

Profile of the Writer

Sherwood Anderson
(1876–1941)

  Sherwood Anderson was born in Camden, Ohio on September 13, 1876. The Andersons traveled from one small town to the next for the first eight years of Sherwood's life, until in 1884 the family settled into Clyde, Ohio, the town which would later be the inspiration behind *Winesburg, Ohio*.

  Anderson's childhood and adolescence witnessed family hardship. His father's business failed and his mother became an alcoholic. Anderson left school at the age of 14 in order to help with the family's finances. The hardships that the boy experienced growing up working and not having a strong father figure in his life, harbored some resentment toward his father. When he was 19, his mother died of tuberculosis and Anderson and his siblings could not keep the family together any longer. So Anderson left for Chicago.

  In Chicago, Sherwood Anderson met and fell in love with Cornelia Lane from Toledo. They married in 1904, and two years later they moved to Cleveland, where he accepted the job as the president of the United Factories Company. After the birth of their first son in 1907, Anderson decided he needed to earn more money to support his family. So he started up his own company and by 1908, the Anderson Manufacturing Company was a success. Around the same time, his passion for literature was growing.

Anderson desperately tried to fulfill both his financial obligations to his family and his personal obsession with literature, but the battle was difficult. Anderson also had problems in his marriage. The tension between his personal gratifications, his troubled marriage, and his family obligations all came to a breakdown in November 1912.

After his recovery, Anderson left the business world and returned to writing in Chicago. With the help of his friends, a publisher soon picked up Anderson. In 1916, Cornelia and Sherwood decided to divorce. While his family life was less than ideal, his career began to take off. His first novel *Windy McPherson's Son* was published that same year. The following year he published *Marching Men*. Finally in 1919, Anderson's finest literary work was created—*Winesburg, Ohio*. While the shocking novel was not appreciated during Anderson's lifetime, the impact of the novel had a great influence on other writers such as Faulkner and Hemingway, and set a new standard for Midwestern literature.

Through Anderson's memoir, readers learn about how almost every single one of his stories or characters are based on people he knew personally or had encountered. Later in his life, Anderson moved to Marion, Virginia, where he bought and ran two newspapers. He died unexpectedly in Panama, on a trip to South America, and was buried in Marion.

Preview Questions

1. In Sherwood Anderson's life, there is an abrupt turn from a successful businessman to a professional writer. In 1912, he left his family to pursue a writing career in Chicago. How did such a sudden change come about?

2. Sherwood Anderson was famous for his characterization of the grotesque. Why do you think the grotesque shall be represented in literature?

Literary Reading: The Egg

My father was, I am sure, intended by nature to be a cheerful, kindly man. Until he was thirty-four years old he worked as a farmhand for a man named Thomas Butterworth whose place lay near the town of Bidwell, Ohio. He had then a horse of his own and on Saturday evenings drove into town to spend a few hours in social intercourse with other farmhands. In town he drank several glasses of beer and stood about in Ben Head's saloon-crowded on Saturday evenings with visiting farmhands. Songs were sung and glasses thumped on the bar. At ten o'clock father drove home along a lonely country road, made his horse comfortable for the night and himself went to bed, quite happy in his position in life. He had at that time no notion of trying to rise in the world.

It was in the spring of his thirty-fifth year that father married my mother, then a country schoolteacher, and in the following spring I came wriggling and crying into the world. Something happened to the two people. They became ambitious. The American passion for getting up in the world took possession of them.

It may have been that mother was responsible. Being a schoolteacher she had no doubt read books and magazines. She had, I presume, read of how Garfield, Lincoln, and other Americans rose from poverty to fame and greatness and as I lay beside her—in the days of her lying—she may have dreamed that I would someday rule men and cities. At any rate she induced father to give up his place as a farmhand, sell his horse and embark on an independent enterprise of his own. She was a tall silent woman with a long nose and troubled grey eyes. For herself she wanted nothing. For father and myself she was incurably ambitious.

The first venture into which the two people went turned out badly. They rented ten acres of poor stony land on Griggs's Road, eight miles from Bidwell, and launched into chicken raising. I grew into boyhood on the place and got my first impressions of life there. From the beginning they were impressions of disaster and if, in my turn, I am a gloomy man inclined to see the darker side of life, I attribute it to the fact that what should have been for me the happy joyous days of childhood were spent on a chicken farm.

One unversed in such matters can have no notion of the many and tragic things that can happen to a chicken. It is born out of an egg, lives for a few weeks as a tiny fluffy thing such as you will see pictured on Easter cards, then becomes hideously naked, eats quantities of corn and meal bought by the sweat of your father's brow, gets diseases called pip, cholera, and other names, stands looking with stupid eyes at the sun, becomes sick and dies. A few hens and now and then a rooster, intended to serve God's mysterious ends, struggle through to maturity. The hens lay eggs out of which come other chickens and the dreadful cycle is thus made complete. It is all unbelievably complex. Most philosophers must have been raised on chicken farms. One hopes for so much from a chicken and is so dreadfully disillusioned. Small chickens, just setting out on the journey of life, look so bright and alert and they are in fact so dreadfully stupid. They are so much like people they mix one up in one's judgments of life. If disease does not kill them they wait until your expectations are thoroughly aroused and then walk under the wheels of a wagon—to go squashed and dead back to their maker. Vermin infest their youth, and fortunes must be spent for curative powders. In later life I have seen how a literature has been built up on the subject of fortunes to be made out of the raising of chickens. It is intended to be read by the gods who have just eaten of the tree of the knowledge of good and evil. It is a hopeful literature and declares that much may be done by simple ambitious people who own a few hens. Do not be led astray by it. It was not written for you. Go hunt for gold on the frozen hills of Alaska, put your faith in the honesty of a politician, believe if you will that the world is daily growing better and that good will triumph over evil, but do not read and believe the literature that is written concerning the hen. It was not written for you.

I, however, digress. My tale does not primarily concern itself with the hen. If correctly told it will center on the egg. For ten years my father and mother struggled to make our chicken farm pay and then they gave up that struggle and began another. They moved into the town of Bidwell, Ohio and embarked in the restaurant business. After ten years of worry with incubators that did not hatch, and with tiny—and in their own way lovely—balls of fluff that passed on into semi-naked pullerhood and from that into dead henhood, we threw all aside and packing our belongings on a wagon drove down Griggs's Road toward Bidwell, a tiny caravan of hope looking for a new place from which to start on our upward journey through life.

We must have been a sad looking lot, not, I fancy, unlike refugees fleeing from a battlefield. Mother and I walked in the road. The wagon that contained our goods had been borrowed for the day from Mr. Albert Griggs, a neighbor. Out of its sides stuck the legs of cheap chairs and at the back of the pile of beds, tables, and boxes filled with kitchen utensils was a crate of live chickens, and on top of that the baby carriage in which I had been wheeled about in my infancy. Why we stuck to the baby carriage I don't know. It was unlikely other children would be born and the wheels were broken. People who have few possessions cling tightly to those they have. That is one of the facts that make life so discouraging.

Father rode on top of the wagon. He was then a bald-headed man of forty-five, a little fat and from long association with mother and the chickens he had become habitually silent and discouraged. All during our ten years on the chicken farm he had worked as a laborer on neighboring farms and most of the money he had earned had been spent for remedies to cure chicken diseases, on Wilmer's White Wonder Cholera Cure or Professor Bidlow's Egg Producer or some other preparations that mother found advertised in the poultry papers. There were two little patches of hair on father's head just above his ears. I remember that as a child I used to sit looking at him when he had gone to sleep in a chair before the stove on Sunday afternoons in the winter. I had at that rime already begun to read books and have notions of my own and the bald path that led over the top of his head was, I fancied, something like a broad road, such a road as Caesar might have made on which to lead his legions out of Rome and into the wonders of an unknown world. The tufts of hair that grew above father's ears were, I thought, like forests. I fell into a half-sleeping, half-waking state and dreamed I was a tiny thing going along the road into a far beautiful place where there were no chicken farms and where life was a happy eggless affair.

One might write a book concerning our flight from the chicken farm into town. Mother and I walked the entire eight miles—she to be sure that nothing fell from the wagon and I to see the wonders of the world. On the seat of the wagon beside father was his greatest treasure. I will tell you of that.

On a chicken farm where hundreds and even thousands of chickens come out of eggs, surprising things sometimes happen. Grotesques are born out of eggs as out of people. The accident does not often occur—perhaps once in a thousand births. A chicken is, you see, born that has four legs, two pairs of wings, two heads or what not. The things do not live. They go quickly back to the hand of their maker that has for a moment trembled. The fact that the poor little things could not live was one of the tragedies of life to father. He had some sort of notion that if he could but bring into henhood or roosterhood a five-legged hen or a two-headed rooster his fortune would be made. He dreamed of taking the wonder about to county fairs and of growing rich by exhibiting it to other farmhands.

At any rate he saved all the little monstrous things that had been born on our chicken farm. They were preserved in alcohol and put each in its own glass bottle. These he had carefully put into a box and on our journey into town it was carried on the wagon seat beside him. He drove the horses with one hand and with the other clung to the box. When we got to our destination the box was taken down at once and the bottles removed. All during our days as keepers of a restaurant in the town of Bidwell, Ohio, the grotesques in their little glass bottles sat on a shelf back of the counter. Mother sometimes protested but father was a rock on the subject of his treasure. The grotesques were, he declared, valuable. People, he said, liked to look at strange and wonderful things.

Did I say that we embarked in the restaurant business in the town of Bidwell, Ohio? I exaggerated a little. The town itself lay at the foot of a low hill and on the shore of a small river. The railroad did not run through the town and the station was a mile away to the north at a place called Pickleville. There had been a cider mill and pickle factory at the station, but before the time of our coming they had both gone out of business. In the morning and in the evening busses came down to the station along a road called Turner's Pike from the hotel on the main street of Bidwell. Our going to the out-of-the-way place to embark in the restaurant business was mother's idea. She talked of it for a year and then one day went off and rented an empty store building opposite the railroad station. It was her idea that the restaurant would be profitable. Travelling men, she said, would be always waiting around to take trains out of town and town people would come to the station to await incoming trains. They would come to the restaurant to buy pieces of pie and drink coffee. Now that I am older I know that she had another motive in going. She was ambitious for me. She wanted me to rise in the world, to get into a town school and become a man of the towns.

At Pickleville father and mother worked hard as they always had done. At first there was the necessity of putting our place into shape to be a restaurant. That took a month. Father built a shelf on which he put tins of vegetables. He painted a sign on which he put his name in large red letters. Below his name was the sharp command—"EAT HERE"—that was so seldom obeyed. A showcase was bought and filled with cigars and tobacco. Mother scrubbed the floor and the walls of the room. I went to school in the town and was glad to be away from the farm and from the presence of the discouraged, sad-looking chickens. Still I was not very joyous. In the evening I walked home from school along Turner's Pike and remembered the children I had seen playing in the town school yard. A troop of little girls had gone hopping about and singing. I tried that. Down along the frozen road I went hopping solemnly on one leg. "Hippity hop to the barber shop," I sang shrilly. Then I stopped and looked doubtfully about. I was afraid of being seen in my gay mood. It must have seemed to me that I was doing a thing that should not be done by one who, like myself, had been raised on a chicken farm where death was a daily visitor.

Mother decided that our restaurant should remain open at night. At ten in the evening a passenger train went north past our door followed by a local freight. The freight crew had switching to do in Pickleville and when the work was done they came to our restaurant for hot coffee and food. Sometimes one of them ordered a fried egg. In the morning at four they returned northbound and again visited us. A little trade began to grow up. Mother slept at night and during the day tended the restaurant and fed our boarders while father slept. He slept in the same bed mother had occupied during the night and I went off to the town of Bidwell and to school. During the long nights, while mother and I slept, father cooked meats that were to go into sandwiches for the lunch baskets of our boarders. Then an idea in regard to getting up in the world came into his head. The American spirit took hold of him. He also became ambitious.

In the long nights when there was little to do father had time to think. That was his undoing. He decided that he had in the past been an unsuccessful man because he had not been cheerful enough and that in the future he would adopt a cheerful outlook on life. In the early morning he came upstairs and got into bed with mother. She woke and the two talked. From my bed in the corner I listened.

It was father's idea that both he and mother should try to entertain the people who came to eat at our restaurant. I cannot now remember his words, but he gave the impression of one about to become in some obscure way a kind of public entertainer. When people, particularly young people from the town of Bidwell, came into our place, as on very rare occasions they did, bright entertaining conversation was to be made. From father's words I gathered that something of the jolly innkeeper effect was to be sought. Mother must have been doubtful from the first, but she said nothing discouraging. It was father's notion that a passion for the company of himself and mother would spring up in the breasts of the younger people of the town of Bidwell. In the evening bright happy groups would come singing down Turner's Pike. They would troop shouting with joy and laughter into our place. There would be song and festivity. I do not mean to give the impression that father spoke so elaborately of the matter. He was as I have said an uncommunicative man. "They want some place to go. I tell you they want some place to go," he said over and over. That was as far as he got. My own imagination has filled in the blanks.

For two or three weeks this notion of father's invaded our house. We did not talk much but in our daily lives tried earnestly to make smiles take the place of glum looks. Mother smiled at the boarders and I, catching the infection, smiled at our cat. Father became a little feverish in his anxiety to please. There was no doubt lurking somewhere in him a touch of the spirit of the showman. He did not waste much of his ammunition on the railroad men he served at night but seemed to be waiting for a young man or woman from Bidwell to come in to show what he could do. On the counter in the restaurant there was a wire basket kept always filled with eggs, and it must have been before his eyes when the idea of being entertaining was born in his brain. There was something pre-natal about the way eggs kept themselves connected with the development of his idea. At any rate an egg ruined his new impulse in life. Late one night I was awakened by a roar of anger coming from father's throat. Both mother and I sat upright in our beds. With trembling hands she lighted a lamp that stood on a table by her head. Downstairs the front door of our restaurant went shut with a bang and in a few minutes father tramped up the stairs. He held an egg in his hand and his hand trembled as though he were having a chill. There was a half insane light in his eyes. As he stood glaring at us I was sure he intended throwing the egg at either mother or me. Then he laid it gently on the table beside the lamp and dropped on his knees beside mother's bed. He began to cry like a boy and I, carried away by his grief, cried with him. The two of us filled the little upstairs room with our wailing voices. It is ridiculous, but of the picture we made I can remember only the fact that mother's hand continually stroked the bald path that ran across the top of his head. I have forgotten what mother said to him and how she induced him to tell her of what had happened downstairs. His explanation also has gone out of my mind. I remember only my own grief and fright and the shiny path over father's head glowing in the lamplight as he knelt by the bed.

As to what happened downstairs. For some unexplainable reason I know the story as well as though I had been a witness to my father's discomfiture. One in time gets to know many unexplainable things. On that evening young Joe Kane, son of a merchant of Bidwell, came to Pickleville to meet his father, who was expected on the ten o'clock evening train from the south. The train was three hours late and Joe came into our place to loaf about and to wait for its arrival. The local freight train came in and the freight crew were fed. Joe was left alone in the restaurant with father.

From the moment he came into our place the Bidwell young man must have been puzzled by my father's actions. It was his notion that father was angry at him for hanging around. He noticed that the restaurant keeper was apparently disturbed by his presence and he thought of going out. However, it began to rain and he did not fancy the long walk to town and back. He bought a five-cent cigar and ordered a cup of coffee. He had a newspaper in his pocket and took it out and began to read. "I'm waiting for the evening train. It's late," he said apologetically.

For a long time father, whom Joe Kane had never seen before, remained silently gazing at his visitor. He was no doubt suffering from an attack of stage fright. As so often happens in life he had thought so much and so often of the situation that now confronted him that he was somewhat nervous in its presence.

For one thing, he did not know what to do with his hands. He thrust one of them nervously over the counter and shook hands with Joe Kane. "How-de-do," he said. Joe Kane put his newspaper down and stared at him. Father's eye lighted on the basket of eggs that sat on the counter and he began to talk. "Well," he began hesitatingly, "well, you have heard of Christopher Columbus, eh?" He seemed to be angry. "That Christopher Columbus was a cheat," he declared emphatically. "He talked of making an egg stand on its end. He talked, he did, and then he went and broke the end of the egg."

My father seemed to his visitor to be beside himself at the duplicity of Christopher Columbus. He muttered and swore. He declared it was wrong to teach children that Christopher Columbus was a great man when, after all, he cheated at the critical moment. He had declared he would make an egg stand on end and then when his bluff had been called he had done a trick. Still grumbling at Columbus, father took an egg from the basket on the counter and began to walk up and down. He rolled the egg between the palms of his hands. He smiled genially. He began to mumble words regarding the effect to be produced on an egg by the electricity that comes out of the human body. He declared that without breaking its shell and by virtue of rolling it back and forth in his hands he could stand the egg on its end. He explained that the warmth of his hands and the gentle rolling movement he gave the egg created a new center of gravity, and Joe Kane was mildly interested. "I have handled thousands of eggs," father said. "No one knows more about eggs than I do."

He stood the egg on the counter and it fell on its side. He tried the trick again and again, each time rolling the egg between the palms of his hands and saying the words regarding the wonders of electricity and the laws of gravity. When after a half hour's effort he did succeed in making the egg stand for a moment, he looked up to find that his visitor was no longer watching. By the time he had succeeded in calling Joe Kane's attention to the success of his effort, the egg had again rolled over and lay on its side.

Afire with the showman's passion and at the same time a good deal disconcerted by the failure of his first effort, father now took the bottles containing the poultry monstrosities down from their place on the shelf and began to show them to his visitor. "How would you like to have seven legs and two heads like this fellow?" he asked, exhibiting the most remarkable of his treasures. A cheerful smile played over his face. He reached over the counter and tried to slap Joe Kane on the shoulder as he had seen men do in Ben Head's saloon when he was a young farmhand and drove to town on Saturday evenings. His visitor was made a little ill by the sight of the body of the terribly deformed bird floating in the alcohol in the bottle and got up to go. Coming from behind the counter, father took hold of the young man's arm and led him back to his seat. He grew a little angry and for a moment had to turn his face away and force himself to smile. Then he put the bottles back on the shelf. In an outburst of generosity he fairly compelled Joe Kane to have a fresh cup of coffee and another cigar at his expense. Then he took a pan and filling it with vinegar, taken from a jug that sat beneath the counter, he declared himself about to do a new trick. "I will heat this egg in this pan of vinegar," he said. "Then I will put it through the neck of a bottle without breaking the shell. When the egg is inside the bottle it will resume its normal shape and the shell will become hard again. Then I will give the bottle with the egg in it to you. You can take it about with you wherever you go. People will want to know how you got the egg in the bottle. Don't tell them. Keep them guessing. That is the way to have fun with this trick."

Father grinned and winked at his visitor. Joe Kane decided that the man who confronted him was mildly insane but harmless. He drank the cup of coffee that had been given him and began to read his paper again. When the egg had been heated in vinegar, father carried it on a spoon to the counter and going into a back room got an empty bottle. He was angry because his visitor did not watch him as he began to do his trick, but nevertheless went cheerfully to work. For a long time he struggled, trying to get the egg to go through the neck of the bottle. He put the pan of vinegar back on the stove, intending to reheat the egg, then picked it up and burned his fingers. After a second bath in the hot vinegar, the shell of the egg had been softened a little but not enough for his purpose. He worked and worked and a spirit of desperate determination took possession of him. When he thought that at last the trick was about to be consummated, the delayed train came in at the station and Joe Kane started to go nonchalantly out at the door. Father made a last desperate effort to conquer the egg and make it do the thing that would establish his reputation as one who knew how to entertain guests who came into his restaurant. He worried the egg. He attempted to be somewhat rough with it. He swore and the sweat stood out on his forehead. The egg broke under his hand. When the contents spurted over his clothes, Joe Kane, who had stopped at the door, turned and laughed.

A roar of anger rose from my father's throat. He danced and shouted a string of inarticulate words. Grabbing another egg from the basket on the counter, he threw it, just missing the head of the young man as he dodged through the door and escaped.

Father came upstairs to mother and me with an egg in his hand. I do not know what he intended to do. I imagine he had some idea of destroying it, of destroying all eggs, and that he intended to let mother and me see him begin. When, however, he got into the presence of mother something happened to him. He laid the egg gently on the table and dropped on his knees by the bed as I have already explained. He later decided to close the restaurant for the night and to come upstairs and get into bed. When he did so he blew out the light and after much muttered conversation both he and mother went to sleep. I suppose I went to sleep also, but my sleep was troubled. I awoke at dawn and for a long time looked at the egg that lay on the table. I wondered why eggs had to be and why from the egg came the hen who again laid the egg. The question got into my blood. It has stayed there, I imagine, because I am the son of my father. At any rate, the problem remains unsolved in my mind. And that, I conclude, is but another evidence of the complete and final triumph of the egg—at least as far as my family is concerned.

Thinking, Talking and Writing About Literature

###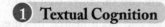

Make an introductory presentation on the following terms related to this literary work.

1) the grotesque in literature
2) the tripartite theory of mind

❷ Textual Reading

Search for evidence in the text and answer the following questions.

1) Critics believe that "The Egg" established Sherwood Anderson's gift for humor or his ability to understand the tragic-comic. What are the comic renditions in the story? Do they conflict with the tragic fate of the family?

2) "The Egg" is written from the point of position of an adult male remembering his childhood. Sigmund Freud's tripartite theory of mind may be employed to analyze the psyche of the three characters. All of the main characters, the kid, the female parent, and the male parent, have an id that emerges at some point in the narrative. Study the story in detail and try to determine what the id of these characters is.

❸ Textual Reading

Discuss in groups the following questions to further explore this literary work.

1) Who is the narrator of the story? Why does the narrator openly admit that he has fabricated the most important elements of the story he is telling?

2) What kind of man was Father as a single farmhand? How did he change into a man full of ambition to rise up?

3) The narrative changes with the personality change of the father. Compare the sentence structures before and after the change to summarize linguistic differences.

4) What are the characteristics of the son and in what way is he affected by the failure of his family?

❹ Writing About Literature

Read the following critical excerpt and then write an essay.

> West, Michael D. "Sherwood Anderson's Triumph: 'The Egg'."
> *Bloom's Major Short Story Writers: Sherwood Anderson.*
> New York: Chelsea House Publishers, 2003. 133–135.

Early reviewers often singled out the story for praise and all modern interpretive biographies recognize its surpassing merit. James Schevill terms it "one of Anderson's greatest stories and one of the outstanding tales in American literature", and Irving Howe states flatly that "of all Anderson's short fictions 'The Egg' most deserves to be placed among the great stories of the world". Yet, hampered by space, critics of the story have dealt only haphazardly with the reasons for its greatness. Even Howe's admirable discussion relies heavily on plot synopsis and cites but one detail to demonstrate that the story is "complex and ironic". Assuming familiarity with the plot as a point of departure, I hope to substantiate the more acute perceptions embodied in the scanty critical literature on the story.

Anderson's greatest fault as a prose stylist is his saturation in the facile, vaguely evocative phrases of advertising. It saps his command of colloquial expression. But in "The Egg" this facility becomes a virtue. Only an adman could have created the pathetic touch of the father's naively simple, straightforward and honest sign, EAT HERE, "the command that was so seldom obeyed". Anderson knew that it takes a come-on to bring in the customers; on top of his paint factory in Elyria was the sign, ROOF-FIX: SEND FOR FREE CATALOG. Or take the words with which the father introduces his attempt to bottle the egg: "People will want to know how you got the egg in the bottle. Don't tell them. Keep them guessing. That is the way to have fun with this trick." The short, choppy sentences and the awkward and unidiomatic failure to contract that is perfectly mimic the prose of the cheap pamphlets promising, to teach you One Hundred and One Easy Tricks which is also the prose of the cheap mail-order catalogues that vend them. Flow moving the tyro entertainer's parrot-like repetition of his patter! A curious coincidence enables us to see exactly how in this story Anderson's mail-order prose (his specialty as a copywriter) is transmuted. Alyse Gregory quite properly stigmatized the effusively meaningless language in which Anderson's ideals are often couched, such as the vague phrase "a kind of white wonder of life". Pure Anderson, admittedly, and pure tin—but note how the same combination of words appears in "The Egg": "Wilmer's White Wonder Cholera Cure... advertised in the poultry papers." Clearly, Anderson's often shoddy lyricism derives from his advertising background; but, just as clearly, in this story the lyric impulse is mastered and directed ironically against that background. Consider in this light the paired adjectives in each of the following sentences:

> If, in my turn, I am a gloomy man inclined to see the darker side of life, I attribute it to the fact that what should have been for me the happy joyous days of childhood were spent on a chicken farm.
>
> I... dreamed I was a tiny thing going along the road into a far beautiful place where there were no chicken farms.
>
> It is a hopeful literature and declares that much may be done by simple ambitious people who own a few hens.
>
> In the evening bright happy groups would come singing down Turner's Pike.

In *Mid-American Chants* Anderson tries to make serious statements in language of such falsified simplicity. Here, the phrases are used, without exception, ironically.

Another strand woven into the irony of "The Egg" is the frequent Biblical phraseology. Anderson publicized his indebtedness to the Bible by tearing pages out of the copies placed in hotel rooms. But when he attempts to use it as a conscious framework, it constricts rather than inspires his imagination, as in the story of Jesse Bentley, the most unsatisfactory section of *Winesburg*. In "The Egg", however, scriptural echoes, beautifully diffused, expand the significance of the characters and their actions. At times the language is not strictly Biblical but merely has an archaic flavor: "in the days of her lying in." Sometimes the echo is more specific; the chicken "born out of an egg" that "lives for a few weeks as a tiny fluffy thing... stands looking with stupid eyes at the sun, becomes sick and dies" does so to the cadences of Job's *Man that is born of woman*. "One might write a book concerning our flight from the chicken-farm into town" suggests, as well as the flight of an army and that of chickens, the Flight into Egypt. Significantly, the first chapters of Genesis bulk largest in Anderson's consciousness. Literature on chicken farms should "be read by the gods who have just eaten of the tree of the knowledge of good and evil". Repeated references to the sweat on the father's brow enhance the meaning of his small life: *In the sweat of thy face shalt thou eat bread*. And the crucial incident of the story is given a weird resonance by the slaying of Abel. After the father has offered the firstlings of his flock, Kane's amused rejection of him, though understandable, is also a re-enactment of Cain's murder. This is, of course, in no sense the "meaning" of the scene; the great effectiveness of the scriptural echoes in this story lies in the fact that they occur with evocative rather than informative value, and with a touch of irony. The father is, after all, the personification of the un-Abel, and there is a twist in having the man whom we know as the "innkeeper" and "restaurant keeper" aspiring to be his *brother's keeper*.

Essay Writing

Read the above selection and write an essay on "The Egg" from the perspective of psychoanalysis with no less than 500 words.

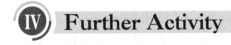

IV Further Activity

Scan the QR code and listen to the audio of "The Book of the Grotesque" in *Winesburg, Ohio*.

Lecture 6
William Golding

🌟 Profile of the Writer

William Golding
(1911–1993)

William Gerald Golding was born in Cornwall, England, in 1911. His father was a schoolteacher and an ardent advocate of rationalism, the idea that reason rather than experience is a necessary and reliable means through which to gain knowledge and to understand the world. This rationalist viewpoint was not tolerant of emotionally based experiences, such as the fear of the dark that Golding had as a child. His father wielded a tremendous influence over him, and, in fact, until leaving for college, Golding attended the school where his father taught.

Golding began reading Tennyson at age seven and steeped himself in Shakespeare's works, dreaming of writing poetry. While still at Oxford, a volume of Golding's poems was published as part of Macmillan's *Contemporary Poets* series. These poems illustrate that he had lost faith in the rationalism of his father with its attendant belief in the perfectibility of humankind. In 1935, he graduated from Oxford with a Bachelor of Arts in English and a diploma in education.

From 1935 to 1939, Golding worked as a writer, actor, and producer with a small theater in London, paying his bills with a job as a social worker. He considered the theater his strongest literary influence, citing Greek tragedians and Shakespeare, rather than other novelists, as his primary influences.

Lecture 6
William Golding

In 1939, Golding began teaching English and philosophy in Salisbury at Bishop Wordsworth's School. With the exception of five years he spent in the Royal Navy during World War II, he remained in the teaching position until 1961 when he left to write full time.

The five years Golding spent in the navy (1940–1945) exposed him to the incredible cruelty and barbarity of which mankind is capable. Thus, his fiction of ten deals with the problem of evil, the conflict between the civilizing influence of reason and man's innate desire to dominate.

In *Lord of the Flies* (1954), Golding combined that perception of humanity with his years of experience with schoolboys. Although not the first novel he wrote, *Lord of the Flies* was the first to be published after having been rejected by 21 publishers. An examination of the duality of savagery and civilization in humanity, Golding uses a pristine tropical island as a protected environment in which a group of marooned British schoolboys act out their worst impulses. The boys loyal to the ways of civilization face persecution by the boys indulging in their innate aggression. As such, the novel illustrates the failure of the rationalism espoused by Golding's father. Because of this novel, Golding was granted membership in the Royal Society of Literature in 1955.

A fast, intense writer, Golding quickly followed *Lord of the Flies* with *The Inheritors* (1955), *Pincher Martin* (1956), *Free Fall* (1959), *The Spire* (1964), *The Pyramid* (1967), *Darkness Visible* (1979), *The Paper Men* (1984). His 1980 novel *Rites of Passage* won the Booker Prize. Golding's greatest honor was being awarded the 1983 Nobel Prize for Literature.

Golding died in Cornwall in 1993.

 Preview Questions

1. Reasoning is encouraged in learning to ensure that we can think clearly and properly. Its significance is seen especially in law and politics. Yet is a human life enjoyable if it is governed by reason? How can we balance between reason and experience?

2. William Golding wrote *Lord of the Flies* in 1954, less than a decade after World War II, when the world was in the midst of the Cold War. The atrocities of the Holocaust, the horrific effects of the atomic bomb, and "the threat of the

Communist countries behind the Iron Curtain" were all present in the minds of the Western public and the author. This environment of fear combined with technology's rapid advances acts as a backdrop to the island experiences. So what do you know about the Cold War?

II Literary Reading: *Lord of the Flies* (Chapter 7)

Shadows and Tall Trees

The pig-run kept close to the jumble of rocks that lay down by the water on the other side and Ralph was content to follow Jack along it. If you could shut your ears to the slow suck down of the sea and boil of the return, if you could forget how dun and unvisited were the ferny coverts on either side, then there was a chance that you might put the beast out of mind and dream for a while. The sun had swung over the vertical and the afternoon heat was closing in on the island. Ralph passed a message forward to Jack and when they next came to fruit the whole party stopped and ate.

Sitting, Ralph was aware of the heat for the first time that day. He pulled distastefully at his grey shirt and wondered whether he might undertake the adventure of washing it. Sitting under what seemed an unusual heat, even for this island, Ralph planned his toilet. He would like to have a pair of scissors and cut this hair—he flung the mass back—cut this filthy hair right back to half an inch. He would like to have a bath, a proper wallow with soap. He passed his tongue experimentally over his teeth and decided that a toothbrush would come in handy too. Then there were his nails—

Ralph turned his hand over and examined them. They were bitten down to the quick though he could not remember when he had restarted this habit nor any time when he indulged it.

"Be sucking my thumb next—"

He looked round, furtively. Apparently no one had heard. The hunters sat, stuffing themselves with this easy meal, trying to convince themselves that they got sufficient kick out of bananas and that other olive-grey, jelly-like fruit. With the memory of his sometime clean self as a standard, Ralph looked them over. They were dirty, not with the spectacular dirt of boys who have fallen into mud or been brought down hard on a rainy day. Not one of them was an obvious subject for a shower, and yet—hair, much too long, tangled here and there, knotted round a dead leaf or a twig; faces cleaned fairly well by the process of eating and sweating but marked in the less accessible angles with a kind of shadow; clothes, worn away, stiff like his own with sweat, put on, not for decorum or comfort but out of custom; the skin of the body, scurfy with brine—

He discovered with a little fall of the heart that these were the conditions he took as normal now and that he did not mind. He sighed and pushed away the stalk from which he had stripped the fruit. Already the hunters were stealing away to do their business in the woods or down by the rocks. He turned and looked out to sea.

Here, on the other side of the island, the view was utterly different. The filmy enchantments of mirage could not endure the cold ocean water and the horizon was hard, clipped blue. Ralph wandered down to the rocks. Down here, almost on a level with the sea, you could follow with your eye the ceaseless, bulging passage of the deep sea waves. They were miles wide, apparently not breakers or the banked ridges of shallow water. They traveled the length of the island with an air of disregarding it and being set on other business; they were less a progress than a momentous rise and fall of the whole ocean. Now the sea would suck down, making cascades and waterfalls of retreating water, would sink past the rocks and plaster down the seaweed like shining hair: then, pausing, gather and rise with a roar, irresistibly swelling over point and outcrop, climbing the little cliff, sending at last an arm of surf up a gully to end a yard or so from him in fingers of spray.

Wave after wave, Ralph followed the rise and fall until something of the remoteness of the sea numbed his brain. Then gradually the almost infinite size of this water forced itself on his attention. This was the divider, the barrier. On the other side of the island, swathed at midday with mirage, defended by the shield of the quiet lagoon, one might dream of rescue; but here, faced by the brute obtuseness of the ocean, the miles of division, one was clamped down, one was helpless, one was condemned, one was—

Simon was speaking almost in his ear. Ralph found that he had rock painfully gripped in both hands, found his body arched, the muscles of his neck stiff, his mouth strained open.

"You'll get back to where you came from."

Simon nodded as he spoke. He was kneeling on one knee, looking down from a higher rock which he held with both hands; his other leg stretched down to Ralph's level.

Ralph was puzzled and searched Simon's face for a clue.

"It's so big, I mean—"

Simon nodded.

"All the same. You'll get back all right. I think so, anyway."

Some of the strain had gone from Ralph's body. He glanced at the sea and then smiled bitterly at Simon.

"Got a ship in your pocket?"

Simon grinned and shook his head.

"How do you know, then?"

When Simon was still silent Ralph said curtly, "You're batty."

Simon shook his head violently till the coarse black hair flew backwards and forwards across his face.

"No, I'm not. I just—think you'll get back all right. —"

For a moment nothing more was said. And then they suddenly smiled at each other.

Roger called from the coverts.

"Come and see!"

The ground was turned over near the pig-run and there were droppings that steamed. Jack bent down to them as though he loved them.

"Ralph—we need meat even if we are hunting the other thing."

"If you mean going the right way, we'll hunt."

They set off again, the hunters bunched a little by fear of the mentioned beast, while Jack quested ahead. They went more slowly than Ralph had bargained for; yet in a way he was glad to loiter, cradling his spear. Jack came up against some emergency of his craft and soon the procession stopped. Ralph leaned against a tree and at once the daydreams came swarming up. Jack was in charge of the hunt and there would be time to get to the mountain—

Once, following his father from Chatham to Devonport, they had lived in a cottage on the edge of the moors. In the succession of houses that Ralph had known, this one stood out with particular clarity because after that house he had been sent away to school. Mummy had still been with them and Daddy had come home every day. Wild ponies came to the stone wall at the bottom of the garden, and it had snowed. Just behind the cottage there was a sort of shed and you could lie up there, watching the flakes swirl past. You could see the damp spot where each flake died, then you could mark the first flake that lay down without melting and watch, the whole ground turn white. You could go indoors when you were cold and look out of the window, past the bright copper kettle and the plate with the little blue men.

When you went to bed there was a bowl of cornflakes with sugar and cream. And the books—they stood on the shelf by the bed, leaning together with always two or three laid flat on top because he had not bothered to put them back properly. They were dog-eared and scratched. There was the bright, shining one about Topsy and Mopsy that he never read because it was about two girls; there was the one about the magician which you read with a kind of tied-down terror, skipping page twenty-seven with the awful picture of the spider; there was a book about people who had dug things up, Egyptian things; there was *The Boy's Book of Trains, The Boy's Book of Ships*. Vividly they came before him; he could have reached up and touched them, could feel the weight and slow slide with which *The Mammoth Book for Boys* would come out and slither down... Everything was all right; everything was good-humored and friendly.

The bushes crashed ahead of them. Boys flung themselves wildly from the pig track and scrabbled in the creepers, screaming. Ralph saw Jack nudged aside and fall. Then there was a creature bounding along the pig track toward him, with tusks gleaming and an intimidating grunt. Ralph found he was able to measure the distance coldly and take aim. With the boar only five yards away, he flung the foolish wooden stick that he carried, saw it hit the great snout and hang there for a moment. The boar's note changed to a squeal and it swerved aside into the covert. The pig-run filled with shouting boys again, Jack came running back, and poked about in the undergrowth.

"Through here—"

"But he'd do us!"

"Through here, I said—"

The boar was floundering away from them. They found another pig-run parallel to the first and Jack raced away. Ralph was full of fright and apprehension and pride.

"I hit him! The spear stuck in—"

Now they came, unexpectedly, to an open space by the sea. Jack cast about on the bare rock and looked anxious.

"He's gone."

"I hit him," said Ralph again, "and the spear stuck in a bit."

He felt the need of witnesses.

"Didn't you see me?"

Maurice nodded.

"I saw you. Right bang on his snout—Wheee!"

Ralph talked on, excitedly.

"I hit him all right. The spear stuck in. I wounded him!"

He sunned himself in their new respect and felt that hunting was good after all.

"I walloped him properly. That was the beast, I think!" Jack came back.

"That wasn't the beast. That was a boar."

"I hit him."

"Why didn't you grab him? I tried—"

Ralph's voice ran up.

"But a boar!"

Jack flushed suddenly.

"You said he'd do us. What did you want to throw for? Why didn't you wait?"

He held out his arm.

"Look."

He turned his left forearm for them all to see. On the outside was a rip; not much, but bloody.

"He did that with his tusks. I couldn't get my spear down in time."

Attention focused on Jack.

"That's a wound," said Simon, "and you ought to suck it. Like Berengaria."

Jack sucked.

"I hit him," said Ralph indignantly. "I hit him with my spear, I wounded him."

He tried for their attention.

"He was coming along the path. I threw, like this—"

Robert snarled at him. Ralph entered into the play and everybody laughed. Presently they were all jabbing at Robert who made mock rushes.

Jack shouted.

"Make a ring!"

The circle moved in and round. Robert squealed in mock terror, then in real pain.

"Ow! Stop it! You're hurting!"

The butt end of a spear fell on his back as he blundered among them.

"Hold him!"

They got his arms and legs. Ralph, carried away by a sudden thick excitement, grabbed Eric's spear and jabbed at Robert with it.

"Kill him! Kill him!"

All at once, Robert was screaming and struggling with the strength of frenzy. Jack had him by the hair and was brandishing his knife. Behind him was Roger, fighting to get close. The chant rose ritually, as at the last moment of a dance or a hunt.

"Kill the pig! Cut his throat! Kill the pig! Bash him in!"

Ralph too was fighting to get near, to get a handful of that brown, vulnerable flesh. The desire to squeeze and hurt was over-mastering.

Jack's arm came down; the heaving circle cheered and made pig-dying noises. Then they lay quiet, panting, listening to Robert's frightened snivels. He wiped his face with a dirty arm, and made an effort to retrieve his status.

"Oh, my bum!"

He rubbed his rump ruefully. Jack rolled over.

"That was a good game."

"Just a game," said Ralph uneasily. "I got jolly badly hurt at rugger once."

"We ought to have a drum," said Maurice, "then we could do it properly."

Ralph looked at him.

"How properly?"

"I dunno. You want a fire, I think, and a drum, and you keep time to the drum.

"You want a pig," said Roger, "like a real hunt."

"Or someone to pretend," said Jack. "You could get someone to dress up as a pig and then he could act—you know, pretend to knock me over and all that."

"You want a real pig," said Robert, still caressing his rump, "because you've got to kill him."

"Use a littlun," said Jack, and everybody laughed.

Ralph sat up.

"Well. We shan't find what we're looking for at this rate."

One by one they stood up, twitching rags into place.

Ralph looked at Jack.

"Now for the mountain."

"Shouldn't we go back to Piggy," said Maurice, "before dark?"

The twins nodded like one boy.

"Yes, that's right. Let's go up there in the morning."

Ralph looked out and saw the sea.

"We've got to start the fire again."

"You haven't got Piggy's specs," said Jack, "so you can't."

"Then we'll find out if the mountain's clear."

Maurice spoke, hesitating, not wanting to seem a funk.

"Supposing the beast's up there?"

Jack brandished his spear.

"We'll kill it."

The sun seemed a little cooler. He slashed with the spear.

"What are we waiting for?"

"I suppose," said Ralph, "if we keep on by the sea this way, we'll come out below the burnt bit and then we can climb the mountain.

Once more Jack led them along by the suck and heave of the blinding sea.

Once more Ralph dreamed, letting his skillful feet deal with the difficulties of the path. Yet here his feet seemed less skillful than before. For most of the way they were forced right down to the bare rock by the water and had to edge along between that and the dark luxuriance of the forest. There were little cliffs to be scaled, some to be used as paths, lengthy traverses where one used hands as well as feet. Here and there they could clamber over wave-wet rock, leaping across clear pools that the tide had left. They came to a gully that split the narrow foreshore like a defense. This seemed to have no bottom and they peered awe-stricken into the gloomy crack where water gurgled. Then the wave came back, the gully boiled before them and spray dashed up to the very creeper so that the boys were wet and shrieking. They tried the forest but it was thick and woven like a bird's nest. In the end they had to jump one by one, waiting till the water sank; and even so, some of them got a second drenching. After that the rocks seemed to be growing impassable so they sat for a time, letting their rags dry and watching the clipped outlines of the rollers that moved so slowly past the island. They found fruit in a haunt of bright little birds that hovered like insects. Then Ralph said they were going too slowly. He himself climbed a tree and parted the canopy, and saw the square head of the mountain seeming still a great way off. Then they tried to hurry along the rocks and Robert cut his knee quite badly and they had to recognize that this path must be taken slowly if they were to be safe. So they proceeded after that as if they were climbing a dangerous mountain, until the rocks became an uncompromising cliff, overhung with impossible jungle and falling sheer into the sea.

Ralph looked at the sun critically.

"Early evening. After tea-time, at any rate."

"I don't remember this cliff," said Jack, crestfallen, "so this must be the bit of the coast I missed."

Ralph nodded.

"Let me think."

By now, Ralph had no self-consciousness in public thinking but would treat the day's decisions as though he were playing chess. The only trouble was that he would never be a very good chess player. He thought of the littluns and Piggy. Vividly he imagined Piggy by himself, huddled in a shelter that was silent except for the sounds of nightmare.

"We can't leave the littluns alone with Piggy. Not all night."

The other boys said nothing but stood round, watching him.

"If we went back we should take hours."

Jack cleared his throat and spoke in a queer, tight voice. "We mustn't let anything happen to Piggy, must we?" Ralph tapped his teeth with the dirty point of Eric's spear.

"If we go across—"

He glanced round him.

"Someone's got to go across the island and tell Piggy we'll be back after dark."

Bill spoke, unbelieving.

"Through the forest by himself? Now?"

"We can't spare more than one."

Simon pushed his way to Ralph's elbow.

"I'll go if you like. I don't mind, honestly."

Before Ralph had time to reply, he smiled quickly, turned and climbed into the forest.

Ralph looked back at Jack, seeing him, infuriatingly, for the first time.

"Jack—that time you went the whole way to the castle rock."

Jack glowered.

"Yes?"

"You came along part of this shore—below the mountain, beyond there."

"Yes."

"And then?"

"I found a pig-run. It went for miles."

"So the pig-run must be somewhere in there."

Ralph nodded. He pointed at the forest.

Everybody agreed, sagely.

"All right then. We'll smash a way through till we find the pig-run."

He took a step and halted.

"Wait a minute though! Where does the pig-run go to?"

"The mountain," said Jack, "I told you." He sneered. "Don't you want to go to the mountain?"

Ralph sighed, sensing the rising antagonism, understanding that this was how Jack felt as soon as he ceased to lead.

"I was thinking of the light. We'll be stumbling about."

"We were going to look for the beast."

"There won't be enough light."

"I don't mind going," said Jack hotly. "I'll go when we get there. Won't you? Would you rather go back to the shelters and tell Piggy?"

Now it was Ralph's turn to flush but he spoke despairingly, out of the new understanding that Piggy had given him.

"Why do you hate me?"

The boys stirred uneasily, as though something indecent had been said. The silence lengthened.

Ralph, still hot and hurt, turned away first.

"Come on."

He led the way and set himself as by right to hack at the tangles. Jack brought up the rear, displaced and brooding.

The pig-track was a dark tunnel, for the sun was sliding quickly toward the edge of the world and in the forest shadows were never far to seek. The track was broad and beaten and they ran along at a swift trot. Then the roof of leaves broke up and they halted, breathing quickly, looking at the few stars that pricked round the head of the mountain.

"There you are."

The boys peered at each other doubtfully. Ralph made a decision.

"We'll go straight across to the platform and climb tomorrow."

They murmured agreement; but Jack was standing by his shoulder.

"If you're frightened of course—"

Ralph turned on him.

"Who went first on the castle rock?"

"I went too. And that was daylight."

"All right. Who wants to climb the mountain now?" Silence was the only answer.

"Samneric? What about you?"

"We ought to go an' tell Piggy—"

"—yes, tell Piggy that—"

"But Simon went!"

"We ought to tell Piggy—in case—"

"Robert? Bill?"

They were going straight back to the platform now. Not, of course, that they were afraid—but tired.

Ralph turned back to Jack.

"You see?"

"I'm going up the mountain." The words came from Jack viciously, as though they were a curse. He looked at Ralph, his thin body tensed, his spear held as if he threatened him.

"I'm going up the mountain to look for the beast—now." Then the supreme sting, the casual, bitter word. "Coming?"

At that word the other boys forgot their urge to be gone and turned back to sample this fresh rub of two spirits in the dark. The word was too good, too bitter, too successfully daunting to be repeated. It took Ralph at low water when his nerve was relaxed for the return to the shelter and the still, friendly waters of the lagoon.

"I don't mind."

Astonished, he heard his voice come out, cool and casual, so that the bitterness of

Jack's taunt fell powerless.

"If you don't mind, of course."

"Oh, not at all."

Jack took a step.

"Well then—"

Side by side, watched by silent boys, the two started up the mountain.

Ralph stopped.

"We're silly. Why should only two go? If we find anything, two won't be enough."

There came the sound of boys scuttling away. Astonishingly, a dark figure moved against the tide.

"Roger?"

"Yes."

"That's three, then."

Once more they set out to climb the slope of the mountain. The darkness seemed to flow round them like a tide. Jack, who had said nothing, began to choke and cough, and a gust of wind set all three spluttering. Ralph's eyes were blinded with tears.

"Ashes. We're on the edge of the burnt patch."

Their footsteps and the occasional breeze were stirring up small devils of dust. Now that they stopped again, Ralph had time while he coughed to remember how silly they were. If there was no beast—and almost certainly there was no beast—in that case, well and good; but if there was something waiting on top of the mountain—what was the use of three of them, handicapped by the darkness and carrying only sticks?

"We're being fools."

Out of the darkness came the answer.

"Windy?"

Irritably Ralph shook himself. This was all Jack's fault.

"'Course I am. But we're still being fools."

"If you don't want to go on," said the voice sarcastically, "I'll go up by myself."

Ralph heard the mockery and hated Jack. The sting of ashes in his eyes, tiredness, fear, enraged him.

"Go on then! We'll wait here."

There was silence.

"Why don't you go? Are you frightened?" A stain in the darkness, a stain that was Jack, detached itself and began to draw away.

"All right. So long."

The stain vanished. Another took its place.

Ralph felt his knee against something hard and rocked a charred trunk that was edgy to the touch. He felt the sharp cinders that had been bark push against the back of his knee and knew that Roger had sat down. He felt with his hands and lowered himself beside Roger, while the trunk rocked among invisible ashes. Roger, uncommunicative by nature, said nothing. He offered no opinion on the beast nor told Ralph why he had chosen to come on this mad expedition. He simply sat and rocked the trunk gently. Ralph noticed a rapid and infuriating tapping noise and realized that Roger was banging his silly wooden stick against something.

So they sat, the rocking, tapping, impervious Roger and Ralph, fuming; round them the close sky was loaded with stars, save where the mountain punched up a hole of blackness.

There was a slithering noise high above them, the sound of someone taking giant and dangerous strides on rock or ash. Then Jack found them, and was shivering and croaking in a voice they could just recognize as his.

"I saw a thing on top."

They heard him blunder against the trunk which rocked violently. He lay silent for a moment, then muttered.

"Keep a good lookout. It may be following."

A shower of ash pattered round them. Jack sat up.

"I saw a thing bulge on the mountain."

"You only imagined it," said Ralph shakily, "because nothing would bulge. Not any sort of creature."

Roger spoke; they jumped, for they had forgotten him.

"A frog."

Jack giggled and shuddered.

"Some frog. There was a noise too. A kind of 'plop' noise. Then the thing bulged."

Ralph surprised himself, not so much by the quality of his voice, which was even, but by the bravado of its intention.

"We'll go and look."

For the first time since he had first known Jack, Ralph could feel him hesitate.

"Now—?"

His voice spoke for him.

"Of course."

He got off the trunk and led the way across the clinking cinders up into the dark, and the others followed.

Now that his physical voice was silent the inner voice of reason, and other voices too, made themselves heard. Piggy was calling him a kid. Another voice told him not to be a fool; and the darkness and desperate enterprise gave the night a kind of dentist's chair unreality.

As they came to the last slope, Jack and Roger drew near, changed from the ink-stains to distinguishable figures. By common consent they stopped and crouched together. Behind them, on the horizon, was a patch of lighter sky where in a moment the moon would rise. The wind roared once in the forest and pushed their rags against them.

Ralph stirred.

"Come on."

They crept forward, Roger lagging a little. Jack and Ralph turned the shoulder of the mountain together. The glittering lengths of the lagoon lay below them and beyond that a long white smudge that was the reef. Roger joined them.

Jack whispered.

"Let's creep forward on hands and knees. Maybe it's asleep."

Roger and Ralph moved on, this time leaving Jack in the rear, for all his brave words. They came to the flat top where the rock was hard to hands and knees.

A creature that bulged.

Ralph put his hand in the cold, soft ashes of the fire and smothered a cry. His hand and shoulder were twitching from the unlooked-for contact. Green lights of nausea appeared for a moment and ate into the darkness. Roger lay behind him and Jack's mouth was at his ear.

"Over there, where there used to be a gap in the rock. A sort of hump—see?"

Ashes blew into Ralph's face from the dead fire. He could not see the gap or anything else, because the green lights were opening again and growing, and the top of the mountain was sliding sideways.

Once more, from a distance, he heard Jack's whisper.

"Scared?"

Not scared so much as paralyzed; hung up there immovable on the top of a diminishing, moving mountain. Jack slid away from him, Roger bumped, fumbled with a hiss of breath, and passed onwards. He heard them whispering.

"Can you see anything?"

"There—"

In front of them, only three or four yards away, was a rock-like hump where no rock should be. Ralph could hear a tiny chattering noise coming from somewhere—perhaps from his own mouth. He bound himself together with his will, fused his fear and loathing into a hatred, and stood up. He took two leaden steps forward.

Behind them the silver of moon had drawn clear of the horizon. Before them, something like a great ape was sitting asleep with its head between its knees. Then the wind roared in the forest, there was confusion in the darkness and the creature lifted its head, holding toward them the ruin of a face.

Ralph found himself taking giant strides among the ashes, heard other creatures crying out and leaping and dared the impossible on the dark slope; presently the mountain was deserted, save for the three abandoned sticks and the thing that bowed.

III Thinking, Talking and Writing About Literature

1 Textual Cognition

Make an introductory presentation on the following terms related to this literary work.

1) allegory
2) rationalism

2 Textual Reading

Search for evidence in the text and answer the following questions.

1) Ralph undergoes significant emotional and psychological development in this chapter. Following his spontaneous participation in a pig hunt, he experiences the exhilarating mixture of emotions which are comparable to those that drive Jack and the other hunters. Then what did these emotions show about Ralph's humanity and how did Ralph's emotions underlie Jack's credibility with the group?

2) There was a direct confrontation between Ralph and Jack. Did Jack answer the question? What is the end of the confrontation? How did it subtly change the situation among the boys?

3) Maurice suggested that they added a drum and a fire to do the dance "properly", and Robert and Roger pointed out that they would need a pig to complete the game. Furthermore, Jack looked for a human, someone who could dress up as a pig. So they all acknowledged on some level that this game would inevitably have fatal consequences. So what can we learn about human beings from the fact mentioned above?

4) Simon's credibility as a mystic is established in this chapter. As if he is reading Ralph's mind, Simon interrupts Ralph's strained and tense regard of the ocean's vastness by telling him, "You'll get back to where you came from." Ralph responds with the opinion all the boys hold of

Simon: "You're batty." Note that Simon uses "you" instead of "we". What does this disclose about Simon?

③ Critical Reading

Discuss in groups the following questions to further explore this literary work.

1) In this allegorical novel, what do the island and the boys and many other objects and events represent?

2) What key aspects of the human experiences does *Lord of the Flies* investigate to form the basis of the themes the author wants to convey?

④ Writing About Literature

Read the following critical excerpt and then write an essay.

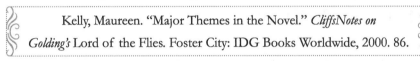

Kelly, Maureen. "Major Themes in the Novel." *CliffsNotes on Golding's* Lord of the Flies. Foster City: IDG Books Worldwide, 2000. 86.

Most societies set up mechanisms to channel aggressive impulses into productive enterprises or projects. On the island, Jack's hunters are successful in providing meat for the group because they tap into their innate ability to commit violence. To the extent that this violence is a reasoned response to the group's needs (for example, to feed for the population), it produces positive effects and outcomes. However, when the violence becomes the motivator and the desired outcome lacks social or moral value beyond itself, as it does with the hunters, at that point the violence becomes evil, savage, and diabolical.

Violence continues to exist in modern society and is institutionalized in the military and politics. Golding develops this theme by having his characters establish a democratic assembly, which is greatly affected by the verbal violence of Jack's power-plays, and an army of hunters, which ultimately forms a small military dictatorship. The boys' assemblies are likened to both ends of the social or civil spectrum, from pre-verbal tribe gatherings to modern governmental institutions, indicating that while the forum for politics has changed over the millennia, the dynamic remains the same. Consider the emotional basis of the boys' choice of leaders: Initially they vote for Ralph not because he has demonstrated leadership skills but because of his charisma and arbitrary possession of the conch. Later they desert him—and the reasoned democracy he promotes—to join Jack's tribe because Jack's way of life, with the war paint and ritualized dance, seems like more fun. Choosing Jack's "fun" tribe indicates a dangerous level of emotionally based self-indulgence. By relying on emotion to decide the island's political format, the boys open themselves up to the possibility of violence because violence lies in the domain of emotion.

Yet Jack's mentality on a larger scale is not fun and games but warfare, a concept made clear at the end: When Ralph encounters the officer on the beach, he notices first not the officer's face but his uniform and revolver, which are the markings of the officer's tribe. The decorative elements of his uniform symbolize his war paint. His ship will be enacting the same sort of manhunt for his enemy that Jack's tribe conducts for Ralph.

Essay Writing

Read the above selection and write an essay on *Lord of the Flies* from the perspective of humanity with no less than 500 words.

IV Further Activity

Scan the QR code and listen to the audio of Chapter 1 of *Lord of the Flies*.

02

第二部分
女性英语成长小说

Female English Bildungsroman

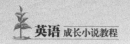

导 言

尽管传统意义上的经典成长小说有跨越时代的魅力，但以白人男性成长经历为主要线索的文学书写显然无法充分表现边缘读者，如女性读者、少数族裔读者、第三世界国家和地区读者的成长经历。美国墨西哥裔女作家希斯内罗丝（Sandra Cisneros，1954—）曾言，她作为贫穷的拉丁裔女性在成长和阅读中常常遇到"文学真空"（literary void），而这成为她创作《芒果街上的小屋》（*The House on Mango Street*）的驱动力。希斯内罗丝解释说，她的计划是要用"从来没有被书写的故事"去填补她的种族、性别、阶级的空白[1]。20 世纪和 21 世纪的很多作者——尤其是女性和少数族裔作者，为了确定替代性的主体性观点和长大成人的方式，对抗并颠覆了传统成长小说。美国学者托比亚斯·伯斯（Tobias Boes）从观念上拓展了成长小说的维度，他认为，尽管成长小说主要被视为 19 世纪的文学和社会现象，但"20 世纪八九十年代女权主义、后殖民和少数族裔研究的兴起拓展了传统的成长小说定义"[2]。

英国女性成长小说

英国女性文学的发展所勾勒出的正是英国女性成长小说温柔突进的进程。简·奥斯丁是第一位真正从女性的心灵深处探索女性成长奥秘的女作家。她的代表作《理智与情感》（*Sense and Sensibility*）、《傲慢与偏见》（*Pride and Prejudice*）、《爱玛》（*Emma*）等塑造了女性成长的群像。奥斯丁从多个层面为女性成长小说的确立奠定了基础。首先，奥斯丁确立了一个女性成长小说的普遍模式："女性青少年的成长困惑和她们的爱情婚姻有

---

[1] Sagel, Jim. "Sandra Cisneros: Conveying the Riches of the Latin American Culture Is the Author's Literary Goal." *Publishers Weekly* 238.15 (1991): 74.

[2] Boes, Tobias. "Modernist Studies and the Bildungsroman: A Historical Survey of Critical Trends." *Literature Compass* 3.2 (2006): 230–243.

密切关系。爱情观、婚姻观的形成和发展成为女性成长小说的共同特点。"[1]其次，奥斯丁确立了教育在女性成长中的重要地位。"奥斯丁认为，妇女天生和男子有同等的智力和理性。在她的笔下，相爱的人们之间通常呈现出一种教育与被教育的关系，妇女和男子一样都能扮演导师的角色。"[2]《傲慢与偏见》中的伊丽莎白（Elizabeth）和达西（Darcy）之间就是这样一种在交互参照的镜像之下，相互影响、相互学习并共同成长的关系。

奥斯丁之后，关注女性成长的另一位女作家是夏洛蒂·勃朗特。她的代表作《简·爱》描写的就是出身卑贱的少女简·爱敢于表达强烈的爱憎、勇于坚守自己的道德和女性独立的人格并最终收获自己的爱情和独立的生活的成长故事。"由于《简·爱》倡导了女性自尊、自强的精神，它被奉为女性成长小说的经典之作"[3]；夏洛蒂·勃朗特也被美国著名女性主义批评家肖瓦尔特（Elaine Showalter）奉为女性文学"三个阶段"中的第一阶段的代表性作家。然而我们不难发现，勃朗特所描述的女性的成长与主流文化对女性美德的心理和社会要求是基本一致的。这说明，在这个阶段，女性作家尚缺乏女性写作的传统可以模仿，她们除了模仿主流文学流行模式并"力求达到男性文化的标准"外别无选择。

英国维多利亚时代著名作家乔治·艾略特的《弗洛斯河上的磨坊》是一部很有代表性的女性成长小说。它通过描述女主人公麦琪（Maggie Tulliver）成长的困惑与挣扎，以及她如何走出一个个困境而步入自我认识完善和情感成熟的过程，揭示出男权社会中的女性为寻求自我和生存空间而面临的种种矛盾冲突及其解决方式。麦琪的成长过程与英国工业化进程平行前进，而麦琪走向成熟也暗指英国社会的现代化。这部小说和大多数成长小说一样，也集中展现了环境与女主人公精神追求之间的矛盾冲突。女主人公最终选择放弃她与菲利普（Philip Wakem）以及新近闯入她生活的斯蒂芬（Stephen Guest）的爱情，找到了控制自我的道德力量，而这一选择标志着麦琪向自我主义的升华迈出了决定性的一步。乔治·艾略特的成长小说在某种意义上修正了英国经典成长小说对阶层上升、财富积累等物质层面的追求，更多地聚焦于精神层面的追求和上升，而女主人公与社会环境格格不入且永远不妥协的精神，也与几乎同时出版的狄更斯的《远大前程》中的皮普有着本质区别。

---

[1] 芮渝萍，《美国成长小说研究》。北京：中国社会科学出版社，2004年，第33页。
[2] 大卫·莫那翰，《简·奥斯丁和妇女地位问题》，朱虹选编《奥斯丁研究》。北京：中国文联出版社，1985年，第336页。
[3] 芮渝萍，《美国成长小说研究》。北京：中国社会科学出版社，2004年，第34页。

"在19世纪八九十年代，女性作家在形成和传播女权主义观念中扮演着中心的角色。"[1] 在与她们同时代的男性作家开始为即将到来的新时代的工业化和商业化对社会的异化而忧心忡忡的时候，女性作家却为即将到来的新时代带给女性的解放的曙光而欢欣鼓舞。女性作家开始从社会责任的层面思考她们写作的目的，正如英国女作家哈维斯（H. R. Haweis）所言："世界的再生存在于女人的手中——在女性作家的手中。让我们用我们的火焰的语言，投身于一项完全神圣的工作，边行动边清洁、修补和美化正在我们面前展开的世界的历史之页。"[2] 此时的女性作家肩负了重新塑造女性社会形象的重任，并开始公开表达对男性中心主义和男性文化的反抗。女人开始认为她们有道义上的权利并拥有领导权，因为她们是精神上的先锋。一些女权主义作家，如英国女作家、女权主义者弗洛伦斯·迪克西夫人（Lady Florence Dixie，1855—1905）、艾利斯·埃塞尔莫（Ellis Ethelmer，1834—1913）等甚至想象世界成为女性一统天下的世界。在迪克西的小说《格劳瑞娜；或1900年的革命》（*Gloriana; or the Revolution of 1900*）中，女主人公格劳瑞娜把自己化装成为一个男孩，用自己的行为和能力证明了女孩与男孩具有同样，甚至是更强的能力。埃塞尔莫的长诗《女人自由》（*Woman Free*）为男权主义的末日而大声欢呼。

肖瓦尔特所界定的第三个阶段是女性文学的成熟期，也是女性成长小说全面探索并取得辉煌成就的时期。在这个时期，女性文学超越了"摹仿"和"反抗"的模式，进入了自我探索的女人阶段。"这个阶段的小说追求女性的自我和艺术的自主，把女权主义的文化分析应用于对文学形式和技巧的分析，而逐渐远离对女性生理经验的探索"。[3] 这一时期的英国女性作家继承了18世纪和19世纪英国女性文学的伟大传统，开始描写曾经是禁区的她们自己的独特经历和感受。"她们努力通过艺术想象把女性经历的片断性连为一体，并且注重自主对于女性作家的含义"。[4] 女性的成长自然成为女性写作的中心和焦

---

[1] Showalter, Elaine. *A Literature of Their Own: British Women Novelists from Bronte to Lessing*. Beijing: Foreign Language Teaching and Research Press, 2004. 182.

[2] Showalter, Elaine. *A Literature of Their Own: British Women Novelists from Bronte to Lessing*. Beijing: Foreign Language Teaching and Research Press, 2004. 183.

[3] 金莉，《她们自己的文学导读》。Showalter, Elaine. *A Literature of Their Own: British Women Novelists from Bronte to Lessing*. Beijing: Foreign Language Teaching and Research Press, 2004. 4.

[4] Showalter, Elaine. *A Literature of Their Own: British Women Novelists from Bronte to Lessing*. Beijing: Foreign Language Teaching and Research Press, 2004. 4.

点。从这个层面来看，女性成长小说的确是"受新女性主义思潮影响最显著的文学形式"[1]。在这个阶段，社会环境为女性成长提供了更为广阔的伸展空间，女性成长小说也因此获得了充分的表达空间。女性书写成为打破沉默、表达独特的女性声音的最恰切的方式。肖瓦尔特也视女性书写为"双声言说"（double-voiced discourse），表达的是父权社会下，压迫者与被压迫者双重的社会和文化诉求。因此，女性成长小说的阅读体验融入的是"女性书写中，被压迫者、被迫害者的潜意识"[2]。

在这个阶段，英国女性文学的代表性人物是弗吉尼亚·伍尔夫（Virginia Woolf, 1882—1941）。在她的短篇小说《遗产》（"The Legacy"）中，安杰拉（Angela）在她的日记里清楚地表达了自己厌倦了作为丈夫附属品的身份，并展现了希望从此走出家庭、走向社会的心路历程。在日记中，她的秘密情人"B.M."出现的频率逐渐高于她的丈夫吉尔伯特（Gilbert）；而在"B.M."去世后，她的日记出现了一片空白，似乎在暗示传统的婚姻关系和贫乏的家庭生活已经无法走进她的内心深处。这一变化展现的正是女性的觉醒和心灵对独立自主的生活的渴望。伍尔夫的另一部小说《远航》（*The Voyage Out*）所关注的同样是女主人公瑞塞尔（Rachel）逐渐意识到婚姻的不平等和帝国侵略的罪恶的心路历程，从这个角度看，这也是一部特征鲜明的女性成长小说。英国在小说中被描述为一个逐渐变小的"岛"，而人则被"囚禁"在这孤岛之上。婚姻生活不会在丈夫或父亲的承诺中改变其不平等的状态。瑞塞尔最后用自己的死亡求得了唯一获得自由的机会，而她的死象征着"拒绝作为承载及复制父权价值的工具"[3]。

美国女性成长小说

19世纪中期最有代表性的美国女性作家是奥尔克特（Louisa May Alcott，1832—1888），她作品中理想的女性既扮演着贤妻良母的角色，又渴望独立与自主。她的代表作《小妇人》（*Little Women*）就是一部典型的女性成长小说。《小妇人》描写了马奇家四姐妹的成长经历。马奇太太（Mrs. March）致力于按照传统的价值标准把四个女儿打造成为符合社会规范的优秀女性，经常启发她们从平凡的日常生活和琐碎的事务中获得人

---

1 Morgan, Ellen. "Humanbecoming: Form & Focus in the Neo-feminist Novel." *Images of Women in Fiction: Feminist Perspectives*. Ed. Susan Koppelman Cornillon. Bowling Green: Bowling Green University Press, 1972.183.
2 Friedman, Susan. "Return of the Repressed in Women's Narrative." *Journal of Narrative Technique* 19 (1989):14.
3 Sage, Lorna. "Introduction." *Virginia Woolf: The Voyage Out*. Oxford: Oxford University Press, 1992. 16.

生的体验和经验。在这四个女儿中，二女儿乔（Joe）的性格中带有某种当时的男孩才有的冒险精神，这与19世纪推崇的淑女形象形成了鲜明的对照。乔的个性独立，努力寻求独立的生活。她充分发掘了自己的写作才能，靠写作赚钱，不但能够支持自己的生活，还能够贴补家用，在经济上获得了充分的独立。在奥尔克特的另一部小说《小男人》（*Little Men*）中，乔与丈夫创办了一所私立学校，这说明乔走出了家庭的小天地，开始融入社会，并承担起传承知识的使命。然而，在乔与丈夫的关系中，我们不难发现，丈夫是处于主导地位的，学校的教学和管理始终以丈夫为中心，而乔却扮演起了辅助的角色，回归了夫唱妇随的传统模式。这种回归说明了奥尔克特最终没能突破时代的局限，在女性人物的定位上经历了一番挣扎之后还是力图回归男性中心的主流文化价值。奥尔克特的文学实践反映的是19世纪中期女性文学"温和的、有限的、实用的女权主义思想"[1]。

在19世纪80年代之后，美国女作家开始活跃于文坛。她们的作品中开始出现"更有独立人格的、勇于冲破传统文化束缚的新型妇女形象"[2]。"成长"成为这一时期美国女性作家创作的共同主题，这在萨拉·奥恩·朱厄特（Sarah Orne Jewett, 1849—1909）、玛丽·威尔金斯·弗里曼（Mary Eleanor Wilkins Freeman, 1852—1930）、凯特·肖邦（Kate Chopin, 1851—1904）、伊迪丝·华顿（Edith Wharton, 1862—1937）和维拉·凯瑟（Willa Cather, 1873—1947）的作品中都有所体现。朱厄特的代表作《乡村医生》（*A Country Doctor*）和《尖尖的枞树之乡》（*The Country of the Pointed Firs*）都是女性成长小说的优秀代表作品。《乡村医生》中的女主人公南·普琳斯利（Nan Prince）的身上不时闪现出作者本人的身影，因此这部作品也被认为是带有自传性的作品。南从小为医生莱斯利（Dr. Leslie）收养，常常跟随他一起出诊，长大后，她在养父的鼓励下开始学习医学，并立志成为一名医生。然而社会不会轻易接受一名女医生，而她也不得不在做职业女性还是做家庭主妇之间进行艰难的抉择。尽管她与乔治（George Gerry）很相爱，但她最终还是拒绝了幸福的婚姻和舒适的家庭所带来的诱惑，开始全身心地投入为社区服务的事业中。为了独立和自由，南付出了巨大的代价；付出同样代价的还有女作家本人——朱厄特终生未婚，她把毕生的精力投入到了文学创作之中。朱厄特的另一部小说《尖尖的枞树之乡》是其晚年的巅峰之作，享有"19世纪美国最优秀的乡土文学"的美誉。这部作品除了对新英格兰浓厚的地域色彩进行厚描外，还以其对女性情感和精神世界的细

---

[1] 转引自吴元迈主编，《20世纪外国文学史第一卷：世纪之交的外国文学》。南京：译林出版社，2004年，第296页。

[2] 吴元迈主编，《20世纪外国文学史第一卷：世纪之交的外国文学》。南京：译林出版社，2004年，第296页。

腻描写见长。这些淳朴、可爱的女人仿佛带着泥土的新鲜气息从朱厄特的小说中走了出来：阿尔米尔·托德夫人（Mrs. Almira Todd）以种植和采集草药为生，热情地帮助村里的医生为大家治病，是一位坚强而独立的女性；她的母亲布莱克特夫人（Mrs. Blackett）是一位热爱生活、乐观自信的可爱老太太。朱厄特的女性人物几乎无一例外地在生活的磨砺中经历了身心的全面成长。与此相对照的是，她小说中的男性人物却往往羸弱、腼腆、沉默。老渔民蒂利（Elijah Tilley）就是一个典型的朱厄特笔下的男性人物：他生活在过去的世界里，沉浸在对妻子的追忆之中，好像他的灵魂与生命已经随着妻子的离去而离开了他的躯体。这样的男性人物仿佛只是为女性人物的衬托而生的，因此体现出明显的"去中心"的特点。"朱厄特在作品中赋予女性在文化中的权力中心和权威地位，这在当时的男权统治社会里是很有超前意义的。"[1]

与朱厄特同时代且同样擅长书写新英格兰地域风情的女作家弗里曼也是一位关注女性成长的作家。与朱厄特不同的是，弗里曼的女性成长小说的成就主要体现在短篇创作上。在弗里曼看来，"狭隘的社会习俗、清教主义传统和男性的权势，共同造成了女性生活的牢笼"[2]。弗里曼在她的女性书写中所要做的就是反抗贫困的生活和男性统治带来的双重压迫。她的名篇《一位新英格兰修女》（*A New England Nun*）中的独孤的老小姐，在社会和世俗的压力下无法敞开心扉去爱，她的独居、自我封闭和沉默成为表达愤怒、维护女性自尊的唯一方式。同年发表的短篇《母亲的反抗》（"The Revolt of 'Mother'"）描写了撒拉·佩恩（Sarah Penn）为了争取更好的生存空间而对丈夫的权威发起挑战的故事。佩恩在丈夫为她盖新房子的承诺中默默地等了40年，然而等到的却是丈夫宁可为牲畜盖新屋也不肯兑现自己的诺言。佩恩决定不再沉默，她带着孩子们搬到了丈夫为牲畜盖的新屋，以此表达自己的愤怒和抗议。然而，为了使自己的作品能够被男权主流文化所认可和接受，朱厄特常常不得不压抑自己的愤怒，用比较含蓄的手法来表达女性的抗争。因此，"她的反抗并未超越父权社会为女性界定的性别范畴"，所以，"还不至于威胁或动摇以男性权力为中心的社会结构"。[3]

19世纪90年代女性的生存空间得到了进一步的拓展，美国女性成长小说也发展得更为成熟，在内容和形式上都超越了传统的创作模式。这一时期，涌现出了吉尔曼（Charlotte Perkins Gilman, 1860—1935）、肖邦、华顿等一批优秀的女性作家。吉尔曼非

---

[1] 吴元迈主编，《20世纪外国文学史第一卷：世纪之交的外国文学》。南京：译林出版社，2004年，第298页。
[2] 吴元迈主编，《20世纪外国文学史第一卷：世纪之交的外国文学》。南京：译林出版社，2004年，第299页。
[3] 吴元迈主编，《20世纪外国文学史第一卷：世纪之交的外国文学》。南京：译林出版社，2004年，第300页。

常注重女性小说的"社会教育功能",她的女权主义小说《女儿国》(Herland)就是一部在女性乌托邦的想象中颠覆男权统治中心地位的作品。在这个"女儿国"中,女人是国家的主宰,她们摒弃了女人的牢笼——家庭,也把男人彻底地排除在生活中心之外,甚至连繁衍后代也不需要男人。《女儿国》以虚幻的方式完成了对男权的颠覆,并为女权主义的奋斗勾勒出了一个具体的理想和目标,从而充分发挥了女性写作的社会教育功能。然而构建在乌托邦想象中的女权主义毕竟如雾里花、水中月,可望而不可即。相比之下,肖邦的《觉醒》(The Awakening)则根植于现实主义的沃土,塑造了一位贴近普通女性生活和思想的新女性形象。爱德娜·蓬迪里埃(Edna Pontellier)是新奥尔良一名商人的妻子,过着中产阶级女性衣食无忧的舒适生活。她仿佛拥有一切,却唯独没有自己。结婚六年之后,她遇到了同性知己和异性恋人,这种情感的丰富使她开始重新审视曾经的生活和迷失的自我。她开始不满足于婚姻中受到种种限制和保守的生活,潜意识里从一名贤妻良母走向了逐渐的觉醒。在这一过程中,爱德娜发现了一个真实的自我,并为了满足对情感和性的欲望而不顾一切。爱德娜的觉醒是精神上的觉醒,也是肉体上的觉醒。她开始摆脱丈夫对自己的控制,并按照自己的意愿去选择精神上的伴侣和性欲上的伙伴。然而爱德娜的觉醒是不见容于当时的社会的,等待她的注定是悲剧的命运;爱德娜的自由只有在死亡的梦魇中才能获得。正如社会对爱德娜的排斥一般,肖邦的命运也随着这本书的出版而发生了骤变。由于在小说中公开讨论了妇女的情感和性的需求,肖邦因此遭到了文学界和评论界人士的蔑视和排斥。肖邦的朋友们视她为洪水猛兽,文学俱乐部将她开除,图书馆也将《觉醒》列为禁书。人们对《觉醒》的否定态度使肖邦受到了深深的伤害,正值创作成熟期的肖邦愤然停止了长篇小说的创作,并于五年后抑郁而死。

被称为亨利·詹姆斯"女继承人"的伊迪丝·华顿的创作始于19世纪末期,却在20世纪末期为女权主义者重新发现,成为瑰宝。出身名门的伊迪丝·华顿深切地体会到了美国上流社会的狭隘、僵化和沉闷,而作为女人,她更清楚这个阶层对妇女的种种无形的羁绊。她最优秀的作品都是把她熟悉的纽约上流社会与她作为女人的深切感受完美融合。"她意识到自己文学创作的理想与作为'装饰物'的上层阶级妇女身份之间的矛盾,从而刻画了妇女的困境。她在创作中以敏锐的目光透过上层阶级的珠光宝气揭露其虚伪堕落的本质,而且对社会流行的传统女性观进行了深刻的剖析和批判,展示了她对女性独特经历的深刻了解。"[1] 华顿的小说中塑造了一系列美国19世纪上层社会的女性形

---

[1] 吴元迈主编,《20世纪外国文学史第一卷:世纪之交的外国文学》。南京:译林出版社,2004年,第304页。

象，从不同的角度关注了这些女性的经历——她们要么在纽约这个浮华都市的大染缸中夭折，要么出淤泥而不染，获得精神上的成长。华顿的代表作《欢乐之家》(*The House of Mirth*)和《纯真年代》(*The Age of Innocence*)被称为关于纽约或欧洲生活的"社会小说"，然而这两部小说的核心却是女性的成长。《欢乐之家》中的莉莉·巴特（Lily Bart）是个受过良好教育但又野心勃勃的漂亮姑娘。在她的母亲去世后，她去和守寡的姑妈佩尼丝顿（Julia Peniston）一起生活，本希望得到姑妈的财产，却不曾想保守的姑妈看不惯莉莉的生活方式，对她的品行也产生了怀疑，因此只留给她一万美元了事。年轻幼稚的莉莉被道貌岸然的特莱纳（Gus Trenor）引入歧途，学会了赌博，并因此欠下特莱纳的钱，只能成为供他消遣的工具。莉莉被上流社会的贵妇人陷害，名誉一落千丈，连一个制帽女工的工作也保不住了。心灰意冷的莉莉在偿还了所有债务之后，自杀身亡。莉莉的死最终向人们证明了她的清白，也实现了她道德层面的升华。莉莉具有典型的双重性格：她既不愿意认同上层社会的价值观，又难以与之彻底决裂，这种犹疑在当时的上层社会妇女中是颇具代表性的。然而，不可否认的是，莉莉是一个最终完成了成长的女人，她的成长恰恰表现在她的生命的完结之中。

维拉·凯瑟是20世纪初美国十分著名的女作家，她以富于特色的创作题材和艺术风格在当时就赢得了普遍的赞誉，而在20世纪末她又赢得了人们的重新关注，并被认为是20世纪美国最杰出的小说家之一。从美国现代文学的角度来看，维拉·凯瑟的贡献虽然不及福克纳（William Faulkner, 1897—1962）和海明威，然而她是第一个着力描写"拓荒时代"的作家，她在作品中刻画了西部草原既苍茫荒凉但又蕴含无穷的生命力的原始风貌，以及拓荒者们虽贫穷、艰难但却质朴、坚强的精神风貌。在凯瑟的作品中，一个永恒的主题是道德和精神力量总是高于物质。她选择美国西部边疆来象征她理想中的生活，所以她最成功的长篇小说，如《我的安东妮亚》(*My Antonia*)、《啊，拓荒者!》(*O Pioneers!*)、《教授的房屋》(*The Professor's House*)以及一些中短篇，如《一个迷途的女人》("A Lost Lady")、《街坊罗西基》("Neighbour Rosicky")等都是以西部为背景的。透过西部的荒原和岩石，她看到的不仅是自然的荒凉和悲壮，更多地看到了岁月的沧桑、人类的足迹和美国历史和现实生活的真正意义。凯瑟的代表作《我的安东妮亚》一直是一部备受关注的女性成长小说。安东妮亚（Antonia）幼时和家人从捷克移民到内布拉斯加州的大草原，从此开始了她坎坷的一生。尽管拓荒的生活艰苦、枯燥，但在广阔的草原上，在自然的怀抱中，安东妮亚生活得幸福快乐；而到城里做工的安东妮亚，却因没有受过教育又轻信他人，被人玩弄，被人抛弃。重新回到大草原的安东妮亚，以她顽强的毅力、坚韧的性格，在那片虽然荒凉但却纯净的土地上开创了一片生机和希望，并嫁给了一个朴实的农民，生育了一群可爱的儿女。安东妮亚离不开自然，就像树木和庄稼离不开土地。可以说，安东妮亚在某种意义上成了自然的化身，代表着凯瑟心中理想的女性形象。与安东妮亚形成鲜明对比的是她幼时的伙伴吉米（Jim Burden），他长大后到东部城市发展，事业有成，但当他回到阔别二十年的草原去看望安东妮亚时，他仍然感到失落，感到自己在东部城市的生活令人烦躁不安，丧失了那份质朴真诚和那种虽然艰苦却又恬淡自怡的真实。吉米幼时与安东妮亚相处时，也像她一样，拥有生活的全部；但时过二十年，他发现安东妮亚仍然有一个灿烂的明天在等待着她，而他自己却只拥有一个曾经美好、但已一去不返的过去。他回去看望安东妮亚，就像去寻找一个逝去的乐园，带着几分怀旧伤感的眷恋和对生活无可奈何的感慨。

从某种程度上说，维拉·凯瑟的女性成长小说代表了美国女性成长小说成熟的开端，也意味着单一的女性成长小说模式的终结。凯瑟在美国女性成长小说的发展历程中是一个承上启下的人物。进入20世纪的美国女性文学开始呈现出多元化的特征，少数族裔美国女性作家开始崭露头角，并结合少数族裔独特的传统文化和女性的特殊经历创作出一大批具有鲜明特色的女性成长小说。同时，女性成长小说在经历了从奥尔克特到维拉·凯瑟的反复书写之后，已经成为美国女性文学中的一个重要文类，并形成了美国女性成长小说的伟大传统。与此同时，对美国女性小说的研究也取得了丰硕成果，而这些研究也进一步推动了美国女性成长小说的繁荣和发展，并不断在艺术和审美上突破传统的模式，迎来了美国女性成长小说的春天。1970年前后，美国开始出现一次空前的出版浪潮，涌现出了一大批由女性作家撰写的、描写女性的小说，这一时期的女性小说把历史越来越多地拖进了自我的书写，目的是让"女性的历史"来取代业已形成的、以男性为主导的历史观。在书写女性历史的过程中，美国女性成长小说的视野、题材、创作手法等都得到了进一步的发展。

20世纪六七十年代以来的女性文学的大量涌现，不仅仅是一场文学革命，也是一场政治革命。这些作品的出现象征着美国妇女的生存意义出现了根本性转变。60年代的女权主义运动所提出的"个人的即是政治的"的口号，使女性作家重新思考女性成长的真正含义，并逐渐从个人倾诉向社会批判转变，从"文化边缘"向"文化中心"温柔而坚定地突进。此时的女性作家更为关注女性写作传统的确立和创新。女权主义运动的初期，女性成长小说主要在较为传统的结构中表现女权主义的视角；这一时期的作品集中描写了男女关系的不平等，婚姻对女性的束缚，甚至也包括大胆的女性性体验。同时，女性作家也意识到女性成长并不是个体的孤独体验，而是女性群体的共同的历史经验。她们越来越清醒地意识到每个人的个体写作体验只有纳入宏大的"妇女文学"的经典才能得到更为广泛的认同和传播，而在她们的作品之中，女性的成长也体现出越来越厚重的历史感和集体感。这种女性群体意识和女性文学经典重构的尝试甚至可以追溯到格特鲁德·斯泰因（Gertrude Stein，1874—1946）用若干妇女的叙述而拼合成的小说。斯泰因的《许许多多的女人》（*Many Many Women*）对女性个体和女性群体以及女性之间的每一种关系进行了详细的描述。斯泰因确立的女性成长小说的女性群体意识日后成为美国女性成长小说的典型的叙述模式。西尔维娅·普拉斯（Sylvia Plath，1932—1963）的《钟形罩》（*The Bell Jar*）、艾丽斯·沃克（Alice Walker，1944— ）的《爱情与烦恼：黑人女性的故事集》（*In Love and Trouble: Stories of Black Women*）、《紫色》（*The Color Purple*）等小说，格洛丽亚·内勒（Gloria Naylor, 1950—2016）的《布鲁斯特街的女人们》（*The Women of Brewster Place*）、托妮·莫里森（Toni Morrison，1931—2019）的《秀拉》（*Sula*）、《宠儿》（*Beloved*）等对女性群体的成长都给予了特别的关注。普拉斯的《钟形罩》被称为"女性版的《麦田里的守望者》"，是一部经典的女性成长小说。尽管该小说具有明显的自传性，但小说女主人公埃斯特（Esther Greenwood）与自我、与社会的抗争历程却是女性的共同经历。《布鲁斯特街的女人们》中的几位女性的故事一开始是并列的、分离的，但她们的经历和思想逐渐交织、融合在一起，以至于她们会梦到彼此的生活，并在梦境之中有共同的经历和感受。这种小说叙事上的尝试体现了女性在狭义和广义上的定义：从广义上讲，"妇女是所有妇女个体的集合"；从狭义上讲，"她是所有妇女共同享有的一种本质"。而这两个层面的含义在美国现当代女性成长小说中往往交织在一起，形成一个立体的女性雕像。

拓展阅读文献

Giffin, Michael. *Female Maturity from Jane Austen to Margaret Atwood: When Bildungsroman Meets Zeitgeist*. CreateSpace Independent Publishing Platform, 2013.

王卓，《投射在文本中的成长丽影——美国女性成长小说研究》。北京：中国书籍出版社，2008年。

Lecture 7
Jane Austen

Profile of the Writer

Jane Austen
(1775–1817)

The daughter of a Hampshire clergyman, Austen was born at Steventon Parsonage on December 16, 1775. As the seventh of eight children, she grew up in a happy and close-knit family, and the careers and families of her brothers (two clergymen, two admirals, and one adopted by wealthy relations) inform her stories. She started writing at a young age, and her juvenilia includes dramatic sketches, spoofs and poems. Friends and family circulated her writings and wooed publishers, but it was over a decade before *Sense and Sensibility* (1811) went into print, soon followed by *Pride and Prejudice* (1813), which she called "my own darling child". Sir Walter Scott contrasted Austen's "exquisite touch" with his own "Big Bow-Wow" approach, praising the way she made "commonplace things and characters interesting from the truth of the description and the sentiment".

Sense and Sensibility and *Pride and Prejudice* both revolve around sisters, and Austen's loving alliance with her only sister Cassandra lasted all her life. Both Jane and Cassandra had romances, but, like Austen's heroines, they refused to marry for the sake of marriage. They remained single, supporting their mother after the death of their father in 1805.

In 1809, Austen moved with her mother and her sister to Chawton, a tranquil Hampshire village. There, in a house given to them by her wealthy brother Edward,

Austen spent her happiest years. All the six of her novels date in their finished form from this period. *Mansfield Park* was published in 1814 and *Emma*, with its heroine whom Austen half-jokingly predicted "no one but myself will much like", in 1815.

Austen died, aged only 41, on July 18, 1817, leaving the subtle *Persuasion* and her Gothic satire *Northanger Abbey* to be published later that year.

Jane Austen's life resembles her novels—at first glance they seem to be composed of a series of quiet, unexceptional events. Such an impression is supported by the comment of her brother, Henry, who wrote after her death that her life was "not by any means a life of event". Similarly, her nephew James added in a biography published fifty years later that "Of events her life was singularly barren: Few changes and no great crisis ever broke the smooth current of its course." However, just as readers find that the complexity of Austen's novel lies in its characters and style, those studying Austen herself discover that the events of her life are secondary to her compelling personality, quick wit, and highly-developed powers of observation. The fact that Austen's life lacked the drama that other authors may have experienced in no way detracted from her skill as a writer. In actuality, Austen's lack of "extraordinary" experiences, as well as of a spouse and children, probably made her writing possible by freeing her time to work on her books. Additionally, because her books were published anonymously, Austen never achieved personal recognition for her works outside of her sphere of family and friends. Such anonymity suited her, for, as literary critic Richard Blythe notes, "literature, not the literary life, was always her intention".

Preview Questions

1. What are the chief concerns of Jane Austen's novels?

2. What is Jane Austen's view on marriage? Do you think her view is out of date in the modern era?

Literary Reading: *Pride and Prejudice* (Chapter 36)

If Elizabeth, when Mr. Darcy gave her the letter, did not expect it to contain a renewal of his offers, she had formed no expectation at all of its contents. But such as they were, it may well be supposed how eagerly she went through them, and what a contrariety of

emotion they excited. Her feelings as she read were scarcely to be defined. With amazement did she first understand that he believed any apology to be in his power; and steadfastly was she persuaded, that he could have no explanation to give, which a just sense of shame would not conceal. With a strong prejudice against everything he might say, she began his account of what had happened at Netherfield. She read with an eagerness which hardly left her power of comprehension, and from impatience of knowing what the next sentence might bring, was incapable of attending to the sense of the one before her eyes. His belief of her sister's insensibility she instantly resolved to be false; and his account of the real, the worst objections to the match, made her too angry to have any wish of doing him justice. He expressed no regret for what he had done which satisfied her; his style was not penitent, but haughty. It was all pride and insolence.

But when this subject was succeeded by his account of Mr. Wickham—when she read with somewhat clearer attention a relation of events which, if true, must overthrow every cherished opinion of his worth, and which bore so alarming an affinity to his own history of himself—her feelings were yet more acutely painful and more difficult of definition. Astonishment, apprehension, and even horror, oppressed her. She wished to discredit it entirely, repeatedly exclaiming, "This must be false! This cannot be! This must be the grossest falsehood!"—and when she had gone through the whole letter, though scarcely knowing anything of the last page or two, put it hastily away, protesting that she would not regard it, that she would never look in it again.

In this perturbed state of mind, with thoughts that could rest on nothing, she walked on; but it would not do; in half a minute the letter was unfolded again, and collecting herself as well as she could, she again began the mortifying perusal of all that related to Wickham, and commanded herself so far as to examine the meaning of every sentence. The account of his connection with the Pemberley family was exactly what he had related himself; and the kindness of the late Mr. Darcy, though she had not before known its extent, agreed equally well with his own words. So far each recital confirmed the other; but when she came to the will, the difference was great. What Wickham had said of the living was fresh in her memory, and as she recalled his very words, it was impossible not to feel that there was gross duplicity on one side or the other; and, for a few moments, she flattered herself that her wishes did not err. But when she read and re-read with the closest attention, the particulars immediately following of Wickham's resigning all pretensions to the living, of his receiving in lieu so considerable a sum as three thousand pounds, again was she forced to hesitate. She put down the letter, weighed every circumstance with what she meant to be impartiality—deliberated on the probability of each statement—but with little success. On both sides it was only assertion. Again she read on; but every line proved more clearly that the affair, which she had believed it impossible that any contrivance could so represent as to render Mr. Darcy's conduct in it less than infamous, was capable of a turn which must make him entirely blameless throughout the whole.

The extravagance and general profligacy which he scrupled not to lay at Mr. Wickham's charge, exceedingly shocked her; the more so, as she could bring no proof of its injustice. She had never heard of him before his entrance into the—shire Militia, in which he had engaged at the persuasion of the young man who, on meeting him accidentally in town, had there renewed a slight acquaintance. Of his former way of life nothing had been known in Hertfordshire but what he told himself. As to his real character, had information been in her power, she had never felt a wish of inquiring. His countenance, voice, and manner had established him at once in the possession of every virtue. She tried to recollect some instance of goodness, some distinguished trait of integrity or benevolence, that might rescue him from the attacks of Mr. Darcy; or at least, by the predominance of virtue, atone for those casual errors under which she would endeavour to class what Mr. Darcy had described as the idleness and vice of many years' continuance. But no such recollection befriended her. She could see him instantly before her, in every charm of air and address; but she could remember no more substantial good than the general approbation of the neighbourhood, and the regard which his social powers had gained him in the mess. After pausing on this point a considerable while, she once more continued to read. But, alas! The story which followed, of his designs on Miss Darcy, received some confirmation from what had passed between Colonel Fitzwilliam and herself only the morning before; and at last she was referred for the truth of every particular to Colonel Fitzwilliam himself—from whom she had previously received the information of his near concern in all his cousin's affairs, and whose character she had no reason to question. At one time she had almost resolved on applying to him, but the idea was checked by the awkwardness of the application, and at length wholly banished by the conviction that Mr. Darcy would never have hazarded such a proposal, if he had not been well assured of his cousin's corroboration.

She perfectly remembered everything that had passed in conversation between Wickham and herself, in their first evening at Mr. Phillips's. Many of his expressions were still fresh in her memory. She was now struck with the impropriety of such communications to a stranger, and wondered it had escaped her before. She saw the indelicacy of putting himself forward as he had done, and the inconsistency of his professions with his conduct. She remembered that he had boasted of having no fear of seeing Mr. Darcy—that Mr. Darcy might leave the country, but that he should stand his ground; yet he had avoided the

Netherfield ball the very next week. She remembered also that, till the Netherfield family had quitted the country, he had told his story to no one but herself; but that after their removal it had been everywhere discussed; that he had then no reserves, no scruples in sinking Mr. Darcy's character, though he had assured her that respect for the father would always prevent his exposing the son.

How differently did everything now appear in which he was concerned! His attentions to Miss King were now the consequence of views solely and hatefully mercenary; and the mediocrity of her fortune proved no longer the moderation of his wishes, but his eagerness to grasp at anything. His behaviour to herself could now have had no tolerable motive; he had either been deceived with regard to her fortune, or had been gratifying his vanity by encouraging the preference which she believed she had most incautiously shown. Every lingering struggle in his favour grew fainter and fainter; and in farther justification of Mr. Darcy, she could not but allow that Mr. Bingley, when questioned by Jane, had long ago asserted his blamelessness in the affair; that proud and repulsive as were his manners, she had never, in the whole course of their acquaintance—an acquaintance which had latterly brought them much together, and given her a sort of intimacy with his ways—seen anything that betrayed him to be unprincipled or unjust—anything that spoke him of irreligious or immoral habits; that among his own connections he was esteemed and valued—that even Wickham had allowed him merit as a brother, and that she had often heard him speak so affectionately of his sister as to prove him capable of some amiable feeling; that had his actions been what Mr. Wickham represented them, so gross a violation of everything right could hardly have been concealed from the world; and that friendship between a person capable of it, and such an amiable man as Mr. Bingley, was incomprehensible.

She grew absolutely ashamed of herself. Of neither Darcy nor Wickham could she think without feeling she had been blind, partial, prejudiced, absurd.

"How despicably I have acted!" she cried; "I, who have prided myself on my discernment! I, who have valued myself on my abilities! who have often disdained the generous candour of my sister, and gratified my vanity in useless or blameable mistrust! How humiliating is this discovery! Yet, how just a humiliation! Had I been in love, I could not have been more wretchedly blind! But vanity, not love, has been my folly. Pleased with the preference of one, and offended by the neglect of the other, on the very beginning of our acquaintance, I have courted prepossession and ignorance, and driven reason away, where either were concerned. Till this moment I never knew myself."

From herself to Jane—from Jane to Bingley, her thoughts were in a line which soon brought to her recollection that Mr. Darcy's explanation there had appeared very insufficient, and she read it again. Widely different was the effect of a second perusal. How could she deny that credit to his assertions in one instance, which she had been obliged to give in the other? He declared himself to be totally unsuspicious of her sister's attachment; and she could not help remembering what Charlotte's opinion had always been. Neither could she deny the justice of his description of Jane. She felt that Jane's feelings, though fervent, were little displayed, and that there was a constant complacency in her air and manner not often united with great sensibility.

When she came to that part of the letter in which her family were mentioned in terms of such mortifying, yet merited reproach, her sense of shame was severe. The justice of the charge struck her too forcibly for denial, and the circumstances to which he particularly alluded as having passed at the Netherfield ball, and as confirming all his first disapprobation, could not have made a stronger impression on his mind than on hers.

The compliment to herself and her sister was not unfelt. It soothed, but it could not console her for the contempt which had thus been self-attracted by the rest of her family; and as she considered that Jane's disappointment had in fact been the work of her nearest relations, and reflected how materially the credit of both must be hurt by such impropriety of conduct, she felt depressed beyond anything she had ever known before.

After wandering along the lane for two hours, giving way to every variety of thought—reconsidering events, determining probabilities, and reconciling herself, as well as she could, to a change so sudden and so important, fatigue, and a recollection of her long absence, made her at length return home; and she entered the house with the wish of appearing cheerful as usual, and the resolution of repressing such reflections as must make her unfit for conversation.

She was immediately told that the two gentlemen from Rosings had each called during her absence; Mr. Darcy, only for a few minutes, to take leave—but that Colonel Fitzwilliam had been sitting with them at least an hour, hoping for her return, and almost resolving to walk after her till she could be found. Elizabeth could but just affect concern in missing him; she really rejoiced at it. Colonel Fitzwilliam was no longer an object; she could think only of her letter.

III Thinking, Talking and Writing About Literature

1 Textual Cognition

Make an introductory presentation on the following terms related to this literary work.

1) irony
2) classic romance

❷ Textual Reading

Search for evidence in the text and answer the following questions.

1) Why did Elizabeth distrust Mr. Darcy at the start, and instead trust Mr. Wickham? What role does Mr. Wickham play in this novel?

2) What function does Mr. Darcy's letter play in changing Elizabeth's attitude towards him?

3) At the end of this chapter, "Colonel Fitzwilliam was no longer an object; she could think only of her letter." Why?

❸ Critical Reading

Discuss in groups the following questions to further explore this literary work.

1) What obstacles does Elizabeth have to overcome in order to attain her personal growth?

2) Explore the developing relationship between Elizabeth and Mr. Darcy. Why do they misunderstand each other, and how do they reach accord?

❹ Writing About Literature

Read the following critical excerpt and then write an essay.

> Baruch, Elaine Hoffman. "The Feminine 'Bildungsroman': Education Through Marriage." *The Massachusetts Review* 22.2 (1981): 335–357.

It has long been a critical commonplace that there is no feminine Bildungsroman. But if the central theme of the Bildungsroman is the education of the hero who is brought to a high level of consciousness through a series of experiences that lead to his development, then many of the great novels that deal with women treat similar themes. From *Emma* to *Jane Eyre* to *Madame Bovary* to *Middlemarch* to *Anna Karenina* to *Portrait of a Lady* to *Lady Chatterley's Lover* and beyond, the novel presents a search for self, an education of the mind and feelings. But unlike the male Bildungsroman, the feminine Bildungsroman takes place in or on the periphery of marriage. That is its most striking characteristic.

In his important book *The Rise of the Novel*, Ian Watt made the point that, starting in the eighteenth century, marriage determined woman's social, economic, and geographic future. In the *Pamela* tradition, which mirrors this social reality, the heroine seeks upward mobility in marriage. In the tradition that I am here treating, which is perhaps equally important, if not as widely recognized, the heroine longs for a love marriage that will increase her knowledge, often in some wide experiential sense.

It is perhaps an index of how much we have changed that we can now dissociate women's education from marriage. However, throughout the nineteenth century things were quite otherwise. Hegel, who is merely one of many spokesmen for the idea, writes that women have their essential destiny in marriage and there only. In a seemingly unrelated passage, he speaks of women and learning:

> Women acquire learning—we know not how—almost as if by breathing ideas, more by living really than by actually taking hold of knowledge. Man, on the other hand, achieves his distinction only by means of advancing thought and much skilled exertion.

Hegel, who admittedly idealizes intuitive knowledge, doesn't recognize the causal connection in the two passages. What other way could women acquire knowledge than to "breathe" it? And what was more natural than for them to seek to make of their marital destiny a means of education, since almost without exception every other institution of higher learning was closed to them?

…

Unlike the lady of the chivalric romance who had merely to sit still in order to find a destiny in the form of some passing knight, modern woman must seek her own hero. The development of the self through marriage involves many trials, for assuredly finding the right man to be one's tutor/lover is far more difficult and dangerous an undertaking than finding the right university.

Essay Writing

Write an essay on Elizabeth's development through marriage with no less than 500 words.

Further Activity

Scan the QR code and listen to the audio of Chapter 36 of *Pride and Prejudice*.

Lecture 8
Charlotte Brontë

Profile of the Writer

Charlotte Brontë
(1816–1855)

Charlotte Brontë was born in 1816, the third daughter of the Rev. Patrick Brontë and his wife Maria. Her brother Patrick Branwell was born in 1817, and her sisters Emily and Anne in 1818 and 1820. In 1820, too, the Brontë family moved to Haworth, Mrs. Brontë dying the following year.

In 1824 the four eldest Brontë daughters were enrolled as pupils at the Clergy Daughter's School at Cowan Bridge. The following year Maria and Elizabeth, the two eldest daughters, became ill, left the school and died: Charlotte and Emily, understandably, were brought home.

In 1826 Mr. Brontë brought home a box of wooden soldiers for Branwell to play with. Charlotte, Emily, Branwell, and Ann, playing with the soldiers, conceived of and began to write in great detail about an imaginary world which they called Angria.

In 1831 Charlotte became a pupil at the school at Roe Head, but she left school the following year to teach her sisters at home. She returned to Roe Head School in 1835 as a governess: for a time her sister Emily attended the same school as a pupil, but became homesick and returned to Haworth. Ann took her place from 1836 to 1837.

In 1838, Charlotte left Roe Head School. In 1839 she accepted a position as governess in the Sidgewick family, but left after three months and returned to Haworth. In 1841 she became governess in the White family, but left, once again, after nine months.

Upon her return to Haworth the three sisters, led by Charlotte, decided to open their own school after the necessary preparations had been completed. In 1842 Charlotte and Emily went to Brussels to complete their studies. After a trip home to Haworth, Charlotte returned alone to Brussels, where she remained until 1844.

Upon her return home the sisters embarked upon their project for founding a school, which proved to be an abject failure: Their advertisements did not elicit a single response from the public. The following year Charlotte discovered Emily's poems, and decided to publish a selection of the poems of all three sisters: 1846 brought the publication of their poems, written under the pseudonyms of Currer, Ellis and Acton Bell. Charlotte also completed *The Professor*, which was rejected for publication. The following year, however, Charlotte's *Jane Eyre*, Emily's *Wuthering Heights*, and Ann's *Agnes Grey* were all published, still under the Bell pseudonyms.

In 1848 Charlotte and Ann visited their publishers in London, and revealed the true identities of the "Bells". In the same year Branwell Brontë, by now an alcoholic and a drug addict, died, and Emily died shortly thereafter. Ann died the following year.

In 1849 Charlotte, visiting London, began to move in literary circles, making the acquaintance, for example, of Thackeray. In 1850 Charlotte edited her sister's various works, and met Mrs. Gaskell. In 1851 she visited the Great Exhibition in London, and attended a series of lectures given by Thackeray.

The Rev. A. B. Nicholls, curate of Haworth since 1845, proposed marriage to Charlotte in 1852. The Rev. Mr. Brontë objected violently, and Charlotte, who, though she may have pitied him, was in any case not in love with him, refused him. Nicholls left Haworth in the following year, the same in which Charlotte's *Villette* was published. By 1854, however, Mr. Brontë's opposition to the proposed marriage had weakened, and Charlotte and Nicholls became engaged. Nicholls returned as curate at Haworth, and they were married, though it seems clear that Charlotte, though she admired him, still did not love him.

In 1854 Charlotte, expecting a child, caught pneumonia. It was an illness which could have been cured, but she seemed to have seized upon it (consciously or unconsciously) as an opportunity of ending her life, and after a lengthy and painful illness, she died, probably of dehydration.

1857 saw the postumous publication of *The Professor*, which had been written in 1845–1846, and in that same year Mrs. Gaskell's *Life of Charlotte Brontë* was published.

I. Preview Questions

1. The women characters in the novel include Mrs. Reed, Miss Temple, Céline Varens, Blanche Ingram, Bertha Mason, and Diana and Mary Rivers. What does Jane Eyre learn about proper feminine behavior from these women? Who are positive role models? Who are negative?

2. The action of the book can be said to be dominated or overshadowed by four strong male characters: John Reed, the Rev. Mr. Brocklehurst, Edward Rochester, and St. John Rivers. What influence or effect does each of these men have on Jane Eyre's moral development? To what extent do these characters constitute Charlotte Brontë's construction of the male gender?

II. Literary Reading: *Jane Eyre* (Chapter 1)

There was no possibility of taking a walk that day. We had been wandering, indeed, in the leafless shrubbery an hour in the morning; but since dinner (Mrs. Reed, when there was no company, dined early) the cold winter wind had brought with it clouds so sombre, and a rain so penetrating, that further outdoor exercise was now out of the question.

I was glad of it; I never liked long walks, especially on chilly afternoons: dreadful to me was the coming home in the raw twilight, with nipped fingers and toes, and a heart saddened by the chidings of Bessie, the nurse, and humbled by the consciousness of my physical inferiority to Eliza, John, and Georgiana Reed.

The said Eliza, John, and Georgiana were now clustered round their mama in the drawing-room: she lay reclined on a sofa by the fireside, and with her darlings about her (for the time neither quarrelling nor crying) looked perfectly happy. Me, she had dispensed from joining the group; saying, "She regretted to be under the necessity of keeping me at a distance; but that until she heard from Bessie, and could discover by her own observation, that I was endeavouring in good earnest to acquire a more sociable and childlike disposition, a more attractive and sprightly manner—something lighter, franker, more natural, as it were—she really must exclude me from privileges intended only for contented, happy, little children."

"What does Bessie say I have done?" I asked.

"Jane, I don't like cavillers or questioners; besides, there is something truly forbidding in a child taking up her elders in that manner. Be seated somewhere; and until you can speak pleasantly, remain silent."

A breakfast-room adjoined the drawing-room, I slipped in there. It contained a bookcase: I soon possessed myself of a volume, taking care that it should be one stored with pictures. I mounted into the window-seat: gathering up my feet, I sat cross-legged, like a Turk; and, having drawn the red moreen curtain nearly close, I was shrined in double retirement.

Folds of scarlet drapery shut in my view to the right hand; to the left were the clear panes of glass, protecting, but not separating me from the drear November day. At intervals, while turning over the leaves of my book, I studied the aspect of that winter afternoon. Afar, it offered a pale blank of mist and cloud; near, a scene of wet lawn and storm-beat shrub, with ceaseless rain sweeping away wildly before a long and lamentable blast.

I returned to my book—*Bewick's History of British Birds*: the letterpress thereof I cared little for, generally speaking; and yet there were certain introductory pages that, child as I was, I could not pass quite as a blank. They were those which treat of the haunts of sea-fowl; of "the solitary rocks and promontories" by them only inhabited; of the coast of Norway, studded with isles from its southern extremity, the Lindeness, or Naze, to the North Cape—

> "Where the Northern Ocean, in vast whirls,
> Boils round the naked, melancholy isles
> Of farthest Thule; and the Atlantic surge
> Pours in among the stormy Hebrides."

Nor could I pass unnoticed the suggestion of the bleak shores of Lapland, Siberia, Spitzbergen, Nova Zembla, Iceland, Greenland, with "the vast sweep of the Arctic Zone, and those forlorn regions of dreary space—that reservoir of frost and snow, where firm fields of ice, the accumulation of centuries of winters, glazed in Alpine heights above heights, surround the pole, and concentre the multiplied rigours of extreme cold". Of these death-white realms I formed an idea of my own: shadowy, like all the half-comprehended notions that float dim through children's brains, but strangely impressive. The words in these introductory pages connected themselves with the succeeding vignettes, and gave significance to the rock standing up alone in a sea of billow and spray; to the broken boat stranded on a desolate coast; to the cold and ghastly moon glancing through bars of cloud at a wreck just sinking.

I cannot tell what sentiment haunted the quite solitary churchyard, with its inscribed headstone; its gate, its two trees, its low horizon, girdled by a broken wall, and its newly-risen crescent, attesting the hour of eventide.

The two ships becalmed on a torpid sea; I believed to be marine phantoms.

The fiend pinning down the thief's pack behind him, I passed over quickly: it was an object of terror.

So was the black horned thing seated aloof on a rock, surveying a distant crowd surrounding a gallows.

Each picture told a story; mysterious often to my undeveloped understanding and imperfect feelings, yet ever profoundly interesting: as interesting as the tales Bessie sometimes narrated on winter evenings, when she chanced to be in good humour; and when, having brought her ironing-table to the nursery hearth, she allowed us to sit about it, and while she got up Mrs. Reed's lace frills, and crimped her nightcap borders, fed our eager attention with passages of love and adventure taken from old fairy tales and other ballads; or (as at a later period I discovered) from the pages of *Pamela*, and *Henry, Earl of Moreland*.

With Bewick on my knee, I was then happy: happy at least in my way. I feared nothing but interruption, and that came too soon. The breakfast-room door opened.

"Boh! Madam Mope!" cried the voice of John Reed; then he paused: he found the room apparently empty.

"Where the dickens is she!" he continued. "Lizzy! Georgy! (calling to his sisters) Jane is not here: tell mama she is run out into the rain—bad animal!"

"It is well I drew the curtain," thought I; and I wished fervently he might not discover my hiding-place: nor would John Reed have found it out himself; he was not quick either of vision or conception; but Eliza just put her head in at the door, and said at once: "She is in the window-seat, to be sure, Jack."

And I came out immediately, for I trembled at the idea of being dragged forth by the said Jack.

"What do you want?" I asked, with awkward diffidence.

"Say, 'What do you want, Master Reed?'" was the answer. "I want you to come here;" and seating himself in an arm-chair, he intimated by a gesture that I was to approach and stand before him.

John Reed was a schoolboy of fourteen years old; four years older than I, for I was but ten: large and stout for his age, with a dingy and unwholesome skin; thick lineaments in a spacious visage, heavy limbs and large extremities. He gorged himself habitually at table, which made him bilious, and gave him a dim and bleared eye and flabby cheeks. He ought now to have been at school; but his mama had taken him home for a month or two, "on account of his delicate health." Mr. Miles, the master, affirmed that he would do very well if he had fewer cakes and sweetmeats sent him from home; but the mother's heart turned from an opinion so harsh, and inclined rather to the more refined idea that John's sallowness was owing to over-application and, perhaps, to pining after home.

John had not much affection for his mother and sisters, and an antipathy to me. He bullied and punished me; not two or three times in the week, nor once or twice in the day, but continually: every nerve I had feared him, and every morsel of flesh in my bones shrank when he came near. There were moments when I was bewildered by the terror he inspired, because I had no appeal whatever against either his menaces or his inflictions; the servants did not like to offend their young master by taking my part against him, and Mrs. Reed was blind and deaf on the subject: she never saw him strike or heard him abuse me, though he did both now and then in her very presence, more frequently, however, behind her back.

Habitually obedient to John, I came up to his chair: he spent some three minutes in thrusting out his tongue at me as far as he could without damaging the roots: I knew he would soon strike, and while dreading the blow, I mused on the disgusting and ugly appearance of him who would presently deal it. I wonder if he read that notion in my face; for, all at once, without speaking, he struck suddenly and strongly. I tottered, and on regaining my equilibrium retired back a step or two from his chair.

"That is for your impudence in answering mama a while since," said he, "and for your sneaking way of getting behind curtains, and for the look you had in your eyes two minutes since, you rat!"

Accustomed to John Reed's abuse, I never had an idea of replying to it; my care was how to endure the blow which would certainly follow the insult.

"What were you doing behind the curtain?" he asked.

"I was reading."

"Show the book."

I returned to the window and fetched it thence.

"You have no business to take our books; you are a dependent, mama says; you have no money; your father left you none; you ought to beg, and not to live here with gentlemen's children like us, and eat the same meals we do, and wear clothes at our mama's expense. Now, I'll teach you to rummage my bookshelves: for they ARE mine; all the house belongs to me, or will do in a few years. Go and stand by the door, out of the way of the mirror and the windows."

I did so, not at first aware what was his intention; but when I saw him lift and poise the book and stand in act to hurl it, I instinctively started aside with a cry of alarm: not soon enough, however; the volume was flung, it hit me, and I fell, striking my head against the door and cutting it. The cut bled, the pain was sharp: my terror had passed its climax; other feelings succeeded.

"Wicked and cruel boy!" I said. "You are like a murderer—you are like a slave-driver—you are like the Roman emperors!"

I had read Goldsmith's *History of Rome*, and had formed my opinion of Nero, Caligula, &c. Also I had drawn parallels in silence, which I never thought thus to have declared aloud.

"What! what!" he cried. "Did she say that to me? Did you hear her, Eliza and Georgiana? Won't I tell mama? but first—"

He ran headlong at me: I felt him grasp my hair and my shoulder: he had closed with a desperate thing. I really saw in him a tyrant, a murderer. I felt a drop or two of blood from my head trickle down my neck, and was sensible of somewhat pungent suffering: these sensations for the time predominated over fear, and I received him in frantic sort. I don't very well know what I did with my hands, but he called me "Rat! Rat!" and bellowed out aloud. Aid was near him: Eliza and Georgiana had run for Mrs. Reed, who was gone upstairs: she now came upon the scene, followed by Bessie and her maid Abbot. We were parted: I heard the words—

"Dear! dear! What a fury to fly at Master John!"

"Did ever anybody see such a picture of passion!"

Then Mrs. Reed subjoined: "Take her away to the red-room, and lock her in there." Four hands were immediately laid upon me, and I was borne upstairs.

III Thinking, Talking and Writing About Literature

1 Textual Cognition

Make an introductory presentation on the following terms related to this literary work.

1) mad woman in the attic
2) Gothic novel

2 Textual Reading

Search for evidence in the text and answer the following questions.

1) What book is Jane Eyre reading when John Reed comes to look for her? Is it relevant to

the theme of the novel?

2) The red curtains that enclose Jane in her isolated window seat connect with the imagery of the red-room to which Jane is banished at the end of the chapter. What symbolic meaning does the color red have?

3) This opening chapter sets up two of the primary themes in the novel: class conflict and gender difference. Can you find some details to illustrate these two themes?

③ Critical Reading

Discuss in groups the following questions to further explore this literary work.

1) The narrator in the novel is an older Jane remembering her childhood. Find a few places where the voice of the older Jane intrudes on the narrative. What is the effect of this older voice's intrusions on the story?

2) Analyze the importance of the five major places where Jane lives on her journey: Gateshead, Lowood, Thornfield, Moor House / Marsh End, and Ferndean. What do their names signify? What lesson does Jane learn at each place?

④ Writing About Literature

Read the following critical excerpt and then write an essay.

> Maier, Sarah E. "Portraits of the Girl-Child: Female Bildungsroman in Victorian Fiction." *Literature Compass* 4.1(2007): 317–335.

Despite this one area of independence, Jane must still operate within the expected boundaries of her position as a governess. Mrs. Fairfax, the housekeeper and sympathetic maternal figure whom Jane meets at Thornfield, educates Jane that she must come and go when told, and must present herself according to the wishes of the Master who "has a gentleman's tastes and habits, and he expects to have things managed in conformity to them". This expected subservience is much like what Jane endured as a child, but it seems that she is ready to trade her teaching position at Lowood in order to be recognised as a capable woman in a somewhat more elevated capacity. The idea of service only becomes dangerous to Jane's autonomy when she is the object of Rochester's affections, and feels him "an influence that quite mastered [her]—that took her feelings from [her] own power and fettered them in his" in a manner which could become subservient. For Jane, when love becomes entwined with duty as the recipient of Rochester's affections, Jane is perfectly aware that she is in danger of being tempted to renounce any degree of autonomy and to repeat the dependence of her childhood. In order to overcome this sense of obligation, Jane

requires status, money and family on her own terms, not those dictated by the passionate, Byronic Rochester. Rochester's breeding and self-mastery threaten to overwhelm her—like Reed and Brocklehurst—except that Rochester also poses the excitement of sexual experience and of a marriage between two minds. With the approach of their marriage, Jane begins to turn inward, exploring her readiness to become a wife in disturbing dreams. In these dreams, she guards a dispossessed child which is strongly suggestive of her own circumstances as a child; significantly, they coincide with the renting of the veil by Jane's hidden doppelgänger, Bertha and prefigure the disruption of the marriage ceremony through the protective agency of Bertha's brother, Richard Mason. These incidents not only reflect Jane's desire to change her situation from dependence to one of independence but, indeed, they are the means of her metamorphosis into a subject who actively seeks individual expression. Jane is propelled forward on her Bildungsroman to question actively the confining parameters of an unsanctioned liaison with Rochester and to escape from Thornfield into flight on a three-day journey across the moors that suggest her educational and spiritual rebirth.

On this journey, Jane enters the female company of Diana and Mary Rivers where she can redefine her subjectivity without the consequence of her history or expectation. With life still in her "possession, with all its requirements and pains, and responsibilities", she can finally set aside "the responsibility fulfilled" and the burden left behind. Her quest is a healthy one and it enables her to articulate her desires now that she has left her girlhood fears behind her. As a teacher at the Morton School, she found "reviving pleasure in this intercourse, of a kind now tasted by [her] for the first time—the pleasure arising from perfect congeniality of tastes, sentiments, and principles" which helps her develop her concepts of self-worth and self-confidence through her increasingly mature independence.

Jane must now confront the next stage in her progression to adult womanhood; in fact, her interaction with and proposal from St. John Rivers is a test of her newly affirmed sense of self. Jane is tempted to succumb to an unhappy relationship out of a sense of duty—perhaps the most pervasive influence in a Victorian woman's mind—but she consciously chooses not to submit to his wishes because they would be self-destructive. Jane realises that she "fell under a freezing spell" but that she "did not love [her] servitude" when accompanied by St. John. His cold, arrogant assumption of moral superiority through his own emotional repression is counter to a life of combined mind and soul. When she "felt daily more and more that [she] must disown half [her] nature, stifle half [her] faculties" to bend to his will, and acknowledges her inner certainty that to "join St. John, [she would] abandon half" herself, Jane resolves to find Rochester. Now an "independent woman" in education and in status because of her uncle, Mr. Eyre of Madeira, left her a legacy of

£20,000, Jane returns to Rochester (now Edward) like equals and proudly declares "I am my own mistress". Self-possessed and self-defined, "in his presence [she] thoroughly lived; and he lived in" hers as a partnership of equals in the "practical" and the "real" business of everyday life through wifehood to motherhood. Jane has grown into an independent woman, not only with the help of fate but because of her continuing attempts to establish herself as an individual.

Essay Writing

Write an essay on *Jane Eyre* from the perspective of coming of age novel with no less than 500 words.

Further Activity

Scan the QR code and listen to the audio of Chapter 1 of *Jane Eyre*.

Lecture 9
George Eliot

Profile of the Writer

**George Eliot
(1819–1880)**

George Eliot came to English novel writing relatively late in life, with her first novel *Adam Bede* (1859) published when she was forty. However, it was an immensely popular work. The lives of her characters are, therefore, viewed from the vantage point of maturity extensive experience; and this perspective is accentuated by her practice of setting her stories back in time to the period of her own childhood. It was Warwickshire countryside that is the place Eliot usually looks back on. There, under her real name, Marian Evans, she spent her childhood at Arbury Farm, of which her father, Robert Evans, was supervisor and land agent. During the decades between 1820s and 1830s, Evans read widely in and out of school and was strongly affected by Evangelism. Her mother's death led to her leaving school at sixteen, and in the next four or five years she seemed to have experienced bouts of depression and self-doubt. She moved with her father to the town of Coventry at the age of twenty-one, and in this new setting her intellectual horizons were extensively widened. As a result of her association with a group of freethinking intellectuals, and her own studies of theology, she reluctantly decided that she could no longer believe in the Christian religion. With a painful decision that caused a rupture with her father, she buried herself in preoccupations with theological issues that led to her first book, a translation in 1846 of *The Life of Jesus* by D. F. Strauss. And for the rest of her life, Evans continued to read extensively in English and Continental philosophy; and when she moved to London after her father's death, her impressive intellectual credentials led to her appointment as an assistant editor of the *Westminster Review*, with a number of essays published in her served years. The Review life brought her into contact with many important writers and thinkers, among whom was George Henry Lewes, a brilliant critic of literature and philosophy, with whom she fell in love. Evans lived with him as a so-called wife, costing her a number of social and families ties, including her relationship with her brother, Isaac, to whom she had been deeply attached since childhood, which became the agonizingly painful experience of *The Mill on the Floss* and lasted happily until his death in 1878.

Eliot brings to her fictions a philosophical and psychological depth that is very different in character from that of the novel of manners. She strives to present her fiction as a mirror that reflects without distortion our experience of life, and defines herself as a historian, leading us to expect her novels to offer considerable insight into contemporary issues. The Woman Question was of particular interest in her, with the typical chosen heroine like Maggie Tulliver of *The Mill on the Floss* having a powerful imagination and a yearning to be more than her society allows her to be. She wrote, "My function is that of the aesthetic, not the doctrinal teacher." It is the breadth of vision through which Eliot enters into the consciousness of all her characters that makes the perspective of her novels on many issues complex. It is the distinctive combination of realism and sympathy that makes her a better realist than her famous French contemporary Flaubert, and she is perhaps often compared to Leo Tolstoy, the greatest English realist.

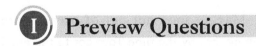

Preview Questions

1. What do you know about George Eliot?

2. *The Mill on the Floss* (1860) mainly deals with the troubled childhood and young adulthood of Maggie Tulliver, but a variety of background details reveal the changing community of the time and so relate to the actual sociological and economic shifts in England in the 1830s. How do you think *The Mill on the Floss* relates to England in the 1830s?

Ⅱ Literary Reading: *The Mill on the Floss* (Chapter 11)

Maggie Tries to Run Away from Her Shadow

Maggie's intentions, as usual, were on a larger scale than Tom imagined. The resolution that gathered in her mind, after Tom and Lucy had walked away, was not so simple as that of going home. No! She would run away and go to the gypsies, and Tom should never see her any more. That was by no means a new idea to Maggie; she had been so often told she was like a gypsy, and "half wild", that when she was miserable it seemed to her the only way of escaping opprobrium, and being entirely in harmony with circumstances, would be to live in a little brown tent on the commons; the gypsies, she considered, would gladly receive her and pay her much respect on account of her superior knowledge. She had once mentioned her views on this point to Tom and suggested that he should stain his face brown, and they should run away together; but Tom rejected the scheme with contempt, observing that gypsies were thieves, and hardly got anything to eat and had nothing to drive but a donkey. Today however, Maggie thought her misery had reached a pitch at which gypsydom was her refuge, and she rose from her seat on the roots of the tree with the sense that this was a great crisis in her life; she would run straight away till she came to Dunlow Common, where there would certainly be gypsies; and cruel Tom, and the rest of her relations who found fault with her, should never see her any more. She thought of her father as she ran along, but she reconciled herself to the idea of parting with him, by determining that she would secretly send him a letter by a small gypsy, who would run away without telling where she was, and just let him know that she was well and happy, and always loved him very much.

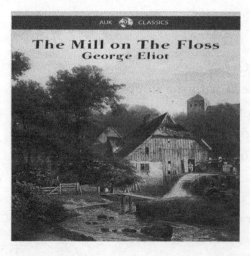

Maggie soon got out of breath with running, but by the time Tom got to the pond again she was at the distance of three long fields, and was on the edge of the lane leading to the highroad. She stopped to pant a little, reflecting that running away was not a pleasant thing until one had got quite to the common where the gypsies were, but her resolution had not abated; she presently passed through the gate into the lane, not knowing where it would lead her, for it was not this way that they came from Dorlcote Mill to Garum Firs, and she felt all the safer for that, because there was no chance of her being overtaken. But she was soon aware, not without trembling, that there were two men coming along the lane in front of her; she had not thought of meeting strangers, she had been too much occupied with the idea of her friends coming after her. The formidable strangers were two shabby-looking men with flushed faces, one of them carrying a bundle on a stick over his shoulder; but to her surprise, while she was dreading their disapprobation as a runaway, the man with the bundle stopped, and in a half-whining, half-coaxing tone asked her if she had a copper to give a poor man. Maggie had a sixpence in her pocket, —her uncle Glegg's present, —which she immediately drew out and gave this poor man with a polite smile, hoping he would feel very kindly toward her as a generous person. "That's the only money I've got," she said apologetically. "Thank you, little miss," said the man, in a less respectful and grateful tone than Maggie anticipated, and she even observed that he smiled and winked at his companion. She walked on hurriedly, but was aware that the two men were standing still, probably to look after her, and she presently heard them laughing loudly. Suddenly it occurred to her that they might think she was an idiot; Tom had said that her cropped hair made her look like an idiot, and it was too painful an idea to be readily forgotten. Besides, she had no sleeves on, —only a cape and bonnet. It was clear that she was not likely to make a favourable impression on passengers, and she thought she would turn into the fields again, but not on the same side of the lane as before, lest they should still be uncle Pullet's fields. She turned through the first gate that was not locked, and felt a delightful sense of privacy in creeping along by the hedgerows, after her recent humiliating encounter. She was used to wandering about the fields by herself, and was less timid there than on the highroad. Sometimes she had to climb over high gates, but that was a small evil; she was getting out of reach very fast, and she should probably soon come within sight of Dunlow Common, or at least of some other common, for she had heard her father say that you couldn't go very far without coming to a common. She hoped so, for she was getting rather tired and hungry, and until she reached the gypsies there was no definite prospect of bread and butter. It was still broad daylight, for aunt Pullet, retaining the early habits of the Dodson family, took tea at half-past four by the sun, and at five by the kitchen clock; so, though it was nearly an hour since Maggie started, there was no gathering gloom on the fields to remind her that the night would come. Still, it seemed to her that she had been walking a very great distance indeed, and it was really surprising that the common did not come within sight. Hitherto she had been in the rich parish of Garum, where was a great deal of pasture-land, and she had only seen one labourer at a distance. That was fortunate in some respects, as labourers might be too ignorant to understand the propriety of her wanting to go to Dunlow Common; yet it would have been better if she could have met some one who would tell her the way without wanting to know anything about her private business. At last, however, the green fields came to an end, and Maggie found herself looking through the bars of a gate into a lane with a wide margin of grass on each side of it. She had never seen such a wide lane before, and, without her knowing why, it gave her the impression that the common could not be far off; perhaps it was because she saw a donkey with a log to his foot feeding on the grassy margin, for she had seen a donkey with that pitiable encumbrance on Dunlow Common when she had been across it in her father's gig. She crept through the bars of the gate and walked on with new spirit, though not without haunting images of Apollyon, and a highwayman with a pistol, and a blinking dwarf in yellow with a mouth from ear to ear, and other miscellaneous dangers. For poor little Maggie had at once the timidity of an active imagination and the daring that comes from overmastering impulse. She had rushed into the adventure of seeking her unknown kindred, the gypsies; and now she was in this strange lane, she hardly dared look on one side of her, lest she should see the diabolical blacksmith in his leathern apron grinning at her with arms akimbo. It was not without a leaping of the heart that she caught sight of a small pair of bare legs sticking up, feet uppermost, by the side of a hillock; they seemed something hideously preternatural, —a diabolical kind of fungus; for she was too much agitated at the first glance to see the ragged clothes and the dark shaggy head attached to them. It was a boy asleep, and Maggie trotted along faster and more lightly, lest she should wake him; it did not occur to her that he was one of her friends the gypsies, who in all probability would have very genial manners. But the fact was so, for at the next bend in the lane Maggie actually saw the little semicircular black tent with the blue smoke rising before it, which was to be her refuge from all the blighting obloquy that had pursued her in civilised life. She even saw a tall female figure by the column of smoke, doubtless the gypsy-mother, who provided the tea and other groceries; it was astonishing to herself that she did not feel more delighted. But it was startling to find the gypsies in a lane, after all, and not on a common; indeed, it was rather disappointing; for a mysterious illimitable common, where there were sand-pits to hide in, and one was out of everybody's reach, had always made part of Maggie's picture of gypsy life. She went on, however, and thought with some comfort that gypsies most likely knew nothing about idiots, so there was no danger of their falling into the mistake of setting her down at the first glance as an idiot. It was plain she had attracted attention; for the tall figure, who proved to be a young woman with a baby on her arm, walked slowly to meet her. Maggie looked up in the new face rather tremblingly as it approached, and was reassured by the thought that her aunt Pullet and the rest were right when they called her a gypsy; for this face, with the bright dark eyes and the long hair, was really something like what she used to see in the glass before she cut her hair off.

"My little lady, where are you going to?" the gypsy said, in a tone of coaxing deference.

It was delightful, and just what Maggie expected; the gypsies saw at once that she was a little lady, and were prepared to treat her accordingly.

"Not any farther," said Maggie, feeling as if she were saying what she had rehearsed in a dream. "I'm come to stay with you, please."

"That's pretty; come, then. Why, what a nice little lady you are, to be sure!" said the gypsy, taking her by the hand. Maggie thought her very agreeable, but wished she had not been so dirty.

There was quite a group round the fire when she reached it. An old gypsy woman was seated on the ground nursing her knees, and occasionally poking a skewer into the round kettle that sent forth an odorous steam; two small shock-headed children were lying prone and resting on their elbows something like small sphinxes; and a placid donkey was bending his head over a tall girl, who, lying on her back, was scratching his nose and indulging him with a bite of excellent stolen hay. The slanting sunlight fell kindly upon them, and the scene was really very pretty and comfortable, Maggie thought, only she hoped they would soon set out the tea-cups. Everything would be quite charming when she had taught the gypsies to use a washing-basin, and to feel an interest in books. It was a little confusing, though, that the young woman began to speak to the old one in a language which Maggie did not understand, while the tall girl, who was feeding the donkey, sat up and stared at her without offering any salutation. At last the old woman said, —

"I'm come from home because I'm unhappy, and I mean to be a gypsy. I'll live with you if you like, and I can teach you a great many things."

"Such a clever little lady," said the woman with the baby sitting down by Maggie, and allowing baby to crawl; "and such a pretty bonnet and frock," she added, taking off Maggie's bonnet and looking at it while she made an observation to the old woman, in the unknown language. The tall girl snatched the bonnet and put it on her own head hind-foremost with a grin; but Maggie was determined not to show any weakness on this subject, as if she were susceptible about her bonnet.

"I don't want to wear a bonnet," she said; "I'd rather wear a red handkerchief, like yours" (looking at her friend by her side). "My hair was quite long till yesterday, when I cut it off; but I dare say it will grow again very soon," she added apologetically, thinking it probable the gypsies had a strong prejudice in favour of long hair. And Maggie had forgotten even her hunger at that moment in the desire to conciliate gypsy opinion.

"Oh, what a nice little lady! —and rich, I'm sure," said the old woman. "Didn't you live in a beautiful house at home?"

"Yes, my home is pretty, and I'm very fond of the river, where we go fishing, but I'm often very unhappy. I should have liked to bring my books with me, but I came away in a hurry, you know. But I can tell you almost everything there is in my books, I've read them so many times, and that will amuse you. And I can tell you something about Geography too, —that's about the world we live in, —very useful and interesting. Did you ever hear about Columbus?"

Maggie's eyes had begun to sparkle and her cheeks to flush, —she was really beginning to instruct the gypsies, and gaining great influence over them. The gypsies themselves were not without amazement at this talk, though their attention was divided by the contents of Maggie's pocket, which the friend at her right hand had by this time emptied without attracting her notice.

"Is that where you live, my little lady?" said the old woman, at the mention of Columbus.

"Oh, no!" said Maggie, with some pity; "Columbus was a very wonderful man, who found out half the world, and they put chains on him and treated him very badly, you know; it's in my Catechism of Geography, but perhaps it's rather too long to tell before tea—I want my tea so."

The last words burst from Maggie, in spite of herself, with a sudden drop from patronizing instruction to simple peevishness.

"Why, she's hungry, poor little lady," said the younger woman. "Give her some o' the cold victual. You've been walking a good way, I'll be bound, my dear. Where's your home?"

"It's Dorlcote Mill, a good way off," said Maggie. "My father is Mr. Tulliver, but we mustn't let him know where I am, else he'll fetch me home again. Where does the queen of the gypsies live?"

"What! do you want to go to her, my little lady?" said the younger woman. The tall girl meanwhile was constantly staring at Maggie and grinning. Her manners were certainly not agreeable.

"No," said Maggie, "I'm only thinking that if she isn't a very good queen you might be glad when she died, and you could choose another. If I was a queen, I'd be a very good queen, and kind to everybody."

"Here's a bit o' nice victual, then," said the old woman, handing to Maggie a lump of dry bread, which she had taken from a bag of scraps, and a piece of cold bacon.

"Thank you," said Maggie, looking at the food without taking it; "but will you give me some bread-and-butter and tea instead? I don't like bacon."

"We've got no tea nor butter," said the old woman, with something like a scowl, as if she were getting tired of coaxing.

"Oh, a little bread and treacle would do," said Maggie.

"We han't got no treacle," said the old woman, crossly, whereupon there followed a sharp dialogue between the two women in their unknown tongue, and one of the small sphinxes snatched at the bread-and-bacon, and began to eat it. At this moment the tall girl, who had gone a few yards off, came back, and said something which produced a strong effect. The old woman, seeming to forget Maggie's hunger, poked the skewer into the pot with new vigor, and the younger crept under the tent and reached out some platters and spoons. Maggie trembled a little, and was afraid the tears would come into her eyes. Meanwhile the tall girl gave a shrill cry, and presently came running up the boy whom Maggie had passed as he was sleeping, —a rough urchin about the age of Tom. He stared at Maggie, and there ensued much incomprehensible chattering. She felt very lonely, and was quite sure she should begin to cry before long; the gypsies didn't seem to mind her at all, and she felt quite weak among them. But the springing tears were checked by new terror, when two men came up, whose approach had been the cause of the sudden excitement. The elder of the two carried a bag, which he flung down, addressing the women in a loud and scolding tone, which they answered by a shower of treble sauciness; while a black cur ran barking up to Maggie, and threw her into a tremor that only found a new cause in the curses with which the younger man called the dog off, and gave him a rap with a great stick he held in his hand.

Maggie felt that it was impossible she should ever be queen of these people, or ever communicate to them amusing and useful knowledge.

Both the men now seemed to be inquiring about Maggie, for they looked at her, and the tone of the conversation became of that pacific kind which implies curiosity on one side and the power of satisfying it on the other. At last the younger woman said in her previous deferential, coaxing tone, —

"This nice little lady's come to live with us; aren't you glad?"

"Ay, very glad," said the younger man, who was looking at Maggie's silver thimble and other small matters that had been taken from her pocket. He returned them all except the thimble to the younger woman, with some observation, and she immediately restored them to Maggie's pocket, while the men seated themselves, and began to attack the contents of the kettle, —a stew of meat and potatoes, —which had been taken off the fire and turned out into a yellow platter.

Maggie began to think that Tom must be right about the gypsies; they must certainly be thieves, unless the man meant to return her thimble by and by. She would willingly have given it to him, for she was not at all attached to her thimble; but the idea that she was among thieves prevented her from feeling any comfort in the revival of deference and attention toward her; all thieves, except Robin Hood, were wicked people. The women saw she was frightened.

"We've got nothing nice for a lady to eat," said the old woman, in her coaxing tone. "And she's so hungry, sweet little lady."

"Here, my dear, try if you can eat a bit o' this," said the younger woman, handing some of the stew on a brown dish with an iron spoon to Maggie, who, remembering that the old woman had seemed angry with her for not liking the bread-and-bacon, dared not refuse the stew, though fear had chased away her appetite. If her father would but come by in the gig and take her up! Or even if Jack the Giant killer, or Mr. Greatheart, or St. George who slew the dragon on the half-pennies, would happen to pass that way! But Maggie thought with a sinking heart that these heroes were never seen in the neighbourhood of St Ogg's; nothing very wonderful ever came there.

Maggie Tulliver, you perceive, was by no means that well trained, well-informed young person that a small female of eight or nine necessarily is in these days; she had only been to school a year at St Ogg's, and had so few books that she sometimes read the dictionary; so that in travelling over her small mind you would have found the most unexpected ignorance as well as unexpected knowledge. She could have informed you that there was such a word as "polygamy," and being also acquainted with "polysyllable," she had deduced the conclusion that "poly" mean "many"; but she had had no idea that gypsies were not well supplied with groceries, and her thoughts generally were the oddest mixture of clear-eyed acumen and blind dreams.

Her ideas about the gypsies had undergone a rapid modification in the last five minutes. From having considered them very respectful companions, amenable to instruction, she had begun to think that they meant perhaps to kill her as soon as it was dark, and cut up her body for gradual cooking; the suspicion crossed her that the fierce-eyed old man was in fact the Devil, who might drop that transparent disguise at any moment, and turn either into the grinning blacksmith, or else a fiery-eyed monster with dragon's wings. It was no use trying to eat the stew, and yet the thing she most dreaded was to offend the gypsies, by betraying her extremely unfavourable opinion of them; and she wondered, with a keenness of interest that no theologian could have exceeded, whether, if the Devil were really present, he would know her thoughts.

"What! you don't like the smell of it, my dear," said the young woman, observing that Maggie did not even take a spoonful of the stew. "Try a bit, come."

"No, thank you," said Maggie, summoning all her force for a desperate effort, and trying to smile in a friendly way. "I haven't time, I think; it seems getting darker. I think I must go home now, and come again another day, and then I can bring you a basket with some jam-tarts and things."

Maggie rose from her seat as she threw out this illusory prospect, devoutly hoping that Apollyon was gullible; but her hope sank when the old gypsy-woman said, "Stop a bit, stop a bit, little lady; we'll take you home, all safe, when we've done supper; you shall ride home, like a lady."

Maggie sat down again, with little faith in this promise, though she presently saw the tall girl putting a bridle on the donkey, and throwing a couple of bags on his back.

"Now, then, little missis," said the younger man, rising, and leading the donkey forward, "tell us where you live; what's the name o' the place?"

"Dorlcote Mill is my home," said Maggie, eagerly. "My father is Mr. Tulliver; he lives there."

"What! A big mill a little way this side o' St Ogg's?"

"Yes," said Maggie. "Is it far off? I think I should like to walk there, if you please."

"No, no, it'll be getting dark, we must make haste. And the donkey'll carry you as nice as can be; you'll see."

He lifted Maggie as he spoke, and set her on the donkey. She felt relieved that it was not the old man who seemed to be going with her, but she had only a trembling hope that she was really going home.

"Here's your pretty bonnet," said the younger woman, putting that recently despised but now welcome article of costume on Maggie's head; "and you'll say we've been very good to you, won't you? and what a nice little lady we said you was."

"Oh yes, thank you," said Maggie, "I'm very much obliged to you. But I wish you'd go with me too." She thought anything was better than going with one of the dreadful men alone; it would be more cheerful to be murdered by a larger party.

"Ah, you're fondest o' me, aren't you?" said the woman. "But I can't go; you'll go too fast for me."

It now appeared that the man also was to be seated on the donkey, holding Maggie before him, and she was as incapable of remonstrating against this arrangement as the donkey himself, though no nightmare had ever seemed to her more horrible. When the woman had patted her on the back, and said "Goodbye," the donkey, at a strong hint from the man's stick, set off at a rapid walk along the lane toward the point Maggie had come from an hour ago, while the tall girl and the rough urchin, also furnished with sticks, obligingly escorted them for the first hundred yards, with much screaming and thwacking.

Not Leonore, in that preternatural midnight excursion with her phantom lover, was more terrified than poor Maggie in this entirely natural ride on a short-paced donkey, with a gypsy behind her, who considered that he was earning half a crown. The red light of the setting sun seemed to have a portentous meaning, with which the alarming bray of the second donkey with the log on its foot must surely have some connection. Two low thatched cottages—the only houses they passed in this lane—seemed to add to its dreariness; they had no windows to speak of, and the doors were closed; it was probable that they were inhabitated by witches, and it was a relief to find that the donkey did not stop there.

At last—oh, sight of joy!—this lane, the longest in the world, was coming to an end, was opening on a broad highroad, where there was actually a coach passing! And there was a finger-post at the corner, —she had surely seen that finger-post before, —"To St. Ogg's, 2 miles." The gypsy really meant to take her home, then; he was probably a good man, after all, and might have been rather hurt at the thought that she didn't like coming with him alone. This idea became stronger as she felt more and more certain that she knew the road quite well, and she was considering how she might open a conversation with the injured gypsy, and not only gratify his feelings but efface the impression of her cowardice, when, as they reached a cross-road. Maggie caught sight of some one coming on a white-faced horse.

"Oh, stop, stop!" she cried out. "There's my father! Oh, father, father!"

The sudden joy was almost painful, and before her father reached her, she was sobbing. Great was Mr. Tulliver's wonder, for he had made a round from Basset, and had not yet been home.

"Why, what's the meaning o' this?" he said, checking his horse, while Maggie slipped from the donkey and ran to her father's stirrup.

"The little miss lost herself, I reckon," said the gypsy. "She'd come to our tent at the far end o' Dunlow Lane, and I was bringing her where she said her home was. It's a good way to come after being on the tramp all day."

"Oh yes, father, he's been very good to bring me home," said Maggie, —"a very kind, good man!"

"Here, then, my man," said Mr. Tulliver, taking out five shillings. "It's the best day's work you ever did. I couldn't afford to lose the little wench; here, lift her up before me."

"Why, Maggie, how's this, how's this?" he said, as they rode along, while she laid her head against her father and sobbed. "How came you to be rambling about and lose yourself?"

"Oh, father," sobbed Maggie, "I ran away because I was so unhappy; Tom was so angry with me. I couldn't bear it."

"Pooh, pooh," said Mr. Tulliver, soothingly, "you mustn't think o' running away from father. What 'ud father do without his little wench?"

"Oh no, I never will again, father—never."

Mr. Tulliver spoke his mind very strongly when he reached home that evening; and the effect was seen in the remarkable fact that Maggie never heard one reproach from her mother, or one taunt from Tom, about this foolish business of her running away to the gypsies. Maggie was rather awe-stricken by this unusual treatment, and sometimes thought that her conduct had been too wicked to be alluded to.

III. Thinking, Talking and Writing About Literature

1 Textual Cognition

Make an introductory presentation on the following terms related to this literary work.

1) feminist novel
2) sympathy

2 Textual Reading

Search for evidence in the text and answer the following questions.

1) Maggie Tulliver is the protagonist of *The Mill on the Floss*. When the novel begins, Maggie is a clever and impetuous child. Eliot presents Maggie as more imaginative and interesting than the rest of her family and, sympathetically, in need of love. How can you understand the character of Maggie through her intentions towards the gypsies?

2) What is the significance of Maggie's encounter with the gypsies when she runs away?

3) In *The Mill on the Floss*, Chapter XI of Book First has an interesting title: "Maggie Tries to Run Away from Her Shadow." Maggie Tulliver, aged 9, a heroine of this novel, tries to escape from her home to the gypsydom, fancying herself to be a queen of the gypsies. What makes her have such a bold and unrealistic attempt? And what does "Her Shadow" in this title mean?

3 Critical Reading

Discuss in groups the following questions to further explore this literary work.

1) What is the significance of the title *The Mill on the Floss*?

2) Eliot remains concerned with the workings of community—both social and economic—and tracks their interrelations, as well as their effect upon characters, as part of her realism. Can you explain the effect of society upon the individuals in *The Mill on the Floss*?

4 Writing About Literature

Read the following critical excerpt and then write an essay.

> Hughes, Kathryn. "Rereading: George Eliot's *Mill on the Floss*."
> *The Guardian*, March 27, 2010.

It is, though, Maggie Tulliver who towers over *The Mill on the Floss*, one of those great literary heroines whom bookish girls grow up wanting to be. Just like Anne of Green Gables or even Jane Eyre, Maggie captures exactly the dilemma of being the clever girl of the family, the ugly duckling, the misplaced foundling who longs to be recognised for the genius she secretly knows herself to be. (Maggie fantasises about writing to Sir Walter Scott, who will naturally recognise her specialness.) Several of the most celebrated incidents in Maggie's life are said to be taken straight from Mary Anne's own emotionally jagged childhood—the hacking off of her unruly hair with the scissors, the running away to join the Gypsies, the mortification of being displaced in her brother's affections by a new pony.

The central crisis of the novel is a reworking of the drama that defined Eliot's own adult life. Towards the end of the book, the adult Maggie goes on an ill-advised boat trip with Stephen Guest, her cousin Lucy's beau. "Nothing happens", as we might say today, apart from Stephen begging Maggie to elope with him by heading to Scotland for a quick marriage. Maggie realises just in time that what she is doing is wrong and returns home. However, her absence has caused a storm of gossip and "the world's wife" is busy painting the blackest picture of what really went on during those missing hours. Respectable women turn away from Maggie in the street, and coarse men laugh knowingly. Tom, who is now head of the family, refuses to let his disgraced sister return to the mill, declaring savagely: "I wash my hands of you for ever."

Here, surely, is a fictional transmutation of Eliot's own "elopement" with Lewes in 1854. That, too, had started with a boat trip—to Germany, where the middle-aged couple spent the first few months of their life together. While Maggie commits no actual sin— she has not slept with Stephen—Eliot seems to be making the provocative case that neither has she. Lewes may technically still have been a married man, but that was because his complicated legal situation made divorce impossible. As far as Eliot was concerned, she and Lewes, whom she always referred to as "my husband", had a sacred bond which was more binding than any piece of paper. The "world's wife", though, saw things very differently.

On returning to Britain in the spring of 1855, Eliot found herself the centre of a storm of vicious finger-pointing. As a "fallen woman" she was not welcome in any respectable home, and several of her women friends were forbidden by their fathers from calling on her. Inveterate gossips such as Elizabeth Gaskell and Harriet Martineau made things even murkier by adding embellishments, including a fictitious illegitimate baby, to this already most juicy of literary scandals.

That Eliot was often writing about herself when she wrote about Maggie is betrayed by the uneven shape of *The Mill on the Floss*. The first two sections are leisurely and detailed, studded with examples of the comical Dodsons and the minute plotting of the changing relationship between the young Tullivers. It is as if Eliot is unable to achieve the critical distance required to move her story briskly forward, but instead lingers lovingly over her memories of those early years with Isaac.

And so the ending, when it comes, is rushed and breathless. A terrible tidal flood has marooned Tom in the mill and, in a reversal of the usual rescue plot, Maggie rows out from the town to save her elder brother. On the way back a piece of flotsam breaks off and heads towards their small boat. "'It is coming, Maggie!' Tom said, in a deep, hoarse voice, loosing the oars, and clasping her." The boat sinks, taking Tom and Maggie down in that final embrace. In real life this reunion of brother and sister never took place. Instead, Isaac and Mary Ann Evans spent their adult lives apart; he on the Warwickshire family farm, she as an increasingly successful and fêted author in London.

Essay Writing

Write an essay on *The Mill on the Floss* from the perspective of the struggle between George Eliot and Maggie Tulliver with no less than 500 words.

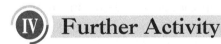 Further Activity

Scan the QR code and watch part of the documentary *George Eliot*, which is about *The Mill on the Floss* produced by Artsmagic Ltd. and directed by Liam Dale.

Lecture 10
Kate Chopin

Profile of the Writer

Kate Chopin
(1851–1904)

Katherine O'Flaherty Chopin, born on February 8, 1851, was a native of St. Louis and spent barely 14 years in Louisiana, but her fiction is identified with the South. At 19, Kate O'Flaherty married Oscar Chopin, a young cotton broker, and moved with him to New Orleans and later to his family home in Cloutierville, Louisiana, near the Red River. After Oscar died in 1882, she returned with their six children to St. Louis. But eight years later, when she began to write, it was the Creoles and Acadians of her Louisiana experiences that animated her fiction.

Distinctly unsentimental in her approach, she often relied on popular period motifs, such as the conflict of the Yankee businessman and the Creole, a theme that informs her first novel, *At Fault* (1890), and several of her short stories. These vivid and economical tales, richly flavored with local dialect, provide penetrating views of the heterogeneous culture of south Louisiana. Many of them were collected in *Bayou Folk* (1894) and *A Night in Acadie* (1897). Chopin's second novel, *The Awakening* (1899), also strongly evokes the region, but is primarily a lyrical, stunning study of a young woman whose deep personal discontents lead to adultery and suicide. Praised for its craft and damned for its content, the novel was a scandal, and Chopin, always sensitive to her critics, gradually lost confidence in her gift and soon ceased to write.

Lecture 10
Kate Chopin

> Chopin died of a brain hemorrhage in 1904 after a strenuous day at the St. Louis World's Fair, where she had been a regular visitor. She was remembered only as one of the southern local colorists of the 1890s until *The Awakening* was rediscovered in the 1970s as an early masterpiece of American realism and a superb rendering of female experience.

Preview Questions

1. Search for the historical context of the novel *The Awakening*. To what extent does Edna's story depend upon its location in America in the 1890s?

2. Readers and scholars have been discussing the novel's themes for a hundred years, and their views vary widely. Early critics condemned the book for its amoral treatment of adultery, and some readers today share that view. But from the 1960s on, most scholars and readers in the US and many other nations have come to think of Kate Chopin as "the first woman writer in her country to accept passion as a legitimate subject for serious, outspoken fiction", to cite the words of Per Seyersted, and they see Chopin as one of America's essential authors. What do you think contributes to this change of attitude towards Kate Chopin?

Literary Reading: *The Awakening* (Chapter 1)

A green and yellow parrot, which hung in a cage outside the door, kept repeating over and over:

"Allez vous-en! Allez vous-en! Sapristi! That's all right!"

He could speak a little Spanish, and also a language which nobody understood, unless it was the mocking-bird that hung on the other side of the door, whistling his fluty notes out upon the breeze with maddening persistence.

Mr. Pontellier, unable to read his newspaper with any degree of comfort, arose with an expression and an exclamation of disgust. He walked down the gallery and across the narrow "bridges" which connected the Lebrun cottages one with the other. He had been seated before the door of the main house. The parrot and the mocking-bird were the property of Madame Lebrun, and they had the right to make all the noise they wished. Mr. Pontellier had the privilege of quitting their society when they ceased to be entertaining.

He stopped before the door of his own cottage, which was the fourth one from the main building and next to the last. Seating himself in a wicker rocker which was there, he once more applied himself to the task of reading the newspaper. The day was Sunday; the paper was a day old. The Sunday papers had not yet reached Grand Isle. He was already acquainted with the market reports, and he glanced restlessly over the editorials and bits of news which he had not had time to read before quitting New Orleans the day before.

Mr. Pontellier wore eye-glasses. He was a man of forty, of medium height and rather slender build; he stooped a little. His hair was brown and straight, parted on one side. His beard was neatly and closely trimmed.

Once in a while he withdrew his glance from the newspaper and looked about him. There was more noise than ever over at the house. The main building was called "the house", to distinguish it from the cottages. The chattering and whistling birds were still at it. Two young girls, the Farival twins, were playing a duet from "Zampa" upon the piano. Madame Lebrun was bustling in and out, giving orders in a high key to a yard-boy whenever she got inside the house, and directions in an equally high voice to a dining-room servant whenever she got outside. She was a fresh, pretty woman, clad always in white with elbow sleeves. Her starched skirts crinkled as she came and went. Farther down, before one of the cottages, a lady in black was walking demurely up and down, telling her beads. A good many persons of the pension had gone over to the Chênière Caminada in Beaudelet's lugger to hear mass. Some young people were out under the water-oaks playing croquet. Mr. Pontellier's two children were there—sturdy little fellows of four and five. A quadroon nurse followed them about with a far-away, meditative air.

Mr. Pontellier finally lit a cigar and began to smoke, letting the paper drag idly from his hand. He fixed his gaze upon a white sunshade that was advancing at snail's pace from the beach. He could see it plainly between the gaunt trunks of the water-oaks and across the stretch of yellow camomile. The gulf looked far away, melting hazily into the blue of the horizon. The sunshade continued to approach slowly. Beneath its pink-lined shelter were his wife, Mrs. Pontellier, and young Robert Lebrun. When they reached the cottage, the two seated themselves with some appearance of fatigue upon the upper step of the porch, facing each other, each leaning against a supporting post.

"What folly! To bathe at such an hour in such heat!" exclaimed Mr. Pontellier. He himself had taken a plunge at daylight. That was why the morning seemed long to him.

"You are burnt beyond recognition," he added, looking at his wife as one looks at a valuable piece of personal property which has suffered some damage. She held up her hands, strong, shapely hands, and surveyed them critically, drawing up her lawn sleeves above the wrists. Looking at them reminded her of her rings, which she had given to her husband before leaving for the beach. She silently reached out to him, and he, understanding, took the rings from his vest pocket and dropped them into her open palm. She slipped them upon her fingers; then clasping her knees, she looked across at Robert and began to laugh. The rings sparkled upon her fingers. He sent back an answering smile.

"What is it?" asked Pontellier, looking lazily and amused from one to the other. It was some utter nonsense; some adventure out there in the water, and they both tried to relate it at once. It did not seem half so amusing when told. They realized this, and so did Mr. Pontellier. He yawned and stretched himself. Then he got up, saying he had half a mind to go over to Klein's hotel and play a game of billiards.

"Come go along, Lebrun," he proposed to Robert. But Robert admitted quite frankly that he preferred to stay where he was and talk to Mrs. Pontellier.

"Well, send him about his business when he bores you, Edna," instructed her husband as he prepared to leave.

"Here, take the umbrella," she exclaimed, holding it out to him. He accepted the sunshade, and lifting it over his head descended the steps and walked away.

"Coming back to dinner?" his wife called after him. He halted a moment and shrugged his shoulders. He felt in his vest pocket; there was a ten-dollar bill there. He did not know; perhaps he would return for the early dinner and perhaps he would not. It all depended upon the company which he found over at Klein's and the size of "the game." He did not say this, but she understood it, and laughed, nodding goodbye to him.

Both children wanted to follow their father when they saw him starting out. He kissed them and promised to bring them back bonbons and peanuts.

III Thinking, Talking and Writing About Literature

1 Textual Cognition

Make an introductory presentation on the following terms related to this literary work.

1) wing imagery
2) female consciousness

❷ Textual Reading

Search for evidence in the text and answer the following questions.

1) The very beginning of the chapter establishes a key symbolism in the novel: Edna is the green-and-yellow parrot telling everyone to "go away, for God's sake". Identify and discuss the bird imagery and symbolism used in this chapter and throughout the book.

2) The nature of Edna's relationships with Léonce and Robert is established in the first chapter. Please identify them.

3) Another motif set up in this chapter is the significance of music in Edna's life and in the novel. What music is heard? Is it relevant to Edna's ultimate fate?

❸ Critical Reading

Discuss in groups the following questions to further explore this literary work.

1) Is Edna Pontellier a wounded victim of her patriarchal society, or is she a triumphant pioneer in her search for freedom?

2) Would Edna be better off if she were living in our times, or is her struggle universal—true for women everywhere at all times?

3) Some people say that Kate Chopin "was an integral part of the evolution of feminism, providing 20th-century readers with feminist literature that is still highly respected and studied today". How do you understand this statement?

❹ Writing About Literature

Read the following critical excerpt and then write an essay.

> Saleh, Ammar Hashim. "Tragic Female Bildungsroman in Kate Chopin's *The Awakening.*" *Journal of Education and Science* 18.2 (2011): 1–14.

Chopin embodied the Bildungsroman genre in her novel *The Awakening* by presenting a heroine, Edna Pontellier, who manages to develop and grow up while upholding the expectations of her society. To Chopin, Edna's formation, as a character, doesn't mean only personal maturation but also consciousness to the meaning of life which intuited early in her character.

Hence Chopin's *The Awakening* depicted the inferior social status of Edna Pontellier, especially in South America in the early 1900s who revolted against her society and led the life of an independent female regardless of all the risks. At that time wealthy women were seen as "trophy wives" of their husbands just as Edna was for Leonce, her husband.

Women were expected to marry, have children, and take care of the house, with no single thought of their own needs.

In *The Awakening*, Edna struggles with the stifling duties imposed on her as a wife of a successful New Orleans businessman, and a mother of six children. *The Awakening* unfolds the two stages of Edna's life. She is in conflict between her exterior world, the role of a wife and a mother that society imposes on her, and her interior reality of emotions and sexuality which are initially asleep and awakened throughout the course of the novel.

Wearing the mask of Bildungsroman, *The Awakening* attacks the tradition of life as narrative development, a tradition that leads inevitably to self-destruction instead of seeking for self-creation and self-understanding of the women to their needs to be individuals rather than mere wives and mothers.

Essay Writing

Write an essay on *The Awakening* from the perspective of coming of age novel with no less than 500 words.

IV. Further Activity

Scan the QR code and listen to the audio of Chapter 1 of *The Awakening*.

Lecture 11
Virginia Woolf

Profile of the Writer

Virginia Woolf
(1882–1941)

Virginia Woolf, original name in full Adeline Virginia Stephen, is an English writer whose novels, through their nonlinear approaches to narrative, exerted a major influence on the genre. While she is best known for her novels, especially *Mrs. Dalloway* (1925) and *To the Lighthouse* (1927), Woolf also wrote pioneering essays on artistic theory, literary history, women's writing, and the politics of power. A fine stylist, she experimented with several forms of biographical writing, kept a lifetime diary, and composed painterly short fictions.

Adeline Virginia Stephen grew up in a remarkable household. Her father, Leslie Stephen, was an eminent literary figure and the first editor (1882–1891) of the *Dictionary of National Biography*. During her childhood, Woolf did not attend school. However, her father gave her private lessons in which he recommended literature and worked on improving her writing. Woolf's childhood was not altogether unhappy; she was sexually abused by her half-brothers, and her mother Julia died in 1895 when Woolf was only 13 years old. In the time after her mother's death she experienced her first, of many, nervous breakdowns. She continued to struggle with mental health issues throughout her life, and a concern for sanity versus madness appears throughout her writing.

Lecture 11
Virginia Woolf

In 1904, the family moved to Bloomsbury Square. It was in this home that Virginia, along with her sister Vanessa and brother Adrian became a part of the Bloomsbury Group, a group of intellectuals interested in avant-garde English modernism. She married a fellow member, political journalist and activist, Leonard Woolf in 1912. Shortly after getting married, Woolf published her first novel *The Voyage Out* (1913). During this time Woolf suffered another near suicidal breakdown. In 1915 the Woolfs moved to the Hogarth House and it was here that in 1917 they founded the Hogarth Press which published all of Woolf's works with the exception of her second novel *Night and Day* (1919). The Hogarth Press published not only the works of Woolf, but also writers Katherine Mansfield, Gertrude Stein, T. S. Eliot, and translations of the works of Sigmund Freud. Woolf continued writing, innovating the form of the novel, and experimenting with stream of consciousness narrative techniques and went on to publish *Jacob's Room* (1922), *Mrs. Dalloway, To the Lighthouse, Orlando* (1928), *The Waves* (1931), and *The Years* (1937). In 1929, Woolf published "A Room of One's Own", a feminist essay based on lectures she had given at women's colleges, in which she examined women's role in literature. Her essay "Three Guineas" continued the feminist themes and addressed Fascism and war. Most of her essays and reviews were collected in *The Common Reader* (1925) and *The Second Common Reader* (1932).

In the 1930s, with the rise of Fascism, Woolf became increasingly despondent, and as World War II began, she committed suicide by weighing her pockets down with stones and walking into the river Ouse, eventually drowning herself on March 28, 1941. *Between the Acts* was published posthumously later that year.

Preview Questions

1. Watch the movie *The Hours* adapted from *Mrs. Dalloway*. Then explore how this movie reflects the theme of the novel, and the artistic creation of Virginia Woolf.

2. Woolf offers us the novel of one character, Clarissa Dalloway: we are invited to follow along for a day in her life—a day that ends with her throwing a society party—to follow her mind as it thinks its way through that day. But what are we to make of her mind? Are these thoughts worth pondering?

II Literary Reading: *Mrs. Dalloway* (Chapter 1)

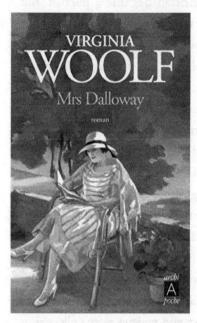

Mrs. Dalloway said she would buy the flowers herself.

For Lucy had her work cut out for her. The doors would be taken off their hinges; Rumpelmayer's men were coming. And then, thought Clarissa Dalloway, what a morning—fresh as if issued to children on a beach.

What a lark! What a plunge! For so it had always seemed to her, when, with a little squeak of the hinges, which she could hear now, she had burst open the French windows and plunged at Bourton into the open air. How fresh, how calm, stiller than this of course, the air was in the early morning; like the flap of a wave; the kiss of a wave; chill and sharp and yet (for a girl of eighteen as she then was) solemn, feeling as she did, standing there at the open window, that something awful was about to happen; looking at the flowers, at the trees with the smoke winding off them and the rooks rising, falling; standing and looking until Peter Walsh said, "Musing among the vegetables?"—was that it?—"I prefer men to cauliflowers"—was that it? He must have said it at breakfast one morning when she had gone out on to the terrace—Peter Walsh. He would be back from India one of these days, June or July, she forgot which, for his letters were awfully dull; it was his sayings one remembered; his eyes, his pocket-knife, his smile, his grumpiness and, when millions of things had utterly vanished—how strange it was!—a few sayings like this about cabbages.

She stiffened a little on the kerb, waiting for Durtnall's van to pass. A charming woman, Scrope Purvis thought her (knowing her as one does know people who live next door to one in Westminster); a touch of the bird about her, of the jay, blue-green, light, vivacious, though she was over fifty, and grown very white since her illness. There she perched, never seeing him, waiting to cross, very upright.

For having lived in Westminster—how many years now? over twenty, —one feels even in the midst of the traffic, or waking at night, Clarissa was positive, a particular hush, or solemnity; an indescribable pause; a suspense (but that might be her heart, affected, they said, by influenza) before Big Ben strikes. There! Out it boomed. First a warning, musical; then the hour, irrevocable. The leaden circles dissolved in the air. Such fools we are, she thought, crossing Victoria Street. For Heaven only knows why one loves it so, how one sees it so, making it up, building it round one, tumbling it, creating it every moment afresh; but the veriest frumps, the most dejected of miseries sitting on doorsteps (drink their downfall) do the same; can't be dealt with, she felt positive, by Acts of Parliament for that very reason: they love life. In people's eyes, in the swing, tramp, and trudge; in the bellow and the uproar; the carriages, motor cars, omnibuses, vans, sandwich men shuffling and swinging; brass bands; barrel organs; in the triumph and the jingle and the strange high singing of some aeroplane overhead was what she loved; life; London; this moment of June.

For it was the middle of June. The War was over, except for some one like Mrs. Foxcroft at the Embassy last night eating her heart out because that nice boy was killed and now the old Manor House must go to a cousin; or Lady Bexborough who opened a bazaar, they said, with the telegram in her hand, John, her favourite, killed; but it was over; thank Heaven—over. It was June. The King and Queen were at the Palace. And everywhere, though it was still so early, there was a beating, a stirring of galloping ponies, tapping of cricket bats; Lords, Ascot, Ranelagh and all the rest of it; wrapped in the soft mesh of the grey-blue morning air, which, as the day wore on, would unwind them, and set down on their lawns and pitches the bouncing ponies, whose forefeet just struck the ground and up they sprung, the whirling young men, and laughing girls in their transparent muslins who, even now, after dancing all night, were taking their absurd woolly dogs for a run; and even now, at this hour, discreet old dowagers were shooting out in their motor cars on errands of mystery; and the shopkeepers were fidgeting in their windows with their paste and diamonds, their lovely old sea-green brooches in eighteenth-century settings to tempt Americans (but one must economise, not buy things rashly for Elizabeth), and she, too, loving it as she did with an absurd and faithful passion, being part of it, since her people were courtiers once in the time of the Georges, she, too, was going that very night to kindle and illuminate; to give her party. But how strange, on entering the Park, the silence; the mist; the hum; the slow-swimming happy ducks; the pouched birds waddling; and who should be coming along with his back against the Government buildings, most appropriately, carrying a despatch box stamped with the Royal Arms, who but Hugh Whitbread; her old friend Hugh—the admirable Hugh!

"Good morning to you, Clarissa!" said Hugh, rather extravagantly, for they had known each other as children. "Where are you off to?"

"I love walking in London," said Mrs. Dalloway. "Really it's better than walking in the country."

They had just come up—unfortunately—to see doctors. Other people came to see pictures; go to the opera; take their daughters out; the Whitbreads came "to see doctors". Times without number Clarissa had visited Evelyn Whitbread in a nursing home. Was Evelyn ill again? Evelyn was a good deal out of sorts, said Hugh, intimating by a kind of pout or swell of his very well-covered, manly, extremely handsome, perfectly upholstered body (he was almost too well dressed always, but presumably had to be, with his little job at Court) that his wife had some internal ailment, nothing serious, which, as an old friend, Clarissa Dalloway would quite understand without requiring him to specify. Ah yes, she did of course; what a nuisance; and felt very sisterly and oddly conscious at the same time of her hat. Not the right hat for the early morning, was that it? For Hugh always made her feel, as he bustled on, raising his hat rather extravagantly and assuring her that she might be a girl of eighteen, and of course he was coming to her party tonight, Evelyn absolutely insisted, only a little late he might be after the party at the Palace to which he had to take one of Jim's boys, —she always felt a little skimpy beside Hugh; schoolgirlish; but attached to him, partly from having known him always, but she did think him a good sort in his own way, though Richard was nearly driven mad by him, and as for Peter Walsh, he had never to this day forgiven her for liking him.

She could remember scene after scene at Bourton—Peter furious; Hugh not, of course, his match in any way, but still not a positive imbecile as Peter made out; not a mere barber's block. When his old mother wanted him to give up shooting or to take her to Bath he did it, without a word; he was really unselfish, and as for saying, as Peter did, that he had no heart, no brain, nothing but the manners and breeding of an English gentleman, that was only her dear Peter at his worst; and he could be intolerable; he could be impossible; but adorable to walk with on a morning like this.

(June had drawn out every leaf on the trees. The mothers of Pimlico gave suck to their young. Messages were passing from the Fleet to the Admiralty. Arlington Street and Piccadilly seemed to chafe the very air in the Park and lift its leaves hotly, brilliantly, on waves of that divine vitality which Clarissa loved. To dance, to ride, she had adored all that.)

For they might be parted for hundreds of years, she and Peter; she never wrote a letter and his were dry sticks; but suddenly it would come over her, If he were with me now what would he say?—some days, some sights bringing him back to her calmly, without the old bitterness; which perhaps was the reward of having cared for people; they came back in the middle of St. James's Park on a fine morning—indeed they did. But Peter—however beautiful the day might be, and the trees and the grass, and the little girl in pink—Peter never saw a thing of all that. He would put on his spectacles, if she told him to; he would look. It was the state of the world that interested him; Wagner, Pope's poetry, people's characters eternally, and the defects of her own soul. How he scolded her! How they argued! She would marry a Prime Minister and stand at the top of a staircase; the perfect hostess he called her (she had cried over it in her bedroom), she had the makings of the perfect hostess, he said.

So she would still find herself arguing in St. James's Park, still making out that she had been right—and she had too—not to marry him. For in marriage a little licence, a little independence there must be between people living together day in day out in the same house; which Richard gave her, and she him. (Where was he this morning for instance? Some committee, she never asked what.) But with Peter everything had to be shared; everything gone into. And it was intolerable, and when it came to that scene in the little garden by the fountain, she had to break with him or they would have been destroyed, both of them ruined, she was convinced; though she had borne about with her for years like an arrow sticking in her heart the grief, the anguish; and then the horror of the moment when some one told her at a concert that he had married a woman met on the boat going to India! Never should she forget all that! Cold, heartless, a prude, he called her. Never could she understand how he cared. But those Indian women did presumably— silly, pretty, flimsy nincompoops. And she wasted her pity. For he was quite happy, he assured her— perfectly happy, though he had never done a thing that they talked of; his whole life had been a failure. It made her angry still.

She had reached the Park gates. She stood for a moment, looking at the omnibuses in Piccadilly.

She would not say of any one in the world now that they were this or were that. She felt very young; at the same time unspeakably aged. She sliced like a knife through everything; at the same time was outside, looking on. She had a perpetual sense, as she watched the taxi cabs, of being out, out, far out to sea and alone; she always had the feeling that it was very, very dangerous to live even one day. Not that she thought herself clever, or much out of the ordinary. How she had got through life on the few twigs of knowledge Fräulein Daniels gave them she could not think. She knew nothing; no language, no history; she scarcely read a book now, except memoirs in bed; and yet to her it was absolutely absorbing; all this; the cabs passing; and she would not say of Peter, she would not say of herself, I am this, I am that.

Her only gift was knowing people almost by instinct, she thought, walking on. If you put her in a room with some one, up went her back like a cat's; or she purred. Devonshire House, Bath House, the house with the china cockatoo, she had seen them all lit up once; and remembered Sylvia, Fred, Sally Seton—such hosts of people; and dancing all night; and the waggons plodding past to market; and driving home across the Park. She remembered once throwing a shilling into the Serpentine. But every one remembered; what she loved was this, here, now, in front of her; the fat lady in the cab. Did it matter then, she asked herself, walking towards Bond Street, did it matter that she must inevitably cease completely; all this must go on without her; did she resent it; or did it not become consoling to believe that death ended absolutely? but that somehow in the streets of London, on the ebb and flow of things, here, there, she survived, Peter survived, lived in each other, she being part, she was positive, of the trees at home; of the house there, ugly, rambling all to bits and pieces as it was; part of people she had never met; being laid out like a mist between the people she knew best, who lifted her on their branches as she had seen the trees lift the mist, but it spread ever so far, her life, herself. But what was she dreaming as she looked into Hatchards' shop window? What was she trying to recover? What image of white dawn in the country, as she read in the book spread open:

Fear no more the heat o' the sun

Nor the furious winter's rages.

This late age of the world's experience had bred in them all, all men and women, a well of tears. Tears and sorrows; courage and endurance; a perfectly upright and stoical bearing. Think, for example, of the woman she admired most, Lady Bexborough, opening the bazaar.

There were Jorrocks's Jaunts and Jollities; there were Soapy Sponge and Mrs. Asquith's Memoirs and Big Game Shooting in Nigeria, all spread open. Ever so many books there were; but none that seemed exactly right to take to Evelyn Whitbread in her nursing home. Nothing that would serve to amuse her and make that indescribably dried-up little woman look, as Clarissa came in, just for a moment cordial; before they settled down for the usual interminable talk of women's ailments. How much she wanted it—that people should look pleased as she came in, Clarissa thought and turned and walked back towards Bond Street, annoyed, because it was silly to have other reasons for doing things. Much rather would she have been one of those people like Richard who did things for themselves, whereas, she thought, waiting to cross, half the time she did things not simply, not for themselves; but to make people think this or that; perfect idiocy she knew (and now the policeman held up his hand) for no one was ever for a second taken in. Oh if she could have had her life over again! she thought, stepping on to the pavement, could have looked even differently!

She would have been, in the first place, dark like Lady Bexborough, with a skin of crumpled leather and beautiful eyes. She would have been, like Lady Bexborough, slow and stately; rather large; interested in politics like a man; with a country house; very dignified, very sincere. Instead of which she had a narrow pea-stick figure; a ridiculous little face, beaked like a bird's. That she held herself well was true; and had nice hands and feet; and dressed well, considering that she spent little. But often now this body she wore (she stopped to look at a Dutch picture), this body, with all its capacities, seemed nothing—nothing at all. She had the oddest sense of being herself invisible; unseen; unknown; there being no more marrying, no more having of children now, but only this astonishing and rather solemn progress with the rest of them, up Bond Street, this being Mrs. Dalloway; not even Clarissa any more; this being Mrs. Richard Dalloway.

Bond Street fascinated her; Bond Street early in the morning in the season; its flags flying; its shops; no splash; no glitter; one roll of tweed in the shop where her father had bought his suits for fifty years; a few pearls; salmon on an iceblock.

"That is all," she said, looking at the fishmonger's. "That is all," she repeated, pausing for a moment at the window of a glove shop where, before the War, you could buy almost perfect gloves. And her old Uncle William used to say a lady is known by her shoes and her gloves. He had turned on his bed one morning in the middle of the War. He had said, "I have had enough." Gloves and shoes; she had a passion for gloves; but her own daughter, her Elizabeth, cared not a straw for either of them.

Not a straw, she thought, going on up Bond Street to a shop where they kept flowers for her when she gave a party. Elizabeth really cared for her dog most of all. The whole house this morning smelt of tar. Still, better poor Grizzle than Miss Kilman; better distemper and tar and all the rest of it than sitting mewed in a stuffy bedroom with a prayer book! Better anything, she was inclined to say. But it might be only a phase, as Richard said, such as all girls go through. It might be falling in love. But why with Miss Kilman? who had been badly treated of course; one must make allowances for that, and Richard said she was very able, had a really historical mind. Anyhow they were inseparable, and Elizabeth, her own daughter, went to Communion; and how she dressed, how she treated people who came to lunch she did not care a bit, it being her experience that the religious ecstasy made people callous (so did causes); dulled their feelings, for Miss Kilman would do anything for the Russians, starved herself for the Austrians, but in private inflicted positive torture, so insensitive was she, dressed in a green mackintosh coat. Year in year out she wore that coat; she perspired; she was never in the room five minutes without making you feel her superiority, your inferiority; how poor she was; how rich you were; how she lived in a slum without a cushion or a bed or a rug or whatever it might be, all her soul rusted with that grievance sticking in it, her dismissal from school during the War—poor embittered unfortunate creature! For it was not her one hated but the idea of her, which undoubtedly had gathered in to itself a great deal that was not Miss Kilman; had become one of those spectres with which one battles in the night; one of those spectres who stand astride us and suck up half our life-blood, dominators and tyrants; for no doubt with another throw of the dice, had the black been uppermost and not the white, she would have loved Miss Kilman! But not in this world. No.

It rasped her, though, to have stirring about in her this brutal monster! to hear twigs cracking and feel hooves planted down in the depths of that leaf-encumbered forest, the soul; never to be content quite, or quite secure, for at any moment the brute would be stirring, this hatred, which, especially since her illness, had power to make her feel scraped, hurt in her spine; gave her physical pain, and made all pleasure in beauty, in friendship, in being well, in being loved and making her home delightful rock, quiver, and bend as if indeed there were a monster grubbing at the roots, as if the whole panoply of content were nothing but self love! this hatred!

Nonsense, nonsense! she cried to herself, pushing through the swing doors of Mulberry's the florists.

She advanced, light, tall, very upright, to be greeted at once by button-faced Miss Pym, whose hands were always bright red, as if they had been stood in cold water with the flowers.

There were flowers: delphiniums, sweet peas, bunches of lilac; and carnations, masses of carnations. There were roses; there were irises. Ah yes—so she breathed in the earthy garden sweet smell as she stood talking to Miss Pym who owed her help, and thought her kind, for kind she had been years ago; very kind, but she looked older, this year, turning her head from side to side among the irises and roses and nodding tufts of lilac with her eyes half closed, snuffing in, after the street uproar, the delicious scent, the exquisite coolness. And then, opening her eyes, how fresh like frilled linen clean from a laundry laid in wicker trays the roses looked; and dark and prim the red carnations, holding their heads up; and all the sweet peas spreading in their bowls, tinged violet, snow white, pale—as if it were the evening and girls in muslin frocks came out to pick sweet peas and roses after the superb summer's day, with its almost blue-black sky, its delphiniums, its carnations, its arum lilies was over; and it was the moment between six and seven when every flower—roses, carnations, irises, lilac—glows; white, violet, red, deep orange; every flower seems to burn by itself, softly, purely in the misty beds; and how she loved the grey-white moths spinning in and out, over the cherry pie, over the evening primroses!

And as she began to go with Miss Pym from jar to jar, choosing, nonsense, nonsense, she said to herself, more and more gently, as if this beauty, this scent, this colour, and Miss Pym liking her, trusting her, were a wave which she let flow over her and surmount that hatred, that monster, surmount it all; and it lifted her up and up when—oh! a pistol shot in the street outside!

"Dear, those motor cars," said Miss Pym, going to the window to look, and coming back and smiling apologetically with her hands full of sweet peas, as if those motor cars, those tyres of motor cars, were all HER fault.

The violent explosion which made Mrs. Dalloway jump and Miss Pym go to the window and apologise came from a motor car which had drawn to the side of the pavement precisely opposite Mulberry's shop window. Passers-by who, of course, stopped and stared, had just time to see a face of the very greatest importance against the dove-grey upholstery, before a male hand drew the blind and there was nothing to be seen except a square of dove grey.

Yet rumours were at once in circulation from the middle of Bond Street to Oxford Street on one side, to Atkinson's scent shop on the other, passing invisibly, inaudibly, like a cloud, swift, veil-like upon hills, falling indeed with something of a cloud's sudden sobriety and stillness upon faces which a second before had been utterly disorderly. But now mystery had brushed them with her wing; they had heard the voice of authority; the spirit of religion was abroad with her eyes bandaged tight and her lips gaping wide. But nobody knew whose face had been seen. Was it the Prince of Wales's, the Queen's, the Prime Minister's? Whose face was it? Nobody knew.

III Thinking, Talking and Writing About Literature

1 Textual Cognition

Make an introductory presentation on the following terms related to this literary work.

1) Flaneuse
2) free indirect speech

2 Textual Reading

Search for evidence in the text and answer the following questions.

1) In the selection, from Mrs. Dalloway's going out to buy flowers to her hearing a pistol shot, her thoughts jump from the present to the past. What does the author try to reveal in the selection?

2) The characters in *Mrs. Dalloway* show much of British society's disenchantment with the old hierarchical class system. Please take Mrs. Dalloway as an example to demonstrate the social shifts taking place in the class system.

3) What do the strokes of Big Ben in the text symbolize?

③ Critical Reading

Discuss in groups the following questions to further explore this literary work.

1) World War I is the historical and political background of *Mrs. Dalloway*. How can the effect of World War I on British society be seen in the characters of *Mrs. Dalloway*?

2) The city London threads through on many levels. How does the urban setting determine both the novel's form and meaning?

④ Writing About Literature

Read the following critical excerpt and then write an essay.

> Brown, Paul Tolliver. "The Spatiotemporal Topography of Virginia Woolf's *Mrs. Dalloway*: Capturing Britain's Transition to a Relative Modernity." *Journal of Modern Literature* 38.4 (2015): 20–38.

Instead of making multiple blunders in an otherwise scrupulously crafted novel, Woolf creates fluid spatiotemporal dimensions to draw attention to the fact that her characters inhabit a relative setting. Just as time and space are dynamic qualities in Einstein's conception of the universe, Woolf's London is incredibly interactive and not always in apparent step with the characters who live there. The relationship between Clarissa, Peter, and Richard and their surroundings may be dynamic, but it is not chaotic. As readers, we tend to assume that Big Ben and the people who roam London's streets share the same perspective of time and space, and we might additionally surmise that because the characters are walking through the city that, if anything, they are moving at a slightly faster pace than their presumably stationary environs. Nevertheless, the characters' thoughts suggest the opposite. They are consumed by their lives before the war while Big Ben persists in announcing the present hour in a London that has moved on despite them. The characters are not traveling too fast. In a metaphorical sense that aligns with the structure of Woolf's narrative, they are traveling too slow.

In a fully relative London, Woolf's slow-moving characters would perceive their own sense of time ticking by at a faster rate than Big Ben's. According to Einstein, time passes more quickly for a relatively stationary observer (in this context, Woolf's characters that remain mostly stuck in the Victorian past) than it does for an observer moving at a more rapid pace (modern London). In accord with relativity, Woolf's characters would perceive that they take a greater amount of time to stroll the streets by their wrist watches than Big Ben would seem to denote to readers. From their subjective points of view, characters' accounting of time and distance would appear wholly rational even if it were incongruous in relation to the city's most famous clock. Readers who note apparent discrepancies do so because they affiliate themselves with Big Ben and base their calculations on a single, accelerated system moving at a much different speed than the characters themselves. Consequently, they assign a unilateral point of view to an otherwise diverse multitude.

Essay Writing

Write an essay on psychological time in *Mrs. Dalloway* with no less than 500 words.

IV Further Activity

Scan the QR code and listen to the BBC Radio "In Our Time: History" by Melvyn Bragg and his guests on Virginia Woolf's novel *Mrs. Dalloway*, published in 1925.

Lecture 12
Sylvia Plath

Profile of the Writer

Sylvia Plath
(1932–1963)

Plath published her first poem at age eight. She entered Smith College on a scholarship in 1951. At Smith Plath achieved considerable artistic, academic, and social success, but she also suffered from severe depression, attempted suicide, and underwent a period of psychiatric hospitalization. She graduated from Smith with highest honors in 1955 and went on to Newnham College in Cambridge, England, on a Fulbright fellowship. In 1956 she married the English poet Ted Hughes; they had two children. The couple separated in 1962, after Hughes's affair with another woman.

During 1957–1958 Plath was an instructor in English at Smith College. In 1960, shortly after she returned to England with Hughes, her first collection of poems appeared as *The Colossus*, which received good reviews. Her novel, *The Bell Jar*, was published in London in 1963 under the pseudonym Victoria Lucas. Strongly autobiographical, the book describes the mental breakdown and eventual recovery of a young college girl and parallels Plath's own breakdown and hospitalization in 1953.

During her last three years, Plath abandoned the restraints and conventions that had bound much of her early work. She wrote with great speed, producing poems of stark self-revelation and confession. The anxiety, confusion, and doubt that haunted her were transmuted into verses of great power and pathos borne on flashes of incisive wit. Her poem "Daddy" and several others explore her conflicted relationship with her father, Otto Plath, who died when she was eight. In 1963, after this burst of productivity, she took her own life.

Ariel (1965)—a collection of Plath's later poems that included "Daddy" and another of her well-known poems, "Lady Lazarus"—sparked the growth of a much broader following of devoted and enthusiastic readers than she had during her lifetime. *The Collected Poems*, which includes many previously unpublished poems, appeared in 1981 and received the 1982 Pulitzer Prize for poetry, making Plath the first to receive the honor posthumously.

Ⅰ Preview Questions

1. What do you know about Sylvia Plath as a poet?
2. *The Bell Jar* chronicles a young woman's mental breakdown and eventual recovery. What is the symbolic meaning of the title?

Ⅱ Literary Reading: *The Bell Jar* (Chapter 1)

It was a queer, sultry summer, the summer they electrocuted the Rosenbergs, and I didn't know what I was doing in New York. I'm stupid about executions. The idea of being electrocuted makes me sick, and that's all there was to read about in the papers—goggle-eyed headlines staring up at me on every street corner and at the fusty, peanut-smelling mouth of every subway. It had nothing to do with me, but I couldn't help wondering what it would be like, being burned alive all along your nerves.

I thought it must be the worst thing in the world.

New York was bad enough. By nine in the morning the fake, country-wet freshness that somehow seeped in overnight evaporated like the tail end of a sweet dream. Mirage-gray at the bottom of their granite canyons, the hot streets wavered in the sun, the car tops sizzled and glittered, and the dry, cindery dust blew into my eyes and down my throat.

I kept hearing about the Rosenbergs over the radio and at the office till I couldn't get them out of my mind. It was like the first time I saw a cadaver. For weeks afterward, the cadaver's head—or what there was left of it—floated up behind my eggs and bacon at breakfast and behind the face of Buddy Willard, who was responsible for my seeing it in the

first place, and pretty soon I felt as though I were carrying that cadaver's head around with me on a string, like some black, noseless balloon stinking of vinegar.

I knew something was wrong with me that summer, because all I could think about was the Rosenbergs and how stupid I'd been to buy all those uncomfortable, expensive clothes, hanging limp as fish in my closet, and how all the little successes I'd totted up so happily at college fizzled to nothing outside the slick marble and plate-glass fronts along Madison Avenue.

I was supposed to be having the time of my life.

I was supposed to be the envy of thousands of other college girls just like me all over America who wanted nothing more than to be tripping about in those same size-seven patent leather shoes I'd bought in Bloomingdale's one lunch hour with a black patent leather belt and black patent leather pocketbook to match. And when my picture came out in the magazine the twelve of us were working on—drinking martinis in a skimpy, imitation silver-lame bodice stuck on to a big, fat cloud of white tulle, on some Starlight Roof, in the company of several anonymous young men with all-American bone structures hired or loaned for the occasion—everybody would think I must be having a real whirl.

Look what can happen in this country, they'd say. A girl lives in some out-of-the-way town for nineteen years, so poor she can't afford a magazine, and then she gets a scholarship to college and wins a prize here and a prize there and ends up steering New York like her own private car.

Only I wasn't steering anything, not even myself. I just bumped from my hotel to work and to parties and from parties to my hotel and back to work like a numb trolleybus. I guess I should have been excited the way most of the other girls were, but I couldn't get myself to react. I felt very still and very empty, the way the eye of a tornado must feel, moving dully along in the middle of the surrounding hullabaloo.

There were twelve of us at the hotel.

We had all won a fashion magazine contest, by writing essays and stories and poems and fashion blurbs, and as prizes they gave us jobs in New York for a month, expenses paid, and piles and piles of free bonuses, like ballet tickets and passes to fashion shows and hair stylings at a famous expensive salon and chances to meet successful people in the field of our desire and advice about what to do with our particular complexions.

I still have the make-up kit they gave me, fitted out for a person with brown eyes and brown hair: an oblong of brown mascara with a tiny brush, and a round basin of blue eye shadow just big enough to dab the tip of your finger in, and three lipsticks ranging from red to pink, all cased in the same little gilt box with a mirror on one side. I also have a white plastic sunglasses case with colored shells and sequins and a green plastic starfish sewed onto it.

I realized we kept piling up these presents because it was as good as free advertising for the firms involved, but I couldn't be cynical. I got such a kick out of all those free gifts showering on to us. For a long time afterward I hid them away, but later, when I was all right again, I brought them out, and I still have them around the house. I use the lipsticks now and then, and last week I cut the plastic starfish off the sunglasses case for the baby to play with.

So there were twelve of us at the hotel, in the same wing on the same floor in single rooms, one after the other, and it reminded me of my dormitory at college. It wasn't a proper hotel—I mean a hotel where there are both men and women mixed about here and there on the same floor.

This hotel—the Amazon—was for women only, and they were mostly girls my age with wealthy parents who wanted to be sure their daughters would be living where men couldn't get at them and deceive them; and they were all going to posh secretarial schools like Katy Gibbs, where they had to wear hats and stockings and gloves to class, or they had just graduated from places like Katy Gibbs and were secretaries to executives and simply hanging around in New York waiting to get married to some career man or other.

These girls looked awfully bored to me. I saw them on the sunroof, yawning and painting their nails and trying to keep up their Bermuda tans, and they seemed bored as hell. I talked with one of them, and she was bored with yachts and bored with flying around in airplanes and bored with skiing in Switzerland at Christmas and bored with the men in Brazil.

Girls like that make me sick. I'm so jealous I can't speak. Nineteen years, and I hadn't been out of New England except for this trip to New York. It was my first big chance, but here I was, sitting back and letting it run through my fingers like so much water.

I guess one of my troubles was Doreen.

I'd never known a girl like Doreen before. Doreen came from a society girls' college down South and had bright white hair standing out in a cotton candy fluff round her head and blue eyes like transparent agate marbles, hard and polished and just about indestructible, and a mouth set in a sort of perpetual sneer. I don't mean a nasty sneer, but an amused, mysterious sneer, as if all the people around her were pretty silly and she could tell some good jokes on them if she wanted to.

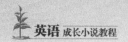

Doreen singled me out right away. She made me feel I was that much sharper than the others, and she really was wonderfully funny. She used to sit next to me at the conference table, and when the visiting celebrities were talking she'd whisper witty sarcastic remarks to me under her breath.

Her college was so fashion conscious, she said, that all the girls had pocketbook covers made out of the same material as their dresses, so each time they changed their clothes they had a matching pocketbook. This kind of detail impressed me. It suggested a whole life of marvelous, elaborate decadence that attracted me like a magnet.

The only thing Doreen ever bawled me out about was bothering to get my assignments in by a deadline.

"What are you sweating over that for?" Doreen lounged on my bed in a peach silk dressing gown, filing her long, nicotine-yellow nails with an emery board, while I typed up the draft of an interview with a best-selling novelist.

That was another thing—the rest of us had starched cotton summer nighties and quilted housecoats, or maybe terrycloth robes that doubled as beach coats, but Doreen wore these full-length nylon and lace jobs you could half see through, and dressing gowns the color of skin, that stuck to her by some kind of electricity. She had an interesting, slightly sweaty smell that reminded me of those scallopy leaves of sweet fern you break off and crush between your fingers for the musk of them.

"You know old Jay Cee won't give a damn if that story's in tomorrow or Monday." Doreen lit a cigarette and let the smoke flare slowly from her nostrils so her eyes were veiled. "Jay Cee's ugly as sin," Doreen went on coolly. "I bet that old husband of hers turns out all the lights before he gets near her or he'd puke otherwise."

Jay Cee was my boss, and I liked her a lot, in spite of what Doreen said. She wasn't one of the fashion magazine gushers with fake eyelashes and giddy jewelry. Jay Cee had brains, so her plug-ugly looks didn't seem to matter. She read a couple of languages and knew all the quality writers in the business.

I tried to imagine Jay Cee out of her strict office suit and luncheon-duty hat and in bed with her fat husband, but I just couldn't do it. I always had a terribly hard time trying to imagine people in bed together.

Jay Cee wanted to teach me something, all the old ladies I ever knew wanted to teach me something, but I suddenly didn't think they had anything to teach me. I fitted the lid on my typewriter and clicked it shut.

Doreen grinned. "Smart girl."

Somebody tapped at the door.

"Who is it?" I didn't bother to get up.

"It's me, Betsy. Are you coming to the party?"

"I guess so." I still didn't go to the door.

They imported Betsy straight from Kansas with her bouncing blonde ponytail and Sweetheart-of-Sigma-Chi smile. I remember once the two of us were called over to the office of some blue-chinned TV producer in a pin-stripe suit to see if we had any angles he could build up for a program, and Betsy started to tell about the male and female corn in Kansas. She got so excited about that damn corn even the producer had tears in his eyes, only he couldn't use any of it, unfortunately, he said.

Later on, the Beauty Editor persuaded Betsy to cut her hair and made a cover girl out of her, and I still see her fare now and then, smiling out of those "P.Q.'s wife wears B.H. Wragge" ads.

Betsy was always asking me to do things with her and the other girls as if she were trying to save me in some way. She never asked Doreen. In private, Doreen called her Pollyanna Cowgirl.

"Do you want to come in our cab?" Betsy said through the door.

Doreen shook her head.

"That's all right, Betsy," I said. "I'm going with Doreen."

"Okay." I could hear Betsy padding off down the hall.

"We'll just go till we get sick of it," Doreen told me, stubbing out her cigarette in the base of my bedside reading lamp, "then we'll go out on the town. Those parties they stage here remind me of the old dances in the school gym. Why do they always round up Yalies? They're so *too-pit!*"

Buddy Willard went to Yale, but now I thought of it, what was wrong with him was that he was stupid. Oh, he'd managed to get good marks all right, and to have an affair with some awful waitress on the Cape by the name of Gladys, but he didn't have one speck of intuition. Doreen had intuition. Everything she said was like a secret voice speaking straight out of my own bones.

We were stuck in the theater-hour rush. Our cab sat wedged in back of Betsy's cab and in front of a cab with four of the other girls, and nothing moved.

Doreen looked terrific. She was wearing a strapless white lace dress zipped up over a snug corset affair that curved her in at the middle and bulged her out again spectacularly above and below, and her skin had a bronzy polish under the pale dusting powder. She smelled strong as a whole perfume store.

I wore a black shantung sheath that cost me forty dollars. It was part of a buying spree I had with some of my scholarship money when I heard I was one of the lucky ones going to New York. This dress was cut so queerly I couldn't wear any sort of a bra under it, but that didn't matter much as I was skinny as a boy and barely rippled, and I liked feeling almost naked on the hot summer nights.

The city had faded my tan, though. I looked yellow as a Chinaman. Ordinarily, I would have been nervous about my dress and my odd color, but being with Doreen made me forget my worries. I felt wise and cynical as all hell.

When the man in the blue lumber shirt and black chinos and tooled leather cowboy boots started to stroll over to us from under the striped awning of the bar where he'd been eyeing our cab, I couldn't have any illusions. I knew perfectly well he'd come for Doreen. He threaded his way out between the stopped cars and leaned engagingly on the sill of our open window.

"And what, may I ask, are two nice girls like you doing all alone in a cab on a nice night like this?"

He had a big, wide, white toothpaste-ad smile.

"We're on our way to a party," I blurted, since Doreen had gone suddenly dumb as a post and was fiddling in a blase way with her white lace pocketbook cover.

"That sounds boring," the man said. "Whyn't you both join me for a couple of drinks in that bar over there? I've some friends waiting as well."

He nodded in the direction of several informally dressed men slouching around under the awning. They had been following him with their eyes, and when he glanced back at them, they burst out laughing.

The laughter should have warned me. It was a kind of low, know-it-all snicker, but the traffic showed signs of moving again, and I knew that if I sat tight, in two seconds I'd be wishing I'd taken this gift of a chance to see something of New York besides what the people on the magazine had planned out for us so carefully.

"How about it, Doreen?" I said.

"How about it, Doreen?" the man said, smiling his big smile. To this day I can't remember what he looked like when he wasn't smiling. I think he must have been smiling the whole time. It must have been natural for him, smiling like that.

"Well, all right," Doreen said to me. I opened the door, and we stepped out of the cab just as it was edging ahead again and started to walk over to the bar.

There was a terrible shriek of brakes followed by a dull thump-thump.

"Hey you!" Our cabby was craning out of his window with a furious, purple expression. "Waddaya think you're doin'?"

He had stopped the cab so abruptly that the cab behind bumped smack into him, and we could see the four girls inside waving and struggling and scrambling up off the floor.

The man laughed and left us on the curb and went back and handed a bill to the driver in the middle of a great honking and some yelling, and then we saw the girls from the magazine moving off in a row, one cab after another, like a wedding party with nothing but bridesmaids.

"Come on, Frankie," the man said to one of his friends in the group, and a short, scrunty fellow detached himself and came into the bar with us.

He was the type of fellow I can't stand. I'm five feet ten in my stocking feet, and when I am with little men I stoop over a bit and slouch my hips, one up and one down, so I'll look shorter, and I feel gawky and morbid as somebody in a sideshow.

For a minute I had a wild hope we might pair off according to size, which would line me up with the man who had spoken to us in the first place, and he cleared a good six feet, but he went ahead with Doreen and didn't give me a second look. I tried to pretend I didn't see Frankie dogging along at my elbow and sat close by Doreen at the table.

It was so dark in the bar I could hardly make out anything except Doreen. With her white hair and white dress she was so white she looked silver. I think she must have reflected the neons over the bar. I felt myself melting into the shadows like the negative of a person I'd never seen before in my life.

"Well, what'll we have?" the man asked with a large smile.

"I think I'll have an old-fashioned," Doreen said to me.

Ordering drinks always floored me. I didn't know whisky from gin and never managed to get anything I really liked the taste of. Buddy Willard and the other college boys I knew were usually too poor to buy hard liquor or they scorned drinking altogether. It's amazing how many college boys don't drink or smoke. I seemed to know them all. The farthest Buddy Willard ever went was buying us a bottle of Dubonnet, which he only did because he was trying to prove he could be aesthetic in spite of being a medical student.

"I'll have a vodka," I said.

The man looked at me more closely. "With anything?"

"Just plain," I said. "I always have it plain."

I thought I might make a fool of myself by saying I'd have it with ice or gin or anything. I'd seen a vodka ad once, just a glass full of vodka standing in the middle of a snowdrift in a blue light, and the vodka looked clear and pure as water, so I thought having vodka plain must be all right. My dream was someday ordering a drink and finding out it tasted wonderful.

The waiter came up then, and the man ordered drinks for the four of us. He looked so at home in that citified bar in his ranch outfit I thought he might well be somebody famous.

Doreen wasn't saying a word, she only toyed with her cork placemat and eventually lit a cigarette, but the man didn't seem to mind. He kept staring at her the way people stare at the great white macaw in the zoo, waiting for it to say something human.

The drinks arrived, and mine looked clear and pure, just like the vodka ad.

"What do you do?" I asked the man, to break the silence shooting up around me on all sides, thick as jungle grass. "I mean what do you do here in New York?"

Slowly and with what seemed a great effort, the man dragged his eyes away from Doreen's shoulder. "I'm a disc jockey," he said. "You prob'ly must have heard of me. The name's Lenny Shepherd."

"I know you," Doreen said suddenly.

"I'm glad about that, honey," the man said, and burst out laughing. "That'll come in handy. I'm famous as hell."

Then Lenny Shepherd gave Frankie a long look.

"Say, where do you come from?" Frankie asked, sitting up with a jerk. "What's your name?"

"This here's Doreen." Lenny slid his hand around Doreen's bare arm and gave her a squeeze.

What surprised me was that Doreen didn't let on she noticed what he was doing. She just sat there, dusky as a bleached-blonde Negress in her white dress, and sipped daintily at her drink.

"My name's Elly Higginbottom," I said. "I come from Chicago." After that I felt safer. I didn't want anything I said or did that night to be associated with me and my real name and coming from Boston.

"Well, Elly, what do you say we dance some?"

The thought of dancing with that little runt in his orange suede elevator shoes and mingy T-shirt and droopy blue sports coat made me laugh. If there's anything I look down on, it's a man in a blue outfit. Black or gray, or brown, even. Blue makes me laugh.

"I'm not in the mood," I said coldly, turning my back on him and hitching my chair over nearer to Doreen and Lenny.

Those two looked as if they'd known each other for years by now. Doreen was spooning up the hunks of fruit at the bottom of her glass with a spindly silver spoon, and Lenny was grunting each time she lifted the spoon to her mouth, and snapping and pretending to be a dog or something, and trying to get the fruit off the spoon. Doreen giggled and kept spooning up the fruit.

I began to think vodka was my drink at last. It didn't taste like anything, but it went straight down into my stomach like a sword swallower's sword and made me feel powerful and godlike.

"I better go now," Frankie said, standing up.

I couldn't see him very clearly, the place was so dim, but for the first time I heard what a high, silly voice he had. Nobody paid him any notice.

"Hey, Lenny, you owe me something. Remember, Lenny, you owe me something, don't you, Lenny?"

I thought it odd Frankie should be reminding Lenny he owed him something in front of us, and we being perfect strangers, but Frankie stood there saying the same thing over and over until Lenny dug into his pocket and pulled out a big roll of green bills and peeled one off and handed it to Frankie. I think it was ten dollars.

"Shut up and scram."

For a minute I thought Lenny was talking to me as well, but then I heard Doreen say, "I won't come unless Elly comes." I had to hand it to her the way she picked up my fake name.

"Oh, Elly'll come, won't you, Elly?" Lenny said, giving me a wink.

"Sure I'll come," I said. Frankie had wilted away into the night, so I thought I'd string along with Doreen. I wanted to see as much as I could.

I liked looking on at other people in crucial situations. If there was a road accident or a street fight or a baby pickled in a laboratory jar for me to look at, I'd stop and look so hard I never forgot it.

I certainly learned a lot of things I never would have learned otherwise this way, and even when they surprised me or made me sick I never let on, but pretended that's the way I knew things were all the time.

III Thinking, Talking and Writing About Literature

1 Textual Cognition

Make an introductory presentation on the following terms related to this literary work.

1) semi-autobiography
2) trauma

2 Textual Reading

Search for evidence in the text and answer the following questions.

1) The very first sentence of the chapter alerts the reader to the conflicts that will be dealt with in this semi-autobiographical novel: "It was a queer, sultry summer, the summer they electrocuted the Rosenbergs, and I didn't know what I was doing in New York." What do you

think contributes to the speaker's adolescent crisis?

2) What kind of social and educational expectations would have shaped the lives of young women in the US in the 1950s? In what ways can our understanding of these issues inform our reading of the first chapter of *The Bell Jar*?

3) Esther herself says, "I was supposed to be having the time of my life." Why is she so miserable with her success? Why does she feel the need to invent another name for herself, "Elly Higginbottom"? Try to figure out why Esther is so filled with conflict, so alienated.

❸ Critical Reading

Discuss in groups the following questions to further explore this literary work.

1) How does *The Bell Jar* relate to the women's liberation movement?
2) What are the sociological/historical/psychological explanations for Esther's problems?
3) Why is this book a wasteland description of women's lives?

❹ Writing About Literature

Read the following critical excerpt and then write an essay.

> Churchwell, Sarah. "An Introduction to *The Bell Jar*."
> The British Library, May 25, 2016.

The Bell Jar is an acidic satire on the madness of 1950s America, exploring the impossibility of living up to the era's contradictory ideals of womanhood. Despite its reputation as the favourite novel of morbidly self-obsessed adolescent girls, it is a much funnier book than many may realise. Among the many ironies surrounding the novel's undeserved reputation for taking itself seriously, one of the sharpest is perhaps the way that it has tended to be dismissed along gender lines, as a book "merely" for women, or petulant teenagers. But although *The Bell Jar* concerns a young woman's eventual breakdown and suicide attempt, it also tells a story of recovery, redemption, rebirth and starting over. And it examines the social expectations and toxic culture of 1950s American culture that makes finding a positive identity as a woman so difficult that its heroine is driven to self-destruction.

Losing any secure sense of herself, Esther Greenwood symbolically tests out a series of possible identities, different selves, through the women she meets; none of them represent her full character, the range of her psyche. As many critics have noted, Plath brings in a series of female "doubles", or alter egos, to suggest possible role models of ideal femininity in the 1950s. In particular, Esther identifies with Doreen, who is described in terms that suggest Marilyn Monroe, and with Betsy, a virginal, wholesome cheerful girl-next-door in the style of Doris Day. A girl in the 1950s could be a virgin or she could be a whore: it was a neo-Victorian era, as evidenced by the crinolines and tiny waists. "Pureness was the great issue when I was nineteen", Esther explains: girls had to be virgins, and yet they were discovering sexual desire.

Esther tries on differing models of femininity and discards them like the clothes she will throw from her window when departing New York, for none of them fit her anymore. The mutually incompatible pressures of individualism and conformity split her apart. As she tells one useless boyfriend: "if neurotic is wanting two mutually exclusive things at one and the same time, then I'm neurotic as hell. I'll be flying back and forth between one mutually exclusive thing and another for the rest of my days." Plath excoriates the women who conformed to the era's rules; "girls like that make me sick", Esther repeats in a refrain that becomes increasingly pointed: her society is indeed making Esther sick.

Essay Writing

Read the above selection and write an essay entitled *How Does the Toxic Culture of 1950s America Determine the Fate of Esther* with no less than 500 words.

 IV ## Further Activity

Why should you read Sylvia Plath? Scan the QR code and watch a TED Talk to find out the answer.

03

第三部分
族裔英语成长小说

Ethnic English Bildungsroman

导 言

拉美文学和加勒比文学研究专家纳迪亚（Nadia Avendaño）认为，"成长小说本身，在最近几十年中，一直由庶民群体，而非西方主流文化中的男性推动转化和复兴，因此充当着社会局外人，尤其是女性和少数族裔群体文学的最为重要的文类。"[1] 比如印度裔英国作家巴里·拉伊（Bali Rai, 1971—）发表于2001年的成长小说《（联合国）包办婚姻》（(Un) arranged Marriage）讲述了旁遮普-英国（Punjabi-British）男孩曼尼（Manny）的成长故事。再比如美籍阿富汗作家卡勒德·胡赛尼（Khaled Hosseini, 1965—）于2003年出版的长篇小说《追风筝的人》（The Kite Runner）也是一部成长小说。小说以主人公阿米尔（Amir）的成长历程为主线，围绕阿米尔和家仆阿里（Ali）的儿子哈桑（Hassan）的童年往事及其对阿米尔的影响展开，叙述了阿米尔犯错、悔过、赎罪的经历，同时再现了20世纪70年代之后阿富汗社会经历的政治动荡与变迁。这些当代文坛十分畅销的小说均是族裔英语成长小说（ethnic Bildungsroman）。

20世纪90年代的"多元文化转向"让人们越来越清楚地意识到，性别、阶级、民族语境、种族、文化、时间等因素深刻地影响着成长小说的创作，而这又反过来促使学界对少数族裔和多元种族的成长叙事给予越来越多的批评关注。

与经典成长小说不同，族裔成长小说讲述的是边缘群体的青少年设法融入主流社会，同时又要保持自己的个性和独立的成长故事。族裔成长小说描写"那些由于性别和肤色难以被主流社会接受的人们的特殊身份和适应问题"[2]，而对于此种新型成长小说中身份定位的特质，族裔小说研究专家布雷德林（Bonnie Braendlin）进行了如下定义：

---

[1] Avendaño, Nadia. "The Chicana Subaltern and the Ethnic Female Bildungsroman in Patricia Santana's *Motorcycle Ride on the Sea of Tranquility*." *Letras Hispanas* 9.1 (2013): 67.

[2] Braendlin, Bonnie. "Bildung in Ethnic Women Writers." *Denver Quarterly* 17 (1983): 75.

这种新的成长小说肯定一种由外来者或者由他们自己的文化所定义的身份，而不是由权威的盎格鲁－美国权力结构来定义；它表明由新的标准和视角对传统成长的再次评估，重新评估[1]。

不同于经典成长小说中通常聚焦于阶级差别，在族裔成长小说中，青少年成长的焦点往往是刻板印象和种族主义。作者在借用传统成长小说主要元素的基础之上，也创造了很多新的模式，其中之一就是主人公成长的核心困境往往来自社会，而不是自我。这一社会的障碍以种族主义、刻板印象等方式表现出来。在传统成长小说中，主人公也会受到来自社会的挑战，但他们对社会价值依旧忠诚。比如，在《简·爱》中，女主人公经历各种人生遭际，却一定要找到一条通往社会认可的成功之路：地位、金钱、名誉、美丽。而在族裔成长小说中，主人公却很难与主流价值观取得一致。

英语族裔成长小说的发展是世界范围内的文学现象，在英国、美国、加拿大、澳大利亚等多民族国家均有不同程度的发展。不过美国这个"大熔炉"汇集了世界文坛中最丰富多彩的文学作品、最多元的文化背景和风格最独特的文学家，美国的多元文化特质成就了美国族裔文学的多元文化特征。因此本章遴选的族裔文学作品主要以美国族裔文学为主，其中涉及美国非裔成长小说、美国印第安成长小说等。

美国非裔成长小说

美国非裔文学的出现本身就是黑人族群不断成长的结果。美国著名黑人学者杜波依斯（W. E. B. Du Bois，1868—1963）早在1903年就在《黑人的灵魂》(*The Souls of Black Folk*)一书中提出："美国黑人的历史是抗争的历史"[2]，因此黑人成长小说的历史也毫无疑问是黑人在抗争中成长的表现史。非裔美国成长小说大多讲述主人公在成长过程中所经历的痛苦，在白人社会中遭遇文化冲突的困惑，以及最后走出困境、获得自由、长大成人的过程。他们在文化冲突中寻找身份认同，最典型的表现为两种成长模式：一是主人公从美国梦的幻灭中追寻自我的迷惘式成长，主人公逐步有了对社会的认识和对自我的定位，但是仍苦于可见抑或不可见的主客观原因而无法突破，无所适从；二是主人公从黑人传统文化中汲取成长的力量，在引路人的帮助下，最后以回归传统的方式确立自己的

---

1 Braendlin, Bonnie. "Bildung in Ethnic Women Writers." *Denver Quarterly* 17 (1983): 75.
2 Du Bois, W. E. B. *The Souls of Black Folk*. Ed. Brent Hayes Edwards. New York: Oxford University Press, 2007. 9.

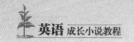

身份，建构主体。

有着黑色大西洋记忆和种植园奴隶制创伤的美国非裔的成长不得不面对最为关键的问题，那就是身份问题。非裔作家们不仅探讨黑人的"身份焦虑"，还通过主人公的经历揭示人在社会中的异化和自我失落。正如美国非裔作家拉尔夫·艾利森（Ralph Ellison, 1914—1994）所言，"小说是我努力要回答这些问题的途径：我是谁？我是干什么的？我该怎样理解我周围的生活？我该如何用我自己对过去历史的了解，用我自己对现在历史的复杂认识去看待我眼中的美国社会？"[1]

1940 年，美国非裔作家理查德·赖特（Richard Wright, 1908—1960）的《土生子》（*Native Son*）出版。小说描述了主人公别格（Bigger Thomas）对白人占据统治地位的主流社会的疯狂反抗，因而这部小说也被归入抗议小说之列，成为控诉种族歧视摧残黑人从而导致悲剧发生的一部具有里程碑意义的作品。正如美国著名文学评论家欧文·豪（Irving Howe）所言："自《土生子》诞生的那一天起，美国文化被永远地改变了。"[2] 值得注意的是，这部小说不仅是一部抗议小说，还是一部很有代表性的黑人成长小说。别格的心理成长践行了美国成长小说的叙述模式：天真—诱惑—出走—迷惘—考验—失去天真—顿悟—认识人生和自我。小说的三个部分——"恐惧""逃亡"和"命运"[3]——都是围绕别格对待生活的不同态度展开的：别格由开始仇视白人的生活，对周围的一切感到厌恶、疏离，到借谋杀展示自我的存在和发泄反抗的情绪，再发展到最后的自我反思。他的成长过程经历了一系列的事件和心理变化，他不仅是美国社会种族问题的牺牲品，是具有反抗精神的黑人青年的代表，更是一个没有找到自己位置和幸福最终导致成长失败的黑人青年。别格的成长是美国黑人在重重重压下的"向死而生"，是一种心理成长。

艾利森的《看不见的人》（*Invisible Man*）也是一部聚焦黑人主人公自我身份追寻的成长小说。主人公从小接受的是白人的价值观，勤奋恭顺，坚信只要有技能在身，生活就会变得越来越好，就能收获应有的尊重和报酬。因此，他想通过"去黑化"实现自己完全"白化"的华丽蜕变。于是他对白人一味听从，尽力迎合，目的就是被主流社会接受。可是事与愿违，他正走上一条不归之路，丢掉了尊严与自我却并未换得他想要的，或者说在当时的历史语境下，他也根本不知自己想要什么。主人公的经历揭示了黑人在成长过程中所遭遇到的异化和自我失落，导致"身份焦虑"。正如主人公开篇所言：

---

[1] 陆钰明，《美国散文经典》，唐根金等译。上海：汉语大辞典出版社，2005 年，第 232 页。
[2] Howe, Irving. "Black Boys and Native Sons." *Dissent*, Autumn (1963): 354.
[3] 理查德·赖特，《土生子》，施咸荣译。南京：译林出版社，1999 年。

第三部分
族裔英语成长小说 导言

> 我是看不见的人。我并不是埃德加·爱伦·坡笔下的幽灵,也不是好莱坞影片中虚无缥缈的幻影。我是一个实实在在的人,一个有血有肉的人——甚至可以说我还有心灵。要知道,人们看不见我,那只是因为他们拒绝看见我。[1]

美国非裔成长小说主人公在文化冲突中所表现出来的无所适从,以及其想有所为而终无为的状态,清晰地昭示着主人公想要做回自己的艰难性。

在美国非裔成长小说的创作中,黑人女作家成就斐然。有评论家言,"从60年代开始,文学的接力棒传到了黑人女性作家手中。"[2] 与黑人男作家相比,黑人女作家似乎更加珍视民族的遗产和文化,而在女性细腻情感的浸润下,黑人民族文化以更加独特、温婉、细碎的方式表达出来,无论是一床带有非洲特色的百纳被,还是一条具有民族特色的裙子,都被巧妙地赋予了承载民族文化和情结的重任。同时,黑人女作家强烈的性别意识也使得她们不但对白人主流社会和文化有着本能的对抗情绪,对黑人男性意识也一直倔强地保持着距离。正如托妮·莫里森所言:"拉尔夫·艾利森、理查德·赖特的作品我挺佩服,可就是感觉不到究竟带给我些什么。我认为他们只是把有关我们黑人的事讲给你们听,讲给大家,讲给白人,讲给男人们听。"[3] 莫里森的言外之意是,黑人男性作家通过把黑人女性排除在写作之外的方式再次使黑人女性边缘化了。与白人女性作家对性别称呼的敏感和反感不同,黑人女作家对"女性"的称呼有着异乎寻常的偏爱,莫里森、沃克等人更是坚称自己是"黑人女作家"。黑人女性作家之所以对种族和性别身份不讳言,反而不断强调和凸现,是因为她们明智地意识到了这个独特视角的介入将给她们的作品带来独特的艺术魅力,正如莫里森所总结的那样:"身为黑人和女性,我能进入到那些不是黑人、不是女性的人所不能进入的一个感情和感受的宽广领域。"[4]

从20世纪二三十年代开始,美国黑人女作家以女性成长为题材的作品就已陆续问世了。佐拉·尼尔·赫斯顿(Zora Neale Hurston,1891—1960)的代表作《他们眼望上苍》(*Their Eyes Were Watching God*)就是其中的优秀作品。《他们眼望上苍》的主人公珍妮(Janie Crawford)从小和曾经是奴隶的祖母南妮(Nanny Crawford)一起生活。为了让珍妮过上富裕的生活,南妮把16岁的珍妮嫁给了有地有房的中年农民洛根·基利克

---

[1] Ellison, Ralph. *Invisible Man*. New York: Vintage Books, 1995. 1.
[2] 王守仁、吴新云,《性别·种族·文化》。北京:北京大学出版社,2004年,第20页。
[3] 查尔斯·鲁亚斯,《美国作家访谈录》,粟旺、李文俊等译。北京:中国对外翻译出版社,1995年,第204页。
[4] Taylor-Guthrie, Danille, ed. *Conversations with Toni Morrison*. Jackson: University Press of Mississippi, 1994. 243.

斯（Logan Killicks）。洛根把珍妮看作干活的骡子，这种毫无爱情的沉闷生活使珍妮的梦想破灭了。珍妮离开洛根，跟着一位英俊小伙乔·斯塔克斯（Jody Starks）到了伊顿维尔。乔成了镇长，还有了漂亮的房子和商店。然而，虽然他们结婚20年，但乔同样不能平等地对待珍妮，还不时地当众嘲笑她。一次，珍妮的反抗情绪爆发了，她的反唇相讥使乔不久便气死了。后来珍妮遇上了一个比她小十几岁的流浪农工迪·凯克（Tea Cake）。他平等地对待珍妮，帮助她找到了自尊和自己的声音。两人结婚后，到了佛罗里达的大沼泽地，在那里快乐且幸福地生活了两年。一场飓风来临，在洪水中，凯克为救珍妮而被疯狗咬伤，患了狂犬病。处于重病中的凯克试图用枪射杀珍妮，珍妮自卫反把他打死了。最后，法庭宣判珍妮无罪。经历了三次婚姻和种种磨难的珍妮终于成长为一位成熟的独立自主的女人。这部作品是一部经典的女性主义的成长小说，探索了女性主义关注的性属、性政治和妇女身份问题。作品的故事中套故事的叙事结构是对民间故事模式的运用。赫斯顿成功地把黑人民间故事和布道词糅合进小说中，采用了自由间接话语、黑人方言土语等种种独特的表达方式，具有鲜明的黑人特性。这部作品的女性主义主题、浓郁的黑人民俗文化特色和叙事策略，使它成为美国文学史上的经典，影响了众多当代黑人女作家。

而有些作品在当时并没有引起人们的注意。波·马歇尔（Paule Marshall，1929—2019）的《棕色姑娘，棕色砖房》（*Brown Girl, Brownstones*）的出版和接受就是一个典型的例证。《棕色姑娘，棕色砖房》出版于1959年，而当时少数族裔女性的生活和成长还没有唤起主流社会的关注。直到1981年，这部被束之高阁的来自巴巴多斯黑人女作家的作品，经女权出版社发掘并经过包装后再版，才引起了人们的关注。这部作品带有很强的自传性，讲述的也是一位有着非洲黑人血统的巴巴多斯女孩塞利娜·博依斯（Selina Boyce）从童年到成年的身心成长历程。这部成长小说以黑人与白人两种文化的冲突为背景来讲述塞利娜的成长故事。塞利娜的母亲希拉（Silla）受到白人中产阶级价值观念的影响，希望通过自己的辛苦劳作攒钱使自己成为纽约棕色砖房的主人。母亲希拉的梦想是一个典型的美国梦，体现了美国白人从富兰克林时代就确立的自我奋斗的务实的价值取向，同时也代表了美国少数族裔，包括像塞利娜的母亲一样的巴巴多斯移民的集体梦想；与母亲不同，塞利娜的父亲戴顿（Deighton）带有更多的理想主义色彩，当他意外得到了一块巴巴多斯的土地之后，他自然想回到故土，做一个享受自由的农民，过一种浪漫的田园生活。塞利娜的母亲和父亲分别代表了"美国文化体系中的理想和务实两个极端"，也代表了"美国梦想和生存、尊严和责任之间的冲突"。塞利娜在情感上更亲近父亲，然而她的理智却告诉她事实上她更像她的母亲，也必须像母亲一样去适应新的环境，才能真正在社会中找到自己的位置并实现自己的价值。父母提供的两个完全不同的生活模式使塞利娜在艰难选择的同时也不得不深刻地内省，因为只有内省和反思才能使她更清晰地认识自我。塞利娜开始思考一张棕色的面孔对她来说到底意味着什么。这张棕色的面孔像一个古老的关于黑夜的寓言拷问着白人同样暗如黑夜的心灵；这是让白人在白日会做噩梦的颜色，却是巴巴多斯人的民族自豪感的源泉和自我发展的动力。父亲和母亲所代表的两种不同的文化心理取向都并非理想的选择，作为新一代的巴巴多斯移民，塞利娜做出了不同的选择。她离开了美国的巴巴多斯人聚居区，前往西印度群岛探寻自己的种族之根。"这一选择表明，她不是要与巴巴多斯文化彻底决裂，同时也表明她与美国主流文化的距离。"[1] 塞利娜的选择说明了她与两种文化割不断、理还乱的复杂关系，她对两种文化都保持着审慎的距离，但又不可避免地受其影响。她的西印度之行表明了她寻求既有别于追寻美国梦的母亲，也有别于对国土眷恋难以自拔的父亲的自我和生活的决心，而这也是她成熟的开始，是她的新生的开始。

非洲裔黑人女性成长小说的成熟期出现在20世纪60年代末，贯穿了整个70年代，并在80年代达到高峰。60年代一部黑人女作家的自传体小说及其姊妹篇对美国黑人女性成长小说的发展起到了强大的推动作用，这位女作家就是有着传奇人生的玛亚·安基罗（Maya Angelou，1928—2014）。安基罗于1969年出版了《我知道笼中的鸟儿为何歌唱》（*I Know Why the Caged Bird Sings*），这部小说是当时刚刚步入不惑之年的安基罗对自己充满不安、屈辱、甚至暴力的童年生活的回忆。记忆的开端是当时只有3岁的安基罗［出生时的名字是玛桂瑞特·约翰森（Marguerite Johnson）］与她的哥哥贝里·约翰森（Bailey Johnson）在父母离异之后，被送到美国南方阿肯色州的乡村小镇斯坦姆坡斯与他们的祖母共同生活。在20世纪30年代的美国，旧南方的体制随着战争"死去"了，但其固有的心理和文化却比以往更顽固、更疯狂地"存活"着。在南北战争结束后半个多世纪的南方，白人仍然在心理上顽固地捍卫着自己曾经的特权，这种偏执的心理致使像斯坦姆坡斯一样的美国南方小镇仍旧笼罩在残酷的种族歧视和种族隔离的阴霾之中。作为一名生活在这种氛围中的黑人女孩，童年的安基罗不得不过早地面对白人种族主义者的凶险和暴力，过早地承受黑人的屈辱和悲惨的命运。在安基罗徐徐拉开的记忆的帷幔中，读者与安基罗共同经历了她对金发碧眼白皮肤的渴望，她被强暴后的惊恐和沉默，

---

[1] 芮渝萍，《美国成长小说研究》。北京：中国社会科学出版社，2004年，第293页。

她故意打碎白人主人花瓶后的愤怒情感的释放，她立志要成为街车售票员的抗争；见证了她面对种族歧视从不知所措到无言的愤怒，从微妙抵抗到积极抗争的过程；目睹了她从黑人身份的错置到黑人的种族骄傲的变化。安基罗的童年记忆在她16岁成为未婚先孕的母亲的体验中拉上了帷幕。因此从题材上来看，这是一部典型的有关童年和青春期的自传性作品，是一部融合了黑人自传和女性成长小说特征的黑人女性自传体成长小说。

黑人女性成长小说的全面成熟要归功于两位黑人女性作家——托妮·莫里森和艾丽斯·沃克。托妮·莫里森用自己丰富而成功的文学实践向全世界证明了非洲女性的写作才华，并以一部又一部的文学作品确立了黑人女性成长小说从主题到叙事的写作传统。莫里森的成名之作《最蓝的眼睛》(*The Bluest Eye*)作为族裔女性成长小说在情节构建和叙事策略上都取得了突破性进展。莫里森创作该书的初衷十分明确，那就是要书写"在文学中任何地方，任何人都未曾认真对待过的人物——书写处于边缘地位的小女孩"[1]。《最蓝的眼睛》的小主人公佩克拉（Pecola Breedlove）是一个黑人姑娘，而她受白人主流审美观念的影响，羡慕好莱坞童星秀兰·邓波儿（Shirley Temple）的一双蓝色的眼睛。她幻想着自己有朝一日也能拥有一双那么蓝的眼睛，这样她的冷漠的母亲就会疼爱她，别人也会喜欢她。佩克拉错误地认为她生活的不幸——父母关系不合，被人嗤笑，被父亲强暴——都是因为自己没有长那样一双美丽的蓝色眼睛。对蓝色眼睛的歇斯底里式的渴望最终使佩克拉神志不清，精神分裂，而在这癫狂的状态中，她觉得自己终于拥有了一双最蓝的眼睛。从社会意义上来说，《最蓝的眼睛》通过佩克拉的毁灭和克劳迪娅的成长故事，"一是要唤起黑人的自省和改变自我命运的勇气，二是要唤起整个社会对改善黑人成长环境的思索"[2]。从美学意义上来说，《最蓝的眼睛》从叙事视角、叙事结构、叙事时间和叙事语言为族裔女性成长小说进行了全方位的探索，极大地丰富了族裔女性成长小说的叙事手段，解构了性别/种族二元对立的局限和破坏性，并将"成长小说带入了众声喧哗之境"[3]。

这个"众声喧哗之境"的最高境界当然是艾丽斯·沃克和她创作的以《紫色》为代表的一系列以黑人女性成长为焦点的小说。沃克的小说之所以流行并区别于很多族裔女性作家的文学创作，主要原因在于她坚决地在女性视角中引入了历史、文化等厚重的因素。这种文学写作策略使得她的女性人物"凭着因对历史的感知而产生的一种时间的透

---

1 Taylor-Guthrie, Danille, ed. *Conversations with Toni Morrison*. Jackson: University Press of Mississippi, 1994. 88.
2 芮渝萍，《美国成长小说研究》。北京：中国社会科学出版社，2004年，第284页。
3 李晶菁，《女性成长小说：文类、性别、主体之对话》，《研究与动态》，2004年第10期，第64页。

明度而相互审视——隔着一扇窗户而不是一面不透明的自恋之镜"。因此，沃克将非裔女性的"唯我论的自我审视变成了感情移入和同胞之情"以及一种"带来转变的力量"。《紫色》就是这样一部在女作家独特的历史视角的介入下写就的女性成长小说。沃克本人对于《紫色》的创作曾经这样写道：

> 我……当初就知道《紫色》会成为一部历史小说，而且想到这一点我就不禁笑起来……一位男性黑人批评家说他曾听说我有一天要写一部历史小说，而且接着说了一句话，大致意思是：老天爷保佑，但愿我们见不到这样一本书。我之所以笑，是因为（他会说）我写的"历史"女人气，这部历史不是从获取土地或是生儿育女、沙场鏖战以及伟人之死写起，而是从一个女人向另一个女人索要内衣写起。[1]

《紫色》的确就是这样一部在女性之间亲密关系的形成和发展中书写的黑人女性成长的历史。女主人公西丽亚（Celie）十四岁时被继父强暴，生下的两个孩子也被强行送人了。已经失去了生育能力的西丽亚不知向谁倾诉，她发泄感情的唯一途径就是给上帝写信。几年后，继父把她嫁给黑人"—"先生。西丽亚在信中有意不提她丈夫的名字，而是以"—"代替，这一细节表明丈夫对她来说完全是一个陌生人。西丽亚承担着繁重的家务，经常被丈夫打骂。不久，西丽亚的妹妹耐蒂（Nettie）为躲避父亲的纠缠逃到她这儿，但被"—"先生赶走。后来她到非洲当传教士，一直给西丽亚写信，但"—"先生把这些信都藏了起来。西丽亚了解实情后，十分气愤。在"—"先生的情人莎格（Shug）的启发帮助下，西丽亚走出家庭做裁缝谋生。继父死后，她继承了家里的一所房子和一家商店，成为经济上独立的女性。"—"先生也逐渐意识到了西丽亚的价值，学会了尊重和善待她。耐蒂带着西丽亚的孩子从非洲回来，与她团聚。

在小说的开端，西丽亚是"作为父权制度的牺牲品"开始写信并讲述自己的故事的。在这本书即将完结之时，她逐渐意识到"上帝并不是男性的强权，而是她周围的美"[2]。这种美最初是莎格传递给她的。在与莎格的温柔恋情中，西丽亚找到了年轻时的感觉和对失去的孩子的那种温柔的情感，同时也从莎格的身上学会了作为女人的魅力和权利。除

---

[1] 转引自萨克文·伯科维奇主编，《剑桥美国文学史第七卷：散文作品1940年—1990年》，孙宏主译。北京：中央编译出版社，2005年，第531页。

[2] 萨克文·伯科维奇主编，《剑桥美国文学史第七卷：散文作品1940年—1990年》，孙宏主译。北京：中央编译出版社，2005年，第530页。

了莎格，西丽亚还发现了一种美，那就是她的故土——非洲大陆，而这一次是通过耐蒂的书信传递给她的。对周围的美的发现使西丽亚经历了精神上的重生。

作为族裔女性成长小说，《紫色》的贡献是多方面的。首先，《紫色》"对黑人妇女摆脱她们的父兄、丈夫或情人所加给她们的伤害，依靠自身的力量和女性间的相互支持求得自我解放，作了迄今为止最为大胆的探索"[1]。其次，书信体的运用使族裔女性成长小说的叙事模式得以融入从理查森开始的书信体小说的传统之中，而沃克对书信体所做的大胆的变异尝试，不但直接体现了女主人公西丽亚的精神成长过程，而且使族裔女性成长小说的叙事模式进一步丰富。再次，《紫色》凸显了非洲裔女性成长小说中的"姐妹情谊"在女性人格的成熟中所起的作用。

从19世纪至今，美国黑人女性成长小说在黑人女作家的笔端日益成熟，不但拥有了大量的读者，也引起了研究者的关注和重视。到了20世纪下半叶，黑人女作家的群体不断壮大——1993年黑人女诗人丽塔·达夫（Rita Dove，1952—）成为美国的桂冠诗人，同年，托妮·莫里森摘得了诺贝尔文学奖的桂冠。美国黑人女作家在书写女性成长的过程中，自身也在悄然地成长，并逐渐走向成熟。

美国印第安成长小说

印第安人是北美大陆最早的居民。在哥伦布和他的探险者们踏上这块神奇的大陆之前，他们已经繁衍生息了两万多年。印第安人不但创造了辉煌的文化，而且形成了悠久的口头文学传统。印第安人的这些口头文学世代相传，反复咏诵，在白人的英语文学统治北美大陆之前一直处于主流地位。可以说，印第安文学是"美国文学不可分割的一部分，没有它就没有真正的美国文学史"[2]。尽管随着白人文化的蛀蚀，印第安口头文学受到了毁灭性的破坏，但"白人对印第安土地的侵占和其后的印第安子女在白人开办的学校里受教育，美国印第安土著作家也随之产生了"[3]。而美国印第安文学也如涅槃的凤凰，从此开始了"转型和再生"的发展阶段[4]。经过长时期的艰难探索，美国印第安作家经历了复杂的心路历程，并最终向着印第安传统回归。1969年，莫马代（N. Scott Momaday,

---

1 吴元迈主编，《20世纪外国文学史第一卷：世纪之交的外国文学》。南京：译林出版社，2004年，第60页。
2 埃默里·埃利奥特主编，《哥伦比亚美国文学史》，朱通伯等译。成都：四川辞书出版社，1994年，第5页。
3 Wiget, Andrew, ed. *Dictionary of Native American Literature*. Boston: Twayne Publishers, 1985. 145.
4 朱振武等，《美国小说本土化的多元因素》。上海：上海外语教育出版社，2006年，第2页。

1934— ）的小说《黎明之屋》（*House Made of Dawn*）的出版标志着印第安文学向主流文学经典的迈进，有越来越多的印第安作家跻身经典作家的行列。

美国印第安文学中的一个重要主题就是关于个人身份的追索和定位，这一主题在美国印第安文艺复兴时期的文学作品中尤其得到了强化：孤独的男主人公在主流社会生活一段时间之后，重返保留地，意识到两个世界之间的差异，从而对自己的多元种族身份有了新的理解。美国印第安人被同化和文化转化是欧洲移民和基督教传播的直接结果；自1879年始建立的印第安寄宿学校强制要求把印第安人送到寄宿学校进行教化。

谢尔曼·阿莱克西（Sherman Alexie，1966— ）的成长小说《飞逸》（*Flight*）和《一个印第安少年的超真实日记》（*The Absolutely True Diary of a Part-Time Indian*）均是美国印第安成长小说中的代表性作品。《一个印第安少年的超真实日记》发表于2007年。故事讲述了一个印第安少年阿诺德（Arnold Spirit, Jr.）离开毫无希望的印第安人居留地，转学到附近一所白人学校去寻求他希望的生活。最初离开居留地的时候，他被印第安部落族人视为叛徒，而白人世界他也无法融入，为此他曾十分彷徨、焦虑；但最终，阿诺德因为优良的品行，不仅得到了部落族人的谅解，也逐渐被美国白人社会所接纳。这部小说是以作者个人真实经历为基础的，很多故事情节都曾实际发生过。阿诺德走出保留地并且赢得白人社会和印第安部落的双重认同，除了依靠个体所具有的品质和能力之外，还在于他顺应了印第安部落和白人社会共同的交流愿望和种族融合的理想。

在印第安文学的发展过程中，男性作家和女性作家一直齐头并进，并肩作战，共同奏响了印第安文学的美妙音符。究其原因，恐怕与很多印第安部族崇尚的女性中心传统不无关系。在印第安传统文化中，女性往往扮演着部落、家族的领袖或是精神领袖的角色。印第安很多神话传说故事都清楚地表明，女性神祇在神的谱系中享有崇高的地位，如拉克纳-普纬布洛人的"蜘蛛女"、玛雅文化中的"光之母"、那瓦霍人的"变形女"等。不过，不可否认的是，殖民化进程摧毁了印第安女性固有的价值和地位，正如印第安裔女评论家波拉·甘·艾伦（Paula Gunn Allen，1939—2008）所言："土著妇女依然必须应对一个事实，一个更难于注意或讲述的事实：如果公众和个人视美国印第安人这一群体是隐形的话，那么印第安妇女则根本不存在。"[1]

印第安女性作家的写作经历了"女性意识萌芽"（1890年至1970年）和"女性身份书写"（1970年至今）两个阶段，而这两个阶段与印第安女性的成长是一致的。"事实上，

---

[1] Allen, Paula. *The Sacred Hoop: Recovering the Feminine in American Indian Traditions*. Boston: Beacon Press, 1986. 9.

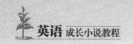

一些本土女作家早在19世纪就已经把文学当作武器了。到了20世纪，美国本土女作家尽其所能去跨越过去与现在、传统与现代之间的界限。"[1]可见，对于印第安女作家来说，文学书写也是她们钟情地为自我、为族群战斗的武器，这一点与非裔女性作家是不谋而合的。

现存的最早由印第安妇女创作的小说是索菲亚·艾丽斯·卡拉汉（S. Alice Callahan, 1868—1894）的《森林之子瓦妮玛》(*Wynema: A Child of the Forest*)，这标志着印第安女性用英语创作文学作品的开始。有趣的是，印第安女性创作的第一部小说就是一部典型的女性成长教育小说。小说讲述了少女瓦妮玛（Wynema Harjo）的成长历程，并通过瓦妮玛与她的白人老师威尔（Genevieve Weir）之间的文化冲突，凸显了瓦妮玛信奉的印第安女性中心与威尔所秉承的白人文化男性中心之间的冲突。而真正被认为是印第安女性经典之作的小说是莫尔·达夫（Mourning Dove, 1888—1936）[又名胡米苏玛（Hum-ishu-ma），或克莱斯德尔·昆塔斯科特（Christine Quintasket）]于1927年出版的《科金维，一个混血儿》(*Cogewea, the Half Blood*)。莫尔·达夫被认为是"第二位将印第安民族日常生活的方方面面、口头传统和宗教信仰等各方面都融入小说创作的美国印第安小说家"[2]。作为印第安女作家，莫尔·达夫对文学的贡献在于她首次引入了"印第安混血儿"这一主题。混血儿科金维（Cogewea）一直徘徊在两种文化之间，她既尊重印第安传统价值理念，也迷恋现代美国人的生活方式。这种犹疑与徘徊在很大程度上是由她的混血儿身份所带来的。莫尔·达夫所确立的"混血儿寻求自我位置的主题"成为"美国印第安小说在20世纪30年代和40年代占主导地位的小说主题"[3]，她也为印第安女性成长小说的发展拓宽了题材的范围，并因此被尊为"美国印第安文艺复兴的文学之母"[4]。这一阶段的印第安女性成长小说与印第安女性的成长一样处于萌芽的状态，她们还没有形成属于自己的文学语言和文学思维模式，只能用"'敌人的语言'书写自己的故事"[5]。面对强大的白人文化风卷残云般地侵入，她们所能做的就是"倾力展现本族文化的光辉传统，试图让白人改变对印第安人的偏见，从而改写印第安人的刻板形

---

1 李美华，《当代美国女性文学述评》，《外国文学研究》，2003年第3期，第153页。

2 Wiget, Andrew, ed. *Dictionary of Native American Literature*. Boston: Twayne Publishers, 1985. 259.

3 Allen, Paula, ed. *Studies in American Indian Literature: Critical Essays and Course Design*. New York: Modern Language Association of America, 1983. 162.

4 朱振武等，《美国小说本土化的多元因素》，上海：上海外语教育出版社，2006年，第11页。

5 刘玉，《美国印第安女性文学述评》，《当代外国文学》，2007年第3期，第93页。

象"[1],因此,这一时期印第安女性书写的假想读者是白人,关注的是白人读者的喜好和价值取向。从这个角度来说,印第安女性的成长是很难在这样亦步亦趋的文学书写中构建起来的。

从 20 世纪 60 年代末开始,印第安女性作家开始关注种族和性别的双重书写,并把创作重心放在了历史和现实的互动与关联上。在这一时期,女性作家开始关注女性身份意识的构建,而印第安民族悠久的历史和伟大的传统则成为她们得天独厚的写作资源。这一时期涌现出了一大批优秀的印第安女性作家;1995 年出版的《青烟升起:北美印第安人文学大全》共收录了 37 位优秀的当代印第安作家,而女性作家居然有 17 位,这一数字清楚地表明印第安女性作家群在印第安文学中的分量。这其中比较有代表性的有莱斯利·马蒙·西尔科(Leslie Marmon Silko,1948—)、波拉·甘·艾伦、路易斯·厄德里奇(Louise Erdrich,1954—)、琳达·霍根(Linda Hogan,1947—)、伊丽莎白·库克琳恩(Elizabeth Cook-Lynn,1930—)、温迪·罗丝(Wendy Rose,1948—)、格洛丽亚·波德(Gloria Bird,1951—)、雪莉·西尔·韦特(Shirley Hill Witt,1934—)等。这些女作家来自不同的印第安部落,有着不尽相同的生活经历和教育背景,然而,"她们同样开始在自己的作品中表达一种更加清晰的女性自己的声音,对过去存在的以及现在才出现的一些已成定论的有关本土女性的论断发出了挑战"[2]。印第安文化传统成为她们的挑战的永不枯竭的源泉。这其中,对印第安女性成长的书写最为成功的作家是西尔科。

从 1969 年至今,西尔科出版了《典仪》(*Ceremony*)、《死者年鉴》(*Almanac of the Dead*)、《沙丘花园》(*Gardens in the Dunes*)三部长篇小说和大量短篇小说。同时,她还是文学创作的多面手,在诗歌、散文等领域也颇有建树。从血统上说,西尔科的身世很是不同寻常。她的身上有印第安人、墨西哥人和美洲白人三种不同的血统,然而在印第安拉古纳保留地的生活经历才是她真正的身份认同之根。边缘化的身份和生活使西尔科立志书写一种新型的民族故事,一种将印第安口头文学与书面文本编织在一起的新型故事。她清楚地意识到,只有这样,才既能够使口头文学借助新的文本焕发新的生命力,又能使新的文学文本在古老的部落传说中唤起读者古老的民族记忆,从而使现当代少数族裔作家的作品在民族文化中占有一席之地。这实际上一直是美国少数族裔作家们的一个心结。西尔科对此给出的回答是颇具代表性的:

---

[1] 刘玉,《美国印第安女性文学述评》,《当代外国文学》,2007 年第 3 期,第 93 页。
[2] 李美华,《当代美国女性文学述评》,《外国文学研究》,2003 年第 3 期,第 153 页。

当我讲故事时，我的意思绝不仅仅是指坐在那儿，讲一个那种总是以"很久很久以前"开头的老故事。我所说的讲故事，是指一种如何看待你自己、你周围的人、你的生活和在更为广阔的背景下看待你在生活中所处的位置的方式。而所谓的背景不仅仅是指你在自然中的位置，还包括你所经历过的，以及在别人身上发生过的事情。[1]

这段话解释了西尔科所定义的故事之间"相互联系的力量"，体现了讲故事的可能性正是理解人类经验的可能性的文学伦理功能，也表达了她探索新型民族故事的远大文学理想。西尔科的新型民族故事关注的是个体体验与民族记忆的关系，个体文化身份的寻求与民族身份重塑的关系，是个体的生命体验穿越了历史时空的超越，总之，是一种充满了口头文学和书面文字互动力量的新型故事。《讲故事的人》(*Storyteller*)中的代表性作品《黄女人》("Yellow Woman")就是集中体现西尔科新型民族故事理念的精致的短篇。故事的主人公是一名来自"高地那边的普韦布洛"的女人，我们不知道她的名字，只知道她被刚刚认识的男人称为"黄女人"。就像《莫比·迪克》的开篇，故事讲述人的那一句"叫我伊斯梅尔吧"而开启的自我寻求的漫长的海上旅程一样，《黄女人》中女主人公被冠以"黄女人"的名字清晰地告诉我们，这似乎又是一个老生常谈的自我寻求的故事。不错，这个故事将满足这类故事的一切基本因素。然而，这似乎并不能概括这个故事的全部。故事中细密编织的印第安部落传说和精心构建的充满印第安典仪色彩的情节不断地唤起读者对古老的印第安民族文化的遥远记忆，以及对"黄女人"故事的深层思考。不难看出，西尔科对印第安女性的成长是十分关注的，并成功地寻找到了一种将印第安历史、印第安神话和社会现实融为一体的女性成长小说的叙事模式。

西尔科的堂姐波拉·甘·艾伦也是一位创作成长小说的高手。她耗时十余年创作的《拥有阴影的女人》(*The Woman Who Owned the Shadows*)就是一部女性成长小说。小说沿袭了莫尔·达夫所确立的混血儿身份意义追寻的主题。主人公伊法妮·阿顿修(Ephanie Atencio)是西班牙和印第安血统的混血儿，在父权的压制下，在对混血儿和对同性恋的排斥的氛围中，伊法妮·阿顿修逐渐迷失了自我，她自暴自弃地试图结束自己的生命。当她最后一次试图自杀时，她与印第安神话中的蜘蛛女始祖相遇，并在她的引领下，走出了被心魔困住的心灵之域，重新找回自我的价值和位置。"《拥有阴影的女人》真切地描绘出伊法妮在现代物质社会里追寻自我、身份的艰难历程，深刻地反思

---

1 Barnes, Kim. "A Leslie Marmon Silko Interview." *"Yellow Woman": Leslie Marmon Silko*. Ed. Melody Graulich. New Brunswick: Rutgers University Press, 1993. 49–50.

了20世纪印第安妇女如何被主流文化、欧美女性主义以及印第安社会男权思想逐步边缘化的事实。"[1]

说到印第安女作家，有一位是不能不被提及的，那就是路易斯·厄德里奇（Louise Erdrich）。与西尔科和艾伦不同，厄德里奇似乎对印第安民族痛苦的记忆不感兴趣。1984年，她的小说《爱药》（*Love Medicine*）获得了"全国图书评论奖"，从此声名鹊起。她的小说构思精巧，布局谋篇讲究，叙事策略新颖独特，对文字精雕细刻，具有很强的艺术性。同时，"她的小说不但符合现当代印第安书面小说的传统，而且也符合在这片土地上一直沿袭下来的口头文学的传统"[2]。从《爱药》开始，她一发不可收地连续发表了《甜菜女王》（*The Beet Queen*）、《足迹》（*Tracks*）、《宾戈宫》（*The Bingo Palace*）等多部小说，从多个层面描写了当代印第安人，尤其是印第安女性的生活，折射出了印第安家庭、族群之间，以及印第安人与白人之间的错综复杂的关系。厄德里奇关注的更多的是印第安人当代的现实生活，而她笔下的印第安民族少了些悲壮和沉重，多了些幽默和轻松，这似乎预示着印第安女性文学的一个转向。

拓展阅读文献

Feng, Pin-chia. *The Female Bildungsroman by Toni Morrison and Maxine Hong Kingston: A Postmodern Reading*. New York: Peter Lang Publishing, 1998.

Japtok, Martin. *Growing up Ethnic: Nationalism and the Bildungsroman in African American and Jewish American Fiction*. Iowa: University of Iowa Press, 2005.

---

1 刘玉，《美国印第安女性文学述评》，《当代外国文学》，2007年，第3期，第95页。
2 Wiget, Andrew, ed. *Dictionary of Native American Literature*. New York: Garland, 1994. 428.

Lecture 13
Ralph Ellison

Profile of the Writer

Ralph Waldo Ellison
(1914–1994)

On March 1, 1914, Ralph Waldo Ellison was born in Oklahoma City, Oklahoma, to Lewis Alfred Ellison, a construction foreman and the former Ida Milsap, a church stewardess. At age 18, he attended Tuskegee Institute in Montgomery, Alabama, and then studied music from 1933 to 1936. Ellison worked at a variety of jobs including janitor, shoeshine boy, jazz musician, and freelance photographer. In 1936 Ellison moved to New York and met Richard Wright and Langston Hughes, which led to his first attempts at fiction and prompted his move to Harlem where he lived for more than 40 years with his wife, Fanny McConnell.

Soon after his move to New York in 1936, his book reviews, short stories, and articles began to appear in numerous magazines and anthologies, and Ellison was on his way to becoming an acclaimed author. As a renowned novelist, short-story writer, and critic, Ellison taught at several colleges and universities and lectured extensively at such prestigious institutions as Yale University. On April 16, 1994, Ellison died of cancer, at his home in New York City.

During the summer of 1945, when Ellison visited friends in Vermont, the opening lines of *Invisible Man* came to him, an entirely different novel from the ones he created before. *Invisible Man* was published in 1952, "a novel about innocence and human error, a struggle through illusion to reality", and a "portrait of the artist as rabble-rouser", as Ellison described. Responding to questions concerning the narrator's journey as a reflection of the black struggle for justice and equality, Ellison contended that he is "not concerned with injustice, but with art", pointing out that there is "no dichotomy between art and protest".

Ellison became known primarily for *Invisible Man*, which won the National Book Award and established him as one of the most important American authors of the twentieth century. His nonfiction works, *Shadow and Act* (1964) and *Going to the Territory* (1986), together with numerous unpublished speeches and writings, were published in 1995 as *The Collected Essays of Ralph Ellison*. He also wrote numerous short stories—including "King of the Bingo Game", "That I Had the Wings", and "Flying Home"—published posthumously in 1996 as *Flying Home and Other Stories*.

Henry Louis Gates Jr., a renowned author and critic, once wrote that Ellison, Richard Wright (1908–1960) and James Baldwin (1924–1987) comprised "the holy male trinity of the black tradition". Wright, most famous for his protest novel *Native Son*, was known for depicting blacks as oppressed victims of white society; Baldwin, best known for his nonfiction works such as *Notes of a Native Son,* and *Nobody Knows My Name*, focused on religious themes and "blackness as salvation". But Ellison, who saw blackness as a metaphor for the human condition, transcended the theme of race by incorporating mythological and supernatural elements into his works. *Invisible Man* explores the narrator's attempt to cope with racism and segregation and to make sense of a society in which both the oppressed and the oppressor become victims of their blindness concerning American identity and the true brotherhood of humanity. Consequently, Ellison is renowned not only as an author and the master of black vernacular, but as an astute commentator on literature, culture, and race.

Preview Questions

1. Beginning with slave narratives, the "running man" is a key theme in black folklore and literature. How does Ellison incorporate this theme into *Invisible Man*?

2. Listen to the song "To Be Invisible" by Curtis Mayfield, included in his musical anthology, *People Get Ready: The Curtis Mayfield Story*. Then explore how the song lyrics reflect the theme of *Invisible Man*.

II. Literary Reading: *Invisible Man* (Chapter 1)

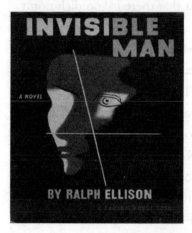

It goes a long way back, some twenty years. All my life I had been looking for something, and everywhere I turned someone tried to tell me what it was. I accepted their answers too, though they were often in contradiction and even self-contradictory. I was naïve. I was looking for myself and asking everyone except myself questions which I, and only I, could answer. It took me a long time and much painful boomeranging of my expectations to achieve a realization everyone else appears to have been born with: That I am nobody but myself. But first I had to discover that I am an invisible man!

And yet I am no freak of nature, nor of history. I was in the cards, other things having been equal (or unequal) eighty-five years ago. I am not ashamed of my grandparents for having been slaves. I am only ashamed of myself for having at one time been ashamed. About eighty-five years ago they were told that they were free, united with others of our country in everything pertaining to the common good, and, in everything social, separate like the fingers of the hand. And they believed it. They exulted in it. They stayed in their place, worked hard, and brought up my father to do the same. But my grandfather is the one. He was an odd old guy, my grandfather, and I am told I take after him. It was he who caused the trouble. On his deathbed he called my father to him and said, "Son, after I'm gone I want you to keep up the good fight. I never told you, but our life is a war and I have been a traitor all my born days, a spy in the enemy's country ever since I give up my gun back in the Reconstruction. Live with your head in the lion's mouth. I want you to overcome 'em with yeses, undermine 'em with grins, agree 'em to death and destruction, let 'em swoller you till they vomit or bust wide open." They thought the old man had gone out of his mind. He had been the meekest of men. The younger children were rushed from the room, the shades drawn and the flame of the lamp turned so low that it sputtered on the wick like the old man's breathing. "Learn it to the younguns," he whispered fiercely; then he died.

But my folks were more alarmed over his last words than over his dying. It was as though he had not died at all, his words caused so much anxiety. I was warned emphatically to forget what he had said and, indeed, this is the first time it has been mentioned outside the family circle. It had a tremendous effect upon me, however. I could never be sure of what he meant. Grandfather had been a quiet old man who never made any trouble, yet on his deathbed he had called himself a traitor and a spy, and he had spoken of his meekness as a dangerous activity. It became a constant puzzle which lay unanswered in the back of my mind. And whenever things went well for me I remembered my grandfather and felt guilty and uncomfortable. It was as though I was carrying out his advice in spite of myself. And to make it worse, everyone loved me for it. I was praised by the most lily-white men of the town. I was considered an example of desirable conduct—just as my grandfather had been. And what puzzled me was that the old man had defined it as treachery. When I was praised for my conduct I felt a guilt that in some way I was doing something that was really against the wishes of the white folks, that if they had understood they would have desired me to act just the opposite, that I should have been sulky and mean, and that that really would have been what they wanted, even though they were fooled and thought they wanted me to act as I did. It made me afraid that some day they would look upon me as a traitor and I would be lost. Still I was more afraid to act any other way because they didn't like that at all. The old man's words were like a curse. On my graduation day I delivered an oration in which I showed that humility was the secret, indeed, the very essence of progress. (Not that I believed this—how could I, remembering my grandfather?—I only believed that it worked.) It was a great success. Everyone praised me and I was invited to give the speech at a gathering of the town's leading white citizens. It was a triumph for our whole community.

It was in the main ballroom of the leading hotel. When I got there I discovered that it was on the occasion of a smoker, and I was told that since I was to be there anyway I might as well take part in the battle royal to be fought by some of my schoolmates as part of the entertainment. The battle royal came first.

All of the town's big shots were there in their tuxedoes, wolfing down the buffet foods, drinking beer and whiskey and smoking black cigars. It was a large room with a high ceiling. Chairs were arranged in neat rows around three sides of a portable boxing ring. The fourth side was clear, revealing a gleaming space of polished floor. I had some misgivings over the battle royal, by the way. Not from a distaste for fighting, but because I didn't care too much for the other fellows who were to take part. They were tough guys who seemed to have no grandfather's curse worrying their minds. No one could mistake their toughness. And besides, I suspected that fighting a battle royal might detract from the dignity of my speech. In those pre-invisible days I visualized myself as a potential Booker T. Washington. But the other fellows didn't care too much for me either, and there were nine of them. I felt superior to them in my way, and I didn't like the manner in which we were all crowded together into the servants' elevator. Nor did they like my being there. In fact, as the warmly lighted floors flashed past the elevator we had words over the fact that I, by taking part in the fight, had knocked one of their friends out of a night's work.

    We were led out of the elevator through a rococo hall into an anteroom and told to get into our fighting togs. Each of us was issued a pair of boxing gloves and ushered out into the big mirrored hall, which we entered looking cautiously about us and whispering, lest we might accidentally be heard above the noise of the room. It was foggy with cigar smoke. And already the whiskey was taking effect. I was shocked to see some of the most important men of the town quite tipsy. They were all there—bankers, lawyers, judges, doctors, fire chiefs, teachers, merchants. Even one of the more fashionable pastors. Something we could not see was going on up front. A clarinet was vibrating sensuously and the men were standing up and moving eagerly forward. We were a small tight group, clustered together, our bare upper bodies touching and shining with anticipatory sweat; while up front the big shots were becoming increasingly excited over something we still could not see. Suddenly I heard the school superintendent, who had told me to come, yell, "Bring up the shines, gentlemen! Bring up the little shines!"

    We were rushed up to the front of the ballroom, where it smelled even more strongly of tobacco and whiskey. Then we were pushed into place. I almost wet my pants. A sea of faces, some hostile, some amused, ringed around us, and in the center, facing us, stood a magnificent blonde—stark naked. There was dead silence. I felt a blast of cold air chill me. I tried to back away, but they were behind me and around me. Some of the boys stood with lowered heads, trembling. I felt a wave of irrational guilt and fear. My teeth chattered, my skin turned to goose flesh, my knees knocked. Yet I was strongly attracted and looked in spite of myself. Had the price of looking been blindness, I would have looked. The hair was yellow like that of a circus kewpie doll, the face heavily powdered and rouged, as though to form an abstract mask, the eyes hollow and smeared a cool blue, the color of a baboon's butt. I felt a desire to spit upon her as my eyes brushed slowly over her body. Her breasts were firm and round as the domes of East Indian temples, and I stood so close as to see the fine skin texture and beads of pearly perspiration glistening like dew around the pink and erected buds of her nipples. I wanted at one and the same time to run from the room, to sink through the floor, or go to her and cover her from my eyes and the eyes of the others with my body; to feel the soft thighs, to caress her and destroy her, to love her and murder her, to hide from her, and yet to stroke where below the small American flag tattooed upon her belly her thighs formed a capital V. I had a notion that of all in the room she saw only me with her impersonal eyes.

    And then she began to dance, a slow sensuous movement; the smoke of a hundred cigars clinging to her like the thinnest of veils. She seemed like a fair bird-girl girdled

Lecture 13
Ralph Ellison

in veils calling to me from the angry surface of some gray and threatening sea. I was transported. Then I became aware of the clarinet playing and the big shots yelling at us. Some threatened us if we looked and others if we did not. On my right I saw one boy faint. And now a man grabbed a silver pitcher from a table and stepped close as he dashed ice water upon him and stood him up and forced two of us to support him as his head hung and moans issued from his thick bluish lips. Another boy began to plead to go home. He was the largest of the group, wearing dark red fighting trunks much too small to conceal the erection which projected from him as though in answer to the insinuating low-registered moaning of the clarinet. He tried to hide himself with his boxing gloves.

And all the while the blonde continued dancing, smiling faintly at the big shots who watched her with fascination, and faintly smiling at our fear. I noticed a certain merchant who followed her hungrily, his lips loose and drooling. He was a large man who wore diamond studs in a shirtfront which swelled with the ample paunch underneath, and each time the blonde swayed her undulating hips he ran his hand through the thin hair of his bald head and, with his arms upheld, his posture clumsy like that of an intoxicated panda, wound his belly in a slow and obscene grind. This creature was completely hypnotized. The music had quickened. As the dancer flung herself about with a detached expression on her face, the men began reaching out to touch her. I could see their beefy fingers sink into the soft flesh. Some of the others tried to stop them and she began to move around the floor in graceful circles, as they gave chase, slipping and sliding over the polished floor. It was mad. Chairs went crashing, drinks were spilt, as they ran laughing and howling after her. They caught her just as she reached a door, raised her from the floor, and tossed her as college boys are tossed at a hazing, and above her red, fixed-smiling lips I saw the terror and disgust in her eyes, almost like my own terror and that which I saw in some of the other boys. As I watched, they tossed her twice and her soft breasts seemed to flatten against the air and her legs flung wildly as she spun. Some of the more sober ones helped her to escape. And I started off the floor, heading for the anteroom with the rest of the boys.

Some were still crying and in hysteria. But as we tried to leave we were stopped and ordered to get into the ring. There was nothing to do but what we were told. All ten of us climbed under the ropes and allowed ourselves to be blindfolded with broad bands of white cloth. One of the men seemed to feel a bit sympathetic and tried to cheer us up as we stood with our backs against the ropes. Some of us tried to grin. "See that boy over there?" one of the men said. "I want you to run across at the bell and give it to him right in the belly. If you don't get him, I'm going to get you. I don't like his looks." Each of us was told the same. The blindfolds were put on. Yet even then I had been going over my speech. In my mind each word was as bright as flame. I felt the cloth pressed into place, and frowned so that it would be loosened when I relaxed.

But now I felt a sudden fit of blind terror. I was unused to darkness. It was as though I had suddenly found myself in a dark room filled with poisonous cottonmouths. I could hear the bleary voices yelling insistently for the battle royal to begin.

"Get going in there!"

"Let me at that big nigger!"

I strained to pick up the school superintendent's voice, as though to squeeze some security out of that slightly more familiar sound.

"Let me at those black sonsabitches!" someone yelled.

"No, Jackson, no!" another voice yelled. "Here, somebody, help me hold Jack."

"I want to get at that ginger-colored nigger. Tear him limb from limb," the first voice yelled.

I stood against the ropes trembling. For in those days I was what they called ginger-colored, and he sounded as though he might crunch me between his teeth like a crisp ginger cookie.

Quite a struggle was going on. Chairs were being kicked about and I could hear voices grunting as with a terrific effort. I wanted to see, to see more desperately than ever before. But the blindfold was as tight as a thick skin-puckering scab and when I raised my gloved hands to push the layers of white aside a voice yelled, "Oh, no you don't, black bastard! Leave that alone!"

"Ring the bell before Jackson kills him a coon!" someone boomed in the sudden silence. And I heard the bell clang and the sound of the feet scuffling forward.

A glove smacked against my head. I pivoted, striking out stiffly as someone went past, and felt the jar ripple along the length of my arm to my shoulder. Then it seemed as though all nine of the boys had turned upon me at once. Blows pounded me from all sides while I struck out as best I could. So many blows landed upon me that I wondered if I were not the only blindfolded fighter in the ring, or if the man called Jackson hadn't succeeded in getting me after all.

Blindfolded, I could no longer control my motions. I had no dignity. I stumbled about like a baby or a drunken man. The smoke had become thicker and with each new blow it seemed to sear and further restrict my lungs. My saliva became like hot bitter glue. A glove connected with my head, filling my mouth with warm blood. It was everywhere. I could not tell if the moisture I felt upon my body was sweat or blood. A blow landed hard against the nape of my neck. I felt myself going over, my head hitting the floor. Streaks of blue light filled the black world behind the blindfold. I lay prone, pretending that I was knocked out, but felt myself seized by hands and yanked to my feet. "Get going, black boy! Mix it up!"

Lecture 13
Ralph Ellison

My arms were like lead, my head smarting from blows. I managed to feel my way to the ropes and held on, trying to catch my breath. A glove landed in my mid-section and I went over again, feeling as though the smoke had become a knife jabbed into my guts. Pushed this way and that by the legs milling around me, I finally pulled erect and discovered that I could see the black, sweat-washed forms weaving in the smoky-blue atmosphere like drunken dancers weaving to the rapid drum-like thuds of blows.

Everyone fought hysterically. It was complete anarchy. Everybody fought everybody else. No group fought together for long. Two, three, four, fought one, then turned to fight each other, were themselves attacked. Blows landed below the belt and in the kidney, with the gloves open as well as closed, and with my eye partly opened now there was not so much terror. I moved carefully, avoiding blows, although not too many to attract attention, fighting from group to group. The boys groped about like blind, cautious crabs crouching to protect their mid-sections, their heads pulled in short against their shoulders, their arms stretched nervously before them, with their fists testing the smoke-filled air like the knobbed feelers of hypersensitive snails. In one corner I glimpsed a boy violently punching the air and heard him scream in pain as he smashed his hand against a ring post. For a second I saw him bent over holding his hand, then going down as a blow caught his unprotected head. I played one group against the other, slipping in and throwing a punch then stepping out of range while pushing the others into the melee to take the blows blindly aimed at me. The smoke was agonizing and there were no rounds, no bells at three minute intervals to relieve our exhaustion. The room spun round me, a swirl of lights, smoke, sweating bodies surrounded by tense white faces. I bled from both nose and mouth, the blood spattering upon my chest.

The men kept yelling, "Slug him, black boy! Knock his guts out!"

"Uppercut him! Kill him! Kill that big boy!"

Taking a fake fall, I saw a boy going down heavily beside me as though we were felled by a single blow, saw a sneaker-clad foot shoot into his groin as the two who had knocked him down stumbled upon him. I rolled out of range, feeling a twinge of nausea.

The harder we fought the more threatening the men became. And yet, I had begun to worry about my speech again. How would it go? Would they recognize my ability? What would they give me?

I was fighting automatically when suddenly I noticed that one after another of the boys was leaving the ring. I was surprised, filled with panic, as though I had been left alone with an unknown danger. Then I understood. The boys had arranged it among themselves. It was the custom for the two men left in the ring to slug it out for the winner's prize. I discovered this too late. When the bell sounded two men in tuxedoes leaped into the ring and removed the blindfold. I found myself facing Tatlock, the biggest of the gang. I felt sick at my stomach. Hardly had the bell stopped ringing in my ears than it clanged again and I saw him moving swiftly toward me. Thinking of nothing else to do I hit him smash on the nose. He kept coming, bringing the rank sharp violence of stale sweat. His face was a black blank of a face, only his eyes alive—with hate of me and aglow with a feverish terror from what had happened to us all. I became anxious. I wanted to deliver my speech and he came at me as though he meant to beat it out of me. I smashed him again and again, taking his blows as they came. Then on a sudden impulse I struck him lightly and as we clinched, I whispered, "Fake like I knocked you out, you can have the prize."

"I'll break your behind," he whispered hoarsely.

"For them?"

"For me, sonofabitch!"

They were yelling for us to break it up and Tatlock spun me half around with a blow, and as a joggled camera sweeps in a reeling scene, I saw the howling red faces crouching tense beneath the cloud of blue-gray smoke. For a moment the world wavered, unraveled, flowed, then my head cleared and Tatlock bounced before me. That fluttering shadow before my eyes was his jabbing left hand. Then falling forward, my head against his damp shoulder, I whispered,

"I'll make it five dollars more."

"Go to hell!"

But his muscles relaxed a trifle beneath my pressure and I breathed, "Seven?"

"Give it to your ma," he said, ripping me beneath the heart.

And while I still held him I butted him and moved away. I felt myself bombarded with punches. I fought back with hopeless desperation. I wanted to deliver my speech more than anything else in the world, felt that only these men could judge truly my ability, and now this stupid clown was ruining my chances. I began fighting carefully now, moving in to punch him and out again with my greater speed. A lucky blow to his chin and I had him going too—until I heard a loud voice yell, "I got my money on the big boy."

Hearing this, I almost dropped my guard. I was confused: Should I try to win against the voice out there? Would not this go against my speech, and was not this a moment for humility, for nonresistance? A blow to my head as I danced about sent my right eye popping like a jack-in-the-box and settled my dilemma. The room went red as I fell. It was a dream fall, my body languid and fastidious as to where to land, until the floor became impatient and smashed up to meet me. A moment later I came to. An hypnotic voice said FIVE emphatically. And I lay there, hazily watching a dark red spot of my own blood shaping itself into a butterfly, glistening and soaking into the soiled gray world of the canvas.

Lecture 13
Ralph Ellison

When the voice drawled TEN I was lifted up and dragged to a chair. I sat dazed. My eye pained and swelled with each throb of my pounding heart and I wondered if now I would be allowed to speak. I was wringing wet, my mouth still bleeding. We were grouped along the wall now. The other boys ignored me as they congratulated Tatlock and speculated as to how much they would be paid. One boy whimpered over his smashed hand. Looking up front, I saw attendants in white jackets rolling the portable ring away and placing a small square rug in the vacant space surrounded by chairs. Perhaps, I thought, I will stand on the rug to deliver my speech.

Then the M.C. called to us, "Come on up here boys and get your money."

We ran forward to where the men laughed and talked in their chairs, waiting. Everyone seemed friendly now.

"There it is on the rug," the man said. I saw the rug covered with coins of all dimensions and a few crumpled bills. But what excited me, scattered here and there, were the gold pieces.

"Boys, it's all yours," the man said. "You get all you grab."

"That's right, Sambo," a blond man said, winking at me confidentially.

I trembled with excitement, forgetting my pain. I would get the gold and the bills, I thought. I would use both hands. I would throw my body against the boys nearest me to block them from the gold.

"Get down around the rug now," the man commanded, "and don't anyone touch it until I give the signal."

"This ought to be good," I heard.

As told, we got around the square rug on our knees. Slowly the man raised his freckled hand as we followed it upward with our eyes.

I heard, "These niggers look like they're about to pray!"

Then, "Ready," the man said. "Go!"

I lunged for a yellow coin lying on the blue design of the carpet, touching it and sending a surprised shriek to join those rising around me. I tried frantically to remove my hand but could not let go. A hot, violent force tore through my body, shaking me like a wet rat. The rug was electrified. The hair bristled up on my head as I shook myself free. My muscles jumped, my nerves jangled, writhed. But I saw that this was not stopping the other boys. Laughing in fear and embarrassment, some were holding back and scooping up the coins knocked off by the painful contortions of the others. The men roared above us as we struggled.

"Pick it up, goddamnit, pick it up!" someone called like a bass-voiced parrot. "Go on, get it!"

I crawled rapidly around the floor, picking up the coins, trying to avoid the coppers and to get greenbacks and the gold. Ignoring the shock by laughing, as I brushed the coins off quickly, I discovered that I could contain the electricity—a contradiction, but it works. Then the men began to push us onto the rug. Laughing embarrassedly, we struggled out of their hands and kept after the coins. We were all wet and slippery and hard to hold. Suddenly I saw a boy lifted into the air, glistening with sweat like a circus seal, and dropped, his wet back landing flush upon the charged rug, heard him yell and saw him literally dance upon his back, elbows beating a frenzied tattoo upon the floor, his muscles twitching like the flesh of a horse stung my many flies. When he finally rolled off, his face was gray and no one stopped him when he ran from the floor amid booming laughter.

"Get the money," the M. C. called. "That's good hard American cash!"

And we snatched and grabbed, snatched and grabbed. I was careful not to come too close to the rug now, and when I felt the hot whiskey breath descend upon me like a cloud of foul air I reached out and grabbed the leg of a chair. It was occupied and I held on desperately.

"Leggo, nigger! Leggo!"

The huge face wavered down to mine as he tried to push me free. But my body was slippery and he was too drunk. It was Mr. Colcord, who owned a chain of movie houses and "entertainment palaces." Each time he grabbed me I slipped out of his hands. It became a real struggle. I feared the rug more than I did the drunk, so I held on, surprising myself for a moment by trying to topple him upon the rug. It was such an enormous idea that I found myself actually carrying it out. I tried not to be obvious, yet when I grabbed his leg, trying to tumble him out of the chair, he raised up roaring with laughter, and, looking at me with soberness dead in the eye, kicked me viciously in the chest. The chair leg flew out of my hand and I felt myself going and rolled. It was as though I had rolled through a bed of hot coals. It seemed a whole century would pass before I would roll free, a century in which I was seared through the deepest levels of my body to the fearful breath within me and the breath seared and heated to the point of explosion. It'll all be over in a flash, I thought as I rolled clear. It'll all be over in a flash.

But not yet, the men on the other side were waiting, red faces swollen as though from apoplexy as they bent forward in their chairs. Seeing their fingers coming toward me I rolled away as a fumbled football rolls off the receiver's fingertips, back into the coals. That time I luckily sent the rug sliding out of place and heard the coins ringing against the floor and the boys scuffling to pick them up and the M.C. calling, "All right, boys, that's all. Go get dressed and get your money."

I was limp as a dish rag. My back felt as though it had been beaten with wires.

Lecture 13
Ralph Ellison

When we had dressed the M.C. came in and gave us each five dollars, except Tatlock, who got ten for being last in the ring. Then he told us to leave. I was not to get a chance to deliver my speech, I thought. I was going out into the dim alley in despair when I was stopped and told to go back. I returned to the ballroom, where the men were pushing back their chairs and gathering in groups to talk.

The M.C. knocked on a table for quiet. "Gentlemen," he said, "we almost forgot an important part of the program. A most serious part, gentlemen. This boy was brought here to deliver a speech which he made at his graduation yesterday..."

"Bravo!"

"I'm told that he is the smartest boy we've got out there in Greenwood. I'm told that he knows more big words than a pocket-sized dictionary."

Much applause and laughter.

"So now, gentlemen, I want you to give him your attention."

There was still laughter as I faced them, my mouth dry, my eye throbbing. I began slowly, but evidently my throat was tense, because they began shouting, "Louder! Louder!"

"We of the younger generation extol the wisdom of that great leader and educator," I shouted, "who first spoke these flaming words of wisdom: 'A ship lost at sea for many days suddenly sighted a friendly vessel. From the mast of the unfortunate vessel was seen a signal: "Water, water; we die of thirst!" The answer from the friendly vessel came back: "Cast down your bucket where you are." The captain of the distressed vessel, at last heeding the injunction, cast down his bucket, and it came up full of fresh sparkling water from the mouth of the Amazon River.' And like him I say, and in his words, "To those of my race who depend upon bettering their condition in a foreign land, or who underestimate the importance of cultivating friendly relations with the Southern white man, who is his next-door neighbor, I would say: "Cast down your bucket where you are—cast it down in making friends in every manly way of the people of all races by whom we are surrounded..."

I spoke automatically and with such fervor that I did not realize that the men were still talking and laughing until my dry mouth, filling up with blood from the cut, almost strangled me. I coughed, wanting to stop and go to one of the tall brass, sand-filled spittoons to relieve myself, but a few of the men, especially the superintendent, were listening and I was afraid. So I gulped it down, blood, saliva and all, and continued. (What powers of endurance I had during those days! What enthusiasm! What a belief in the rightness of things!) I spoke even louder in spite of the pain. But still they talked and still they laughed, as though deaf with cotton in dirty ears. So I spoke with greater emotional emphasis. I closed my ears and swallowed blood until I was nauseated. The speech seemed a hundred times as long as before, but I could not leave out a single word. All had to be said, each memorized nuance considered, rendered. Nor was that all. Whenever I uttered a word of three or more syllables a group of voices would yell for me to repeat it. I used the phrase "social responsibility" and they yelled:

"What's that word you say, boy?"

"Social responsibility," I said.

"What?"

"Social..."

"Louder."

"... responsibility."

"More!"

"Respon—"

"Repeat!"

"—sibility."

The room filled with the uproar of laughter until, no doubt, distracted by having to gulp down my blood, I made a mistake and yelled a phrase I had often seen denounced in newspaper editorials, heard debated in private.

"Social..."

"What?" they yelled.

"...equality—"

The laughter hung smokelike in the sudden stillness. I opened my eyes, puzzled. Sounds of displeasure filled the room. The M.C. rushed forward. They shouted hostile phrases at me. But I did not understand.

A small dry mustached man in the front row blared out, "Say that slowly, son!"

"What sir?"

"What you just said!"

"Social responsibility, sir," I said.

"You weren't being smart, were you, boy?" he said, not unkindly.

"No, sir!"

"You sure that about 'equality' was a mistake?"

"Oh, yes, sir," I said. "I was swallowing blood."

"Well, you had better speak more slowly so we can understand. We mean to do right by you, but you've got to know your place at all times. All right, now, go on with your speech."

I was afraid. I wanted to leave but I wanted also to speak and I was afraid they'd snatch me down.

"Thank you, sir," I said, beginning where I had left off, and having them ignore me as before.

Yet when I finished there was a thunderous applause. I was surprised to see the superintendent come forth with a package wrapped in white tissue paper, and, gesturing for quiet, address the men.

"Gentlemen, you see that I did not overpraise this boy. He makes a good speech and some day he'll lead his people in the proper paths. And I don't have to tell you that that is important in these days and times. This is a good, smart boy, and so to encourage him in the right direction, in the name of the Board of Education I wish to present him a prize in the form of this..."

He paused, removing the tissue paper and revealing a gleaming calfskin brief case.

"... in the form of this first-class article from Shad Whitmore's shop."

"Boy," he said, addressing me, "take this prize and keep it well. Consider it a badge of office. Prize it. Keep developing as you are and some day it will be filled with important papers that will help shape the destiny of your people."

I was so moved that I could hardly express my thanks. A rope of bloody saliva forming a shape like an undiscovered continent drooled upon the leather and I wiped it quickly away. I felt an importance that I had never dreamed.

"Open it and see what's inside," I was told.

My fingers a-tremble, I complied, smelling the fresh leather and finding an official-looking document inside. It was a scholarship to the state college for Negroes. My eyes filled with tears and I ran awkwardly off the floor.

I was overjoyed; I did not even mind when I discovered that the gold pieces I had scrambled for were brass pocket tokens advertising a certain make of automobile.

When I reached home everyone was excited. Next day the neighbors came to congratulate me. I even felt safe from grandfather, whose deathbed curse usually spoiled my triumphs. I stood beneath his photograph with my brief case in hand and smiled triumphantly into his stolid black peasant's face. It was a face that fascinated me. The eyes seemed to follow everywhere I went.

That night I dreamed I was at a circus with him and that he refused to laugh at the clowns no matter what they did. Then later he told me to open my brief case and read what was inside and I did, finding an official envelope stamped with the state seal; and inside the envelope I found another and another, endlessly, and I thought I would fall of weariness. "Them's years," he said. "Now open that one." And I did and in it I found an engraved document containing a short message in letters of gold. "Read it," my grandfather said. "Out loud."

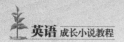

"To Whom It May Concern," I intoned. "Keep This Nigger-Boy Running."

I awoke with the old man's laughter ringing in my ears.

(It was a dream I was to remember and dream again for many years after. But at that time I had no insight into its meaning. First I had to attend college.)

III Thinking, Talking and Writing About Literature

1 Textual Cognition

Make an introductory presentation on the following terms related to this literary work.

1) narrative of ascent

2) wordplay

2 Textual Reading

Search for evidence in the text and answer the following questions.

1) Chapter 1 consists of six key episodes. Please find them.

2) How do you interpret "the calfskin brief case" in the sentence, "He paused, removing the tissue paper and revealing a gleaming calfskin brief case"?

3) What does the narrator's dream in the text symbolize?

3 Critical Reading

Discuss in groups the following questions to further explore this literary work.

1) Why is *Invisible Man* considered a Bildungsroman?

2) Analyze the novel's three-part structure. How does it represent the narrator's movement from "purpose to passion to perception"?

4 Writing About Literature

Read the following critical excerpt and then write an essay.

> Rodnon, Stewart. "*The Adventures of Huckleberry Finn* and *Invisible Man:* Thematic and Structural Comparisons."
> *Negro American Literature Forum* 4.2 (1970): 45–51.

"By far the best novel yet written by an American Negro," declared Robert A. Bone,

"*Invisible Man* is quite possibly the best American novel since World War II." Sustaining this assertion, some two hundred editors, creative writers, and critics in 1965 voted it the most significant work of fiction published in post-war America. Praise, indeed, for any novel, much less a first novel; yet the praise is merely a trickle of approbation when compared to the flood of critical admiration for Mark Twain's *The Adventures of Huckleberry Finn*, an acknowledged American classic which is almost universally required reading in high school and college American Literature courses. Because a comparison of American literary classics and a modern black artist's novel is one fruitful and intelligent approach to the teaching of black culture, I am offering here an analysis of the two novels, focusing on the thematic and stylistic similarities.

The thematic similarities may be divided into three sections: the journey concept, the education motif, and the essential theme. Probably the most immediately apparent similarity between the two novels is the protagonist-as-traveler idea. "Movement is one of the great consolers of human woe" is an aphorism which, perhaps, accounts for the permanence of the picaresque. Each novel follows the picaresque tradition of having its central figure (or figures) travel a long road (or moving road, as Pascal defined a river) in which he is an onlooker, or more frequently a participant, in a series of episodes. Huck's trip down the river is clearly picaresque. So, too, the protagonist of *Invisible Man* moves physically and emotionally through his series of separate experiences; in order, we see him, a Negro, as high school boy in a Southern state, college student in a Southern Negro college, employee in a paint factory, leader of a Communist-type group called the Brotherhood, and self-exile in a brightly lighted basement.

 Essay Writing

Please compare and contrast the journey concept as represented in *The Adventures of Huckleberry Finn* and *Invisible Man* with no less than 500 words.

 Further Activity

Scan the QR code and watch a video clip "Crash Course Literature" by John Green on *Invisible Man*.

Lecture 14
Zora Neale Hurston

Profile of the Writer

Zora Neale Hurston
(1891–1960)

Zora Neale Hurston was a world-renowned writer and anthropologist, whose novels, short stories, and plays often depicted African American life in the South. Her work in anthropology examined black folklore. Hurston's influence on many writers cemented her place in history as one of the foremost female writers of the 20th century.

Zora Neale Hurston was born in Notasulga, Alabama on January 7, 1891, to an enslaved couple. At a young age, her family relocated to Eatonville, Florida where they flourished. Eventually, her father became one of the town's first mayors. In 1917, Hurston enrolled at Morgan College, where she completed her high school studies. She then attended Howard University and earned an associate's degree. In 1925, Hurston received a scholarship to Barnard College and graduated three years later with a BA in anthropology. During her time as a student in New York City, Hurston befriended other writers such as Langston Hughes and Countee Cullen. Together, the group of writers joined the black cultural renaissance in Harlem.

Throughout her life, Hurston dedicated herself to promoting and studying black culture. She traveled to both Haiti and Jamaica to study the religions of the African diaspora. Hurston often incorporated her research into her fictional writing. As an author, Hurston started publishing short stories as early as 1920. Unfortunately, her work was ignored by the mainstream literary audience for years. However, she gained a following among African Americans. In 1935, she published *Mules and Men*. Between 1934 and 1939, she published three books including her most popular work, *Their Eyes Were Watching God*. The fictional story chronicled the tumultuous life of Janie Crawford through which Hurston broke literary norms by focusing her work on the experience of a black woman.

Was Hurston ahead of her time in her writings, or was she, as one of her characters puts it, "a mite too previous"? Although publication many years after one's death does not bring a promise of wealth or an audience for any writer, there are more opportunities for black female writers today than were open to Hurston while she was alive. When the feminist (or womanist) critics, led by Walker, reintroduced Hurston's work to the public's attention in 1975, they opened not just a narrow path to Eatonville, but a broad national highway for black female writers to travel. Hurston would have reveled in their journeys.

Although Hurston eventually received praise for her works, she was often underpaid. Therefore, she remained in debt and poverty. After years of writing, Hurston had to enter the St. Lucie County Welfare Home as she was unable to take care of herself. She died of heart disease on January 28, 1960. At first, her remains were placed in an unmarked grave. In 1972, Alice Walker located her grave and created a marker. Although Hurston's work was not widely known during her life, in death she ranks among the best writers of the 20th century.

Preview Questions

1. Zora Neale Hurston was greatly involved in the literary movement known as the Harlem Renaissance. Research Hurston's activities and her contributions to the Renaissance.

2. "Now, women forget all those things they don't want to remember and remember everything they don't want to forget. The dream is the truth. Then they act and do things accordingly." How do you interpret "The dream is the truth"?

II Literary Reading: *Their Eyes Were Watching God*
(Chapter 1)

Ships at a distance have every man's wish on board. For some they come in with the tide. For others they sail forever on the horizon, never out of sight, never landing until the Watcher turns his eyes away in resignation, his dreams mocked to death by Time. That is the life of men.

Now, women forget all those things they don't want to remember, and remember everything they don't want to forget. The dream is the truth. Then they act and do things accordingly.

So the beginning of this was a woman and she had come back from burying the dead. Not the dead of sick and ailing with friends at the pillow and the feet. She had come back from the sodden and the bloated; the sudden dead, their eyes flung wide open in judgment.

The people all saw her come because it was sundown. The sun was gone, but he had left his footprints in the sky. It was the time for sitting on porches beside the road. It was the time to hear things and talk. These sitters had been tongueless, earless, eyeless conveniences all day long. Mules and other brutes had occupied their skins. But now, the sun and the bossman were gone, so the skins felt powerful and human. They became lords of sounds and lesser things. They passed nations through their mouths. They sat in judgment.

Seeing the woman as she was made them remember the envy they had stored up from other times. So they chewed up the back parts of their minds and swallowed with relish. They made burning statements with questions, and killing tools out of laughs. It was mass cruelty. A mood come alive. Words walking without masters; walking altogether like harmony in a song.

"What she doin' coming back here in dem overhalls? Can't she find no dress to put on?—Where's dat blue satin dress she left here in?—Where all dat money her husband took and died and left her?—What dat ole forty year ole 'oman doin' wid her hair swingin' down her back lak some young gal?—Where she left dat young lad of a boy she went off here wid?—Thought she was going to marry?—Where he left her?—What he done wid all her money?—Betcha he off wid some gal so young she ain't even got no hairs—Why she don't stay in her class?—"

When she got to where they were she turned her face on the bander log and spoke. They scrambled a noisy "good evenin' " and left their mouths setting open and their ears full of hope. Her speech was pleasant enough, but she kept walking straight on to her gate. The porch couldn't talk for looking.

The men noticed her firm buttocks like she had grape fruits in her hip pockets; the great rope of black hair swinging to her waist and unraveling in the wind like a plume; then her pugnacious breasts trying to bore holes in her shirt. They, the men, were saving with the mind what they lost with the eye. The women took the faded shirt and muddy overalls and laid them away for remembrance. It was a weapon against her strength and if it turned out of no significance, still it was a hope that she might fall to their level some day.

But nobody moved, nobody spoke, nobody even thought to swallow spit until after her gate slammed behind her.

Pearl Stone opened her mouth and laughed real hard because she didn't know what else to do. She fell all over Mrs. Sumpkins while she laughed. Mrs. Sumpkins snorted violently and sucked her teeth.

"Humph! Y'all let her worry yuh. You ain't like me. Ah ain't got her to study 'bout. If she ain't got manners enough to stop and let folks know how she been makin' out, let her g'wan!"

"She ain't even worth talkin' after," Lulu Moss drawled through her nose. "She sits high, but she looks low. Dat's what Ah say 'bout dese ole women runnin' after young boys."

Pheoby Watson hitched her rocking chair forward before she spoke. "Well, nobody don't know if it's anything to tell or not. Me, Ah'm her best friend, and Ah don't know."

"Maybe us don't know into things lak you do, but we all know how she went 'way from here and us sho seen her come back. 'Tain't no use in your tryin' to cloak no ole woman lak Janie Starks, Pheoby, friend or no friend."

"At dat she ain't so ole as some of y'all dat's talking."

"She's way past forty to my knowledge, Pheoby."

"No more'n forty at de outside."

"She's 'way too old for a boy like Tea Cake."

"Tea Cake ain't been no boy for some time. He's round thirty his ownself."

"Don't keer what it was, she could stop and say a few words with us. She act like we done done something to her," Pearl Stone complained. "She de one been doin' wrong."

"You mean, you mad 'cause she didn't stop and tell us all her business. Anyhow, what you ever know her to do so bad as y'all make out? The worst thing Ah ever knowed her to do was taking a few years offa her age and dat ain't never harmed nobody. Y'all makes me tired. De way you talkin' you'd think de folks in dis town didn't do nothin' in de bed 'cept praise de Lawd. You have to 'scuse me, 'cause Ah'm bound to go take her some supper." Pheoby stood up sharply.

"Don't mind us," Lulu smiled, "just go right ahead, us can mind yo' house for you till you git back. Mah supper is done. You bettah go see how she feel. You kin let de rest of us know."

"Lawd," Pearl agreed, "Ah done scorched-up dat lil meat and bread too long to talk about. Ah kin stay 'way from home long as Ah please. Mah husband ain't fussy."

"Oh, er, Pheoby, if youse ready to go, Ah could walk over dere wid you," Mrs. Sumpkins volunteered. "It's sort of duskin' down dark. De booger man might ketch yuh."

"Naw, Ah thank yuh. Nothin' couldn't ketch me dese fewsteps Ah'm goin'. Anyhow mah husband tell me say no first class booger would have me. If she got anything to tell yuh, you'll hear it."

Pheoby hurried on off with a covered bowl in her hands. She left the porch pelting her back with unasked questions. They hoped the answers were cruel and strange. When she arrived at the place, Pheoby Watson didn't go in by the front gate and down the palm walk to the front door. She walked around the fence corner and went in the intimate gate with her heaping plate of mulatto rice. Janie must be round that side.

She found her sitting on the steps of the back porch with the lamps all filled and the chimneys cleaned.

"Hello, Janie, how you comin'?"

"Aw, pretty good, Ah'm tryin' to soak some uh de tiredness and de dirt outa mah feet." She laughed a little.

"Ah see you is. Gal, you sho looks good. You looks like youse yo' own daughter." They both laughed. "Even wid dem overhalls on, you shows yo' womanhood."

"G'wan! G'wan! You must think Ah brought yuh somethin'. When Ah ain't brought home a thing but mahself."

"Dat's a gracious plenty. Yo' friends wouldn't want nothin' better."

"Ah takes dat flattery offa you, Pheoby, 'cause Ah know it's from de heart." Janie extended her hand. "Good Lawd, Pheoby! ain't you never goin' tuh gimme dat lil rations you brought me? Ah ain't had a thing on mah stomach today exceptin' mah hand." They both laughed easily. "Give it here and have a seat."

"Ah knowed you'd be hongry. No time to be huntin' stove wood after dark. Mah mulatto rice ain't so good dis time. Not enough bacon grease, but Ah reckon it'll kill hongry."

"Ah'll tell you in a minute," Janie said, lifting the cover. "Gal, it's too good! you switches a mean fanny round in a kitchen."

"Aw, dat ain't much to eat, Janie. But Ah'm liable to have something sho nuff good tomorrow, 'cause you done come."

Janie ate heartily and said nothing. The varicolored cloud dust that the sun had stirred up in the sky was settling by slow degrees.

"Here, Pheoby, take yo' ole plate. Ah ain't got a bit of use for a empty dish. Dat grub sho come in handy."

Pheoby laughed at her friend's rough joke. "Youse just as crazy as you ever was."

"Hand me dat wash-rag on dat chair by you, honey. Lemme scrub mah feet." She took the cloth and rubbed vigorously. Laughter came to her from the big road.

"Well, Ah see Mouth-Almighty is still sittin' in de same place. And Ah reckon they got me up in they mouth now."

"Yes indeed. You know if you pass some people and don't speak tuh suit 'em dey got tuh go way back in yo' life and see whut you ever done. They know mo' 'bout yuh than you do yo' self. An envious heart makes a treacherous ear. They done 'heard' 'bout you just what they hope done happened."

"If God don't think no mo' 'bout 'em then Ah do, they's a lost ball in de high grass."

"Ah hears what they say 'cause they just will collect round mah porch 'cause it's on de big road. Mah husband git so sick of 'em sometime he makes 'em all git for home."

"Sam is right too. They just wearin' out yo' sittin' chairs."

"Yeah, Sam say most of 'em goes to church so they'll be sure to rise in Judgment. Dat's de day dat every secret is s'posed to be made known. They wants to be there and hear it all."

"Sam is *too* crazy! You can't stop laughin' when youse round him."

"Uuh hunh. He says he aims to be there hisself so he can find out who stole his corn-cob pipe."

"Pheoby, dat Sam of your'n just won't quit! Crazy thing!"

"Most of dese zigaboos is so het up over yo' business till they liable to hurry theyself to Judgment to find out about you if they don't soon know. You better make haste and tell 'em 'bout you and Tea Cake gittin' married, and if he taken all yo' money and went off wid some young gal, and where at he is now and where at is all yo' clothes dat you got to come back here in overhalls."

"Ah don't mean to bother wid tellin' 'em nothin', Pheoby. 'Tain't worth de trouble. You can tell 'em what Ah say if you wants to. Dat's just de same as me 'cause mah tongue is in mah friend's mouf."

"If you so desire Ah'll tell 'em what you tell me to tell 'em."

"To start off wid, people like dem wastes up too much time puttin' they mouf on things they don't know nothin' about. Now they got to look into me loving Tea Cake and see whether it was done right or not! They don't know if life is a mess of corn-meal

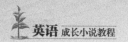

dumplings, and if love is a bed-quilt!"

"So long as they get a name to gnaw on they don't care whose it is, and what about, 'specially if they can make it sound like evil."

"If they wants to see and know, why they don't come kiss and be kissed? Ah could then sit down and tell 'em things. Ah been a delegate to de big 'ssociation of life. Yessuh! De Grand Lodge, de big convention of livin' is just where Ah been dis year and a half y'all ain't seen me."

They sat there in the fresh young darkness close together. Pheoby eager to feel and do through Janie, but hating to show her zest for fear it might be thought mere curiosity. Janie full of that oldest human longing—self-revelation. Pheoby held her tongue for a long time, but she couldn't help moving her feet. So Janie spoke.

"They don't need to worry about me and my overhalls long as Ah still got nine hundred dollars in de bank. Tea Cake got me into wearing 'em—following behind him. Tea Cake ain't wasted up no money of mine, and he ain't left me for no young gal, neither. He give me every consolation in de world. He'd tell 'em so too, if he was here. If he wasn't gone."

Pheoby dilated all over with eagerness, "Tea Cake gone?"

"Yeah, Pheoby, Tea Cake is gone. And dat's de only reason you see me back here— cause Ah ain't got nothing to make me happy no more where Ah was at. Down in the Everglades there, down on the muck."

"It's hard for me to understand what you mean, de way you tell it. And then again Ah'm hard of understandin' at times."

"Naw, 'tain't nothin' lak you might think. So 'tain't no use in me telling you somethin' unless Ah give you de understandin' to go 'long wid it. Unless you see de fur, a mink skin ain't no different from a coon hide. Looka heah, Pheoby, is Sam waitin' on you for his supper?"

"It's all ready and waitin'. If he ain't got sense enough to eat it, dat's his hard luck."

"Well then, we can set right where we is and talk. Ah got the house all opened up to let dis breeze get a little catchin'."

"Pheoby, we been kissin'-friends for twenty years, so Ah depend on you for a good thought. And Ah'm talking to you from dat standpoint."

Time makes everything old so the kissing, young darkness became a monstropolous old thing while Janie talked.

III Thinking, Talking and Writing About Literature

1 Textual Cognition

Make an introductory presentation on the following terms related to this literary work.

1) gender dynamics
2) language and voice

2 Textual Reading

Search for evidence in the text and answer the following questions.

1) *Their Eyes Were Watching God* opens with the gossip of the porch sitters about Janie, when she returns to Eatonville after a lengthy absence. What do you think of the writing purpose?

2) What is the role of the porch sitters in *Their Eyes Were Watching God*? How do they contribute to the novel?

3) What's your understanding of Janie Mae Crawford Killicks Starks Woods based on the text?

3 Critical Reading

Discuss in groups the following questions to further explore this literary work.

1) What is the significance of the title *Their Eyes Were Watching God* to the novel?

2) *Their Eyes Were Watching God* focuses its plot both on Janie's series of romantic relationships as well as on Janie's individual quest for self-fulfillment and spiritual nourishment. Discuss the relation between her romance and personal growth.

4 Writing About Literature

Read the following critical excerpt and then write an essay.

> Chinn, Nancy. "Like Love, 'A Movin Thing': Janie's Search for Self and God in *Their Eyes Were Watching God.*" *South Atlantic Review* 60.1 (1995): 77–95.

Echoes of the title appear in the novel's opening passage, which reveals Hurston's understanding of traditional male and female roles. According to Du Plessis, "the absolute beginning of the book begins playing with the title materials and meanings by opening issues about words and the Word in relation to gender and racial power". A man is "the

Watcher" who has the possibility of heading toward the horizon, while, for women, "[t]he dream is the truth". Unnamed, Janie appears as a woman who "had come back from the sodden and the bloated; the sudden dead, their eyes flung wide open in judgment". This passage is puzzling to the first time reader who does not know about the hurricane that occurs late in the novel, but the notion that death comes unexpectedly and perhaps undeservedly is clearly suggested. Also implied is the idea that the dead blame others or God for their deaths. These dead judges are replaced in the first chapter by living watchers, the people on the porch who observe Janie as she returns to her house in Eatonville. Janie refers to them as "Mouth-Almighty" and tells her friend Phoeby that she knows they are judging her. Their attempt to emulate God by judging is described as "mass cruelty. A mood comes alive. Words walking without masters; walking altogether like harmony in a song". The final image ends this passage on an ambiguous note and suggests that this cruelty has achieved a kind of artistry perhaps because it has been practiced so often. After working as "tongueless, earless, eyeless conveniences all day long", the people transform themselves into godlike judges, missing in the process, the narrator suggests, the intermediary stage—humanity. These judges imply that God too is a severe judge who causes death and destruction. This view of God produces the traditional view of women by which they judge Janie harshly. Hurston has subverted stereotypes, however, by moving from men to women to a specific, but unnamed, woman: "So the beginning of this was a woman".

Essay Writing

It is stated that the novel's opening passage reveals Hurston's understanding of male and female roles. Then what's your understanding of the statement? Please write an essay on it with no less than 500 words.

IV Further Activity

Scan the QR code and watch a video clip "Crash Course Literature" by John Green on *Their Eyes Were Watching God*.

Lecture 15
Maya Angelou

Profile of the Writer

Maya Angelou
(1928–2014)

Maya Angelou, a poet, dancer, singer, activist, and scholar, was a world-famous author, best known for her unique and pioneering autobiographical writing style.

Marguerite Ann Johnson (Maya Angelou), was born in St. Louis, Missouri on April 4, 1928. After her parents divorced, Angelou went to live with her paternal grandmother in Stamps, Arkansas at an early age. Her older brother gave Angelou her nickname "Maya". At the age of seven, Angelou was raped by her mother's boyfriend who was later jailed and killed when released. Believing that her confession of the trauma had a hand in the man's death, Angelou became mute for six years. Angelou's interest in the written word and the English language was evident from an early age. Throughout her childhood, she wrote essays, poetry, and kept a journal.

Despite a 15-year-old girl, she decided to apply for the position of a streetcar conductor, but was rejected at first because of her race. Every day for three weeks, she requested a job application, and finally, she was accepted for the position and became the first African American woman to work as a streetcar conductor in San Francisco. In the summer of 1944, she graduated from Mission High School and soon after gave birth to her only child, Clyde Bailey (Guy) Johnson. Angelou undertook a series of odd jobs to support herself and her son. In 1949, she married Tosh Angelos and adopted a form of his surname and kept it throughout her life.

Angelou was noted for her talents as a singer and dancer, particularly in the calypso and cabaret styles. In the 1950s, she performed professionally in the US, Europe, and northern Africa, and sold albums of her recordings. In 1959 Angelou joined the Harlem Writers Guild that African American writers in New York City formed to nurture and support the publication of black authors. She also became active in the Civil Rights Movement and served as the northern coordinator of the Southern Christian Leadership Conference, a prominent African American advocacy organization.

In 1969, Angelou published *I Know Why the Caged Bird Sings*, an autobiography of her early life. Her tale of personal strength amid childhood trauma and racism resonated with readers and was nominated for the National Book Award. Many schools sought to ban the book for its frank depiction of sexual abuse, but it is credited with helping other abuse survivors tell their stories. *I Know Why the Caged Bird Sings* has been translated into numerous languages and has sold over a million copies worldwide. Angelou eventually published six more autobiographies, culminating in 2013s' *Mom & Me & Mom*.

She wrote numerous poetry volumes, such as the Pulitzer Prize-nominated *Just Give Me a Drink of Water 'fore I Diiie* (1971), as well as several essay collections. She also recorded spoken albums of her poetry, including "On the Pulse of the Morning", for which she won a Grammy for Best Spoken Word Album.

Angelou died on May 28, 2014. Several memorials were held in her honor for Angelou's remarkable and inspiring career in the arts.

I Preview Questions

1. Discuss autobiography as an art form.
2. Compare Angelou's depiction of Southern culture with that of Zora Neale Hurston, or other Southern writers.

II Literary Reading: *I Know Why the Caged Bird Sings* (Chapter 4)

What sets one Southern town apart from another, or from a Northern town or hamlet, or city high-rise? The answer must be the experience shared between the unknowing majority (it) and the knowing minority (you). All of childhood's unanswered questions must finally be passed back to the town and answered there. Heroes and bogey men, values and dislikes, are first encountered and labeled in that early environment. In later years they change faces, places and maybe races, tactics, intensities and goals, but beneath those penetrable masks they wear forever the stocking-capped faces of childhood.

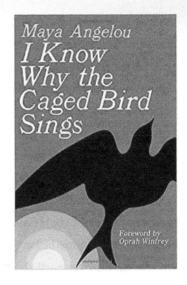

Mr. McElroy, who lived in the big rambling house next to the Store, was very tall and broad, and although the years had eaten away the lesh from his shoulders, they had not, at the time of my knowing him, gotten to his high stomach, or his hands or feet.

He was the only Negro I knew, except for the school principal and the visiting teachers, who wore matching pants and jackets. When I learned that men's clothes were sold like that and called suits, I remember thinking that somebody had been very bright, for it made men look less manly, less threatening and a little more like women.

Mr. McElroy never laughed, and seldom smiled, and to his credit was the fact that he liked to talk to Uncle Willie. He never went to church, which Bailey and I thought also proved he was a very courageous person. How great it would be to grow up like that, to be able to stare religion down, especially living next door to a woman like Momma.

I watched him with the excitement of expecting him to do anything at any time. I never tired of this, or became disappointed or disenchanted with him, although from the perch of age, I see him now as a very simple and uninteresting man who sold patent medicine and tonics to the less sophisticated people in towns (villages) surrounding the metropolis of Stamps.

There seemed to be an understanding between Mr. McElroy and Grandmother. This was obvious to us because he never chased us off his land. In summer's late sunshine I often sat under the chinaberry tree in his yard, surrounded by the bitter aroma of its fruit and lulled by the drone of flies that fed on the berries. He sat in a slotted swing on his porch, rocking in his brown three-piece, his wide Panama nodding in time with the whir of insects.

One greeting a day was all that could be expected from Mr. McElroy. After his "Good morning, child," or "Good afternoon, child," he never said a word, even if I met him again on the road in front of his house or down by the well, or ran into him behind the house escaping in a game of hide-and-seek.

He remained a mystery in my childhood. A man who owned his land and the big

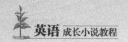

many-windowed house with a porch that clung to its sides all around the house. An independent Black man. A near anachronism in Stamps.

Bailey was the greatest person in my world. And the fact that he was my brother, my only brother, and I had no sisters to share him with, was such good fortune that it made me want to live a Christian life just to show God that I was grateful. Where I was big, elbowy and grating, he was small, graceful and smooth. When I was described by our playmates as being shit color, he was lauded for his velvet-black skin. His hair fell down in black curls, and my head was covered with black steel wool. And yet he loved me.

When our elders said unkind things about my features (my family was handsome to a point of pain for me), Bailey would wink at me from across the room, and I knew that it was a matter of time before he would take revenge. He would allow the old ladies to finish wondering how on earth I came about, then he would ask, in a voice like cooling bacon grease, "Oh Mizeriz Coleman, how is your son? I saw him the other day, and he looked sick enough to die."

Aghast, the ladies would ask, "Die? From what? He ain't sick."

And in a voice oilier than the one before, he'd answer with a straight face, "From the Uglies."

I would hold my laugh, bite my tongue, grit my teeth and very seriously erase even the touch of a smile from my face. Later, behind the house by the black-walnut tree, we'd laugh and laugh and howl.

Bailey could count on very few punishments for his consistently outrageous behavior, for he was the pride of the Henderson/Johnson family.

His movements, as he was later to describe those of an acquaintance, were activated with oiled precision. He was also able to find more hours in the day than I thought existed. He finished chores, homework, read more books than I and played the group games on the side of the hill with the best of them. He could even pray out loud in church, and was apt at stealing pickles from the barrel that sat under the fruit counter and Uncle Willie's nose.

Once when the Store was full of lunchtime customers, he dipped the strainer, which we also used to sift weevils from meal and flour, into the barrel and fished for two fat pickles. He caught them and hooked the strainer onto the side of the barrel where they dripped until he was ready for them. When the last school bell rang, he picked the nearly dry pickles out of the strainer, jammed them into his pockets and threw the strainer behind the oranges. We ran out of the Store. It was summer and his pants were short, so the pickle juice made clean streams down his ashy legs, and he jumped with his pockets full of loot and his eyes laughing a "How about that?" He smelled like a vinegar barrel or a sour angel.

After our early chores were done, while Uncle Willie or Momma minded the Store, we were free to play the children's games as long as we stayed within yelling distance. Playing hide-and-seek, his voice was easily identified, singing, "Last night, night before, twenty-four robbers at my door. Who all is hid? Ask me to let them in, hit 'em in the head with a rolling pin. Who all is hid?" In follow the leader, naturally he was the one who created the most daring and interesting things to do. And when he was on the tail of the pop the whip, he would twirl off the end like a top, spinning, falling, laughing, finally stopping just before my heart beat its last, and then he was back in the game, still laughing.

Of all the needs (there are none imaginary) a lonely child has, the one that must be satisfied, if there is going to be hope and a hope of wholeness, is the unshaking need for an unshakable God. My pretty Black brother was my Kingdom Come.

In Stamps the custom was to can everything that could possibly be preserved. During the killing season, after the first frost, all neighbors helped each other to slaughter hogs and even the quiet, big-eyed cows if they had stopped giving milk.

The missionary ladies of the Christian Methodist Episcopal Church helped Momma prepare the pork for sausage. They squeezed their fat arms elbow deep in the ground meat, mixed it with gray nose-opening sage, pepper and salt, and made tasty little samples for all obedient children who brought wood for the slick black stove. The men chopped off the larger pieces of meat and laid them in the smokehouse to begin the curing process. They opened the knuckle of the hams with their deadly-looking knives, took out a certain round harmless bone ("it could make the meat go bad") and rubbed salt, coarse brown salt that looked like fine gravel, into the flesh, and the blood popped to the surface.

Throughout the year, until the next frost, we took our meals from the smokehouse, the little garden that lay cousin-close to the Store and from the shelves of canned foods. There were choices on the shelves that could set a hungry child's mouth to watering. Green beans, snapped always the right length, collards, cabbage, juicy red tomato preserves that came into their own on steaming buttered biscuits, and sausage, beets, berries and every fruit grown in Arkansas.

But at least twice yearly Momma would feel that as children we should have fresh meat included in our diets. We were then given money—pennies, nickels, and dimes entrusted to Bailey—and sent to town to buy liver. Since the whites had refrigerators, their butchers bought the meat from commercial slaughterhouses in Texarkana and sold it to the wealthy even in the peak of summer.

Crossing the Black area of Stamps which in childhood's narrow measure seemed a whole world, we were obliged by custom to stop and speak to every person we met, and Bailey felt constrained to spend a few minutes playing with each friend. There was a joy in going to town with money in our pockets (Bailey's pockets were as good as my own) and time on our hands. But the pleasure fled when we reached the white part of town. After we left Mr. Willie Williams' Do Drop Inn, the last stop before whitefolksville, we had to cross the pond and adventure the railroad tracks. We were explorers walking without weapons into man-eating animals' territory.

In Stamps the segregation was so complete that most Black children didn't really, absolutely know what whites looked like. Other than that they were different, to be dreaded, and in that dread was included the hostility of the powerless against the powerful, the poor against the rich, the worker against the worked for and the ragged against the well dressed.

I remember never believing that whites were really real.

Many women who worked in their kitchens traded at our Store, and when they carried their finished laundry back to town they often set the big baskets down on our front porch to pull a singular piece from the starched collection and show either how graceful was their ironing hand or how rich and opulent was the property of their employers.

I looked at the items that weren't on display. I knew, for instance, that white men wore shorts, as Uncle Willie did, and that they had an opening for taking out their "things" and peeing, and that white women's breasts weren't built into their dresses, as some people said, because I saw their brassieres in the baskets. But I couldn't force myself to think of them as people. People were Mrs. LaGrone, Mrs. Hendricks, Momma, Reverend Sneed, Lillie B, and Louise and Rex. Whitefolks couldn't be people because their feet were too small, their skin too white and see-throughy, and they didn't walk on the balls of their feet the way people did—they walked on their heels like horses.

People were those who lived on my side of town. I didn't like them all, or, in fact, any of them very much, but they were people. These others, the strange pale creatures that lived in their alien unlife, weren't considered folks. They were whitefolks.

III Thinking, Talking and Writing About Literature

1 Textual Cognition

Make an introductory presentation on the following terms related to this literary work.

1) segregation
2) home and displacement

❷ Textual Reading

Search for evidence in the text and answer the following questions.

1) What do you think of Marguerite's attitudes towards her blackness?

2) Contrast Bailey and Maya Johnson in terms of their coping skills.

3) How do you understand the sentence, "I remember never believing that whites were really real" in the chapter?

❸ Critical Reading

Discuss in groups the following questions to further explore this literary work.

1) *I Know Why the Caged Bird Sings* underscores meaning through the stylistic details that illuminate its themes and action. What literary devices does Angelou utilize in the text?

2) Discuss how female role models in Maya's life significantly influence her growth and emotional well-being in the novel.

❹ Writing About Literature

Read the following critical excerpt and then write an essay.

> Lupton, Mary Jane. "Singing the Black Mother: Maya Angelou and Autobiographical Continuity." *Black American Literature Forum* 24.2 (1990): 257–276.

I Know Why the Caged Bird Sings is the first and most highly praised volume in the series. It begins with the humiliations of childhood and ends with the birth of a child. At its publication, critics, not anticipating a series, readily appreciated the clearly developed narrative form. In 1973, for example, Sidonie Smith discussed the "sense of an ending" in *Caged Bird* as it relates to Angelou's acceptance of Black womanhood: "With the birth of her child Maya is herself born into a mature engagement with the forces of life". But with the introduction in 1974 of Angelou's second autobiographical volume, *Gather Together in My Name*, the tight structure appeared to crumble; childhood experiences were replaced by episodes which a number of critics consider disjointed or bizarre. Selwyn Cudjoe, for instance, noted the shift from the "intense solidity and moral center" in *Caged Bird* to the "conditions of alienation and fragmentation" in *Gather Together*, conditions which affect its organization and its quality, making it "conspicuously weak". Lynn Z. Bloom found the sequel "less satisfactory" because the narrator "abandons or jeopardizes the maturity, honesty, and intuitive good judgment toward which she had been moving in *Caged Bird*". Crucial to Bloom's judgment is her concept of movement toward, which insinuates the achievement of an ending.

Essay Writing

Please write an essay on the "sense of an ending" in *I Know Why the Caged Bird Sings* from the perspective of its narrative form with no less than 500 words.

IV Further Activity

Scan the QR code and listen to the audio of Chapter 1 of *I Know Why the Caged Bird Sings*.

Lecture 16
Paule Marshall

Profile of the Writer

Paule Marshall
(1929–2019)

Paule Marshall, original name Valenza Pauline Burke, was born on April 9, 1929, in Brooklyn and died on August 12, 2019, Richmond, Virginia. Although she was born in the United States of America, her parents and extended family were from Barbados. Many of Paule Marshall's novels are located in the West Indies, the homeland of her ancestors, and Brooklyn, where she grew up. Her works emphasized a need for black Americans to reclaim their African heritage.

The Barbadian background of Marshall's parents informed all of her works. She spent her early years in her parents' home country and returned several times as a young adult. After graduating from Brooklyn College in 1953, she worked briefly as a librarian before joining *Our World*, an African American magazine, where she worked from 1953 to 1956 as a food and fashion editor. She married Kenneth Marshall in 1957 and divorced six years later. Her autobiographical novel, *Brown Girl, Brownstones* (1959), tells of the American daughter of Barbadian parents who travels to their homeland as an adult. The book was critically acclaimed for its acute rendition of dialogue, gaining widespread recognition when it was reprinted in 1981.

Soul Clap Hands and Sing, a 1961 collection of four novellas, presents four aging men who come to terms with their earlier refusal to affirm lasting values.

Marshall's 1962 short story "Reena" was one of the first pieces of fiction to feature a college-educated, politically active black woman as its protagonist; it was frequently anthologized and was also included in her collection *Reena and Other Stories* (1983). *The Chosen Place, the Timeless People* (1969) is set on a fictional Caribbean island and concerns a philanthropic attempt to modernize an impoverished and oppressed society.

Marshall's most eloquent statement of her belief in African Americans' need to rediscover their heritage was *Praisesong for the Widow*, a highly regarded 1983 novel that established her reputation as a major writer. Its protagonist, Avatara (Avey) Johnson, a middle-class woman, undergoes a spiritual rebirth on the island of Grenada. *Daughters* (1991) concerns a West Indian woman in New York who returns home to assist her father's reelection campaign. The protagonist, like those of Marshall's other works, has an epiphany after confronting her personal and cultural past. *The Fisher King* (2000) is a cross-generational tale about a rift between two black Brooklyn families.

In addition to her career as a writer, Marshall had a long career as a teacher. She has served as a faculty member at Yale University, Virginia Commonwealth University, the University of California, Berkeley, and the renowned Iowa Writer's Workshop at the University of Iowa.

Over the course of her impressive writing career, Paule Marshall has been honored with numerous awards and accolades. She has been selected as a MacArthur Fellow and is also past recipient of the Dos Passos Prize for Literature.

I. Preview Questions

1. The American Dream is the belief that anyone, including immigrants, can achieve material prosperity and a better life for the next generation through hard work and education. Discuss if and how the novel *Brown Girl, Brownstones* calls into question the idea of the American Dream for immigrants.

2. Search for the cultural and historical context for the novel. What impact do these contexts have on the events of the novel?

II. Literary Reading: *Brown Girl, Brownstones* (Chapter 1)

In the somnolent July afternoon the unbroken line of brown stone houses down the long Brooklyn street resembled an army massed at attention. They were all one uniform red-brown stone. All with high massive stone stoops and black iron-grille fences staving off the sun. All draped in ivy as though mourning. Their somber façades, indifferent to the summer's heat and passion, faced a park while their backs reared dark against the sky. They were only three or four stories tall—squat—yet they gave the impression of formidable height.

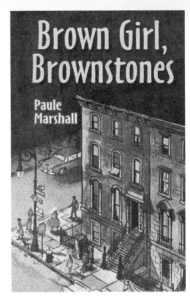

Glancing down the interminable Brooklyn street you thought of those joined brownstones as one house reflected through a train of mirrors, with no walls between the houses but only vast rooms yawning endlessly one into the other. Yet, looking close, you saw that under the thick ivy each house had something distinctively its own. Some touch that was Gothic, Romanesque, baroque or Greek triumphed amid the Victorian clutter. Here, Ionic columns framed the windows while next door gargoyles scowled up at the sun. There, the cornices were hung with carved foliage while Gorgon heads decorated others. Many houses had bay windows or Gothic stonework; a few boasted turrets raised high above the other roofs. Yet they all shared the same brown monotony. All seemed doomed by the confusion in their design.

Behind those grim façades, in those high rooms, life soared and ebbed. Bodies crouched in the postures of love at night, children burst from the womb's thick shell, and death, when it was time, shuffled through the halls. First, there had been the Dutch-English and Scotch-Irish who had built the houses. There had been tea in the afternoon then and skirts rustling across the parquet floors and mild voices. For a long time it had been only the whites, each generation unraveling in a quiet skein of years behind the green shades.

But now in 1939 the last of them were discreetly dying behind those shades or selling the houses and moving away. And as they left, the West Indians slowly edged their way in. Like a dark sea nudging its way onto a white beach and staining the sand, they came. The West Indians, especially the Barbadians who had never owned anything perhaps but a few poor acres in a poor land, loved the houses with the same fierce idolatry as they had the land on their obscure islands. But, with their coming, there was no longer tea in the afternoon, and their odd speech clashed in the hushed rooms, while underneath the ivy the old houses remained as indifferent to them as to the whites, as aloof...

Her house was alive to Selina. She sat this summer afternoon on the upper landing on the top floor, listening to its shallow breathing—a ten-year-old girl with scuffed legs and a body as straggly as the clothes she wore. A haze of sunlight seeping down from the skylight through the dust and dimness of the hall caught her wide full mouth, the small but strong nose, the eyes set deep in the darkness of her face. They were not the eyes of a child. Something too old lurked in their centers. They were weighted, it seemed, with scenes of a long life. She might have been old once and now, miraculously, young again—but with the memory of that other life intact. She seemed to know the world down there in the dark hall and beyond for what it was. Yet knowing, she still longed to leave this safe, sunlit place at the top of the house for the challenge there.

Suddenly the child, Selina, leaped boldly to the edge of the step, her lean body quivering. At the moment she hurled herself forward, her hand reached back to grasp the bannister, and the contradiction of her movement flung her back on the step. She huddled there, rubbing her injured elbow and hating her cowardice. Slowly she raised her arm, thin and dark in the sun-haze, circled by two heavy silver bangles which had come from "home" and which every Barbadian-American girl wore from birth. Glaring down, she shook her fist, and the bangles sounded her defiance with a thin clangor. When her arm dropped, the house, stunned by the noise, ceased breathing and a pure silence fell.

She smiled, for this was the silence she loved. It came when the old white servant upstairs slept amid her soiled sheets, when her father read and napped in the sun parlor, her sister slept in their basement bedroom and the new tenant Suggie was out. Above all, it was a silence which came when the mother was at work.

She rose, her arms lifted in welcome, and quickly the white family who had lived here before, whom the old woman upstairs always spoke of, glided with pale footfalls up the stairs. Their white hands trailed the bannister; their mild voices implored her to give them a little life. And as they crowded around, fusing with her, she was no longer a dark girl alone and dreaming at the top of an old house, but one of them, invested with their beauty and gentility. She threw her head back until it trembled proudly on the stalk of her neck and, holding up her imaginary gown, she swept downstairs to the parlor floor.

At the bottom step she paused in the entrance hall, which was a room in itself with its carpet, wallpaper and hushed dimness. Opening off the hall was the parlor, full of ponderous furniture and potted ferns which the whites had left, with an aged and inviolate silence. It was the museum of all the lives that had ever lived here. The floor-to-ceiling mirror retained their faces as the silence did their voices.

As Selina entered, the chandelier which held the sunlight frozen in its prisms rushed at her, and the mirror flung her back at herself. The mood was broken. The gown dropped from her limp hands. The illusory figures fled and she was only herself again. A truculent face and eyes too large and old, a flat body perched on legs that were too long. A torn middy blouse, dirty shorts, and socks that always worked down into the heel of her sneakers. That was all she was. She did not belong here. She was something vulgar in a holy place. The room was theirs, she knew, glancing up at the frieze of cherubs and angels on the ceiling; it belonged to the ghost shapes hovering in the shadows. But not to her. As she left, her shorts, bagging around her narrow behind, defined her sadness.

She made only a cursory tour of the master bedroom next door, opening the drawers to smell the lavender amid the seldom-used things, running a finger along the fluted edges of the high bed in which she had been born—the only piece of furniture they had brought with them. Whenever she was sick enough to have the doctor she slept there. Then the mother put on sheets that smelled of lavender and her father brought her up through the hall and laid her gently down. And it was always like falling out of herself into its soft depth...

Going downstairs to the basement she leaned against one of the high-back chairs ranged solemnly around the table in the dining room. Her eyes reflected the stained-glass wisteria lamp, the special crystal in the china closet and the family photograph, which did not include her, on the buffet. She wanted suddenly to send up a loud importunate cry to declare herself, to bring someone running. With the impulse strong in her she burst into the bedroom she shared with her sister.

Her sister, Ina, lay under the sheet, her body limp in sleep and her tight-clustered curls glistening. Watching her, Selina felt an inexplicable resentment. It flowed out from her, across the room, finally penetrating Ina's sleep. Ina opened her eyes, suddenly, apprehensively, awake.

"Whaddya want?" she cried. "Go away."

Selina bared her teeth and drew closer.

Ina scrambled up, gathering the sheet around her. "You heard what Mother said. You're not to bother me today. I'm sick," she cried from behind the sheet, shying away from Selina as though she embodied all that was rough and loud and undisciplined in the world.

Selina, remembering the mother's admonition, stopped, rubbed her sneaker on her leg and glared.

Ina was thin but soft, passing gracefully through adolescence, being spared its awkwardness. But she seemed somehow defenseless because of this—as though she would never really be fit for the roughness of life. Sensing this softness, Selina said, "You were sure ugly as a baby. Didja ever take a good look at yourself in that picture on the buffet? You were sure ugly."

The fear eased from Ina's face at the frailty of her attack. "Go away, pestilence, you're not to bother me when I have my pains." She was deeply involved with the changes taking place in her body and loved giving herself up to them, matching the summer heat with the blood-heat of her body. She had no patience with Selina and her boy's shape. Her voice stiffened with sarcasm now. "Look who's talking about somebody being ugly as a baby! You were ugly then, you're uglier now and you'll get worse. There!" And laughing, she rolled over and burrowed her face in the pillow.

Outrage clogged Selina's throat. She wanted to leap on Ina, pin her to the bed and then ground her fists and knees in that softness until the tears came and the whimpers and the apologies, until her own anger drained from her. But behind the blur of her tears she knew there was nothing she could do—for Ina was sick with some mysterious thing that made her unassailable.

Outside in the dining room she tried to swallow the impotence that was like hardened phlegm in her throat, and the room, like a dark, fragrant mother tried to soothe her. But she would not be comforted. She snatched up the family photograph from the buffet and stared at it bitterly in the scant light.

It was her father, mother, Ina and the brother she had never known. The picture of a neat, young family and she did not believe it. The small girl under the drooping bow did not resemble her sister. The young woman in the 1920's dress with a headband around her forehead could not be the mother. This mother had a shy beauty, there was a girlish expectancy in her smile. Then there was the baby on her lap, who stared out at Selina with round blank eyes. His hair capped his head like fur and his tiny fists held tightly onto nothing.

"He's like a girl with all that hair," she muttered contemptuously. He had been frail and dying with a bad heart while she had been stirring into life. She had lain curled in the mother's stomach, waiting for his dying to be complete, she knew, peering through the pores as the box containing his body was lowered into the ground. Then she had come, strong and well-made, to take his place. But they had taken no photographs...

Her father was the only one she believed in the picture. Despite the old-fashioned suit and the spats, it was her father. The angle at which he held the cane, his detached air, the teasing smile proclaimed him. For her, he was the one constant in the flux and unreality of life. The day was suddenly bright with the thought of him upstairs in the sun parlor, and slamming down the photograph she bounded from the room, taking the steps two at a time.

They were very proud of the sun parlor. Not many of the old brownstones had them. It was the one room in the house given over to the sun. Sunlight came spilling through the glass walls, swayed like a dancer in the air and lay in a yellow rug on the floor.

Her father was there, stretched dark and limp on a narrow cot like someone drunk with sun. He had lain there since the mother left, studying a correspondence course in accounting that he had just started, reading the newspapers and letters, listening to the radio. Selina sat on the floor facing him, waiting, watching his lids move as his eyes moved under them.

Lecture 16
Paule Marshall

Deighton Boyce's face was like his eyelids—a closed blind over the man beneath. He was well-hidden behind the high slanted facial bones, flared nose and thin lips, within the lean taut body, and his dark skin, burnished to a high fine gloss, completed the mystery.

"How the lady-folks?" he called finally, his eyes reaching over the letter he was reading. They were a deeper brown than his skin with the sun in their centers.

His tone was the signal that they had stepped into an intimate circle and were joined together in the pause and beat of life. Selina scratched where the elastic of her sock made ridges in her flesh. "I couldn't go to the movies today because old Ina has her pains. I don't see why I can't go with my girl friend, but Mother says not without Ina."

"You got to heed yuh mother."

"I know, but I still don't understand why. Ina doesn't look after me."

"Yuh mother know best."

He returned to his letter and she closed her eyes. The sun on her lids created an orange void inside her and she wanted to remain like this always with the sun on her eyes and bound with her father in their circle.

"I don know what wunna New York children does find in a movie," he said after a time. "Sitting up in a dark place when the sun shining bright-bright outside."

"There's nothing else to do on Saturday."

"We had Sat'day home too and found plenty to do when we was boys coming up."

She opened her eyes and there was a halo of bluish orange around his head. She blinked. "I don't see what you could do that's better than the movies."

"How you mean? You think people din make sport before there was movie? Come Sat'day, when we was boys coming up, we would get piece of stick and a lime and a big stone and play cricket. If we had little change in we pocket we would pick up weself and go up Kensington Field to football..."

"What else?"

"How you mean? I's a person live in town and always had plenty to do. I not like yuh mother and the 'mounts of these Bajan that come from down some gully or up some hill behind God back and ain use to nothing. 'Pon a Sat'day I would walk 'bout town like I was a full-full man. All up Broad Street and Swan Street like I did own the damn place."

"What else?"

"How you mean?"

"Didja play any games?"

"Game? How you mean? Tha's all we did. Rolling the roller and cork-sticking..."

"What's that?"

"But how many times I must tell you, nuh? It some rough-up something. Throwing a tennis ball hard-hard at each other and you had to move fast, if not it would stun you good..."

"What else?"

"Plenty else!" he cried, angered that she remained unimpressed. "We would pick up weself and go sea-bathing all down Christ Church where the rich white people live. Stay in the water all day shooting the waves, mahn, playing cricket on the sand, playing lick-corn..." Anticipating her, he lifted his hand. "Don ask, I gon tell you just-now. Lick-cork is just play-fighting in the sea after a cork."

He paused, lifting his head, and the sunlight lanced his eyes. "And when a tourist ship come into Carlisle Bay we would swim out to it and the rich white people from America would throw money in the water just to see we dive for it. Some them would throw a shilling and all. I tell you, those people had so much of money it did turn them foolish." He smiled, his teeth a dry white against his darkness, and abruptly returned to his letter.

Selina closed her eyes again and in the orange void tried to see him diving after the coins. But thoughts of the mother intruded. What had she and the others who lived down in the gullies and up on the hills behind God's back done on Saturdays? She could never think of the mother alone. It was always the mother and the others, for they were alike—those watchful, wrathful women whose eyes seared and searched and laid bare, whose tongues lashed the world in unremitting distrust. Each morning they took the train to Flatbush and Sheepshead Bay to scrub floors. The lucky ones had their steady madams while the others wandered those neat blocks or waited on corners—each with her apron and working shoes in a bag under her arm until someone offered her a day's work. Sometimes the white children on their way to school laughed at their blackness and shouted "nigger," but the Barbadian women sucked their teeth, dismissing them. Their only thought was of the "few raw-mout' pennies" at the end of the day which would eventually "buy house".

They returned home laden with throw-offs: the old clothes which the Jews had given them. Whenever the mother forced her to wear them, Selina spent the day hating the unknown child to whom they belonged. Anger flashed now within the orange depth and it was only her father's voice which restored her.

"Yes, lady-folks, we did make plenty sport when we was boys coming up..." he was saying, his eyes pierced with memories.

"What is it like—home?"

"What I must say, nuh? Barbados is poor-poor but sweet enough. That's why I going back."

"When?"

"Soon as I catch my hand here. You see this?" He held up the accounting manual. "This gon do it. I gon breeze through this course 'cause I was always good in figures. I ain even gon bother my head with all this preliminary work they sending now." He tossed aside the manual. "I gon wait till they send the real facts and study them. Then a job making decent money and we gone."

"Taking me?"

"How you mean! And we gon live in style, mahn. No little board and shingle house with a shed roof to cook in. We gon have the best now." He waved the letter he had been reading, then as quickly dropped it, turning suspiciously to the door. "Where yuh sister?"

"Downstairs, I think."

"You sure? 'Cause I thought I did hear somebody outside... You know how she does sneak 'bout listening to what we say and then lick she mouth to your mother."

"She's supposed to be sick and sleeping."

Reassured, he held up the letter again. "You see this? Don't broadcast it to the Sammy-cow-and-Duppy but my sister that just dead leave me piece of ground. Now how's that for news?" His teeth flashed in a strong smile. "Now let these bad-minded Bajan here talk my name 'cause I only leasing this house while they buying theirs. One thing I got good land home!"

For a moment she did not understand. From his smile and the way his eyes glowed she knew that it was important. She should have leaped up and pirouetted and joined his happiness. But a strange uneasiness kept her seated with her knees drawn tight against her chest. She asked cautiously, "You mean we're rich?"

"We ain rich but we got land."

"Is it a lot?"

"Two acres almost. I know the piece of ground good. You could throw down I-don-know-what on it and it would grow. And we gon have a house there—just like the white people own. A house to end all house!"

"Are you gonna tell Mother?"

His smile faltered and failed; his eyes closed in a kind of weariness. "How you mean! I got to tell she, nuh."

"Whaddya think she's gonna say?"

"How I could know? Years back I could tell but not any more."

She turned away from the pain darkening his eyes.

"Ah come nuh!" he cried after a long pause. "What I frighten for? It my piece of ground, ain it? And I can do what I please with it. So come, lady-folks, let we celebrate with something from the candy store..."

"Hootons!"

He brought the coins from his pocket. "I tell you, this Hooton is the one thing you children here have that I wish we did have when we was boys coming up."

She laughed and shoved the coins around in his palm until she found a nickel. With her hand still in his, she suddenly sat on the bed and, leaning close, whispered, "Look, I know you told me not to tell the Sammy-cow-and-Duppy about the land, but might I tell Beryl since she's my best friend? I'll make her swear and hope to die not to tell anyone…"

"Tell she," he said tenderly and closed his fist tight around her hand. "Your mother will know soon and then the world and it wife gon know." He freed her and swiftly she was gone, through the master bedroom, hurtling through the hall, her arms pumping, stopping only on the stoop to pull her socks out of the backs of her sneakers.

Chauncey Street languished in the afternoon heat, and across from it Fulton Park rose in a cool green wall. After the house, Selina loved the park. The thick trees, the grass— shrill-green in the sun—the statue of Robert Fulton and the pavilion where the lovers met and murmured at night formed, for her, the perfect boundary for her world; the park was the fitting buffer between Chauncey Street's gentility and Fulton Street's raucousness.

The sun was always loud on Fulton Street. It hung low and dead to the pavement, searing the trolley tracks and store windows, bearing down until the street spun helplessly in an eddy of cars, voices, neon signs and trolleys. Selina responded to the turbulence, rushing and leaping in a dark streak through the crowd. Passing the beauty parlor she saw the new tenant Suggie and turned in.

Suggie Skeete's full-fleshed legs and arms, her languorous pose, all the liquid roundness of her body under the sheer summer dress hinted that love, its rituals and its passion, was her domain. As Selina's shadow slanted across her she looked up, greeting her with a laugh murmurous as water. "Wha'lah, wha'lah, Selina? But where you always running to with yuh head down like a goat when it ready to butt? Look the clothes in strings like you belong to some string band society. The eyes wild like a tearcat. The hair like it curse comb, damn oil and blast the hairdresser. Come, let Miss Thompson slap the hot comb in it."

"Not me, Miss Suggie. I'd never get my hair done in this heat."

"Well you best put a comb to it before your mother come and put that mouth of hers 'pon you."

"Selina?" A voice hurdled above the tangled voices and the angry clicking of the hot curling tongs inside the shop.

"Yes, Miss Thompson, it's me."

A tall drawn woman—a faded brown in color and no longer young—came from behind the partition, whirling a smoking curling tong in one thin hand and flicking perspiration from her face with the other. The soiled nurse's uniform fell straight down her fleshless body, hiding the bones jutting under the skin. Her long lean shadow cut into the sunlight and brought a sudden darkness into the waiting room. Amidst the noise, she and Selina shared a quiet tender smile.

"I'm on my way to the candy store," she said softly. "You want me to bring you a Pepsi?"

"No thanks, honey. Just had one. That damn Pepsi don't do nothing but fill me with gas anyways. What I needs..." She thought a moment, her sunken eyes with the circles of age and weariness under them turned toward the sun in the doorway. "What I needs is to be sitting out in the park with them cool breezes blowing over me. That's what I needs. One of them c-o-o-l breezes. Then I'd feel human instead of like some old mule. That's all I needs," she repeated, sighing and turning away, "and it don't cost nothing and don't gimme no gas..."

On her way back through the park, Selina heard her name rising in a strident chant behind. Turning, she saw the girls waving their bright movie handbills and recognized her best friend Beryl. She was suddenly jealous of the others for the hours they had spent with her in the dark theater. She gave them a disinterested wave and hurried on.

"You missed the best Tarzan chapter today, Selina," one shouted. "Tarzan was captured and he..."

"I'm bored with Tarzan," she cried and wanted to shout that she would be leaving them soon to live in a big house in a sweet land and that they would miss her. She walked faster.

At the park gate Beryl caught up with her. "I knew you'd be mad. I was gonna come and ask your mother if you could go but I knew she'd of said no. And I knew you'd be mad."

Something in Beryl always soothed her and destroyed her anger. Perhaps it was the way Beryl's thick braids rested quietly on her shoulders or the way her tiny breasts nudged her middy blouse. They made Selina shy, those breasts, and ashamed of her own shapelessness. "I'm not mad."

"Yes you are. But I didn't have any fun today without you. And Tarzan is boring because he always escapes. Today he..."

As she talked Selina watched the shifting pattern of sun and shade on her face. She wished suddenly that her eyes could pierce Beryl's skin and roam inside her. What would Beryl be like inside? Like a small well-lighted room with the furniture neatly arranged around it.

"You're not listening."

"I was too. Look, I gotta give my father these Hootons. You want one?"

"No, it's too hot for chocolate. Can you come out later?"

"Maybe, if you come ask my mother. Oh, do come, I've got something to tell you."

She grabbed her arm, remembering, and felt Beryl's warmth rush into her. "Something very, very special. Come later and ask," she shouted, running up the stoop.

She found her father asleep, seduced like her sister and the old woman upstairs by the siren call of the afternoon. He still held the letter, and she slipped it away and placed it on the pillow beside his face. Downstairs she put his share of the candy in the icebox, then went up to the parlor and sat in the window seat behind the curtains. She ate slowly, melting the chocolate between her hands and then carefully licking it up from each palm and finger. As it slipped warmly down, her mind filled with warm thoughts of the secret she would share with Beryl. When she finished she watched a train of ants move along the ledge and wondered whether to kill them and make it rain...

She had decided to kill them when she sensed the mother, and her hand paused mid-air. It was strange how Selina always sensed her. Even before she looked up and over to the park she knew that she would see the mother there striding home under the trees.

Silla Boyce brought the theme of winter into the park with her dark dress amid the summer green and the bright-figured house-dresses of the women lounging on the benches there. Not only that, every line of her strong-made body seemed to reprimand the women for their idleness and the park for its senseless summer display. Her lips, set in a permanent protest against life, implied that there was no time for gaiety. And the park, the women, the sun even gave way to her dark force; the flushed summer colors ran together and faded as she passed.

There was something else today in the angle of her head that added to Selina's uneasiness. It was as though the mother knew all that had transpired in the house since morning—her father's idleness, her quarrel with Ina, the news of the land—and was coming to chastise them all. Selina's eyes dropped to the mother's legs, and with drawn breath she sought the meaning in that purposeful stride. Suddenly in one swift pure movement she was in front of the mirror, struggling out of her shorts and tugging at her matted braids.

III Thinking, Talking and Writing About Literature

1 Textual Cognition

Make an introductory presentation on the following terms related to this literary work.

1) metaphor
2) ethnic solidarity

❷ Textual Reading

Search for evidence in the text and answer the following questions.

1) "Glancing down the interminable Brooklyn street you thought of those joined brownstones as one house reflected through a train of mirrors, with no walls between the houses but only vast rooms yawning endlessly one into the other. Yet, looking close, you saw that under the thick ivy each house had something distinctively its own. […] Yet they all shared the same brown monotony. All seemed doomed by the confusion in their design." What's your understanding of the sentences in Paragraph 2?

2) "The West Indians, especially the Barbadians who had never owned anything perhaps but a few poor acres in a poor land, loved the houses with the same fierce idolatry as they had the land on their obscure islands." What does "idolatry" mean here?

3) What do Deighton's constant dreams about returning to Barbados foreshadow?

❸ Critical Reading

Discuss in groups the following questions to further explore this literary work.

1) How do you interpret the symbolism of the brownstone houses in the novel?

2) Selina goes from being a ten-year-old at the start of the novel to being an eighteen-year-old at the end. How does she change over the course of the novel? What events and decisions cause her to change?

❹ Writing About Literature

Read the following critical excerpt and then write an essay.

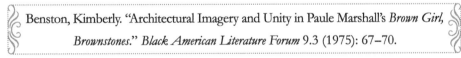

Benston, Kimberly. "Architectural Imagery and Unity in Paule Marshall's *Brown Girl, Brownstones*." *Black American Literature Forum* 9.3 (1975): 67–70.

Thus *Brown Girl, Brownstones* is a work dominated by two major stories, but not consistently unified by either one of them. What, then, holds the work together, and what gives this unity dynamism and scope? Like the prose symphonies of Novalis and Broch, Toomer and Baldwin, the truly important unifying (and most impressive) element in Miss Marshall's work is its precise, consistent use of imagery and symbolism. Several images (which, through repeated use in specific contexts, grow into symbols) recur throughout the novel and give its otherwise slightly disjointed structure shape and homogeneity. The elements of plot and action are strung together with such ease that the narrative seems to call special attention to its basic language and image patterns and to challenge the reader to understand the characters and their stories with reference to the very words that give them life. Moreover, it is exactly this relationship between character, story, and image that defines the texture of *Brown Girl, Brownstones*; and it is surely this texture multifarious, dense, and extremely suggestive beyond the primary recognitions of action and emotion—which gives overall significance to the novel.

Essay Writing

Please write an essay on the architectural imagery in *Brown Girl, Brownstones* with no less than 500 words.

IV Further Activity

Scan the QR code and read the text "An Interview of Paule Marshall" by Daryl Cumber Dance.

Lecture 17
Toni Morrison

Profile of the Writer

Toni Morrison
(1931–2019)

Toni Morrison was the first African-American woman to win the Nobel Prize in Literature in 1993. In addition to writing plays, and children's books, her novels have earned her countless prestigious awards including the Pulitzer Prize and the Presidential Medal of Freedom from President Barack Obama. Morrison's work has inspired a generation of writers to follow in her footsteps.

Toni Morrison was born on February 18, 1931 in Lorain, Ohio. The second of four children, Morrison's birth name was Chloe Anthony Wofford. Although she grew up in a semi-integrated area, racial discrimination was a constant threat. When she was twelve years old, she converted to Catholicism and was baptized under the name Anthony after Saint Anthony of Padua. She later went by the nickname "Toni" after this saint.

In 1949, Morrison decided to attend a historically black institution for her college education at Howard University in Washington, D.C. While in college, Morrison experienced racial segregation in a new way. She joined the university's theatrical group called the Howard University Players, and frequently toured the segregated South with the play. In addition, she witnessed how racial hierarchy divided people of color based on their skin tone. However, the community at Howard University also allowed her to make connections with other writers, artists, and activists that influenced her work. After graduating with a bachelor's degree in English, Morrison attended Cornell University to earn the Master of Arts in English. When she graduated in 1955, she began teaching English at Texas Southern University but returned to Howard University as a professor. While back at the university, Morrison met her husband Harold Morrison. The couple had two children, Harold and Slade.

Later, she transferred to the New York City branch of Random House Publishing and began to edit fiction and books by African-American authors. When Morrison was 39 years old, she published her first novel *The Bluest Eye*. Three years later, Morrison published her second novel *Sula*, which was nominated for the National Book Award. By her third novel *Song of Solomon* in 1977, Toni Morrison became a household name and earned critical acclaim as well as the National Book Critics Circle Award. The success of her books encouraged Morrison to become a writer full time.

In 1987, Morrison released her novel called *Beloved*, based on the true story of an African-American enslaved woman. This book was a best seller for 25 weeks and won countless awards including the Pulitzer Prize for Fiction. In 1993, Morrison became the first black woman to win the Nobel Prize in Literature.

Morrison's works continued to influence writers and artists through her focus on African-American life and her commentary on race relations. In June of 2019, director Timothy Greenfield-Sanders released a documentary of her life called *Toni Morrison: The Pieces I Am*. Morrison passed away two months later from complications of pneumonia.

I Preview Questions

1. Search for the historical context of the novel *The Bluest Eye*. What social movements were closely linked to the novel?

2. Discuss the narrative structure of the novel. Why might Morrison have chosen to present the events in a non-chronological way?

II Literary Reading: *The Bluest Eye* (Chapter 11)

LOOKLOOKHERECOMESAFRIENDTHE
FRIENDWILLPLAYWITHJANETHEYWI

Lecture 17
Toni Morrison

LLPLAYAGOODGAMEPLAYJANEPLAY

How many times a minute are you going to look inside that old thing?

I didn't look in a long time.

You did too—

So what? I can look if I want to.

I didn't say you couldn't. I just don't know why you have to look every minute. They aren't going anywhere.

I know it. I just like to look.

You scared they might go away?

Of course not. How can they go away?

The others went away.

They didn't go away. They changed.

Go away. Change. What's the difference?

A lot. Mr. Soaphead said they would last forever.

Forever and ever Amen?

Yes, if you want to know.

You don't have to be so smarty when you talk to me.

I'm not being smarty. You started it.

I'd just like to do something else besides watch you stare in that mirror.

You're just jealous.

I am not.

You are. You wish you had them.

Ha. What would I look like with blue eyes?

Nothing much.

If you're going to keep this up, I may as well go on off by myself.

No. Don't go. What you want to do? We could go outside and play, I guess. But it's too hot.

You can take your old mirror. Put it in your coat pocket, and you can look at yourself up and down the street.

Boy! I never would have thought you'd be so jealous.

Oh, come on!

You are.

Are what?

Jealous.

O.K. So I'm jealous.

See. I told you.

No. I told you.

Are they really nice?

Yes. Very nice.

Just "very nice"?

Really, truly, very nice.

Really, truly, bluely nice?

Oh, God. You are crazy.

I am not!

I didn't mean it that way.

Well, what did you mean?

Come on. It's too hot in here.

Wait a minute. I can't find my shoes.

Here they are. Oh. Thank you. Got your mirror?

Yes dearie...

Well, let's go then   Ow!

What's the matter?

The sun is too bright. It hurts my eyes.

Not mine. I don't even blink. Look. I can look right at the sun.

Don't do that.

Why not? It doesn't hurt. I don't even have to blink.

Well, blink anyway. You make me feel funny, staring at the sun like that.

Feel funny how?

I don't know.

Yes, you do. Feel funny how?

I told you, I don't know.

Why don't you look at me when you say that? You're looking drop-eyed like Mrs. Breedlove.

Mrs. Breedlove look drop-eyed at you?

Yes. Now she does. Ever since I got my blue eyes, she look away from me all of the time. Do you suppose she's jealous too?

Could be. They are pretty, you know.

I know. He really did a good job. Everybody's jealous.

Every time I look at somebody, they look off.

Is that why nobody has told you how pretty they are?

Sure it is. Can you imagine? Something like that happening to a person, and nobody but nobody saying anything about it? They all try to pretend they don't see them. Isn't that funny? I said, isn't that funny?

Yes.

You are the only one who tells me how pretty they are.

Yes.

You are a real friend. I'm sorry about picking on you before. I mean, saying you were jealous and all.

That's all right.

No. Really. You are my very best friend. Why didn't I know you before?

You didn't need me before.

Didn't need you?

I mean... you were so unhappy before. I guess you didn't notice me before.

I guess you're right. And I was so lonely for friends. And you were right here. Right before my eyes.

No, honey. Right after your eyes.

What?

What does Maureen think about your eyes?

She doesn't say anything about them. Has she said anything to you about them?

No. Nothing.

Do you like Maureen?

Oh. She's all right. For a half-white girl, that is.

I know what you mean. But would you like to be her friend? I mean, would you like to go around with her or anything?

No.

Me neither. But she sure is popular.

Who wants to be popular?

Not me.

Me neither.

But you couldn't be popular anyway. You don't even go to school.

You don't either.

I know. But I used to. *What did you stop for?*

They made me.

Who made you?

I don't know. After that first day at school when I had my blue eyes. Well, the next day they had Mrs. Breedlove come out. Now I don't go anymore. But I don't care.

You don't?

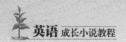

No, I don't. They're just prejudiced, that's all.

Yes, they sure are prejudiced.

Just because I got blue eyes, bluer than theirs, they're prejudiced.

That's right.

They are bluer, aren't they?

Oh, yes. Much bluer. Bluer than Joanna's? Much bluer than Joanna's.

And bluer than Michelena's?

Much bluer than Michelena's.

I thought so. Did Michelena say anything to you about my eyes?

No. Nothing.

Did you say anything to her?

No.

How come?

How come what?

How come you don't talk to anybody?

I talk to you.

Besides me.

I don't like anybody besides you.

Where do you live?

I told you once.

What is your mother's name?

Why are you so busy meddling me?

I just wondered. You don't talk to anybody. You don't go to school. And nobody talks to you.

How do you know nobody talks to me?

They don't. When you're in the house with me, even Mrs. Breedlove doesn't say anything to you. Ever. Sometimes I wonder if she even sees you.

Why wouldn't she see me?

I don't know. She almost walks right over you.

Maybe she doesn't feel too good since Cholly's gone.

Oh, yes. You must be right.

She probably misses him.

I don't know why she would. All he did was get drunk and beat her up.

Well, you know how grown-ups are.

Yes. No. How are they?

Well, she probably loved him anyway.

Lecture 17
Toni Morrison

HIM?

Sure. Why not? Anyway, if she didn't love him, she sure let him do it to her a lot.

That's nothing.

How do you know?

I saw them all the time. She didn't like it.

Then why'd she let him do it to her?

Because he made her.

How could somebody make you do something like that?

Easy.

Oh, yeah? How easy?

They just make you, that's all.

I guess you're right. And Cholly could make anybody do anything.

He could not.

He made you, didn't he?

Shut up!

I was only teasing.

Shut up!

O.K. O.K.

He just tried, see? He didn't do anything. You hear me?

I'm shutting up.

You'd better. I don't like that kind of talk.

I said I'm shutting up.

You always talk so dirty. Who told you about that, anyway?

I forget.

Sammy?

No. You did.

I did not.

You did. You said he tried to do it to you when you were sleeping on the couch.

See there! You don't even know what you're talking about. It was when I was washing dishes.

Oh, yes. Dishes.

By myself. In the kitchen.

Well, I'm glad you didn't let him.

Yes.

Did you?

Did I what?

Let him.

Now who's crazy?

I am, I guess.

You sure are.

Still...

Well. Go ahead. Still what?

I wonder what it would be like.

Horrible.

Really?

Yes. Horrible.

Then why didn't you tell Mrs. Breedlove?

I did tell her!

I don't mean about the first time. I mean about the second time, when you were sleeping on the couch.

I wasn't sleeping! I was reading!

You don't have to shout.

You don't understand anything, do you? She didn't even believe me when I told her.

So that's why you didn't tell her about the second time?

She wouldn't have believed me then either.

You're right. No use telling her when she wouldn't believe you.

That's what I'm trying to get through your thick head.

O.K. I understand now. Just about.

What do you mean, just about?

You sure are mean today.

You keep on saying mean and sneaky things. I thought you were my friend.

I am. I am.

Then leave me alone about Cholly.

O.K.

There's nothing more to say about him, anyway. He's gone, anyway.

Yes. Good riddance. Yes. Good riddance. And Sammy's gone too.

And Sammy's gone too.

So there's no use talking about it. I mean them.

No. No use at all.

It's all over now.

Yes.

And you don't have to be afraid of Cholly coming at you anymore.

No.
That was horrible, wasn't it?
Yes.
The second time too?
Yes.
Really? The second time too?
Leave me alone! You better leave me alone.
Can't you take a joke? I was only funning.
I don't like to talk about dirty things.
Me neither. Let's talk about something else.
What? What will we talk about?
Why, your eyes.
Oh, yes. My eyes. My blue eyes. Let me look again.
See how pretty they are.
Yes. They get prettier each time I look at them.
They are the prettiest I've ever seen.
Really?
Oh, yes.
Prettier than the sky?
Oh, yes. Much prettier than the sky.
Prettier than Alice-and-Jerry Storybook eyes?
Oh, yes. Much prettier than Alice-and-Jerry Storybook eyes.
And prettier than Joanna's?
Oh, yes. And bluer too.
Bluer than Michelena's?
Yes.
Are you sure?
Of course I'm sure.
You don't sound sure...
Well, I am sure. Unless...
Unless what?
Oh, nothing. I was just thinking about a lady I saw yesterday. Her eyes sure were blue. But no. Not bluer than yours.
Are you sure?
Yes. I remember them now. Yours are bluer.
I'm glad.

Me too. I'd hate to think there was anybody around with bluer eyes than yours. I'm sure there isn't. Not around here, anyway.

But you don't know, do you? You haven't seen everybody, have you?

No. I haven't.

So there could be, couldn't there?

Not hardly.

But maybe. Maybe. You said "around here". Nobody "around here" probably has bluer eyes. What about some place else? Even if my eyes are bluer than Joanna's and bluer than Michelena's and bluer than that lady's you saw, suppose there is somebody way off somewhere with bluer eyes than mine?

Don't be silly.

There could be. Couldn't there?

Not hardly.

But suppose. Suppose a long way off. In Cincinnati, say, there is somebody whose eyes are bluer than mine? Suppose there are two people with bluer eyes?

So what? You asked for blue eyes. You got blue eyes.

He should have made them bluer.

Who?

Mr. Soaphead.

Did you say what color blue you wanted them?

No. I forgot.

Oh. Well.

Look. Look over there. At that girl. Look at her eyes. Are they bluer than mine?

No, I don't think so. Did you look real good?

Yes.

Here comes someone. Look at his. See if they're bluer.

You're being silly. I'm not going to look at everybody's eyes.

You have to.

No I don't.

Please. If there is somebody with bluer eyes than mine, then maybe there is somebody with the bluest eyes. The bluest eyes in the whole world.

That's just too bad, isn't it?

Please help me look.

No.

But suppose my eyes aren't blue enough?

Blue enough for what?

Blue enough for... I don't know. Blue enough for something. Blue enough... for you!
I'm not going to play with you anymore.
Oh. Don't leave me.
Yes. I am.
Why? Are you mad at me?
Yes.
Because my eyes aren't blue enough? Because I don't have the bluest eyes?
No. Because you're acting silly.
Don't go. Don't leave me. Will you come back if I get them?
Get what?
The bluest eyes. Will you come back then?
Of course I will. I'm just going away for a little while.
You promise?
Sure. I'll be back. Right before your very eyes.

So it was.

A little black girl yearns for the blue eyes of a little white girl, and the horror at the heart of her yearning is exceeded only by the evil of fulfillment.

We saw her sometimes. Frieda and I—after the baby came too soon and died. After the gossip and the slow wagging of heads. She was so sad to see. Grown people looked away; children, those who were not frightened by her, laughed outright.

The damage done was total. She spent her days, her tendril, sap-green days, walking up and down, up and down, her head jerking to the beat of a drummer so distant only she could hear. Elbows bent, hands on shoulders, she flailed her arms like a bird in an eternal, grotesquely futile effort to fly. Beating the air, a winged but grounded bird, intent on the blue void it could not reach—could not even see—but which filled the valleys of the mind.

We tried to see her without looking at her, and never, never went near. Not because she was absurd, or repulsive, or because we were frightened, but because we had failed her. Our flowers never grew. I was convinced that Frieda was right, that I had planted them too deeply. How could I have been so sloven? So we avoided Pecola Breedlove—forever.

And the years folded up like pocket handkerchiefs. Sammy left town long ago; Cholly died in the workhouse; Mrs. Breedlove still does housework. And Pecola is somewhere in that little brown house she and her mother moved to on the edge of town, where you can see her even now, once in a while. The birdlike gestures are worn away to a mere picking and plucking her way between the tire rims and the sunflowers, between Coke bottles and milkweed, among all the waste and beauty of the world—which is what she herself was. All of our waste which we dumped on her and which she absorbed. And all of our beauty, which was hers first and which she gave to us. All of us—all who knew her—felt so wholesome after we cleaned ourselves on her. We were so beautiful when we stood astride her ugliness. Her simplicity decorated us, her guilt sanctified us, her pain made us glow with health, her awkwardness made us think we had a sense of humor. Her inarticulateness made us believe we were eloquent. Her poverty kept us generous. Even her waking dreams we used—to silence our own night-mares. And she let us, and thereby deserved our contempt. We honed our egos on her, padded our characters with her frailty, and yawned in the fantasy of our strength.

And fantasy it was, for we were not strong, only aggressive; we were not free, merely licensed; we were not compassionate, we were polite; not good, but well behaved. We courted death in order to call ourselves brave, and hid like thieves from life. We substituted good grammar for intellect; we switched habits to simulate maturity; we rearranged lies and called it truth, seeing in the new pattern of an old idea the Revelation and the Word.

She, however, stepped over into madness, a madness which protected her from us simply because it bored us in the end.

Oh, some of us "loved" her. The Maginot Line. And Cholly loved her. I'm sure he did. He, at any rate, was the one who loved her enough to touch her, envelop her, give something of himself to her. But his touch was fatal, and the something he gave her filled the matrix of her agony with death. Love is never any better than the lover. Wicked people love wickedly, violent people love violently, weak people love weakly, stupid people love stupidly, but the love of a free man is never safe. There is no gift for the beloved. The lover alone possesses his gift of love. The loved one is shorn, neutralized, frozen in the glare of the lover's inward eye.

And now when I see her searching the garbage—for what? The thing we assassinated? I talk about how I did not plant the seeds too deeply, how it was the fault of the earth, the land, of our town. I even think now that the land of the entire country was hostile to marigolds that year. This soil is bad for certain kinds of flowers. Certain seeds it will not nurture, certain fruit it will not bear, and when the land kills of its own volition, we acquiesce and say the victim had no right to live. We are wrong, of course, but it doesn't matter. It's too late. At least on the edge of my town, among the garbage and the sunflowers of my town, it's much, much, much too late.

Lecture 17
Toni Morrison

Ⅲ Thinking, Talking and Writing About Literature

❶ Textual Cognition

Make an introductory presentation on the following terms related to this literary work.
1) whiteness
2) black stereotype

❷ Textual Reading

Search for evidence in the text and answer the following questions.
1) What happened to Pecola Breedlove based on the dialog in the text?
2) How do you interpret the sentence, "Just because I got blue eyes, bluer than theirs, they're prejudiced"?
3) Discuss Pecola's dream in terms of its worth. Is her dream attainable, or will it eventually be deferred and dry up "like a raisin in the sun", as Hughes's poem ("Dream Deferred") suggests?

❸ Critical Reading

Discuss in groups the following questions to further explore this literary work.
1) What does "the bluest eyes" in the novel symbolize?
2) Discuss the mother-daughter relationships in the novel.

❹ Writing About Literature

Read the following critical excerpt and then write an essay.

 Wong, Shelley. "Transgression as Poesis in *The Bluest Eye*."
Callaloo 13.3 (1990): 471–481.

In an interview, Morrison commented that she had "used the primer, with its picture of a happy family, as a frame acknowledging the outer civilization. The primer with white children was the way life was presented to black people" (LeClair 28–29). The lesson of this passage in fact goes well beyond acknowledging or presenting white bourgeois values—it goes as far as enacting the very conditions of alienated self-containment which underlie those values. We might note, for instance, that the "house" precedes the "family" in order of both appearance and discussion. In this scheme of things, human relations are preempted by property and commodity relations. The space of ownership engulfs the time of human development and fellowship. The body of human relationships is drawn into the marketplace of being, an essentially timeless space which fosters a frightening commensurability between people and units of exchange, a commensurability which renders family members falsely individualized moments of a social and material whole. In the school of bourgeois economics, the child's first lesson in cultural literacy teaches the primacy of the singular and the discrete. The lesson works against memory and history, and collapses the structure of desire and communitas, while simultaneously promoting the desirability of discrete repetition, the wish to be always equal to some measure of ideality divorced from one's own physical and spiritual needs.

Essay Writing

Write an essay on the narrative features of the primer passage in *The Bluest Eye* with no less than 500 words.

IV. Further Activity

Scan the QR code and watch a video clip "Open Yale Course" by Amy Hungerford on *The Bluest Eye*.

Lecture 18
Sandra Cisneros

Profile of the Writer

Sandra Cisneros
(1954–)

    Sandra Cisneros has won multiple awards, fellowships, and honors as an internationally recognized writer. Her book called *The House on Mango Street* (1984), has sold over six million copies and has been translated into over twenty languages.

    Sandra Cisneros was born on December 20, 1954 in Chicago. Although her parents met in Chicago, they were both from Mexico. Cisneros was the only girl of seven children. When Cisneros was ten years old, she wrote her first poem. While in school, she was an active writer and was known as "the poet". After high school, Cisneros attended Loyola University of Chicago and graduated in 1976 with a Bachelor of Arts degree in English. Cisneros continued on to the University of Iowa where she graduated in 1978 with a Master of Fine Arts degree in Creative Writing. After graduation with her second degree, Cisneros worked at many universities including California State University at Chico, the University of California, Berkeley, the University of Michigan Ann Arbor, and the University of New Mexico.

    In 1980, Cisneros published the first book, a short book of poetry called *Bad Boys*. *The House on Mango Street*, a fiction novel, was published in 1984. This book won the American Book Award from the Before Columbus Foundation. She published her first full-length poetry book called *My Wicked Wicked Ways* in 1987. In 1991,

Cisneros published a collection of short stories called *Woman Hollering Creek and Other Stories*. This book won the PEN Center West Award for Best Fiction of 1991, and was nominated as the Best Book of Fiction of 1991 by *The Los Angeles Times*.

In 1994 Cisneros wrote her first children's book called *Pelitos/Hairs* in both Spanish and English. That same year, she wrote another book of poetry called *Loose Woman* that won the Mountains & Plains Booksellers' Award. She wrote her second novel in 2002 that was called *Caramelo*. This book won the Premio Napoli Award, and was selected as an important book of the year by *The New York Times*. She wrote a picture book for "grown-ups" in 2012 called *Have You Seen Marie?*. Her latest book called *A House of My Own: Stories from My Life*, a collection of her personal essays, won the 2016 PEN Center USA Literary Award for creative nonfiction.

Sandra Cisneros' work has been praised by critics for many reasons, from the authenticity of her characters' voices and experience to the marvelous simplicity of her style. Perhaps more important than critics are ordinary readers, who find Cisneros' writing to be moving, funny, direct, and true on the most basic of human levels. Her fiction, *The House on Mango Street*, is often compared to poetry—or even identified as poetry.

I Preview Questions

1. What is the time span of the story in *The House on Mango Street*?
2. Esperanza is the most fully developed character in the book. Search for the meaning of the name "Esperanza".

II Literary Reading: *The House on Mango Street*

We didn't always live on Mango Street. Before that we lived on Loomis on the third floor, and before that we lived on Keeler. Before Keeler it was Paulina, and before that I can't remember. But what I remember most is moving a lot. Each time it seemed there'd be one more of us. By the time we got to Mango Street we were six—Mama, Papa, Carlos, Kiki, my sister Nenny and me.

The house on Mango Street is ours, and we don't have to pay rent to anybody, or share the yard with the people downstairs, or be careful not to make too much noise, and there isn't a landlord banging on the ceiling with a broom. But even so, it's not the house we'd thought we'd get.

We had to leave the flat on Loomis quick. The water pipes broke and the landlord wouldn't fix them because the house was too old. We had to leave fast. We were using the washroom next door and carrying water over in empty milk gallons. That's why Mama and Papa looked for a house, and that's why we moved into the house on Mango Street, far away, on the other side of town.

They always told us that one day we would move into a house, a real house that would be ours for always so we wouldn't have to move each year. And our house would have running water and pipes that worked. And inside it would have real stairs, not hallway stairs, but stairs inside like the houses on TV. And we'd have a basement and at least three washrooms so when we took a bath, we wouldn't have to tell everybody. Our house would be white with trees around it, a great big yard and grass growing without a fence. This was the house Papa talked about when he held a lottery ticket and this was the house Mama dreamed up in the stories she told us before we went to bed.

But the house on Mango Street is not the way they told it at all. It's small and red with tight steps in front and windows so small you'd think they were holding their breath. Bricks are crumbling in places, and the front door is so swollen you have to push hard to get in. There is no front yard, only four little elms the city planted by the curb. Out back is a small garage for the car we don't own yet and a small yard that looks smaller between the two buildings on either side. There are stairs in our house, but they are ordinary hallway stairs, and the house has only one washroom. Everybody has to share a bedroom—Mama and Papa, Carlos and Kiki, me and Nenny.

Once when we were living on Loomis, a nun from my school passed by and saw me playing out front. The laundromat downstairs had been boarded up because it had been robbed two days before and the owner had painted on the wood YES WE'RE OPEN so as not to lose business.

Where do you live? she asked.

There, I said pointing up to the third floor.

You live there?

There. I had to look to where she pointed—the third floor, the paint peeling, wooden bars Papa had nailed on the windows so we wouldn't fall out. You live there? The way she said it made me feel like nothing. There. I lived there. I nodded.

I knew then I had to have a house. A real house. One I could point to. But this isn't it. The house on Mango Street isn't it. For the time being, Mama says. Temporary, says Papa. But I know how those things go.

A House of My Own

Not a flat. Not an apartment in back. Not a man's house. Not a daddy's. A house all my own. With my porch and my pillow, my pretty purple petunias. My books and my stories. My two shoes waiting beside the bed. Nobody to shake a stick at. Nobody's garbage to pick up after.

Only a house quiet as snow, a space for myself to go, clean as paper before the poem.

Mango Says Goodbye Sometimes

I like to tell stories. I tell them inside my head. I tell them after the mailman says, Here's your mail. Here's your mail he said.

I make a story for my life, for each step my brown shoe takes. I say, "And so she trudged up the wooden stairs, her sad brown shoes taking her to the house she never liked."

I like to tell stories. I am going to tell you a story about a girl who didn't want to belong.

We didn't always live on Mango Street. Before that we lived on Loomis on the third floor, and before that we lived on Keeler. Before Keeler it was Paulina, but what I remember most is Mango Street, sad red house, the house I belong but do not belong to.

I put it down on paper and then the ghost does not ache so much. I write it down and Mango says goodbye sometimes. She does not hold me with both arms. She sets me free.

One day I will pack my bags of books and paper. One day I will say goodbye to Mango. I am too strong for her to keep me here forever. One day I will go away.

Friends and neighbors will say, What happened to that Esperanza? Where did she go with all those books and paper? Why did she march so far away?

They will not know I have gone away to come back. For the ones I left behind. For the ones who cannot out.

III Thinking, Talking and Writing About Literature

1 Textual Cognition

Make an introductory presentation on the following terms related to this literary work.

1) alienation and displacement
2) Hispanic

❷ Textual Reading

Search for evidence in the text and answer the following questions.

1) What does the text state explicitly and implicitly? Cite textual evidence in support of your views.

2) Why did Esperanza leave Mango Street?

3) Why do you think Esperanza wanted a house of her own?

❸ Critical Reading

Discuss in groups the following questions to further explore this literary work.

1) What is Sandra Cisneros's purpose in writing *The House on Mango Street*?

2) Clearly Esperanza is a typical adolescent girl, but at some moments she is a child and at some moments an adult. How do you understand this?

❹ Writing About Literature

Read the following critical excerpt and then write an essay.

> Poey, Delia. "Coming of Age in the Curriculum: *The House on Mango Street* and *Bless Me, Ultima* as Representative Texts." *Critical Insights:* The House on Mango Street *by Sandra Cisneros*. Ed. María Herrera-Sobek. New York: Salem Press, 2010. 265–284.

In the traditional Bildungsroman, attention remains focused exclusively on the protagonist, while *Mango Street* disperses the spotlight to include the community as inseparable from the protagonist's identity. As the three sisters tell Esperanza: "You will always be Esperanza. You will always be Mango Street" (Cisneros 105).

Unlike the protagonist of the traditional Bildungsroman, Esperanza does not travel during the course of the book, nor does the text end with an escape. This is significant in that her psychic movement from childhood to adolescence to adulthood takes place within the geographic and cultural boundaries of her community. Her individuation is undertaken, like Antonio's in *Bless Me, Ultima*, in a community-centered context, a marked difference from the master plot of the genre in which the protagonist physically travels outward. This community centeredness demonstrates a point of negotiation of the conflict, for the Latina/o author working within the Bildungsroman tradition, between the valorization of the individual inherent in the genre and its incompatibility with the political and cultural implications that valorization carries for minority intellectuals.

Generalized readings of these two texts that connect them solely to the familiar mapping of the novel, and more specifically to the Bildungsroman with its assumption and valorization of the autonomous individual, reduce reader frustration at moments of difference, be it content based as in Anaya's text, or structural difference as in Cisneros's. This diminished frustration leads to a higher degree of intelligibility, and the assigning of a higher status for these two texts, relative to that of other Latina/o texts. By isolating these texts from their discursive and historical contexts, they can also function as mirrors of the hegemonic and confirmations of stereotypic representations. Thus, it is not the texts themselves that are problematic, since they do engage in layered critiques and propose their own aesthetics. Rather, it is their acceptance as representative that is troubling, given that they do provide opportunities for easy incorporation, which erases their transformative possibilities.

Essay Writing

Write an essay on community centeredness in *The House on Mango Street* as a Bildungsroman with no less than 500 words.

IV Further Activity

Scan the QR code and listen to the audio of *The House on Mango Street*.

04

第四部分
殖民／后殖民
英语成长小说

Colonial/Postcolonial English Bildungsroman

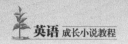

导 言

在经典成长小说中,主人公通过受教育和完成考验,实现从少年到青年的自我成长,适应社会秩序。而在后殖民成长小说中,身份建构是一个复杂的跨文化交流、碰撞的过程。后殖民作家用成长小说回应殖民主义和新殖民主义的创伤,表达在种族压迫语境中成长的艰难。后殖民成长小说研究专家埃里卡·霍格兰(Ericka A. Hoagland)认为,后殖民文学把经典成长小说的叙事改造成为一种对抗殖民的政治行为[1]。拉尔夫·奥斯丁(Ralph A. Austen)在谈到非洲的殖民和后殖民成长小说时,明确表示,尽管与传统的欧洲经典成长小说有很大不同,但在非洲文学中的确存在一个可以被认定为成长小说的类型群[2]。而霍格兰也在《后殖民成长小说》("The Postcolonial Bildungsroman")一文中明确指出,非洲成长小说的确存在[3]。在特定的历史背景下,成长小说不断与时代、空间、时间、社会协商与对话,而其外延与内涵也在不断发生变化。在后殖民非洲文学中,一种丰富的成长小说传统的出现正是这一事实的有力例证。

霍格兰等批评家在非洲小说中看到了对经典成长小说的偏离和改写。很多评论家都注意到非洲文学中的一个独特现象,那就是大部分非洲作家的作品都涉及青春主题,第三代非洲作家的作品更是如此。从"现代非洲文学之父"、尼日利亚作家钦努阿·阿契贝(Chinua Achebe,1930—2013)的《分崩离析》(*Things Fall Apart*),到津巴布韦作家、电影制片人特西提·丹格瑞姆加(Tsitsi Dangarembga,1959—)的《不安之地》(*Nervous Conditions*),再到尼日利亚作家本·奥克瑞(Ben Okri,1959—)的《饥饿之路》(*The Famished Road*)、乌干达女作家戈雷蒂·久姆亨多(Goretti Kyomuhendo,1965—)的《不再有秘密》(*Secrets No More*)、尼日利亚小说家乌诺马·阿祖阿(Unoma

---

[1] Hoagland, Ericka A. "The Postcolonial Bildungsroman." *A History of the Bildungsroman*. Ed. Sarah Graham. Oxford: Cambridge University Press, 2018. 227.

[2] Austen, Ralph A. "Struggling with the African Bildungsroman." *Research in African Literatures* 46.3 (2015): 215.

[3] Hoagland, Ericka A. "The Postcolonial Bildungsroman." *A History of the Bildungsroman*. Ed. Sarah Graham. Oxford: Cambridge University Press, 2018. 227.

Azuah，1969— ）的《冲天火焰》（*Sky-High Flames*）以及尼日利亚"80后"作家基戈泽·欧比奥马（Chigozie Obioma，1986— ）的《钓鱼的男孩》（*The Fishermen*）等，均是非洲成长小说的代表作品。第三代非洲作家中的代表人物阿迪契（Chimamanda Ngozi Adichie，1977— ）更是对成长小说情有独钟。阿迪契的第一部小说《紫木槿》（*Purple Hibiscus*）就是一部经典的非洲女性成长小说。这部小说描写了主人公、伊博族少女卡姆比丽（Kambili）努力打破父权制社会为非洲女性成长设置的种种障碍而寻求自由和个人发展的故事。阿迪契2013年的小说《美国佬》（*Americanah*）讲述的是跨文化语境下一个尼日利亚中学生伊菲米鲁（Ifemelu）的成长故事。另外她的短篇小说集《绕颈之物》（*The Thing Around Your Neck*）中也有多篇故事涉及成长主题。

然而一个值得认真思考的问题是，缘起于18世纪欧洲的成长小说是典型的西方叙事和欧洲文化转型的产物，却在殖民和后殖民的非洲蓬勃发展，其原因何在？美国犹他大学成长小说研究专家大卫·米克尔森（David J. Mickelsen）在谈到非洲喀麦隆作家蒙戈·贝蒂（Mongo Beti，1932—2001）的非洲法语成长小说《完成使命》（*Mission Terminée*）时的一番话很有启发性：

> 当第三世界作家把传统的、地方的形式和继承的欧洲形式结合起来，产生融合的结果常常挑战我们安全的、西方的传统文类观。在这个方面，来自于前殖民地的成长小说毫无疑问是非常有趣的，因为他们的主题以及他们的形式突出了传统和继承的成长小说之间的冲突。例如，非洲成长小说主要检视的是文化的冲突，青年人试图在殖民权力的"文明"教育和他的祖先的传统文化之间求得一种平衡。[1]

显然，非洲成长小说在某种意义上是对欧洲成长小说传统的继承、挪用、颠覆和超越。非洲成长小说兴起的一个重要原因是非洲剧烈的社会转型。事实上，非洲小说的诞生与社会、文化、历史等几个元素机缘巧合。意大利文学批评家莫雷蒂（Franco Moretti）在探讨欧洲社会现代转型时期的文化形态时，将"青春"（youth）看作现代性的"本质"，其理由是"青春"具有永恒的"内在的不满足"（inner dissatisfaction）与"变动性"（mobility），青春的反抗与革命可以毁灭任何既定体制。[2] 非洲成长小说大规模兴起的时间是20世纪

---

[1] Mickelsen, David J. "The Bildungsroman in Africa: The Case of Mission Terminée." *The French Review* 59.3 (1986): 418.

[2] Moretti, Franco. *The Way of the World: The Bildungsroman in European Culture*. New York: Verso, 2000.

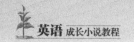

60年代，而非洲国家自20世纪五六十年代相继独立后，开始进入寻求民主国家建立和民主化进程的转型时期。两个时间点的重叠并非机缘巧合，而是因为成长小说的特点之一就是个人成长和历史发展之间强有力的联系纽带。换言之，个人的发展常常以一种寓言的方式和民族发展并行。因此在某种程度上，非洲成长小说大规模兴起是青春主题与社会现代转型在非洲碰撞的结果。

非洲成长小说兴起的另一个重要原因是黑人女性的解放运动。黑人成长小说和白人成长小说的共性之一就是"男性作家，不管肤色和国籍如何，都控制着早期传统"[1]。20世纪30年代之前，几乎所有的欧洲和美国的成长小说都是由男性作家创作的关于男性主人公成长的作品；尽管黑人作家进入到成长小说传统较晚，但也复制了讲述男性主人公故事的模式。1966年，随着被称为"非洲现代文学之母"的尼日利亚小说家弗洛拉·恩瓦帕（Flora Nwapa，1931—1993）的《埃弗鲁》（*Efuru*）的出版，成长小说在非洲女性作家中成为一种流行的文类，而她们的作品也开始在20世纪70年代享有盛誉，拥有越来越广泛的读者群体。非洲女性以欧洲语言写作的现象出现在20世纪70年代和80年代的国际文学场景之中。在此之前，非洲和西方批评家都主要关注男性作家的作品。就像瓦尔特·考林斯（Walt Collins）所指出的那样，恩瓦帕的《埃弗鲁》和肯尼亚的女作家格瑞斯·奥高特（Grace Ogot，1930—2015）创作的《希望之地》（*The Promised Land*）都出版于1966年，但这些作品并没有引起人们的关注，因为人们的目光都聚焦于受人尊重的男性作家，如尼日利亚的钦努阿·阿契贝、肯尼亚的恩古齐·瓦·提安哥（Ngugi wa Thiong'O，1938— ）等。

我们不难发现，非洲成长小说传统和欧洲成长小说传统在很多方面一脉相承，具体体现在如下几个方面。其一，旅行主题。在欧洲成长小说中，主人公常常在不同的城市之间辗转，以解开生命的谜团或者追寻生活的意义。狄更斯的大卫·科波菲尔、劳伦斯的保罗·莫雷尔（Paul Morel）等主人公的生活经历莫不如此。这一特点在非洲、西印度群岛和美国非裔成长小说中得以延续。比如迈克·安东尼（Michael Anthony，1932— ）的《在圣费尔南多的一年》（*The Year in San Fernando*）中的弗朗西斯（Francis），乔治·拉明（George Lamming，1927—2022）的《在我皮肤中的城堡》（*In the Castle of My Skin*）的主人公G和特拉姆普尔（Trumper），詹姆斯·鲍德温（James Baldwin，1924—1987）的《向苍天呼吁》（*Go Tell It on the Mountain*）中的约翰·格赖姆斯（John Grimes），以

---

[1] LeSeur, Geta. *Ten Is the Age of Darkness: The Black Bildungsroman*. Columbia: University of Missouri Press, 1995. 21.

及拉尔夫·艾利森的《看不见的人》中的无名主人公都有相似的人生旅程。

第二个明显相似之处是主人公均出生在闭塞、落后的乡下，身世或凄凉或不明，不知父亲是谁或身在何处。特立尼达作家莫尔·霍奇（Merle Hodge，1944—）的《克里特裂痕，猴子》（*Crick Crack, Monkey*）中的蒂（Tee）、巴巴多斯作家乔治·拉明的《冒险季节》（*Season of Adventure*）中的弗拉（Fola）、美国非裔作家理查德·赖特的《黑孩子》（*Black Boy*）中的理查德（Richard）等都是和大卫、皮普有着相同或相似身世的主人公。

非洲及非洲流散成长小说和经典成长小说的另一个共同特点是与母亲的那种既依赖又对抗的关系。在多部关于西印度男孩成长的小说中，如奥斯汀·克拉克（Austin C. Clarke，1934—）的《在荆棘丛中》（*Amongst Thistles and Thorns*）中的弥尔顿·苏波斯（Milton Sobers）和《在我皮肤中的城堡》中的主人公 G 等都是母亲和儿子关系密切，而这种密切的关系与情节和男孩的成长紧密相连；而在《冒险季节》和马歇尔的《棕色姑娘，棕色砖房》中母亲和女儿的关系却势不两立。正是这些家族相似性使得非洲及非洲流散成长小说传统得以确立。

非洲成长小说与非洲的自传书写有着密切联系。霍格兰认为，非洲成长小说根植于非洲自传传统之中，而几内亚作家卡马·拉雷（Camara Laye，1928—1980）的自传《黑孩子》（*L'Enfant Noir*）往往被认为是非洲成长小说的"原文本"[1]。而之所以把这部自传定位为非洲成长小说的"原文本"，是因为非洲自传和非洲成长小说都参与到殖民与后殖民非洲社会的对话和协商之中。批评家拉尔夫·奥斯丁对非洲成长小说的研究也是从非洲的自传性作品传统谈起的。奥斯丁指出，非洲自传的通常模式是：一名男孩在殖民地出生，父母都受过欧洲教育，男孩本人也到欧洲学校读书，而这给他造成了相当的痛苦，但也促使他经历了对祖父母文化的重新认识；最后他带着对归属的不安和对未来的期待，离开了殖民地，奔向大城市或者欧洲的宗主国，遭遇新的挑战，体验不同人生。[2]

这种基本情节模式对大多数非洲自传读者并不陌生。它在两部广为流传的作品中都有一定呈现：一部是前文提到的卡马拉雷的《黑孩子》，另一部是尼日利亚作家、诺奖得主沃莱·索因卡（Wole Soyinka，1934—）的《在阿凯的童年时光》（*Aké: The Years of Childhood*）。这些自传性作品均以第一人称记录"殖民主义下的成长"[3]。在世界的其他

---

1 Graham, Sarah. "Introduction." *A History of the Bildungsroman*. Cambridge: Cambridge University Press, 2019. 2.
2 Austen, Ralph A. "Coming of Age Through Colonial Education: African Autobiography as Reluctant Bildungsroman (the Case of Camara Laye)." *Mande Studies* 12 (2010): 1–18.
3 Austen, Ralph A. "Struggling with the African Bildungsroman." *Research in African Literatures* 46.3 (2015): 214.

地方的自传作品，包括印裔英国作家尼拉德·C. 乔杜里（Nirad C. Chaudhuri，1897—1999）的《一个不知名的印度人自传》（*Autobiography of an Unknown Indian*），也运用了相似的模式。这样的非洲模式和其他后殖民叙事，不论是纪实的还是虚构的，都与在欧洲传统中确立的成长小说有颇多相似性，这一点已被越来越多的学者认可。

在非洲国家中，尼日利亚的小说创作传统最为完整，而第三代尼日利亚作家的大部分小说都涉及主人公的成长。很多尼日利亚的成长小说都讲述了年轻的主人公在尼日利亚的战争和动荡环境中作为公民、作为牺牲者的经历；随着他们的成熟，逐渐获得自我认知，开始理解尼日利亚社会文化秩序的真正本质，因为他们发现，自己生存的环境在任何时刻都会影响到他们的世界观。除了成长叙事的特点之外，这些小说还表现了一种自传特点。这一点从文学创作的角度不难理解。作为初出茅庐的年轻作家，开始创作的方式之一就是书写和重新包装自我。尼日利亚作家伊·班德勒-托马斯（Biyi Bandele-Thomas，1967—）的《同情的承诺和其他梦想》（*The Sympathetic Undertaker and Other Dreams*）、《来自苍穹后面的人》（*The Man Who Came in from the Back of the Beyond*），赫朗·哈比拉（Helon Habila，1967—）的《等待天使》（*Waiting for an Angel*），尼日利亚作家、戏剧家瑟斐·阿塔（Sefi Atta，1964—）的《一切美好都会来到》（*Everything Good Will Come*），克里斯·阿巴尼（Chris Abani，1966—）的《雅园》（*Graceland*），乌诺马·阿祖阿的《冲天火焰》，阿迪契的《紫木槿》《半轮黄日》（*Half of a Yellow Sun*），乌佐丁玛·伊维拉（Uzodinma Iweala，1982—）的《无境之兽》（*Beasts of No Nation*）等作品均体现出以自传为基本框架和元素的成长主题。

然而，尽管非洲殖民/后殖民小说与欧洲成长小说传统有很多相似性，但更多的是差异。为了在后殖民语境中说明独特的非洲经历，非洲作家将成长小说这种源自西方的叙事形式进行非洲化，并以反讽、挪用等写作策略解构了欧洲经典成长小说。反殖民和反对新殖民（anti-neocolonial）之间对立又协商的关系在非洲成长小说中一直存在。正如杰德·埃斯蒂（Jed Esty）所言，后殖民成长小说显然通过"解构"的过程，塑形了近代成长小说史[1]。非洲成长小说，比如南非女作家奥利芙·施赖纳（Olive Schreiner，1855—1920）的《一个非洲农场的故事》（*The Story of an African Farm*），索马里作家努鲁丁·法拉赫（Nuruddin Farah，1945—）的小说《地图》（*Maps*），尼日利亚作家阿迪契的《紫木槿》，津巴布韦作家、电影制片人特西提·丹格瑞姆加的《不安之地》，尼

---

[1] Esty, Jed. *Unseasonable Youth: Modernism, Colonialism and the Fiction of Development*. Oxford & New York: Oxford University Press, 2012. 18.

第四部分
殖民 / 后殖民英语成长小说　导言

日利亚作家、社会活动家肯·萨罗-维瓦（Ken Saro-Wiwa, 1941—1995）的《乡村男孩索扎》（*Sozaboy*）都反映了这些模式。例如，《一个非洲农场的故事》中人物的成长模式就和经典成长小说有着本质区别。该小说是南非乃至整个非洲文坛的第一部现代长篇小说，对非洲文学产生了深远影响。它对非洲殖民地乡村的描写具有开创性意义，同时也是一部极具创新性的女权主义成长小说。小说聚焦于两位主人公：充满困惑的艺术家瓦尔多（Waldo）和被父权制社会束缚的新女性林德尔（Lyndall）。20世纪70年代，英美女权主义批评的重要著作、肖瓦尔特的《她们自己的文学》（*A Literature of Their Own*）将林德尔视为"英语小说史上第一位严肃的女权主义女主人公"[1]。这部小说基本秉承了成长小说的叙述模式，但人物的成长模式却与传统成长小说，尤其是欧洲男性成长小说中的模式有着本质区别[2]。对此，曼迪·特莱格斯特（Mandy Treagus）在其研究殖民地女性成长的专著《帝国女孩》（*Empire Girls: The Colonial Heroine Comes of Age*）中指出，尽管每一位女主人公都分享了成长小说主人公的渴望，但其性别和殖民性却不能让她充分经历英国男性主人公所获得的成长。林德尔目睹来自帝国殖民冒险者的压迫，也遭遇到父权制社会的歧视。她在不断的抗争中深感无力，以至于发出"我是沉睡的，被包裹起来，被锁扣在自我之中"[3]的悲叹。林德尔的命运以付出生命的代价来抵制殖民压迫和父权压迫而告终。这种"停滞的"成长模式正如杰德·埃斯蒂所言，"在帝国疆界中生活的年轻人受到阻碍或者停滞的成长是不能用经典成长的概念来定义的"[4]。

非洲成长小说在多个方面偏离、解构、颠覆了西方经典成长小说，其中对主人公的个人主义模式及其与社会的和解模式等方面的颠覆、偏离表现得最为突出。成长小说具有内在的颠覆性潜质。对此约瑟·伍兹奎兹（José Santiago Fernández Vázquez）提供了一种可资借鉴的观点："后殖民作家转向成长小说的原因之一就是想要把帝国主义的主代码（master codes）编入文本，从而更有效地捣毁它们。"[5] 伍兹奎兹的观点突出了该文类蕴含的颠覆性潜质（subversive potential）[6]，而这一潜质一直以来的最大特征就是对主流秩序的

1　Showalter, Elaine. *A Literature of Their Own*. Princeton: Princeton University Press, 1977. 199.
2　Treagus, Mandy. *Empire Girls: The Colonial Heroine Comes of Age*. Adelaide: University of Adelaide Press, 2014.
3　Schreiner, Olive. *The Story of an African Farm*. London: Penguin, 1995. 195–196.
4　Esty, Jed. "The Colonial Bildungsroman: *The Story of an African Farm* and the *Ghost of Goethe*." *Victorian Studies* 49 (2007): 407–430.
5　Vázquez, José Santiago Fernández. "Recharting the Geography of Genre: Ben Okri's *The Famished Road* as a Postcolonial Bildungsroman." *Journal of Commonwealth Literature* 27.2 (2002): 86.
6　Hoagland, Ericka A. "The Postcolonial Bildungsroman." *A History of the Bildungsroman*. Ed. Sarah Graham. Oxford: Cambridge University Press, 2018. 219.

反思性批判。

后殖民成长小说在自我与族群的关系、个人对社会的认同方式、个人成长与国家民族成长之间的关系等方面，与经典成长小说有着本质不同，其中最大的不同在于自我和社会之间的关系的定位。自我和自我塑形从其开始被书写就一直是一个令人困惑的、复杂的观念：你是谁、你在社会和世界中的位置、你如何与他人沟通交流等问题引起了越来越多的检视和思考。非洲成长小说更多地涉及复杂的自我观以及自我与社会之间复杂的关系。例如，奥耶坎·奥沃莫耶拉（Oyekan Owomoyela）就曾提醒读者，非洲社会是天然的群体社会（intrinsically communal），非洲人通常都是群体驱动的，在非洲传统文化中，"事实上并不存在个人主义"[1]。同样地，凯瑟琳·菲什伯恩（Katherine Fishburn）在谈到两位重要的非洲作家——塞内加尔女作家玛利亚玛·芭（Mariama Ba, 1929—1981）和尼日利亚裔女作家布奇·埃梅切塔（Buchi Emecheta, 1944—2017）时补充说：

> 因为我们一开始就从一种歌颂个人主义却保留对社会的深深的怀疑的哲学假设出发，我们西方读者还没有准备好理解这些女性的文本。如果我们希望理解这样的文学，那么我们必须至少从理智上（如果不是情感上）承认，不仅有一种方式概念化个人和社会之间的关系。我们一定要愿意接受一个事实，那就是社会从定义上并非对个人有害也不是敌对的，而个人也的确不能与他们的社会截然分开。[2]

约瑟·伍兹奎兹在谈到尼日利亚小说家本·奥克瑞的《饥饿之路》时，也指出这部小说以集体纽带之名批评了成长小说的个人主义终极目的："成长小说原型那关于孤独的、自私的个人，他们对其他人不那么关心。相反，在《饥饿之路》中，主人公对族群的同情之感随着叙事的发展而不断增强。"[3]

大多数情况下，非洲文学中个人的发展和群体生活的延续并不矛盾。阿契贝的《分崩离析》提供了一个经典的范例：主人公奥贡喀沃（Okonkwo）有效地平衡了以个人卓越为目的的个人目标和对身处的族群的责任。尽管奥贡喀沃没有取得成功，小说也以他的自缢结束，但个人和群体之间的内在关联性却依旧很明显。从"伊博文化"（Ibgo

---

1 Owomoyela, Oyekan. *African Literatures: An Introduction*. Waltham: Crossroads Press, 1979. 80.

2 Fishburn, Katherine. *Reading Buchi Emecheta: Cross-Cultural Conversations*. Westport: Greenwood Press, 1995. 37.

3 Vázquez, José Santiago Fernández. "Recharting the Geography of Genre: Ben Okri's *The Famished Road* as a Postcolonial Bildungsroman." *Journal of Commonwealth Literature* 37 (2002): 93.

culture)的角度来看，奥贡喀沃试图以"传统强人气质"来振兴他的部落和族人，而一种强势的部落之爱，则是这种强人气质的主要内涵。

后殖民小说与经典成长小说的另一个不同在于个人成长往往成为国族重构的隐喻。当代非洲国家版图和边界的大部分是殖民者按照经纬在图纸上画就的。这造成了非洲民众对国家的认同缺乏内生基础，国家认同普遍成为国家建构进程中一个棘手的问题。在很多非洲成长小说中，个人成长和国家民族成长之间都存在明显的关联性和同构性。事实上，成长小说常常被非洲作家用于"革命"的隐喻，而个人解放和民族独立也往往更受世人关注。古尔纳（Abdulrazak Gurnah, 1948—）的《天堂》(*Paradise*)、阿契贝的《分崩离析》、阿迪契的《半轮黄日》、奥比奥玛的《钓鱼的男孩》等非洲成长小说均以尼日利亚的国家政治变迁为背景，以中心人物的成长与国族重构为线索，展示人的成长。

比如，《天堂》就是一个小人物的小故事和国家大环境的大故事高度融合的成长小说。十二岁那年，斯瓦希里男孩优素福（Yusuf）离开父母，跟随阿齐兹叔叔（Uncle Aziz）乘火车前往海滨城市。抵达阿齐兹叔叔家后，优素福成为其店铺的一名帮手，并很快和店铺伙计哈利勒成为好友。在叔叔家这个小环境中，他体验到寄人篱下生活的艰辛，也逐渐意识到自己的生活是被设计、被交易、被摆布、被需要的，他始终无法把握自己的命运。小说最后，优素福遵从内心的声音，离开叔叔家，寻找尽管希望渺茫却有可能拥有主动权的人生。与这一小人物的小故事同时展开的是坦桑尼亚被殖民的历史。优素福一家人的悲惨生活就是国家被殖民历史的缩影。优素福未经世事而不加滤镜的视角将殖民者带给坦桑尼亚的灾难尽收眼底。小说通过将个人小故事嵌入社会生活的大故事中，提供了非洲后殖民成长小说将个人与国族同构的生动例证。

再比如《钓鱼的男孩》就以M.K.O.阿比奥拉（M.K.O. Abiola）在1993年竞选尼日利亚总统为历史背景，构建了个人成长和国家发展命运与共的关联性。小说开篇讲述人、主人公本杰明（Benjamin）说，他于"1996年1月"成为一名"渔夫"，而这个时间恰好是尼日利亚前军事独裁者萨尼·阿巴查（Sani Abacha）任职期间。尽管阿比奥拉是民主选举出的，结果却被宣布无效，阿巴查将军同年夺取了权力。本杰明这样解释了他记忆中的国家动乱对个人生活和成长的影响：

> 我们才知道自己安全了，从一九九三年的大选暴动中逃了出来。这次暴动，阿库雷死了一百多人。六月十二日发生的事对尼日利亚的历史产生了深远的影响。从此以后，每年这一天快要来到时，就好像有一千个武装到牙齿的隐形的外科医生带

着手术刀、环锯、针筒和不同寻常的麻醉药品,随着北风降临到阿库雷。[1]

这短短的几行文字就将主人公的命运与民族的命运紧紧地捆绑在一起了。

《半轮黄日》是尼日利亚第三代作家的杰出代表奇玛曼达·阿迪契的第二部重要小说作品。该小说一经问世便好评如潮,并引起评论界的持续关注。对该作品的研究主要聚焦于战争书写、历史书写、创伤书写、身份书写等层面。以上研究关注的焦点大多集中于女主人公、双胞胎姐妹奥兰娜(Olanna)和凯内内(Kainene),或者男主人公、民族主义斗士奥登尼博(Odenigbo)身上。然而事实上,这部小说贯穿始终的灵魂人物却是作为小说"全知叙述意识"的少年乌古(Ugwu)。之所以说少年乌古是《半轮黄日》的灵魂人物,主要原因有以下两点。其一,少年乌古几乎是小说中所有重要事件的见证者和亲历者:他不但以旁观者的身份见证了包括他自己的家庭和奥登尼博的家庭在内的多个尼日利亚家庭、多个人物在战争中的命运和悲欢离合,而且作为士兵亲历了尼日利亚内战(Nigeria-Biafra War)的残酷和暴力。也正是基于此,乌古是阿迪契情感认同最深的人物。阿迪契本人的话印证了这一点。她曾说,乌古是她最认同的形象,并想让他成为小说的灵魂:"一个将所有角色聚合在一起的人物"。[2]其二,乌古是小说中唯一一个经历了"转变"和成长的人物。他不仅经历了战争创伤的洗礼,还经历了一个复杂的自我认知和转化的过程:从自我怀疑、自我否定到自我认知、自我肯定,再到部分地与自我和世界达成和解,最后从懵懂的乡村少年成长为立志书写非洲历史的作家。

内战的爆发从根本上改变了少年乌古的成长轨迹,也改变了所有比亚法拉人的命运。在某种意义上,决定少年乌古成长历程的正是这场深刻地影响了整个尼日利亚人命运的内战。尼日利亚内战不仅对尼日利亚这个国家来说是一个分水岭,对尼日利亚后殖民文学来说也是如此,而正是那些内战中和内战后的"大胆的虚构化的姿态",才使得这场战争不断地被人们从记忆深处挖掘出来,免于被遗忘、被遮蔽的命运。从成长的角度来看,少年乌古的成长随着他在战争中的强暴行为停滞了。唐纳德·邓森(Donald H. Dunson)在《儿童、牺牲者和士兵》(*Child, Victim, Soldier*)一书中说,战争通过暴力阻碍了青少

---

[1] 奇戈希·奥比奥玛,《钓鱼的男孩》,吴晓真译。长沙:湖南文艺出版社,2016年,第123页。
[2] Adichie, Chimamanda Ngozi. "Memory, Witness, and War: Chimamanda Ngozi Adichie Talks with Bookforum." *Bookforum* 14.4 (Dec. 2007–Jan. 2008): 37.

年的社会化[1]。对于此种现象,杰德·埃斯蒂用了"受阻的成长"(arrested development)[2],而莎拉·哈里森(Sarah K. Harrison)则用了"搁置状态"(suspended state)来定位和描述此种成长现象[3]。而这种"停滞"的成长或称为"反成长"经历,是战争创伤带来的难以治愈的青春之痛。从战场归来的乌古生活中最为重要的事情就是写作,他把所听、所见、所想一一记录下来,利用一切间隙在小本子上书写。书写成为少年乌古拯救自己停滞的成长的方式,也是他治愈战争创伤的方式。

成长小说是一种不断"成长"的文类。这一文类经历了从特定的18世纪晚期和19世纪早期的德国现象到包括欧洲其他国家相似题材的演化,再到包括女性作家和少数族裔作家作品的漫长演化过程。在长达三个多世纪的历史流变中,作为亚文类的成长小说显示出不同寻常的"适应性"(adaptability)和"多元性"(diversity)[4],以至于成长小说研究专家拉尔夫·奥斯丁认为,现在完全可以用小写的"bildungsroman"来代替大写的"Bildungsroman",以复数代替单数了[5]。殖民/后殖民成长小说的蓬勃发展恰恰是成长小说文类不断"成长"的经典例证。

拓展阅读文献

Austen, Ralph A. "Struggling with the African Bildungsroman." *Research in African Literatures* 46.3 (2015): 214–231.

Hoagland, Ericka A. "The Postcolonial Bildungsroman." *A History of the Bildungsroman*. Ed. Sarah Graham. Oxford: Cambridge University Press, 2018. 217–238.

王卓,《个人成长与国族重构——后殖民语境下〈半轮黄日〉的成长书写》,《外国文学》,2022年第2期,第25–36页。

---

[1] Dunson, Donald. *Child, Victim, Soldier: The Loss of Innocence in Uganda*. Mary Knoll: Orbis Books, 2008. 6.

[2] Esty, Jed. *Unseasonable Youth: Modernism, Colonialism, and the Fiction of Development*. Oxford: Oxford University Press, 2012.

[3] Harrison, Sarah K. "'Suspended City': Personal, Urban and National Development in Chris Abani's *Graceland*." *Research in African Literatures* 43.2 (2012): 95.

[4] Graham, Sarah. "Introduction." *A History of the Bildungsroman*. Cambridge: Cambridge University Press, 2019. 1.

[5] Austen, Ralph A. "Coming of Age Through Colonial Education: African Autobiography as Reluctant Bildungsroman (the Case of Camara Laye)." *Mande Studies* 12 (2010): 1–18.

Lecture 19
Olive Schreiner

Profile of the Writer

Olive Schreiner
(1855–1920)

 Olive Schreiner was the major South African novelist to emerge in the late nineteenth century. She was the ninth of twelve children born to a German father and an English mother, and was raised as a strict Calvinist on a mission station. However, her religious faith wavered when she was still a young child. After her father was declared insolvent in 1866, she had to part from her parents. Between the ages of 15 and 26 she held a succession of posts as a governess. Her spare time was devoted to writing stories, reading the major Victorian intellectuals, and developing her own distinctive brand of free thought. Over a period of eight years, Schreiner saved for her passage to Britain to find a publisher for *The Story of an African Farm* and to train in medicine.

 Olive Schreiner is remembered as the first and probably the greatest South African novelist. She grew up in a "colonial culture almost bare of serious books", and as her compatriot, Dan Jacobson, has written, "a colonial culture is one which has no memory". Like Katherine Mansfield, born thirty years later, she got much of her material from a people and a landscape that had never yet appeared in literature. She has had a deep and lasting influence on younger South African writers. Her influence on other women, as novelist and thinker, has been just as important.

Lecture 19
Olive Schreiner

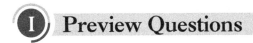 Preview Questions

1. Olive Schreiner is termed as "Charlotte Brontë of South Africa". How do you understand this statement?

2. Set in the barren landscape of the Great Karoo, a vast sandy plain in South Africa in the 1860s, *The Story of an African Farm* begins as a plaasroman (the farm novel), but soon turns into a bildungsroman. What do you think is the significance of this transformation?

#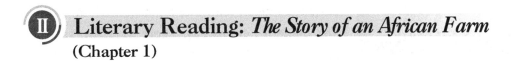
(Chapter 1)

Shadows from Child-Life

THE WATCH.

The full African moon poured down its light from the blue sky into the wide, lonely plain. The dry, sandy earth, with its coating of stunted "karroo" bushes a few inches high, the low hills that skirted the plain, the milk-bushes with their long finger-like leaves, all were touched by a weird and an almost oppressive beauty as they lay in the white light.

In one spot only was the solemn monotony of the plain broken. Near the centre a small solitary "kopje" rose. Alone it lay there, a heap of round ironstones piled one upon another, as over some giant's grave. Here and there a few tufts of grass or small succulent plants had sprung up among its stones, and on the very summit a clump of prickly-pears lifted their thorny arms, and reflected, as from mirrors, the moonlight on their broad fleshy leaves. At the foot of the "kopje" lay the homestead. First, the stone-walled "sheep kraals" and Kaffer huts; beyond them the dwelling-house—a square, red-brick building with thatched roof. Even on its bare red walls, and the wooden ladder that led up to the loft, the moonlight cast a kind of dreamy beauty, and quite etherealized the low brick wall that ran before the house, and which enclosed a bare patch of sand and two straggling sunflowers. On the zinc roof of the great open wagon-house, on the roofs of the outbuildings that jutted from its side, the moonlight glinted with a quite peculiar brightness, till it seemed that every rib in the metal was of burnished silver.

Sleep ruled everywhere, and the homestead was not less quiet than the solitary plain.

In the farm-house, on her great wooden bedstead, Tant Sannie, the Boer-woman, rolled heavily in her sleep.

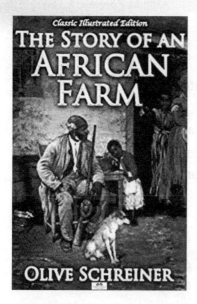

She had gone to bed, as she always did, in her clothes, and the night was warm and the room close, and she dreamed bad dreams. Not of the ghosts and devils that so haunted her waking thoughts; not of her second husband, the consumptive Englishman, whose grave lay away beyond the ostrich-camps; nor of her first, the young Boer; but only of the sheep's trotters she had eaten for supper that night. She dreamed that one stuck fast in her throat, and she rolled her huge form from side to side, and snorted horribly.

In the next room, where the maid had forgotten to close the shutter, the white moonlight fell in in a flood, and made it light as day. There were two small beds against the wall. In one lay a yellow-haired child, with a low forehead and a face of freckles; but the loving moonlight hid defects here as elsewhere, and showed only the innocent face of a child in its first sweet sleep.

The figure in the companion bed belonged of right to the moonlight, for it was of quite elfin-like beauty. The child had dropped her cover on the floor, and the moonlight looked in at the naked little limbs. Presently she opened her eyes and looked at the moonlight that was bathing her.

"Em!" she called to the sleeper in the other bed; but received no answer. Then she drew the cover from the floor, turned her pillow, and pulling the sheet over her head, went to sleep again.

Only in one of the outbuildings that jutted from the wagon-house there was some one who was not asleep. The room was dark; door and shutter were closed; not a ray of light entered anywhere. The German overseer, to whom the room belonged, lay sleeping soundly on his bed in the corner, his great arms folded, and his bushy grey and black beard rising and falling on his breast. But one in the room was not asleep. Two large eyes looked about in the darkness, and two small hands were smoothing the patchwork quilt. The boy, who slept on a box under the window, had just awakened from his first sleep. He drew the quilt up to his chin, so that little peered above it but a great head of silky black curls and the two black eyes. He stared about in the darkness. Nothing was visible, not even the outline of one worm-eaten rafter, nor of the deal table, on which lay the Bible from which his father had read before they went to bed. No one could tell where the tool-box was, and where the fireplace. There was something very impressive to the child in the complete darkness.

At the head of his father's bed hung a great silver hunting watch. It ticked loudly. The boy listened to it, and began mechanically to count. Tick—tick—tick! one, two, three, four!

He lost count presently, and only listened. Tick—tick—tick—tick!

It never waited; it went on inexorably; and every time it ticked *a man died!* He raised himself a little on his elbow and listened. He wished it would leave off.

How many times had it ticked since he came to lie down? A thousand times, a million times, perhaps.

He tried to count again, and sat up to listen better.

"Dying, dying, dying!" said the watch; "dying, dying, dying!"

He heard it distinctly. Where were they going to, all those people?

He lay down quickly, and pulled the cover up over his head; but presently the silky curls reappeared.

"Dying, dying, dying!" said the watch; "dying, dying, dying!"

He thought of the words his father had read that evening—"*For wide is the gate, and broad is the way, that leadeth to destruction, and many there be which go in thereat.*"

"Many, many, many!" said the watch.

"*Because strait is the gate, and narrow is the way, that leadeth unto life, and few there be that find it.*"

"Few, few, few!" said the watch.

The boy lay with his eyes wide open. He saw before him a long stream of people, a great dark multitude, that moved in one direction; then they came to the dark edge of the world and went over. He saw them passing on before him, and there was nothing that could stop them. He thought of how that stream had rolled on through all the long ages of the past—how the old Greeks and Romans had gone over; the countless millions of China and India, they were going over now. Since he had come to bed, how many had gone!

And the watch said, "Eternity, eternity, eternity!"

"Stop them! stop them!" cried the child.

And all the while the watch kept ticking on; just like God's will, that never changes or alters, you may do what you please.

Great beads of perspiration stood on the boy's forehead. He climbed out of bed and lay with his face turned to the mud floor.

"Oh, God, God! save them!" he cried in agony. "Only some; only a few! Only for each moment I am praying here one!" He folded his little hands upon his head. "God! God! save them!"

He grovelled on the floor.

Oh, the long, long ages of the past, in which they had gone over! Oh, the long, long future, in which they would pass away! Oh, God! the long, long, long eternity, which has no end!

The child wept, and crept closer to the ground.

THE SACRIFICE.

The farm by daylight was not as the farm by moonlight. The plain was a weary flat of loose red sand, sparsely covered by dry karroo bushes, that cracked beneath the tread like tinder, and showed the red earth everywhere. Here and there a milk-bush lifted its pale-coloured rods, and in every direction the ants and beetles ran about in the blazing sand. The red walls of the farmhouse, the zinc roofs of the outbuildings, the stone walls of the "kraals", all reflected the fierce sunlight, till the eye ached and blenched. No tree or shrub was to be seen far or near. The two sunflowers that stood before the door, out-stared by the sun, drooped their brazen faces to the sand; and the little cicada-like insects cried aloud among the stones of the "kopje".

The Boer-woman, seen by daylight, was even less lovely than when, in bed, she rolled and dreamed. She sat on a chair in the great front room, with her feet on a wooden stove, and wiped her flat face with the corner of her apron, and drank coffee, and in Cape Dutch swore that the beloved weather was damned. Less lovely, too, by daylight was the dead Englishman's child, her little step-daughter, upon whose freckles and low, wrinkled forehead the sunlight had no mercy.

"Lyndall," the child said to her little orphan cousin, who sat with her on the floor threading beads, "how is it your beads never fall off your needle?"

"I try," said the little one gravely, moistening her tiny finger. "That is why."

The overseer, seen by daylight, was a huge German, wearing a shabby suit, and with a childish habit of rubbing his hands and nodding his head prodigiously when pleased at anything. He stood out at the kraals in the blazing sun, explaining to two Kaffer boys the approaching end of the world. The boys, as they cut the cakes of dung, winked at each other, and worked as slowly as they possibly could; but the German never saw it.

Away, beyond the "kopje", Waldo his son herded the ewes and lambs—a small and dusty herd—powdered all over from head to foot with red sand, wearing a ragged coat and shoes of undressed leather, through whose holes the toes looked out. His hat was too large, and had sunk down to his eyes, concealing completely the silky black curls. It was a curious small figure. His flock gave him little trouble. It was too hot for them to move far; they gathered round every little milk-bush as though they hoped to find shade, and stood there motionless in clumps. He himself crept under a shelving rock that lay at the foot of the "kopje", stretched himself on his stomach, and waved his dilapidated little shoes in the air.

Soon, from the blue bag where he kept his dinner, he produced a fragment of slate, an arithmetic, and a pencil. Proceeding to put down a sum with solemn and earnest demeanour, he began to add it up aloud: "Six and two is eight—and four is twelve—and two is fourteen—and four is eighteen." Here he paused. "And four is eighteen—and—four—is, eighteen." The last was very much drawled. Slowly the pencil slipped from his fingers, and the slate followed it into the sand. For a while he lay motionless, then began muttering to himself, folded his little arms, laid his head down upon them, and might have been asleep, but for the muttering sound that from time to time proceeded from him. A curious old ewe came to sniff at him; but it was long before he raised his head. When he did, he looked at the far-off hills with his heavy eyes.

"Ye shall receive—ye shall receive—shall, shall, shall," he muttered.

He sat up then. Slowly the dullness and heaviness melted from his face; it became radiant. Mid-day had come now, and the sun's rays were poured down vertically; the earth throbbed before the eye.

The boy stood up quickly, and cleared a small space from the bushes which covered it. Looking carefully, he found twelve small stones of somewhat the same size; kneeling down, he arranged them carefully on the cleared space in a square pile, in shape like an altar. Then he walked to the bag where his dinner was kept; in it was a mutton chop and a large slice of brown bread. The boy took them out and turned the bread over in his hand, deeply considering it. Finally he threw it away and walked to the altar with the meat, and laid it down on the stones. Close by in the red sand he knelt down. Sure, never since the beginning of the world was there so ragged and so small a priest. He took off his great hat and placed it solemnly on the ground, then closed his eyes and folded his hands. He prayed aloud:

"Oh, God, my Father, I have made Thee a sacrifice. I have only twopence, so I cannot buy a lamb. If the lambs were mine, I would give Thee one; but now I have only this meat; it is my dinner-meat. Please, my Father, send fire down from heaven to burn it. Thou hast said, Whosoever shall say unto this mountain, Be thou cast into the sea, nothing doubting, it shall be done. I ask for the sake of Jesus Christ. Amen."

He knelt down with his face upon the ground, and he folded his hands upon his curls. The fierce sun poured down its heat upon his head and upon his altar. When he looked up he knew what he should see—the glory of God! For fear his very heart stood still, his breath came heavily; he was half suffocated. He dared not look up. Then at last he raised himself. Above him was the quiet blue sky, about him the red earth; there were the clumps of silent ewes and his altar—that was all.

He looked up—nothing broke the intense stillness of the blue overhead. He looked round in astonishment, then he bowed again, and this time longer than before.

When he raised himself the second time all was unaltered. Only the sun had melted the fat of the little mutton chop, and it ran down upon the stones.

Then, the third time he bowed himself. When at last he looked up, some ants had come to the meat on the altar. He stood up and drove them away. Then he put his hat on his hot curls, and sat in the shade. He clasped his hands about his knees. He sat to watch what would come to pass. The glory of the Lord God Almighty! He knew he should see it.

"My dear God is trying me," he said; and he sat there through the fierce heat of the afternoon. Still he watched and waited when the sun began to slope; and when it neared the horizon and the sheep began to cast long shadows across the karroo, he still sat there. He hoped when the first rays touched the hills till the sun dipped behind them and was gone. Then he called his ewes together, and broke down the altar, and threw the meat far, far away into the field.

He walked home behind his flock. His heart was heavy. He reasoned so: "God cannot lie. I had faith. No fire came. I am like Cain—I am not His. He will not hear my prayer. God hates me."

The boy's heart was heavy. When he reached the "kraal" gate the two girls met him.

"Come," said the yellow-haired Em, "let us play 'coop'. There is still time before it gets quite dark. You, Waldo, go and hide on the 'kopje'; Lyndall and I will shut eyes here, and we will not look."

The girls hid their faces in the stone wall of the sheep-kraal, and the boy clambered half way up the "kopje". He crouched down between two stones and gave the call. Just then the milk-herd came walking out of the cow-kraal with two pails. He was an ill-looking Kaffer.

"Ah!" thought the boy, "perhaps he will die tonight, and go to hell! I must pray for him, I must pray!"

Then he thought—"Where am I going to?" and he prayed desperately.

"Ah! this is not right at all," little Em said, peeping between the stones, and finding him in a very curious posture. "What are you doing Waldo? It is not the play, you know. You should run out when we come to the white stone. Ah, you do not play nicely."

"I—I will play nicely now," said the boy, coming out and standing sheepishly before them; "I—I only forgot; I will play now."

"He has been to sleep," said freckled Em.

"No," said beautiful little Lyndall, looking curiously at him: "he has been crying."

She never made a mistake.

THE CONFESSION.

One night, two years after, the boy sat alone on the "kopje". He had crept softly from his father's room and come there. He often did, because, when he prayed or cried aloud, his father might awake and hear him; and none knew his great sorrow, and none knew his grief, but he himself, and he buried them deep in his heart.

He turned up the brim of his great hat and looked at the moon, but most at the leaves of the prickly pear that grew just before him. They glinted, and glinted, and glinted, just like his own heart—cold, so hard, and very wicked. His physical heart had pain also; it seemed full of little bits of glass, that hurt. He had sat there for half an hour, and he dared not go back to the close house.

He felt horribly lonely. There was not one thing so wicked as he in all the world, and he knew it. He folded his arms and began to cry—not aloud; he sobbed without making any sound, and his tears left scorched marks where they fell. He could not pray; he had prayed night and day for so many months; and tonight he could not pray. When he left off crying, he held his aching head with his brown hands. If one might have gone up to him and touched him kindly; poor, ugly little thing! Perhaps his heart was almost broken.

With his swollen eyes he sat there on a flat stone at the very top of the "kopje"; and the tree, with every one of its wicked leaves, blinked, and blinked, and blinked at him. Presently he began to cry again, and then stopped his crying to look at it. He was quiet for a long while, then he knelt up slowly and bent forward. There was a secret he had carried in his heart for a year. He had not dared to look at it; he had not whispered it to himself, but for a year he had carried it. "I hate God!" he said. The wind took the words and ran away with them, among the stones, and through the leaves of the prickly pear. He thought it died away half down the "kopje". He had told it now!

"I love Jesus Christ, but I hate God."

The wind carried away that sound as it had done the first. Then he got up and buttoned his old coat about him. He knew he was certainly lost now; he did not care. If half the world were to be lost, why not he too? He would not pray for mercy any more. Better so—better to know certainly. It was ended now. Better so.

He began scrambling down the sides of the "kopje" to go home.

Better so! But oh, the loneliness, the agonized pain! for that night, and for nights on nights to come! The anguish that sleeps all day on the heart like a heavy worm, and wakes up at night to feed!

There are some of us who in after years say to Fate, "Now deal us your hardest blow, give us what you will; but let us never again suffer as we suffered when we were children."

The barb in the arrow of childhood's suffering is this: its intense loneliness, its intense agony.

III Thinking, Talking and Writing About Literature

1 Textual Cognition

Make an introductory presentation on the following terms related to this literary work.

1) plaasroman
2) regional novel

❷ Textual Reading

Search for evidence in the text and answer the following questions.

1) The opening paragraphs of *The Story of an African Farm* present the depressive bleakness and monotony of the local landscape. What is the function of this description of local landscape?

2) The narrative contains a number of proto-African words, which add local color. Please read the text and find those words and explain their functions.

3) At the outset Waldo is described listening anxiously to the ticking of a watch. What does this description symbolize?

4) The excerpt describes the childhood of Lyndall, Em and Waldo against the backdrop of everyday life on the secluded farm. In what ways are the three young protagonists different in terms of personality?

❸ Critical Reading

Discuss in groups the following questions to further explore this literary work.

1) Olive Schreiner was rediscovered by feminist scholars in the 1970s and 1980s. Why did she appeal to feminist scholars?

2) Some critics believe that Olive Schreiner made great contributions to the development of Anglophone South African literature. How do you understand her contribution?

❹ Writing About Literature

Read the following critical excerpt and then write an essay.

> Gordon, Lyndall. *Outsiders*. Baltimore: Johns Hopkins University Press, 2019.

In a bare room, a woman prods memory with her pen. The shutters are closed against the sun and by night against the voices of the guards under her window. It was "so dark that even the physical act of writing was difficult". Future readers will know how she has to "crush down indignation" if she is to write.

Constrained under martial law, she means to remake a book that took many years and now has been burnt by troops looting her home in Johannesburg. Report has reached her that the manuscript cannot be salvaged: the first half burnt away; the rest charred—the pages crumbled when touched. For nine months she has put it from her mind, but isolated as she is now in March 1901, regrets for her lost work stir. What memory can retrieve for a short book—she will call it *Woman and Labour*—can occupy this time of confinement and darkness by night when the law forbids a candle and even to strike a match. A resolve firms to rescue her challenge to authority from the ashes.

Twenty years ago she'd sat alone in another room with miles of veld stretching to the horizon. There too, filled with purpose, her pen had traveled over the page as she finished her novel *The Story of an African Farm*. She'd carried it to London and, pressing her manuscript under her waterproof, trod from one London publisher to another. Chapman & Hall, who had turned down another of her novels, accepted the *African Farm* on the advice of their reader, the novelist George Meredith. The publisher of Dickens, Thackeray and Anthony Trollope, they paid this unknown colonial only eighteen pounds, in contrast with the hundreds of pounds that George Henry Lewes had secured for each of the *Scenes* by the unknown George Eliot.

Chapman & Hall's sole editorial suggestion was that the heroine marry her seducer, otherwise "Smith's, the railway booksellers, would not put it on their stalls."

The author refused. And she was right, for political and literary figures like Gladstone, Wilde and Shaw had only praise for the *African Farm*. Workers liked its care for obscure lives, and women its outrage over subjection. Its moral vision had the appeal of scripture. The uneducated shepherd boy Waldo and the orphan girl Lyndall, whose souls are awake, continue to suffer: Waldo in silence; Lyndall compelled to raise a voice not heard before. This is no counseling angel. She becomes a fearless speaker, defying authority and refusing to marry an unworthy man even though he has fathered her child.

Essay Writing

The above selection is from the *Outsiders* by Lyndall Gordon. How do you understand the title "Outsiders"? Write an essay on "Olive Schreiner as an Outsider" with no less than 500 words.

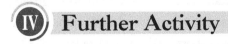

IV Further Activity

Scan the QR code and read an introduction to Olive Schreiner.

Lecture 20
Chinua Achebe

Profile of the Writer

Chinua Achebe
(1930–2013)

Chinua Achebe, one of the world's leading writers, was born in eastern Nigeria, West Africa, in 1930. As the first African writer to win broad critical acclaim in Europe and America and the most widely read African novelist, Chinua Achebe has shaped the world's understanding of Africa and its literature.

A prolific author who has also been widely discussed from various perspectives, Achebe has excited a large body of work. He wrote more than 20 books—novels, short stories, essays and collections of poetry—including *Things Fall Apart* (1958), which has sold more than 10 million copies worldwide and been translated into more than 50 languages; *Arrow of God* (1964); *Beware, Soul Brother and Other Poems* (1971), winner of the Commonwealth Poetry Prize; *Anthills of the Savannah* (1987), which was shortlisted for the Booker Prize for Fiction; *Hopes and Impediments: Selected Essays* (1988); and *Home and Exile* (2000).

Chinua Achebe received numerous honors from around the world, including the Honorary Fellowship of the American Academy of Arts and Letters, as well as honorary doctorates from more than 30 colleges and universities. He was also the recipient of Nigeria's highest award for intellectual achievement, the Nigerian National Merit Award. In 2007, he won the Man Booker International Prize. He died on March 21, 2013, at the age of 82, in Boston, Massachusetts.

Lecture 20
Chinua Achebe

I. Preview Questions

1. Achebe chose to take the title of his novel, *Things Fall Apart*, from William Butler Yeats' poem "The Second Coming" as shown below. How do you interpret the title of the book?

> Turning and turning in the widening gyre
> The falcon cannot hear the falconer;
> Things fall apart; the centre cannot hold;
> Mere anarchy is loosed upon the world

2. Achebe has described how he became a writer: "At the university I read some appalling novels about Africa (including Joyce Cary's much praised *Mister Johnson*) and decided that the story we had to tell could not be told for us by anyone else no matter how gifted or well intentioned." How do you understand this statement?

II. Literary Reading: *Things Fall Apart* (Chapter 1)

Okonkwo was well known throughout the nine villages and even beyond. His fame rested on solid personal achievements. As a young man of eighteen he had brought honour to his village by throwing Amalinze the Cat. Amalinze was the great wrestler who for seven years was unbeaten, from Umuofia to Mbaino. He was called the Cat because his back would never touch the earth. It was this man that Okonkwo threw in a fight which the old men agreed was one of the fiercest since the founder of their town engaged a spirit of the wild for seven days and seven nights.

The drums beat and the flutes sang and the spectators held their breath. Amalinze was a wily craftsman, but Okonkwo was as slippery as a fish in water. Every nerve and every muscle stood out on their arms, on their backs and their thighs, and one almost heard them stretching to breaking point. In the end Okonkwo threw the Cat.

That was many years ago, twenty years or more, and during this time Okonkwo's fame had grown like a bush-fire in the harmattan. He was tall and huge, and his bushy eyebrows and wide nose gave him a very severe look. He breathed heavily, and it was said that, when he slept, his wives and children in their houses could hear him breathe. When

he walked, his heels hardly touched the ground and he seemed to walk on springs, as if he was going to pounce on somebody. And he did pounce on people quite often. He had a slight stammer and whenever he was angry and could not get his words out quickly enough, he would use his fists. He had no patience with unsuccessful men. He had had no patience with his father.

Unoka, for that was his father's name, had died ten years ago. In his day he was lazy and improvident and was quite incapable of thinking about tomorrow. If any money came his way, and it seldom did, he immediately bought gourds of palm-wine, called round his neighbours and made merry. He always said that whenever he saw a dead man's mouth he saw the folly of not eating what one had in one's lifetime. Unoka was, of course, a debtor, and he owed every neighbour some money, from a few cowries to quite substantial amounts.

He was tall but very thin and had a slight stoop. He wore a haggard and mournful look except when he was drinking or playing on his flute. He was very good on his flute, and his happiest moments were the two or three moons after the harvest when the village musicians brought down their instruments, hung above the fireplace. Unoka would play with them, his face beaming with blessedness and peace. Sometimes another village would ask Unoka's band and their dancing egwugwu to come and stay with them and teach them their tunes. They would go to such hosts for as long as three or four markets, making music and feasting. Unoka loved the good hire and the good fellowship, and he loved this season of the year, when the rains had stopped and the sun rose every morning with dazzling beauty. And it was not too hot either, because the cold and dry harmattan wind was blowing down from the north. Some years the harmattan was very severe and a dense haze hung on the atmosphere. Old men and children would then sit round log fires, warming their bodies. Unoka loved it all, and he loved the first kites that returned with the dry season, and the children who sang songs of welcome to them. He would remember his own childhood, how he had often wandered around looking for a kite sailing leisurely against the blue sky. As soon as he found one he would sing with his whole being, welcoming it back from its long, long journey, and asking it if it had brought home any lengths of cloth.

That was years ago, when he was young. Unoka, the grown-up, was a failure. He was poor and his wife and children had barely enough to eat. People laughed at him because he was a loafer, and they swore never to lend him any more money because he never paid back. But Unoka was such a man that he always succeeded in borrowing more, and piling up his debts.

One day a neighbor called Okoye came in to see him. He was reclining on a mud bed in his hut playing on the flute. He immediately rose and shook hands with Okoye, who then unrolled the goatskin which he carried under his arm, and sat down. Unoka went into an inner room and soon returned with a small wooden disc containing a kola nut, some alligator pepper and a lump of white chalk.

"I have kola," he announced when he sat down, and passed the disc over to his guest.

"Thank you. He who brings kola brings life. But I think you ought to break it," replied Okoye, passing back the disc.

"No, it is for you, I think," and they argued like this for a few moments before Unoka accepted the honour of breaking the kola. Okoye, meanwhile, took the lump of chalk, drew some lines on the floor, and then painted his big toe.

As he broke the kola, Unoka prayed to their ancestors for life and health, and for protection against their enemies. When they had eaten they talked about many things: about the heavy rains which were drowning the yams, about the next ancestral feast and about the impending war with the village of Mbaino. Unoka was never happy when it came to wars. He was in fact a coward and could not bear the sight of blood. And so he changed the subject and talked about music, and his face beamed. He could hear in his mind's ear the blood-stirring and intricate rhythms of the ekwe and the udu and the ogene, and he could hear his own flute weaving in and out of them, decorating them with a colourful and plaintive tune. The total effect was gay and brisk, but if one picked out the flute as it went up and down and then broke up into short snatches, one saw that there was sorrow and grief there.

Okoye was also a musician. He played on the ogene. But he was not a failure like Unoka. He had a large barn full of yams and he had three wives. And now he was going to take the Idemili title, the third highest in the land. It was a very expensive ceremony and he was gathering all his resources together. That was in fact the reason why he had come to see Unoka. He cleared his throat and began: "Thank you for the kola. You may have heard of the title I intend to take shortly."

Having spoken plainly so far, Okoye said the next half a dozen sentences in proverbs. Among the Ibo the art of conversation is regarded very highly, and proverbs are the palm-oil with which words are eaten. Okoye was a great talker and he spoke for a long time, skirting round the subject and then hitting it finally. In short, he was asking Unoka to return the two hundred cowries he had borrowed from him more than two years before. As soon as Unoka understood what his friend was driving at, he burst out laughing. He laughed loud and long and his voice rang out clear as the ogene, and tears stood in his eyes. His visitor was amazed, and sat speechless. At the end, Unoka was able to give an answer between fresh outbursts of mirth.

"Look at that wall," he said, pointing at the far wall of his hut, which was rubbed with red earth so that it shone. "Look at those lines of chalk," and Okoye saw groups of short perpendicular lines drawn in chalk. There were five groups, and the smallest group had ten lines. Unoka had a sense of the dramatic and so he allowed a pause, in which he took a pinch of snuff and sneezed noisily, and then he continued: "Each group there represents a debt to someone, and each stroke is one hundred cowries. You see, I owe that man a thousand cowries. But he has not come to wake me up in the morning for it. I shall pay you, but not today. Our elders say that the sun will shine on those who stand before it shines on those who kneel under them. I shall pay my big debts first." And he took another pinch of snuff, as if that was paying the big debts first. Okoye rolled his goatskin and departed.

When Unoka died he had taken no title at all and he was heavily in debt. Any wonder then that his son Okonkwo was ashamed of him? Fortunately, among these people a man was judged according to his worth and not according to the worth of his father. Okonkwo was clearly cut out for great things. He was still young but he had won fame as the greatest wrestler in the nine villages. He was a wealthy farmer and had two barns full of yams, and had just married his third wife. To crown it all he had taken two titles and had shown incredible prowess in two inter-tribal wars. And so although Okonkwo was still young, he was already one of the greatest men of his time. Age was respected among his people, but achievement was revered. As the elders said, if a child washed his hands he could eat with kings. Okonkwo had clearly washed his hands and so he ate with kings and elders. And that was how he came to look after the doomed lad who was sacrificed to the village of Umuofia by their neighbours to avoid war and bloodshed. The ill-fated lad was called Ikemefuna.

III Thinking, Talking and Writing About Literature

1 Textual Cognition

Make an introductory presentation on the following terms related to this literary work.

1) stereotype of African cultures
2) African community

2 Textual Reading

Search for evidence in the text and answer the following questions.

1) Although not indicated in this chapter, the events of *Things Fall Apart* take place in the late 1800s and early 1900s, just before and during the early days of the British Empire's expansion in Nigeria. The novel depicts details about life in an African culture much different

from Western culture. Please find some examples of these differences in this excerpt.

2) Achebe presents details of daily village life in Umuofia, as well as details concerning the Igbo culture. What are the functions of these detailed representations?

3) Chapter 1 describes Okonkwo's principal accomplishments that establish his important position in Igbo society. These details alone provide insight into Okonkwo's character and motivation. Could you sum up Okonkwo's character and motivation?

❸ Critical Reading

Discuss in groups the following questions to further explore this literary work.

1) Achebe notes that his *Things Fall Apart* "was an act of atonement with my past, the ritual return and homage of a prodigal son". How do you understand Achebe's statement?

2) Though the novel is written in English, Achebe often sprinkles words from the Igbo language (the native tongue of the Umuofians and one of the most common languages in Nigeria in general) into the text. What do you think are the functions of this use of African vocabulary?

❹ Writing About Literature

Read the following critical excerpt and then write an essay.

> Gosling, Jonathan. "Resilience and Response to the End of a Way of Life: Lessons from Chinua Achebe's *Things Fall Apart*." *Fictional Leaders: Heroes, Villains and Absent Friends*. New York: Palgrave, 2012. 99–112.

Father to Son

These opening words of the novel introduce the hero thus:

> Okonkwo was well known throughout the nine villages and even beyond. His fame rested on solid personal achievements. (Page 3)

We learn what is meant by his fame, and the measure of his achievements, and also about his poise and character.

> When he walked his heels hardly touched the ground and he seemed to walk on springs as if he was going to pounce on somebody. And he did pounce on people quite often. He had a slight stammer and whenever he was angry and could not get his words out quickly enough he would use his fists. He had no patience with unsuccessful men. He had no patience with his father. (Pages 3–4)

Okonkwo's drama begins with longing to repair the shame he feels about his father Unoka, described as "lazy... improvident... a debtor... a slight sloop. He wore a haggard and mournful look except when he was drinking or playing on his flute" (Page 4). Okonkwo found little charm in his father's fecklessness: "Unoka, the grown-up, was a failure. He was poor and his wife and children had barely enough to eat. People laughed at him because he was a loafer, and they swore never to lend him any money because he never paid it back" (Page 5).

"Unoka was never happy when it came to wars. He was in fact a coward and could not bear the sight of blood. And so he changed the subject and talked about music, and his face beamed" (Page 6). Thus he remained outside the circle of great men who exemplified the virtues and accomplishments of leadership.

When Unoka died he had taken no title at all and he was heavily in debt. Any wonder then that his son Okonkwo was ashamed of him? Fortunately, among these people a man was judged according to his worth and not according to the worth of his father, Okonkwo was clearly cut out for great things. (Pages 7–8)

Okonkwo had no need to figure out what counts as greatness: everyone in the village knew how to assess his prowess and his hard work; and from these early passages we see that his ambition to achieve was driven by a relentless desire to exorcise his shame about his father. He goes on to amass great wealth; but it is reputation that matters to him, especially because it brings inclusion in the cadre of leading citizens. The thing he most wants is to belong; and one of the personal tragedies of the novel is that he never learns to recognise the humanity in his father, or to feel sympathy for the weak. His rise to leadership is accomplished by unremitting attention to being strong, physically and morally, and we have a narrator's voice to give us an account of the complex motives that lie beneath his observable behaviour.

The ambition and drive that is so often admired in leaders may often be fuelled by inner demons akin to Okonkwo's, as revealed in psychoanalytically informed accounts of, for example, Enron (Stein, 2007), Alexander the Great (Kets de Vries, 2004) and the CEOs of finance firms in the years preceding the 2008 financial collapse (Sievers, 2010; Stein, 2011). Part of the appeal of *Things Fall Apart* is that it gives us insight into such inner complexes, and how these help to explain self-destructive and emotionally painful behaviour. We see in Okonkwo a man for whom suffering and cruelty are an acceptable defence against shame: "Okonkwo never showed any emotion openly unless it be the emotion of anger. To show affection was a sign of weakness; the only thing worth demonstrating was strength" (Page 27).

His predicament is recognisable across the cultural divide between his way of life and our own. One strand to the narrative, concerning a boy called Ikemefuma, gives a particularly poignant example of this; although the details seem to emphasise the cultural differences between Okonkwo and we readers, the dénouement is painfully resonant.

In Chapter 2 we hear how the village of Umuofia found cause for war with a neighbouring village but in accord with tradition, accepted instead two young people, a boy and a girl, as hostage. The boy, Ikemefuma, was placed in Okonkwo's charge and brought up in his family, becoming a close friend with the oldest son, Nwoye. Okonkwo comes to love the boy, who excels his own son in skill and aspiration. Perhaps Ikemefuma's need to please his adoptive father, having been torn from his own family, is resonant with Okonkwo's felt need to create his own role models; maybe it is the shame that their fathers were not able to protect and fend for them. In any case, Ikemefuma becomes the recipient for Okonkwo's paternal hopes, in contrast to which Nwoye appears to him as increasingly inadequate.

Thus shame about his father is reflected in shame about his own son, and emerges as the inescapable accompaniment of his greatness. Its potency becomes terrifyingly apparent when the village elders determine that Ikemefuma should be killed in sacrifice; they advise Okonkwo to stay home, to excuse himself from participating in this communal duty: "That boy calls you father, bear no hand in his death" (Page 54). But he accompanies the men to the forest, and when the blow is struck "he heard Ikemefuma cry 'my father, they have killed me!' as he ran towards him. Dazed with fear, Okonkwo drew his matchet and cut him down. He was afraid of being thought weak" (Page 57). How often do we witness displays of ruthlessness in our leaders, fearful of being seen as weak, or even worse, of recognising their own weakness?

Essay Writing

Make an analogy of father and son in *Things Fall Apart* based on your reading of the above selection and write an essay with no less than 500 words.

 ## Further Activity

Scan the QR code and watch a video clip "Poetry Lecture" about Chinua Achebe's poem "Refugee Mother and Child".

Lecture 21
Abdulrazak Gurnah

Profile of the Writer

Abdulrazak Gurnah
(1948–)

Born in 1948, Abdulrazak Gurnah grew up on the island of Zanzibar but arrived in England as a refugee in the late 1960s because of a revolution. Gurnah has until his recent retirement been Professor of English and Postcolonial Literatures at the University of Kent in Canterbury.

Gurnah has published ten novels and a number of short stories. Gurnah's fourth novel, *Paradise* (1994), marks his breakthrough as a writer, which is shortlisted for the 1994 Booker Prize. Because of his own experience, Gurnah always focuses on identity and self-image in his treatment of the refugee experience, which is apparent in *Admiring Silence* (1996), *By the Sea* (2001) and *The Last Gift* (2011). His latest novel, *Afterlives* (2020), takes up where *Paradise* ends and focuses on German colonisation of East Africa.

Gurnah is the first black African author to have won the Nobel Prize in Literature since Wole Soyinka (1934–) in 1986. His award means issues such as the refugee crisis and colonialism, which Gurnah has experienced, will be "discussed". Anders Olsson, Chairman of the Nobel Committee, claims that Gurnah's novels recoil from stereotypical descriptions and open our gaze to a culturally diversified East Africa unfamiliar to many in other parts of the world.

Lecture 21
Abdulrazak Gurnah

I. Preview Questions

1. The Nobel Prize in Literature 2021 was awarded to Abdulrazak Gurnah "for his uncompromising and compassionate penetration of the effects of colonialism and the fate of the refugee in the gulf between cultures and continents". How do you understand this statement?

2. Gurnah's fourth novel *Paradise* (1994) is considered one of his most influential novels. Why does Gurnah entitle his story "Paradise"? How do you understand the title?

II. Literary Reading: *Paradise* (Chapter 6)

…

It was he who built the garden, Mzee Hamdani. Not from nothing, of course. Some of the older trees were already here, but he cleared the ground and built the pools, and played out there all hours of the day like a child. His singing used to drive her husband crazy, so she had to forbid it. Her father gave him to her as a wedding gift. She had known him since she was a child, him and another older slave called Shebe who died several years ago, may God have mercy on him. At her marriage to the seyyid, more than ten years ago, she offered Mzee Hamdani his freedom, as a gift. For although the law at that time forbade buying and selling of people, it did not require that those held as slaves should be released from their obligations. But when she offered Mzee Hamdani his freedom he refused, and there he is, still in the garden singing his qasidas, the poor old man.

"She says do you know why he was called Hamdani?" Amina said, her eyes dull with distance. "Because his mother, who was a slave-woman, had him late in her life. She called him Hamdani in gratitude for his birth. When the mother died, her father bought Hamdani from the family which owned him. It was a poor family, deep in debt."

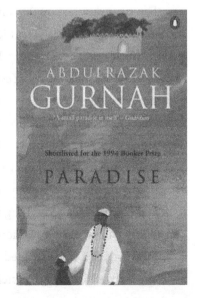

In the silence, the Mistress stared at Yusuf for a long

moment, smiling cheerfully. The smile remained on her face as she continued, but this time she did not speak for long.

"She asks that you should come and sit nearer," Amina said. He tried to look into her eyes, to seek guidance, but she busied herself and avoided looking at him. The Mistress patted the rug a foot or so from her, smiling at him as if he were a shy child. After he had seated himself, she took his hand and placed it on her wound, keeping her hand on his. She shut her eyes and made a long hissing noise, between relief and pleasure. Sitting so close to her, he saw that the flesh on her face and neck was firm and moist. In a moment she released his hand and he rose quickly and retreated.

"She says you have not said a prayer," Amina said, her voice small and distant. He mumbled his usual pretence and hurried away, his hand still warm from the face of the Mistress.

It was after that he asked Khalil about Amina. Khalil looked at him with hate, his thin face twisted with such scorn that Yusuf thought he would spit at him. "Let her speak for herself," he said, and returned to the packets of sugar he was arranging on the counter. A hard silence lay between them all evening. Yusuf was not anxious to broach it, although there were moments when he thought Khalil would speak, to vent his anger and anxiety at him. He felt a calm obstinacy about what he was doing, even if he felt anxious and unsure about how far he would allow matters to take him. At least he would know about the intrigues and the whisperings if he could, and he found an irresistible pleasure in seeing and listening to Amina. He did not know where he had found the strength to act in this way. Despite what Khalil said, and what he himself knew and said to himself, he would not refuse to go when he was called inside.

The next day he sought out Mzee Hamdani as he sat in the shade of the date-palm with his book of qasidas. The old man was irritated and looked around him, as if selecting another tree to move to, under which he could sit in peace.

"Please don't go away," Yusuf said, and something intimate in his voice made the old man hesitate. Mzee Hamdani waited a moment and then allowed the taut muscles of his face to slacken. He nodded impatiently, reluctant as always to suffer anyone's words. *Get on with it*.

"Why did you refuse your freedom when she offered it to you? The Mistress?" Yusuf asked, frowning at the old man as he leaned forward, annoyed with him.

The old man waited a long time, looking at the ground. He smiled, his few teeth long and yellow with age. "This is how life found me," he said.

Yusuf refused to be palmed off with what he thought was an evasion and he shook his head urgently at the old gardener. "But you were her slave… are her slave. Is that how you want to be? Why did you not accept your freedom when she offered it?"

Mzee Hamdani sighed. "Don't you know anything?" he asked sharply, and then paused as if he would say no more. After a while he began again. "They offered me freedom as a gift. She did. Who told her she had it to offer? I know the freedom you are talking about. I had that freedom the moment I was born. When these people say you belong to me, I own you, it is like the passing of the rain, or the setting of the sun at the end of the day. The following morning the sun will rise again whether they like it or not. The same with freedom. They can lock you up, put you in chains, abuse all your small longings, but freedom is not something they can take away. When they have finished with you, they are still as far away from owning you as they were on the day you were born. Do you understand me? This is the work I have been given to do, what can that one in there offer me that is freer than that?"

Yusuf thought it was the talk of an old man. No doubt there was wisdom in it, but it was a wisdom of endurance and impotence, admirable in its way perhaps, but not while the bullies are still sitting on you and releasing their foul gases on you. He kept silent, but he saw that he had saddened the old man, who had never spoken so many words to him before, and now probably wished he had not.

"Where are you from?" Yusuf asked the old man, to flatter and placate him, and because he wanted to ask him about his mother. He wanted to tell Mzee Hamdani about what had happened to him, about how he too had lost his mother. Mzee Hamdani picked up his book of qasidas without replying, and after a moment he waved Yusuf away.

For three days he went inside every evening, braving Khalil's silent disdain. All his attempts to persuade Khalil into conversation had failed. Even the customers were asking solicitously after him. On the third night, as Yusuf approached the darkness that led to the garden, Khalil called out to him. Yusuf paused for a moment and then ignored him and walked down the invisible path which led to the courtyard door which was now kept ajar for him. He answered the questions the Mistress put to him, about his mother, about the journey to the interior and about his time in the mountain town. She leaned back against the wall, smiling as she listened to him. Even when Amina translated, she kept her eyes on him. Her shawl sometimes slid down her shoulders, revealing her bruised neck and her chest, and she seemed unconcerned to retrieve it. As he watched her reclining, he felt a cold hard core of loneliness in him. He asked questions too, intended for Amina, who deflected them with long replies that elaborated on the Mistress. He was content to listen. "The wound came on her when she was young, soon after she was married to her first husband," Amina said. "To begin with it was only a mark, but as time passed it bit deeper and deeper until it reached her heart. The pain was so great that she could not bear to be with people, who would only mock her disfigurement and laugh at her cries of anguish. But now you are healing her with your prayers and your touch, and she can feel the relief."

"How was it when you first came here? What did you think... about what you had come to?" he asked Amina.

"I was too young to think," she said calmly. "And as I was among civilized people, there was nothing to fear. My Aunt Zulekha was renowned for her kindness and piety, and the garden and this house were like paradise, especially to a poor country girl as I was. When people came to visit, they cut themselves with envy for the beauty of the garden. Ask anyone in the town if you don't believe what I say. And every year during the time of alms, Aunt Zulekha gave more and more to the poor. No one was ever turned away without something from this house. The seyyid's affairs were blessed, while the Mistress suffered from this strange disease. It's the way of God, whose wisdom we have no way of judging."

He could not help smiling. "Why do you talk in this queer way when I asked you such a simple question?" he asked.

The Mistress spoke suddenly, her voice edged with restraint. After a moment it softened, and Yusuf saw Amina pause uncertainly before she began to translate. "She says she does not want to hear me speak so much, but to listen to you. How beautifully you speak, she says, even though the words you say are unknown to her. Even when you sit still, light glows in your eyes and from your flesh. And how beautiful is your hair."

Yusuf glanced at the Mistress in astonishment. He saw that her eyes were watering and that her face was bright with daring. When he looked back at Amina, he found that she had lowered her face. "She asks that you put your breath upon her face and so restore her," she said.

"Perhaps I had better go now," Yusuf said after a long, frightening silence.

"She says that the sight of you gives her so much pleasure it causes her pain," Amina said, her face still lowered, but the laughter in her voice now unmistakable.

The Mistress spoke angrily, and even though Yusuf could not understand the words, he knew that she was telling Amina to leave. He too rose a moment after Amina left the room, uncertain how to make his exit. The Mistress was sitting upright with anger, her face pinched with misery. The bubble of her rage slowly subsided, then she beckoned him nearer. Before he left the room he touched her glowing purple wound and felt it throbbing under his hand.

Amina was waiting for him in the shadows by the courtyard door. He stopped in front of her, wanting to put out a hand towards her but afraid she would have no more to do with him if he did. "I have to go back," she said in a whisper. "Wait for me in the garden. Wait."

He waited in the garden, his mind racing with possibilities. A light breeze blew through the trees and bushes, and the deep, contented throbbing of night insects filled the scented air. She would reprimand him about the Mistress, echoing Khalil's warnings and prohibitions. Or she would tell him that she knew that he returned to the house every evening to sit with her, Amina, because he nurtured naïve dreams. As time passed and the waiting seemed interminable, his anxieties grew. He would be discovered lurking in the garden at the dead of night, plotting a shameful robbery. A sudden, surreptitious crack made him think Khalil had come looking for him and would make a scene. Several times he had to restrain himself from leaving. When at last he heard a noise at the door, he hurried towards it with relief.

Amina hushed at him as he approached. "I can't stay long," she whispered. "You see what she means to do now. I shouldn't have told you what she said, but at least you see what she means to do now. She is obsessed with this... You have to be careful... and keep away from her."

"If I keep away I won't see you," he said. After a long silence he continued, "And I want to keep seeing you, even though you won't answer any of my questions."

"What questions?" she asked, and he thought he saw her smile in the dark. "There's no time for questions. She'll hear."

"Later," he said, his body singing. "After she's gone to sleep. You can walk in the garden."

"She's angry. We sleep in the same room. She'll hear..."

"I'll wait for you here," Yusuf said.

"No. I don't know," Amina said, moving away and shutting the courtyard door. She returned after a few minutes. "She's dozing, or pretending to. What questions?"

He could not have cared less about any questions, but he was afraid that if he reached out to touch her she would never let him near her again. "Why do you and Khalil look so unalike? And you speak so differently... for a brother and sister. Almost as if you're speaking different languages."

"We're not brother and sister. Hasn't he told you? Why hasn't he told you? His father saw some men struggling to load two little girls into a boat. They were wading out in the shallows, and the little girls were crying. His father called out and ran into the water. The kidnappers abandoned one of the girls but managed to run off with the other one. He took me home and later I was adopted into the family. So we grew up like brother and sister, but there is no blood between us."

"No, he didn't tell me," Yusuf said quietly. "And the other one? The other girl?"

"My sister? I don't know what happened to her. Or to my mother. I don't remember anything about my father. Nothing. I remember we were taken away in our sleep and we walked for a few days. Do you have any other questions?" she asked with a bitter mockery which he heard clearly in the dark and which made him wince.

"Do you remember your home... where it is, I mean?" he asked.

"I think I remember what it was called... Vumba or Fumba, and I think it was near the sea. I was only three or four years old. I don't even think I can remember how my mother looked. Listen, I have to go now."

"Wait," he said, and reached out a hand to delay her. He held her by the arm, and she made no effort to release herself. "Are you married to him? Is he your husband?"

"Yes," she said calmly.

"No," he said, his voice filled with pain.

"Yes," she said. "But did you not know that either? It was always understood... She explained it all to me when I first came here. Her! That amulet which you found, it was given to me when Khalil's father adopted me. They had a man come and prepare the adoption papers, and he also made an amulet for me. He said it would protect me always, but it didn't. I've got my life, at least. But I only know I have it because of its emptiness, because of what I'm denied. He, the seyyid, he likes to say that most of the occupants of Heaven are the poor and most of the occupants of Hell are women. If there is Hell on earth, then it is here."

He could think of nothing to say, and after a moment he let go of her arm, overwhelmed by the intense calm with which she spoke of her bitterness and defeat. He would never have guessed from her quiet smiles and self-assured silences that she had to keep such miseries in check.

"I used to watch you working in the garden," she said. "Khalil spoke about you and how you were brought here. And I used to imagine that the shade and the water and the earth helped you ease the pain of what had been stolen from you. I envied you, and thought that one day you would catch sight of me at the door and force me to come out too. Come out and play, I imagined you saying. But then they sent you away because she began to get crazy about you. Anyway, enough of all that... Did you want to ask any other questions? Then I must go."

"Yes," he said. "Will you leave him?"

She laughed softly and touched him on the cheek. "I could tell you were a dreamer," she said. "When I watched you in the garden I imagined you were a dreamer. I'd better return before she begins again. Keep away from her. Do you hear?"

"Wait! How will I see you? Unless I come."

"No," she said. "What is there to see? I don't know."

After she had gone he felt the touch of her hand like a mark on his cheek, and touched it to feel it glow.

"Why did you make such a mystery of it and go into such terrible sulks? You could've told me all this simply," Yusuf said, sitting by Khalil, who was already stretched out on his mat.

"I could've," Khalil said reluctantly.

"Why didn't you?" Yusuf asked.

Khalil sat up, drawing the sheet round his shoulders to protect himself from the mosquitoes which were howling round them. "Because it isn't simple. Nothing is, and this wasn't something I could just say to you, hey, how about this one?" Khalil said. "And as for what you call terrible sulking, it is because you make me feel ashamed of you."

"All right, I'm sorry you were ashamed and not really sulking, but perhaps you can now tell me a little more about what is not simple."

"Has she said anything to you? About herself..." Khalil asked.

"She said your father rescued her from kidnappers, and then adopted her as his daughter."

"Is that all? Oh well, that's nothing much," Khalil said, hunching his shoulders sulkily. "I don't know where that skinny old shopkeeper found the courage. Those people had guns... perhaps. And he ran splashing into the waters screaming at them to let the children go. He couldn't even swim.

"We lived in a small town south of here, a poor place. I told you about it. The shop traded with fishermen and small farmers who came to sell their vegetables and eggs for a handful of nails or a piece of cloth or a pound of sugar. And any lucky little bit of smuggling that turned up was always welcome. That's what she was, magendo to be sold off somewhere, like her sister was sold off. I remember when she came, crying and dirty... terrified. Everybody in the town knew her story, but nobody came to ask for her, so she lived with us. My Ba called her kifa urongo," Khalil said and then smiled. "In the morning, my Ba called for her as soon as he was ready to eat his bread, and she brought it and sat with him while he fed little pieces to her. Like she was a little bird. Millet bread and melted ghee every morning, and she sat nearby chattering and opening her mouth wide for the small pieces he broke off for her. She followed my mother while she did her work, or came with me when I went out. Then one day my father said that we would give her our name, so she would become one of us. God made us all from a clot of blood, he used to say. She could speak better with the people there than any of us. She's a Mswahili, like you, although she spoke a little differently.

"Then the seyyid came. This part is very simple. When she was seven years old, my poor stupid Ba, may God have mercy on him, offered her to the seyyid as part of the payment. And I was to be rehani to him until she was of an age to be married, unless my Ba could redeem me before then. But he died, and my Ma and my brothers went back to Arabia and left me here with our shame. When that devil Mohammed Abdalla came to collect us, he made her undress and stroked her with his filthy hands."

Khalil began to weep gently, tears sliding gently down his face.

"The seyyid told me after the marriage that if I wished to stay I could," Khalil continued. "So I stayed to serve that poor girl whom my Ba sold into bondage, may God have mercy on his soul."

"But there is no need for either of you to stay here any more. She can leave if she wants. Who can stop her?" Yusuf cried.

"My brother, how brave you are," Khalil said, laughing through his tears. "We can all run away to live on the mountain. It is up to her to leave. If she goes without the seyyid's will I have to go back to being rehani, or pay the debt. This was the agreement, and this is what honour requires. So she won't leave, and while she stays, I stay."

"How can you talk about honour...?"

"What else do you think I should talk about?" Khalil asked. "My poor Ba, may God have mercy on him, and the seyyid have taken everything else from me. If it was not they who made me into the useless coward you see here, then who did? Perhaps I just have the nature for it, or it is the way we live... our custom. But her, they broke her heart. What else is there to hold above that? If you don't want me to call it honour, then call it anything else you like."

"I'm not at all concerned about your honour," Yusuf said angrily. "It's just another noble word to hide behind. I'm going to take her away from this place."

Khalil lay down on the mat and stretched. "The night the seyyid married her I was happy," he said. "Even though it was not such a sight as that Indian wedding we saw many years ago. There was no singing and no jewels... nor even any guests. I thought that now she would no longer be like a little bird in a cage, singing those broken songs of hers. Did you hear her singing at night sometimes? The marriage would wipe away her shame, I thought. She can leave if she wants! Who has stopped you leaving all these years? Where will you go with her? The seyyid will not even need to raise a hand against you. You'll be condemned in the eyes of all people, rightly so. A criminal. If you stay in this town, you'll not even be safe. Has she said anything to you? I mean has she committed herself?"

Yusuf did not reply, but he could feel his indignation subsiding and sensed the beginning of relief that his reckless resolve was being challenged. Perhaps there was nothing for him to do about it. And though the memory of Amina standing in the dark by the courtyard door was still warm in his hands, he could already feel it cooling into something more quiescent, a fond treasure to be unwrapped at a quiet moment. How could he talk about going away with her? She would laugh in his face and then call for help. Then he heard the bitterness in her voice as she spoke of Uncle Aziz and as she spoke of her life as Hell. He felt her hand on his cheek, her hand on his cheek. Her laughter at his question if she would leave Uncle Aziz…

"No, she has not said anything. She thinks I'm a dreamer," Yusuf said after a long silence. He thought Khalil would ask more questions, but after a moment he heard him sigh and settle himself for sleep.

Yusuf woke up feeling tired and at fault. Throughout the night as he dozed and surfaced, he had debated whether he should leave matters alone or speak to Amina and force the issue with her. He thought she would not turn away from him with scorn, the way she had spoken of her life and of his, how she had watched him and run their lives together. There was something like that in the desire he felt for her too, and although he did not have all the words to hand to speak to her about his desire, he knew that it was not something slight which arose entirely at his own bidding. But all that was only gentle murmuring compared with what would follow if she were willing. Despite that, he was resolved to speak to her. He would say to her: *If this is Hell, then leave. And let me come with you. They've raised us to be timid and obedient, to honour them even as they misuse us. Leave and let me come with you. We're both in the middle of nowhere. Where else can be worse? There would be no walled garden there, wherever we go, with sturdy cypresses and restless bushes, and fruit trees and unexpectedly bright flowers. Nor the bitter scent of orange sap in the day and the deep embrace of jasmine fragrance at night, nor fragrance of pomegranate seeds or the sweet herbaceous grasses in the borders. Nor the music of the water in the pool and the channels. Nor the contentment of the date grove at the cruel height of the day. There would be no music to ravish the senses. It would be like banishment, but how could it be worse than this?* And she would smile and touch his cheek with her hand, making it glow. You're a dreamer, she would say to him, and then promise that they would build a garden of their own more complete than that.

He would feel no remorse about his parents, he said to himself. He would not. They had abandoned him years ago to win their own freedom, and now he would abandon them. If they had gained any relief from his captivity, it would now end while he went to make a life for himself. While he was freely roaming the plains he might even call in on them and thank them for giving him some tough lessons to set him up in life.

4

The shop was busy that day, and Khalil threw himself at the work with a gaiety and abandon which made even the most cast-down customers smile. He's recovered his spirits, they said. God be praised! His banter reached a new daring, at times on the verge of mockery, but delivered with such irresistible amiability that no one felt able to take offence. "What's got into him?" the customers asked. Yusuf smiled and shrugged, then lightly touched his left temple. Several explanations were advanced. It was youthful enthusiasm, misplaced but healthy and pleasing. Might as well laugh now before life knots you up. Some sticks of hashish had done the trick, suggested someone else. He's probably not used to it and his mind has developed a fever. A woman who came to buy two ounces of coconut oil for her hair, and to whom Khalil delivered a rhapsodic allegory on the joys of a massage, wondered if someone had put pepper on the young man's penis. The old men on the terrace watched and cackled happily. Though Khalil avoided his eye, Yusuf could see the gleeful frenzy in his darting glances and stepped out of his way.

In the afternoon, when the pace slackened, Khalil ostentatiously wedged a box into a corner of the shop and sat on it for a doze. Yusuf could never remember him doing that before, and took this sudden slump to be a continuation of his sulks and craziness. He saw Mzee Hamdani struggling with buckets of water and guessed that he would be replenishing the pools. The water spilled and sloshed over the sides of the buckets before the old man had taken the few steps to the garden, splashing his feet and turning the ground muddy. Yusuf watched him with envy and irritation, not bothering to rush to his aid, but the old man was as preoccupied as ever and made no sign that he was aware of him. Later he saw him leave without a backward glance, shuffling across the clearing at the steady pace of a charging millipede. His voice rose intermittently in a chant that was impossible to hear clearly, and which sounded like words sung backwards.

At the usual time in the evening Yusuf went inside. He told himself it would be for the last time. He would say a quick prayer for the Mistress and see Amina and then... ask her to leave with him, if he dared. The courtyard door was ajar and he walked in, calling out gently to announce his arrival. The room was fragrant with incense and the Mistress was sitting alone waiting for him. He stopped at the door, afraid to enter. She smiled and beckoned him in. He saw that she was richly dressed, her long cream dress glittering with amber thread. She pulled her shawl away and leaned forward, waving him nearer with insistent urgency. He took two steps forward and stopped, his heart pounding, knowing he should leave. She began to talk quietly to him. Her voice was rich with feeling, and her smile grew softer as she spoke. Yusuf could not be sure what she wanted him to do, but he could not mistake the look of passion and longing on her face. She pressed the palms of her hand on her bosom and then rose to her feet. When she put her hand on his shoulder he shivered. He began to retreat and she followed. He turned to flee, but she clutched his shirt from behind and he felt it tear in her hands. As he ran out of the room, he heard her screams of agony but did not look back or hesitate.

"What have you done?" Khalil shouted as he ran past him in the darkening garden. Yusuf sat on the terrace feeling numb and disgusting, overcome with the unbearable squalor of his situation. He waited on the terrace for what seemed hours, veering between shame and anger. Perhaps he should leave at once, he thought, before all the messy consequences began. But he had done nothing shameful, it was the way they had forced him to live, forced all of them to live, which was shameful. Their intrigues and hatreds and vengeful acquisitiveness had forced even simple virtues into tokens of exchange and barter. He would go away, there was nothing simpler. Somewhere where he could escape the oppressive claims everything made on him. But he knew that a hard lump of loneliness had long ago formed in his displaced heart, that wherever he went it would be with him, to diminish and disperse any plot he could hatch for small fulfilment. He could go to the mountain town, where Hamid could torture him with self-righteous questions and Kalasinga could divert him with his fantasies. Or join Hussein in his mountain retreat. He could find small enough fulfilment there. Or go to Chatu, to become the court clown of his ramshackle fiefdom. Or to Witu, to find Mohammed the hashish smoker's mother and the sweet land he had lost by his transgressions. And everywhere he would be asked about his father and his mother, and his sister and his brother, and what he had brought and what he hoped to take away. To none of the questions would he have anything but evasive answers. The seyyid could travel deep into strange lands in a cloud of perfume, armed only with bags of trinkets and a sure knowledge of his superiority. The white man in the forest feared nothing as he sat under his flag, ringed by armed soldiers. But Yusuf had neither a flag nor righteous knowledge with which to claim superior honour, and he thought he understood that the small world he knew was the only one available to him.

Khalil came striding at him out of the darkness, his arm raised as if he would strike him. "I told you this would only bring trouble," he said angrily. He pulled him to his feet and started to drag him away. "Let's get out of here. Let's go to town. You stupid, stupid... Shall I tell you what she is saying? That you attacked her and tore her clothes like an animal, after she had treated you with such kindness. She wants me to fetch people from the town so she can make this accusation to witnesses. They will beat you and spit on you... and who knows what else."

"I didn't touch her," Yusuf said.

Khalil let go of his arm and began to punch at him, falling all over him in his rage. "I know that, I know that! Why didn't you listen?" he cried. "I didn't touch her! Try telling that to the crowd she'll gather here."

"What will happen?" Yusuf asked, pushing Khalil angrily away and rising to his feet.

"You must leave."

"Like a criminal? Where will I go? I'll leave when I want. And what will happen when I'm found?"

"Everyone will believe her," Khalil said. "I said I would fetch the people she wants from the town. She'll scream for help otherwise. They will believe what she says. Maybe she'll stop by tomorrow morning if we ignore her, but I don't think so. You should go. Don't you know these people? They'll kill you."

"She tore my shirt from behind. That proves I was running away from her," Yusuf said.

"Don't be ridiculous!" Khalil cried, laughing with disbelief. "Who'll have time to ask you that? Who cares? From behind?" He glanced at Yusuf's back and was then unable to restrain a demented grin. He fell into thought for a moment, trying to remember something.

They hurried to the waterfront and chose a dark spot where they sat talking for hours. Yusuf refused to leave in the middle of the night as if he really was a criminal, and despite Khalil's urging insisted that he would wait until the accusation had been made so he could make a defence before going. No, no, no, Khalil shouted at him, his voice cutting across the hissing of the unresting sea battering the wall at their feet.

It was almost midnight by the time they made their way back to the shop. The town was battened down and silent, patrolled by the lean dogs which haunted Yusuf's dreams. As soon as they arrived at the shop Yusuf sensed a disturbance in the air, as if something had happened while they had been away. After a moment he knew without any uncertainty what had happened. It was the perfume which announced Uncle Aziz's presence. He glanced at Khalil and saw that he knew too. The Pharaoh was back.

"The seyyid," Khalil said in a strained whisper. "He must've come during the evening. Now only God can help you."

Despite everything, Yusuf felt a thrill of pleasure that Uncle Aziz was back. It surprised him that he felt no fear of the merchant, just excited curiosity to see how he would talk to him about the accusations. Would he turn him into an ape and send him to the summit of a barren mountain as the jinn had treated the woodcutter? While Khalil talked about the dire fate awaiting him, Yusuf spread out his mat and lay down with such exasperating calm that Khalil was forced into silence.

Uncle Aziz came out at first light. When he appeared, Khalil threw himself at the merchant's hand with his habitual zeal, kissing it in between his excited greetings. Uncle Aziz was wearing a kanzu and sandals, but was without his cap, a small informality which made him seem comfortable and benign. The face he turned to Yusuf, though, was severe, and he did not offer his hand to be kissed as he usually did.

"What is this bizarre behaviour I hear about?" he asked, motioning for Yusuf to sit down again on the mat from which he had risen. "You appear to have lost your senses. Do you have an explanation for me?"

"I did her no wrong. I sat with her because she invited me in. My shirt was torn from behind," Yusuf said, his voice shaking in an unexpected and annoying way. "That shows I was running away."

Uncle Aziz smiled and then grinned, unable to restrain himself. "Oh, Yusuf," he said mockingly. "Did I not tell you that our natures are base? Why did you have to live through it all again? Who could've thought such a thing of you? From behind? That proves it, then. No harm was intended or done because your shirt was torn from behind."

Khalil launched into explanations in Arabic, which Uncle Aziz listened to for a few moments and then waved down. "Let him speak for himself," he said.

"I did nothing," Yusuf said.

"You went inside often," Uncle Aziz said, his face hardening again. "Where did you learn such manners? I leave you my house and you turn it into a place of gossip and dishonour."

"I went inside because she wanted me to, to say prayers... for her wound."

Uncle Aziz looked silently at him, as if debating what he should say or do next. It was a look Yusuf was familiar with from the journey into the interior. After such reflection, the merchant almost always decided to let matters take their course rather than intervene. It was the silent moment before allowing havoc to have its head. "I should have taken you with me," he said at last. "I should have anticipated... The Mistress is not well. If nothing dishonourable has happened, then we should leave matters there. Especially as your shirt was torn from behind. But this whole matter is not to be spoken of to outsiders. It was still wrong of you to go inside so often."

Khalil again spoke quickly in Arabic. Uncle Aziz nodded sharply a few times, and then spoke back in Arabic. After a few exchanges, Uncle Aziz pointed to the shop by a curt movement of his chin.

"Why did you go inside so often?" Uncle Aziz asked after Khalil had gone to open the shop.

Yusuf looked at the merchant without replying. Uncle Aziz was now sitting on the mat which Khalil had been lying on. One leg was folded under him and he was leaning on an outstretched arm. Yusuf saw that as he waited for him to speak, the calm amused smile began to take shape on Uncle Aziz's face.

"To catch sight of Amina," Yusuf said. The words took a long time to come out of his mouth, and he saw the smile broaden and then settle comfortably on Uncle Aziz's lips. The merchant glanced towards the shop and Yusuf followed his gaze. Khalil was by the counter, staring at them with a look of rage and hate. He turned away and continued opening the shutters.

"Is there more?" Uncle Aziz asked, returning again to Yusuf. "You really have been brave, haven't you? How you've distinguished yourself in these last few weeks!"

Because Yusuf took so long to make a reply, debating how much he should say and what difference it would make, the merchant began to speak again. "I visited your old town while I was on my journey and called on your father. I wanted to make an arrangement with him, to have you stay here and work for me for payment, and in return I would forgive all his obligations to me. But I found out that your father has passed on, may God have mercy on his soul. Your mother no longer lives there and no one could tell me where she has gone. Perhaps she has gone back to her home town. Where is that?"

"I don't know," Yusuf said. He felt no sense of loss, but a sudden sadness that his mother too was now abandoned somewhere. His eyes watered at the thought, and he saw Uncle Aziz give a small nod of approval at this display of grief. The merchant waited, as if content to let Yusuf decide how far he wanted matters to go. In the long silence Yusuf could not make himself say the words that were burning in him. *I want to take her away. It was wrong of you to marry her. To abuse her as if she has nothing which belongs to her. To own people the way you own us.* In the end Uncle Aziz rose to his feet and offered Yusuf his hand to kiss. As Yusuf bent forward into the clouds of perfume, he felt Uncle Aziz's other hand rest on the back of his head for a second and then give him a sharp pat.

"We'll discuss the plans later, to see what work you can best do for me," Uncle Aziz said pleasantly. "I'm getting tired of all this travelling. You can do some of that for me. You might even get to meet your old friend Chatu again. By the way, take care, both of you. Khalil! You too. There's talk of war between the Germans and the English, up there on the northern border. I heard this from the merchants in town when I came in yesterday afternoon. Any day now the Germans are going to start kidnapping people to make them porters for their army. So keep your eyes open. If you see them coming shut up the shop at once and get out of sight. You've heard what the Germans can do, haven't you? All right, get on with your work."

…

III Thinking, Talking and Writing About Literature

❶ Textual Cognition

Make an introductory presentation on the following terms related to this literary work.

1) "garden" metaphor
2) twisted Bildungsroman

❷ Textual Reading

Search for evidence in the text and answer the following questions.

1) How do you understand Mzee Hamdani's statement: "They can lock you up, put you in chains, abuse all your small longings, but freedom is not something they can take away. When they have finished with you, they are still as far away from owning you as they were on the day you were born."?

2) The exchange economy is an important historical, economic, and political issue in early 20th-century East Africa. What is the function of this social background?

3) After learning more about the gardener and two wives of Uncle Aziz, Yusuf begins to realize the power structure in the world of Aziz's house. At the end of the novel, Yusuf voluntarily joins the German army. How do you understand Yusuf's choice?

4) What are the relations between Yusuf's personal experience and national crisis in this book?

❸ Critical Reading

Discuss in groups the following questions to further explore this literary work.

1) Abdulrazak Gurnah delivered his Nobel Prize lecture in literature on December 7 2021. He claims that "writing also has to show what can be otherwise, what it is that the hard domineering eye cannot see, what makes people, apparently small in stature, feel assured in themselves regardless of the disdain of others". How does the point of view of this story help the reader understand this statement?

2) Gurnah found it necessary to write "truthfully", "so that both the ugliness and the virtue come through, and the human being appears out of the simplification and stereotype". How do you understand historical truth and artistic truth?

4 Writing About Literature

Read the following critical excerpt and then write an essay.

> Kearney, Jack. "The Representation of Child Deprivation in Three Contemporary African Novels: An Exploration." *English in Africa* 39.1 (2012). 125–144.

Gurnah's *Paradise* is set in early twentieth-century Tanganyika, the late colonial period in Africa. Yusuf, an only child, is sold by his father at the age of about ten in lieu of financial compensation (*rehani*) to a trader named Aziz (meaning "powerful, respected, beloved"). He proves himself useful to Aziz as a shop assistant (together with another *rehani* victim, Khalil, meaning "friend"). Because Yusuf's *rehani* experience is the major subject of the novel, he is the dominant focalizer throughout. On account of his male physical beauty, he is also a lure to be subtly exploited during Aziz's trading journeys. Abruptly cut off from his childhood sense of himself and of his world, Yusuf's *rehani* status inevitably leads him to see himself as unwanted or worthless except as a form of trading commodity. However, having proved a most useful asset to Aziz, Yusuf wins his approval and support until the trader's own survival comes under threat, at which point he does not hesitate to betray the young man. The name Yusuf is clearly intended to have a symbolic connection with the biblical Joseph and the Qur'anic Yusuf, youngest of the patriarch Jacob's sons, who was sold into slavery (although by his brothers, not by his father). In the Qur'an account Aziz is actually the name of Yusuf's master, and his wife's name is also Zulekha. The very different ultimate fate of Jacob's son, however, helps to heighten the pathos of Gurnah's denouement.

Essay Writing

Read the above selection and write an essay on *Paradise* from the perspective of coming of age in the context of colonial East Africa with no less than 500 words.

IV Further Activity

Scan the QR code and watch a video clip "Nobel Prize lecture in literature" by Abdulrazak Gurnah on December 7 2021.

Lecture 22
Chimamanda Ngozi Adichie

Profile of the Writer

Chimamanda Ngozi Adichie
(1977–)

  Novelist and feminist campaigner Chimamanda Ngozi Adichie was born in 1977 to a middle-class Igbo family in Enugu, Nigeria. She has a Master's degree in Creative Writing from Johns Hopkins University and a Master of Arts in African History from Yale University. She was awarded a Hodder fellowship at Princeton University for the 2005–2006 academic year, and a fellowship at the Radcliffe Institute of Harvard University for the 2011–2012 academic year. In 2008, she received a MacArthur Fellowship.

  Her work has been translated into over 30 languages. Her first novel, *Purple Hibiscus* (2003), won the Commonwealth Writers' Prize, and her second novel, *Half of a Yellow Sun* (2006), won the Orange Prize. Her 2013 novel *Americanah* won the US National Book Critics Circle Award and was named one of *The New York Times* Top Ten Best Books of 2013. She has delivered two landmark TED talks: her 2009 TED Talk "The Danger of a Single Story" and her 2012 TEDx Euston talk "We Should All Be Feminists", which started a worldwide conversation about feminism and was published as a book in 2014. *Dear Ijeawele, or a Feminist Manifesto in Fifteen Suggestions,* was published in March 2017. Her most recent work, *Notes on Grief,* an essay about losing her father, has just been published.

I Preview Questions

1. *Half of a Yellow Sun* (2006) is Adichie's most influential novel and most widely read book in China. How do you understand the title of the book?

2. Nigeria-Biafra Civil War is one of the most important historical background in Adichie's novels. Do you know anything about this war?

II Literary Reading: *Half of a Yellow Sun* (Chapter 1)

Master was a little crazy; he had spent too many years reading books overseas, talked to himself in his office, did not always return greetings, and had too much hair. Ugwu's aunty said this in a low voice as they walked on the path. "But he is a good man," she added. "And as long as you work well, you will eat well. You will even eat meat every day." She stopped to spit; the saliva left her mouth with a sucking sound and landed on the grass.

Ugwu did not believe that anybody, not even this master he was going to live with, ate meat *every day*. He did not disagree with his aunty, though, because he was too choked with expectation, too busy imagining his new life away from the village. They had been walking for a while now, since they got off the lorry at the motor park, and the afternoon sun burned the back of his neck. But he did not mind. He was prepared to walk hours more in even hotter sun. He had never seen anything like the streets that appeared after they went past the university gates, streets so smooth and tarred that he itched to lay his cheek down on them. He would never be able to describe to his sister Anulika how the bungalows here were painted the colour of the sky and sat side by side like polite, well-dressed men, how the hedges separating them were trimmed so flat on top that they looked like tables wrapped with leaves.

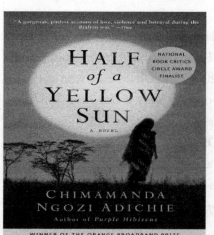

His aunty walked faster, her slippers making *slap-slap* sounds that echoed in the silent street. Ugwu wondered if she, too, could feel the coal tar getting hotter underneath, through her thin soles. They went past a sign, ODIM STREET, and Ugwu mouthed *street*, as he did whenever he saw an English word that was not too long. He smelt something sweet, heady, as they walked into a compound, and was sure it came from the white flowers clustered on the bushes at the entrance. The bushes were shaped like slender hills. The lawn glistened. Butterflies hovered above.

"I told Master you will learn everything fast, *osiso-osiso*," his aunty said. Ugwu nodded attentively although she had already told him this many times, as often as she told him the story of how his good fortune came about: While she was sweeping the corridor in the Mathematics Department a week ago, she heard Master say that he needed a houseboy to do his cleaning, and she immediately said she could help, speaking before his typist or office messenger could offer to bring someone.

"I will learn fast, Aunty," Ugwu said. He was staring at the car in the garage; a strip of metal ran around its blue body like a necklace.

"Remember, what you will answer whenever he calls you is *Yes, sah*!"

"Yes, sah!" Ugwu repeated.

They were standing before the glass door. Ugwu held back from reaching out to touch the cement wall, to see how different it would feel from the mud walls of his mother's hut that still bore the faint patterns of moulding fingers. For a brief moment, he wished he were back there now, in his mother's hut, under the dim coolness of the thatch roof; or in his aunty's hut, the only one in the village with a corrugated-iron roof.

His aunty tapped on the glass. Ugwu could see the white curtains behind the door. A voice said, in English, "Yes? Come in."

They took off their slippers before walking in. Ugwu had never seen a room so wide. Despite the brown sofas arranged in a semicircle, the side tables between them, the shelves crammed with books, and the centre table with a vase of red and white plastic flowers, the room still seemed to have too much space. Master sat in an armchair, wearing a singlet and a pair of shorts. He was not sitting upright but slanted, a book covering his face, as though oblivious that he had just asked people in.

"Good afternoon, sah! This is the child," Ugwu's aunty said.

Master looked up. His complexion was very dark, like old bark, and the hair that covered his chest and legs was a lustrous, darker shade. He pulled off his glasses. "The child?"

"The houseboy, sah."

"Oh, yes, you have brought the houseboy. I *kpotago ya*." Master's Igbo felt feathery in Ugwu's ears. It was Igbo coloured by the sliding sounds of English, the Igbo of one who spoke English often.

"He will work hard," his aunty said. "He is a very good boy. Just tell him what he should do. Thank, sah!"

Master grunted in response, watching Ugwu and his aunty with a faintly distracted expression, as if their presence made it difficult for him to remember something important. Ugwu's aunty patted Ugwu's shoulder, whispered that he should do well, and turned to the door. After she left, Master put his glasses back on and faced his book, relaxing further into a slanting position, legs stretched out. Even when he turned the pages he did so with his eyes on the book.

Ugwu stood by the door, waiting. Sunlight streamed in through the windows, and from time to time, a gentle breeze lifted the curtains. The room was silent except for the rustle of Master's page turning. Ugwu stood for a while before he began to edge closer and closer to the bookshelf, as though to hide in it, and then, after a while, he sank down to the floor, cradling his raffia bag between his knees. He looked up at the ceiling, so high up, so piercingly white. He closed his eyes and tried to reimagine this spacious room with the alien furniture, but he couldn't. He opened his eyes, overcome by a new wonder, and looked around to make sure it was all real. To think that he would sit on these sofas, polish this slippery-smooth floor, wash these gauzy curtains.

"*Kedu afa gi*? What's your name?" Master asked, startling him.

Ugwu stood up.

"What's your name?" Master asked again and sat up straight. He filled the armchair, his thick hair that stood high on his head, his muscled arms, his broad shoulders; Ugwu had imagined an older man, somebody frail, and now he felt a sudden fear that he might not please this master who looked so youthfully capable, who looked as if he needed nothing.

"Ugwu, sah."

"Ugwu. And you've come from Obukpa?"

"From Opi, sah."

"You could be anything from twelve to thirty." Master narrowed his eyes. "Probably thirteen." He said *thirteen* in English.

"Yes, sah."

Master turned back to his book. Ugwu stood there. Master flipped past some pages and looked up. "*Ngwa*, go to the kitchen; there should be something you can eat in the fridge."

"Yes, sah."

Ugwu entered the kitchen cautiously, placing one foot slowly after the other. When he saw the white thing, almost as tall as he was, he knew it was the fridge. His aunty had told him about it. A cold barn, she had said, that kept food from going off. He opened it and gasped as the cool air rushed into his face. Oranges, bread, beer, soft drinks: many things in packets and cans were arranged on different levels and, at the top, a roasted, shimmering chicken, whole but for a leg. Ugwu reached out and touched the chicken. The fridge breathed heavily in his ears. He touched the chicken again and licked his finger before he yanked the other leg off, eating it until he had only the cracked, sucked pieces of bones left in his hand. Next, he broke off some bread, a chunk that he would have been excited to share with his siblings if a relative had visited and brought it as a gift. He ate quickly, before Master could come in and change his mind. He had finished eating and was standing by the sink, trying to remember what his aunty had told him about opening it to have water gush out like a spring, when Master walked in. He had put on a print shirt and a pair of trousers. His toes, which peeked through leather slippers, seemed feminine, perhaps because they were so clean; they belonged to feet that always wore shoes.

"What is it?" Master asked.

"Sah?" Ugwu gestured to the sink.

Master came over and turned the metal tap. "You should look around the house and put your bag in the first room on the corridor. I'm going for a walk, to clear my head, *i nugo*?"

"Yes, sah." Ugwu watched him leave through the back door. He was not tall. His walk was brisk, energetic, and he looked like Ezeagu, the man who held the wrestling record in Ugwu's village.

Ugwu turned off the tap, turned it on again, then off. On and off and on and off until he was laughing at the magic of the running water and the chicken and bread that lay balmy in his stomach. He went past the living room and into the corridor. There were books piled on the shelves and tables in the three bedrooms, on the sink and cabinets in the bathroom, stacked from floor to ceiling in the study, and in the storeroom, old journals were stacked next to crates of Coke and cartons of Premier beer. Some of the books were placed face down, open, as though Master had not yet finished reading them but had hastily gone on to another. Ugwu tried to read the titles, but most were too long, too difficult. *Non-Parametric Methods. An African Survey. The Great Chain of Being. The Norman Impact Upon England.*

He walked on tiptoe from room to room, because his feet felt dirty, and as he did so he grew increasingly determined to please Master, to stay in this house of meat and cool floors. He was examining the toilet, running his hand over the black plastic seat, when he heard Master's voice.

"Where are you, my good man?" He said *my good man* in English. Ugwu dashed out to the living room. "Yes, sah!"

"What's your name again?"

"Ugwu, sah."

"Yes, Ugwu. Look here, *nee anya*, do you know what that is?" Master pointed, and

Ugwu looked at the metal box studded with dangerous-looking knobs.

"No, sah," Ugwu said.

"It's a radiogram. It's new and very good. It's not like those old gramophones that you have to wind and wind. You have to be very careful around it, very careful. You must never let water touch it."

"Yes, sah."

"I'm off to play tennis, and then I'll go on to the staff club." Master picked up a few books from the table. "I may be back late. So get settled and have a rest."

"Yes, sah."

After Ugwu watched Master drive out of the compound, he went and stood beside the radiogram and looked at it carefully, without touching it. Then he walked around the house, up and down, touching books and curtains and furniture and plates, and when it got dark, he turned the light on and marvelled at how bright the bulb that dangled from the ceiling was, how it did not cast long shadows on the wall like the palm oil lamps back home. His mother would be preparing the evening meal now, pounding *akpu* in the mortar, the pestle grasped tightly with both hands. Chioke, the junior wife, would be tending the pot of watery soup balanced on three stones over the fire. The children would have come back from the stream and would be taunting and chasing one another under the breadfruit tree. Perhaps Anulika would be watching them. She was the oldest child in the household now, and as they all sat around the fire to eat, she would break up the fights when the younger ones struggled over the strips of dried fish in the soup. She would wait until all the *akpu* was eaten and then divide the fish so that each child had a piece, and she would keep the biggest for herself, as he had always done.

Ugwu opened the fridge and ate some more bread and chicken, quickly stuffing the food in his mouth while his heart beat as if he were running; then he dug out extra chunks of meat and pulled out the wings. He slipped the pieces into his shorts' pockets before going to the bedroom. He would keep them until his aunty visited and he would ask her to give them to Anulika. Perhaps he could ask her to give some to Nnesinachi too. That might make Nnesinachi finally notice him. He had never been sure exactly how he and Nnesinachi were related, but he knew they were from the same *umunna* and therefore could never marry. Yet he wished that his mother would not keep referring to Nnesinachi as his sister, saying things like, "Please take this palm oil down to Mama Nnesinachi, and if she is not in, leave it with your sister."

Nnesinachi always spoke to him in a vague voice, her eyes unfocused, as if his presence made no difference to her either way. Sometimes she called him Chiejina, the name of his cousin who looked nothing at all like him, and when he said, "It's me," she would say, "Forgive me, Ugwu my brother," with a distant formality that meant she had no wish to make further conversation. But he liked going on errands to her house. They were opportunities to find her bent over, fanning the firewood or chopping *ugu* leaves for her mother's soup pot, or just sitting outside looking after her younger siblings, her wrapper hanging low enough for him to see the tops of her breasts. Ever since they started to push out, those pointy breasts, he had wondered if they would feel mushy—soft or hard like the unripe fruit from the *ube* tree. He often wished that Anulika wasn't so flat-chested—he wondered what was taking her so long anyway, since she and Nnesinachi were about the same age—so that he could feel her breasts. Anulika would slap his hand away, of course, and perhaps even slap his face as well, but he would do it quickly—squeeze and run—and that way he would at least have an idea and know what to expect when he finally touched Nnesinachi's.

But he was worried that he might never get to touch them, now that her uncle had asked her to come and learn a trade in Kano. She would be leaving for the North by the end of the year, when her mother's last child, whom she was carrying, began to walk. Ugwu wanted to be as pleased and grateful as the rest of the family. There was, after all, a fortune to be made in the North; he knew of people who had gone up there to trade and came home to tear down huts and build houses with corrugated-iron roofs. He feared, though, that one of those pot-bellied traders in the North would take one look at her, and the next thing he knew somebody would bring palm wine to her father and he would never get to touch those breasts. They—her breasts—were the images saved for last on the many nights when he touched himself, slowly at first and then vigorously, until a muffled moan escaped him. He always started with her face, the fullness of her cheeks and the ivory tone of her teeth, and then he imagined her arms around him, her body moulded to his. Finally, he let her breasts form; sometimes they felt hard, tempting him to bite into them, and other times they were so soft he was afraid his imaginary squeezing caused her pain.

For a moment, he considered thinking of her tonight. He decided not to. Not on his first night in Master's house, on this bed that was nothing like his hand-woven raffia mat. First, he pressed his hands into the springy softness of the mattress. Then, he examined the layers of cloth on top of it, unsure whether to sleep on them or to remove them and put them away before sleeping. Finally, he climbed up and lay on top of the layers of cloth, his body curled in a tight knot.

He dreamed that Master was calling him—*Ugwu, my good man!*—and when he woke up Master was standing at the door, watching him. Perhaps it had not been a dream. He scrambled out of bed and glanced at the windows with the drawn curtains, in confusion. Was it late? Had that soft bed deceived him and made him oversleep? He usually woke with the first cockcrows.

"Good morning, sah!"

"There is a strong roasted-chicken smell here."

"Sorry, sah."

"Where is the chicken?"

Ugwu fumbled in his shorts' pockets and brought out the chicken pieces.

"Do your people eat while they sleep?" Master asked. He was wearing something that looked like a woman's coat and was absently twirling the rope tied round his waist.

"Sah?"

"Did you want to eat the chicken while in bed?"

"No, sah."

"Food will stay in the dining room and the kitchen."

"Yes, sah."

"The kitchen and bathroom will have to be cleaned today."

"Yes, sah."

Master turned and left. Ugwu stood trembling in the middle of the room, still holding the chicken pieces with his hand outstretched. He wished he did not have to walk past the dining room to get to the kitchen. Finally, he put the chicken back in his pockets, took a deep breath, and left the room. Master was at the dining table, the teacup in front of him placed on a pile of books.

"You know who really killed Lumumba?" Master said, looking up from a magazine. "It was the Americans and the Belgians. It had nothing to do with Katanga."

"Yes, sah," Ugwu said. He wanted Master to keep talking, so he could listen to the sonorous voice, the musical blend of English words in his Igbo sentences.

"You are my houseboy," Master said. "If I order you to go outside and beat a woman walking on the street with a stick, and you then give her a bloody wound on her leg, who is responsible for the wound, you or me?"

Ugwu stared at Master, shaking his head, wondering if Master was referring to the chicken pieces in some roundabout way.

"Lumumba was prime minister of Congo. Do you know where Congo is?" Master asked.

"No, sah."

Master got up quickly and went into the study. Ugwu's confused fear made his eyelids quiver. Would Master send him home because he did not speak English well, kept chicken in his pocket overnight, did not know the strange places Master named? Master came back with a wide piece of paper that he unfolded and laid out on the dining table, pushing aside books and magazines. He pointed with his pen. "This is our world, although the people who drew this map decided to put their own land on top of ours. There is no top or bottom, you see." Master picked up the paper and folded it, so that one edge touched the other, leaving a hollow between. "Our world is round, it never ends. *Nee anya*, this is all water, the seas and oceans, and here's Europe and here's our own continent, Africa, and the Congo is in the middle. Farther up here is Nigeria, and Nsukka is here, in the southeast; this is where we are." He tapped with his pen.

"Yes, sah."

"Did you go to school?"

"Standard two, sah. But I learn everything fast."

"Standard two? How long ago?"

"Many years now, sah. But I learn everything very fast!"

"Why did you stop school?"

"My father's crops failed, sah."

Master nodded slowly. "Why didn't your father find somebody to lend him your school fees?"

"Sah?"

"Your father should have borrowed!" Master snapped, and then, in English, "Education is a priority! How can we resist exploitation if we don't have the tools to understand exploitation?"

"Yes, sah!" Ugwu nodded vigorously. He was determined to appear as alert as he could, because of the wild shine that had appeared in Master's eyes.

"I will enrol you in the staff primary school," Master said, still tapping on the piece of paper with his pen.

Ugwu's aunty had told him that if he served well for a few years, Master would send him to commercial school where he would learn typing and shorthand. She had mentioned the staff primary school, but only to tell him that it was for the children of the lecturers, who wore blue uniforms and white socks so intricately trimmed with wisps of lace that you wondered why anybody had wasted so much time on mere socks.

"Yes, sah," he said. "Thank, sah."

"I suppose you will be the oldest in class, starting in standard three at your age," Master said. "And the only way you can get their respect is to be the best. Do you understand?"

"Yes, sah!"

"Sit down, my good man."

Ugwu chose the chair farthest from Master, awkwardly placing his feet close together.

He preferred to stand.

"There are two answers to the things they will teach you about our land: the real answer and the answer you give in school to pass. You must read books and learn both answers. I will give you books, excellent books." Master stopped to sip his tea. "They will teach you that a white man called Mungo Park discovered River Niger. That is rubbish. Our people fished in the Niger long before Mungo Park's grandfather was born. But in your exam, write that it was Mungo Park."

"Yes, sah." Ugwu wished that this person called Mungo Park had not offended Master so much.

"Can't you say anything else?"

"Sah?"

"Sing me a song."

"Sah?"

"Sing me a song. What songs do you know? Sing!" Master pulled his glasses off. His eyebrows were furrowed, serious. Ugwu began to sing an old song he had learned on his father's farm. His heart hit his chest painfully. *Nzogbo nzogbu enyimba, enyi...*

He sang in a low voice at first, but Master tapped his pen on the table and said "Louder!" so he raised his voice, and Master kept saying "Louder!" until he was screaming. After singing over and over a few times, Master asked him to stop. "Good, good," he said. "Can you make tea?"

"No, sah. But I learn fast," Ugwu said. The singing had loosened something inside him, he was breathing easily and his heart no longer pounded. And he was convinced that Master was mad.

"I eat mostly at the staff club. I suppose I shall have to bring more food home now that you are here."

"Sah, I can cook."

"You cook?"

Ugwu nodded. He had spent many evenings watching his mother cook. He had started the fire for her, or fanned the embers when it started to die out. He had peeled and pounded yams and cassava, blown out the husks in rice, picked out the weevils from beans, peeled onions, and ground peppers. Often, when his mother was sick with the coughing, he wished that he, and not Anulika, would cook. He had never told anyone this, not even Anulika; she had already told him he spent too much time around women cooking, and he might never grow a beard if he kept doing that.

"Well, you can cook your own food then," Master said. "Write a list of what you'll need."

"Yes, sah."

"You wouldn't know how to get to the market, would you? I'll ask Jomo to show you."

"Jomo, sah?"

"Jomo takes care of the compound. He comes in three times a week. Funny man, I've seen him talking to the croton plant." Master paused. "Anyway, he'll be here tomorrow."

Later, Ugwu wrote a list of food items and gave it to Master.

Master stared at the list for a while. "Remarkable blend," he said in English. "I suppose they'll teach you to use more vowels in school."

Ugwu disliked the amusement in Master's face. "We need wood, sah," he said.

"Wood?"

"For your books, sah. So that I can arrange them."

"Oh, yes, shelves. I suppose we could fit more shelves somewhere, perhaps in the corridor. I will speak to somebody at the Works Department."

"Yes, sah."

"Odenigbo. Call me Odenigbo."

Ugwu stared at him doubtfully. "Sah?"

"My name is not Sah. Call me Odenigbo."

"Yes, sah."

"Odenigbo will always be my name. *Sir* is arbitrary. You could be the *sir* tomorrow."

"Yes, sah-Odenigbo."

Ugwu really preferred *sah*, the crisp power behind the word, and when two men from the Works Department came a few days later to install shelves in the corridor, he told them that they would have to wait for Sah to come home; he himself could not sign the white paper with typewritten words. He said *Sah* proudly.

"He's one of these village houseboys," one of the men said dismissively, and Ugwu looked at the man's face and murmured a curse about acute diarrhoea following him and all of his offspring for life. As he arranged Master's books, he promised himself, stopping short of speaking aloud, that he would learn how to sign forms.

In the following weeks, the weeks when he examined every corner of the bungalow, when he discovered that a beehive was lodged in the cashew tree and that the butterflies converged in the front yard when the sun was brightest, he was just as careful in learning the rhythms of Master's life. Every morning, he picked up the *Daily Times* and *Renaissance* that the vendor dropped off at the door and folded them on the table next to Master's tea and bread. He had the Opel washed before Master finished breakfast, and when Master came back from work and was taking a siesta, he dusted the car over again, before Master left for the tennis courts. He moved around silently on the days that Master retired to the study for hours. When Master paced the corridor talking in a loud voice, he made sure that there was hot water ready for tea. He scrubbed the floors daily. He wiped the louvres until they sparkled in the afternoon sunlight, paid attention to the tiny cracks in the bathtub, polished the saucers that he used to serve kola nut to Master's friends. There were at least two visitors in the living room each day, the radiogram turned on low to strange flutelike music, low enough for the talking and laughing and glass clinking to come clearly to Ugwu in the kitchen or in the corridor as he ironed Master's clothes.

He wanted to do more, wanted to give Master every reason to keep him, and so one morning, he ironed Master's socks. They didn't look rumpled, the black ribbed socks, but he thought they would look even better straightened. The hot iron hissed and when he raised it, he saw that half of the sock was glued to it. He froze. Master was at the dining table, finishing up breakfast, and would come in any minute now to pull on his socks and shoes and take the files on the shelf and leave for work. Ugwu wanted to hide the sock under the chair and dash to the drawer for a new pair but his legs would not move. He stood there with the burnt sock, knowing Master would find him that way.

"You've ironed my socks, haven't you?" Master asked. "You stupid ignoramus." *Stupid ignoramus* slid out of his mouth like music.

"Sorry, sah! Sorry, sah!"

"I told you not to call me sir." Master picked up a file from the shelf. "I'm late."

"Sah? Should I bring another pair?" Ugwu asked. But Master had already slipped on his shoes, without socks, and hurried out. Ugwu heard him bang the car door and drive away. His chest felt weighty; he did not know why he had ironed the socks, why he had not simply done the safari suit. Evil spirits, that was it. The evil spirits had made him do it. They lurked everywhere, after all. Whenever he was ill with the fever, or once when he fell from a tree, his mother would rub his body with *okwuma*, all the while muttering, "We shall defeat them, they will not win."

He went out to the front yard, past stones placed side by side around the manicured lawn. The evil spirits would not win. He would not let them defeat him. There was a round, grassless patch in the middle of the lawn, like an island in a green sea, where a thin palm tree stood. Ugwu had never seen any palm tree that short, or one with leaves that flared out so perfectly. It did not look strong enough to bear fruit, did not look useful at all, like most of the plants here. He picked up a stone and threw it into the distance. So much wasted space. In his village, people farmed the tiniest plots outside their homes and planted useful vegetables and herbs. His grandmother had not needed to grow her favourite herb, *arigbe*, because it grew wild everywhere. She used to say that *arigbe* softened a man's heart. She was the second of three wives and did not have the special position that came with being the

Lecture 22
Chimamanda Ngozi Adichie

first or the last, so before she asked her husband for anything, she told Ugwu, she cooked him spicy yam porridge with arigbe. It had worked, always. Perhaps it would work with Master.

Ugwu walked around in search of *arigbe*. He looked among the pink flowers, under the cashew tree with the spongy beehive lodged on a branch, the lemon tree that had black soldier ants crawling up and down the trunk, and the pawpaw trees whose ripening fruits were dotted with fat, bird-burrowed holes. But the ground was clean, no herbs; Jomo's weeding was thorough and careful, and nothing that was not wanted was allowed to be.

The first time they met, Ugwu had greeted Jomo and Jomo nodded and continued to work, saying nothing. He was a small man with a tough, shrivelled body that Ugwu felt needed a watering more than the plants that he targeted with his metal can. Finally, Jomo looked up at Ugwu. "*Afa m bu Jomo*," he announced, as if Ugwu did not know his name. "Some people call me Kenyatta, after the great man in Kenya. I am a hunter."

Ugwu did not know what to say in return because Jomo was staring right into his eyes, as though expecting to hear something remarkable that Ugwu did.

"What kind of animals do you kill?" Ugwu asked. Jomo beamed, as if this was exactly the question he had wanted, and began to talk about his hunting. Ugwu sat on the steps that led to the backyard and listened. From the first day, he did not believe Jomo's stories—of fighting off a leopard barehanded, of killing two baboons with a single shot—but he liked listening to them and he put off washing Master's clothes to the days Jomo came so he could sit outside while Jomo worked. Jomo moved with a slow deliberateness. His raking, watering, and planting all somehow seemed filled with solemn wisdom. He would look up in the middle of trimming a hedge and say, "That is good meat," and then walk to the goatskin bag tied behind his bicycle to rummage for his catapult. Once, he shot a bush pigeon down from the cashew tree with a small stone, wrapped it in leaves, and put it into his bag.

"Don't go to that bag unless I am around," he told Ugwu. "You might find a human head there."

Ugwu laughed but had not entirely doubted Jomo. He wished so much that Jomo had come to work today. Jomo would have been the best person to ask about *arigbe*—indeed, to ask for advice on how best to placate Master.

He walked out of the compound, to the street, and looked through the plants on the roadside until he saw the rumpled leaves close to the root of a whistling pine. He had never smelt anything like the spicy sharpness of *arigbe* in the bland food Master brought back from the staff club; he would cook a stew with it, and offer Master some with rice, and afterwards plead with him. *Please don't send me back home, sah. I will work extra for the burnt* sock. *I will earn the money to replace it.* He did not know exactly what he could do to earn money for the sock, but he planned to tell Master that anyway.

If the *arigbe* softened Master's heart, perhaps he could grow it and some other herbs in the backyard. He would tell Master that the garden was something to do until he started school, since the head-mistress at the staff school had told Master that he could not start midterm. He might be hoping for too much, though. What was the point of thinking about a herb garden if Master asked him to leave, if Master would not forgive the burnt sock? He walked quickly into the kitchen, laid the *arigbe* down on the counter, and measured out some rice.

Hours later, he felt a tautness in his stomach when he heard Master's car: the crunch of gravel and the hum of the engine before it stopped in the garage. He stood by the pot of stew, stirring, holding the ladle as tightly as the cramps in his stomach felt. Would Master ask him to leave before he had a chance to offer him the food? What would he tell his people?

"Good afternoon, sah—Odenigbo," he said, even before Master had come into the kitchen.

"Yes, yes," Master said. He was holding books to his chest with one hand and his briefcase with the other. Ugwu rushed over to help with the books. "Sah? You will eat?" he asked in English.

"Eat what?"

Ugwu's stomach got tighter. He feared it might snap as he bent to place the books on the dining table. "Stew, sah."

"Stew?"

"Yes, sah. Very good stew, sah."

"I'll try some, then."

"Yes, sah!"

"Call me Odenigbo!" Master snapped before going in to take an afternoon bath.

After Ugwu served the food, he stood by the kitchen door, watching as Master took a first forkful of rice and stew, took another, and then called out, "Excellent, my good man."

Ugwu appeared from behind the door. "Sah? I can plant the herbs in a small garden. To cook more stews like this."

"A garden?" Master stopped to sip some water and turn a journal page. "No, no, no. Outside is Jomo's territory, and inside is yours. Division of labour, my good man. If we need herbs, we'll ask Jomo to take care of it." Ugwu loved the sound of *Division of labour, my good man*, spoken in English.

"Yes, sah," he said, although he was already thinking of what spot would be best for

Lecture 22
Chimamanda Ngozi Adichie

the herb garden: near the Boys' Quarters where Master never went. He could not trust Jomo with the herb garden and would tend it himself when Master was out, and this way, his *arigbe*, his herb of forgiveness, would never run out. It was only later in the evening that he realized Master must have forgotten about the burnt sock long before coming home.

Ugwu came to realize other things. He was not a normal houseboy; Dr. Okeke's houseboy next door did not sleep on a bed in a room, he slept on the kitchen floor. The houseboy at the end of the street with whom Ugwu went to the market did not decide what would be cooked, he cooked whatever he was ordered to. And they did not have masters or madams who gave them books, saying, "This one is excellent, just excellent."

Ugwu did not understand most of the sentences in the books, but he made a show of reading them. Nor did he entirely understand the conversations of Master and his friends but listened anyway and heard that the world had to do more about the black people killed in Sharpeville, that the spy plane shot down in Russia served the Americans right, that De Gaulle was being clumsy in Algeria, that the United Nations would never get rid of Tshombe in Katanga. Once in a while, Master would stand up and raise his glass and his voice—"To that brave black American led into the University of Mississippi!" "To Ceylon and to the world's first woman prime minister!" "To Cuba for beating the Americans at their own game!"—and Ugwu would enjoy the clink of beer bottles against glasses, glasses against glasses, bottles against bottles.

More friends visited on weekends, and when Ugwu came out to serve their drinks, Master would sometimes introduce him—in English, of course. "Ugwu helps me around the house. Very clever boy." Ugwu would continue to uncork bottles of beer and Coke silently, while feeling the warm glow of pride spread up from the tips of his toes. He especially liked it when Master introduced him to foreigners, like Mr. Johnson, who was from the Caribbean and stammered when he spoke, or Professor Lehman, the nasal white man from America who had eyes that were the piercing green of a fresh leaf. Ugwu was vaguely frightened the first time he saw him because he had always imagined that only evil spirits had grass-coloured eyes.

He soon knew the regular guests and brought out their drinks before Master asked him to. There was Dr. Patel, the Indian man who drank Golden Guinea beer mixed with Coke. Master called him *Doc*. Whenever Ugwu brought out the kola nut, Master would say, "Doc, you know the kola nut does not understand English," before going on to bless the kola nut in Igbo. Dr. Patel laughed each time, with great pleasure, leaning back on the sofa and throwing his short legs up as if it were a joke he had never heard before. After Master broke the kola nut and passed the saucer around, Dr. Patel always took a lobe and put it into his shirt pocket; Ugwu had never seen him eat one.

There was tall, skinny Professor Ezeka, with a voice so hoarse he sounded as if he spoke in whispers. He always picked up his glass and held it up against the light, to make sure Ugwu had washed it well. Sometimes, he brought his own bottle of gin. Other times, he asked for tea and then went on to examine the sugar bowl and the tin of milk, muttering, "The capabilities of bacteria are quite extraordinary."

There was Okeoma, who came most often and stayed the longest. He looked younger than the other guests, always wore a pair of shorts, and had bushy hair with a parting at the side that stood higher than Master's. It looked rough and tangled, unlike Master's, as if Okeoma did not like to comb it. Okeoma drank Fanta. He read his poetry aloud on some evenings, holding a sheaf of papers, and Ugwu would look through the kitchen door to see all the guests watching him, their faces half frozen, as if they did not dare breathe. Afterwards, Master would clap and say, in his loud voice, "The voice of our generation!" and the clapping would go on until Okeoma said sharply, "That's enough!"

And there was Miss Adebayo, who drank brandy like Master and was nothing like Ugwu had expected a university woman to be. His aunty had told him a little about university women. She would know, because she worked as a cleaner at the Faculty of Sciences during the day and as a waitress at the staff club in the evenings; sometimes, too, the lecturers paid her to come in and clean their homes. She said university women kept framed photos of their student days in Ibadan and Britain and America on their shelves. For breakfast, they had eggs that were not cooked well, so that the yolk danced around, and they wore bouncy, straight-hair wigs and maxi-dresses that grazed their ankles. She told a story once about a couple at a cocktail party in the staff club who climbed out of a nice Peugeot 404, the man in an elegant cream suit, the woman in a green dress. Everybody turned to watch them, walking hand in hand, and then the wind blew the woman's wig off her head. She was bald. They used hot combs to straighten their hair, his aunty had said, because they wanted to look like white people, although the combs ended up burning their hair off.

Ugwu had imagined the bald woman: beautiful, with a nose that stood up, not the sitting-down, flattened noses that he was used to. He imagined quietness, delicacy, the kind of woman whose sneeze, whose laugh and talk, would be soft as the under feathers closest to a chicken's skin. But the women who visited Master, the ones he saw at the supermarket and on the streets, were different. Most of them did wear wigs (a few had their hair plaited or braided with thread), but they were not delicate stalks of grass. They were loud. The loudest was Miss Adebayo. She was not an Igbo woman; Ugwu could tell from her name, even if he had not once run into her and her housegirl at the market and heard them both speaking rapid, incomprehensible Yoruba. She had asked him to wait so that she could give him a ride back to the campus, but he thanked her and said he still had many things left to buy and would take a taxi, although he had finished shopping. He did not want to ride in her car, did not like how her voice rose above Master's in the living room, challenging and arguing. He often fought the urge to raise his own voice from behind the kitchen door and tell her to shut up, especially when she called Master a sophist. He did not know what *sophist* meant, but he did not like that she called Master that. Nor did he like the way she looked at Master. Even when somebody else was speaking and she was supposed to be focused on that person, her eyes would be on Master. One Saturday night, Okeoma dropped a glass and Ugwu came in to clean up the shards that lay on the floor. He took his time cleaning. The conversation was clearer from here and it was easier to make out what Professor Ezeka said. It was almost impossible to hear the man from the kitchen.

"We should have a bigger pan-African response to what is happening in the American South really—" Professor Ezeka said.

Master cut him short. "You know, pan-Africanism is fundamentally a European notion."

"You are digressing," Professor Ezeka said, and shook his head in his usual superior manner.

"Maybe it *is* a European notion," Miss Adebayo said, "but in the bigger picture, we are all one race."

"What bigger picture?" Master asked. "The bigger picture of the white man! Can't you see that we are not all alike except to white eyes?" Master's voice rose easily, Ugwu had noticed, and by his third glass of brandy, he would start to gesture with his glass, leaning forwards until he was seated on the very edge of his armchair. Late at night, after Master was in bed, Ugwu would sit on the same chair and imagine himself speaking swift English, talking to rapt imaginary guests, using words like *decolonize* and *pan-African*, moulding his voice after Master's, and he would shift and shift until he too was on the edge of the chair.

"Of course we are all alike, we all have white oppression in common," Miss Adebayo said dryly. "Pan-Africanism is simply the most sensible response."

"Of course, of course, but my point is that the only authentic identity for the African is the tribe," Master said. "I am Nigerian because a white man created Nigeria and gave me that identity. I am black because the white man constructed *black* to be as different as possible from his *white*. But I was Igbo before the white man came."

Professor Ezeka snorted and shook his head, thin legs crossed. "But you became aware that you were Igbo because of the white man. The pan-Igbo idea itself came only in the face of white domination. You must see that tribe as it is today is as colonial a product as nation and race." Professor Ezeka recrossed his legs.

"The pan-Igbo idea existed long before the white man!" Master shouted. "Go and ask the elders in your village about your history."

"The problem is that Odenigbo is a hopeless tribalist. We need to keep him quiet," Miss Adebayo said.

Then she did what startled Ugwu: she got up laughing and went over to Master and pressed his lips close together. She stood there for what seemed a long time, her hand to his mouth. Ugwu imagined Master's brandy-diluted saliva touching her fingers. He stiffened as he picked up the shattered glass. He wished that Master would not sit there shaking his head as if the whole thing were very funny.

Miss Adebayo became a threat after that. She began to look more and more like a fruit bat, with her pinched face and cloudy complexion and print dresses that billowed around her body like wings. Ugwu served her drink last and wasted long minutes drying his hands on a dishcloth before he opened the door to let her in. He worried that she would marry Master and bring her Yoruba-speaking housegirl into the house and destroy his herb garden and tell him what he could and could not cook. Until he heard Master and Okeoma talking.

"She did not look as if she wanted to go home today," Okeoma said. "*Nwoke m*, are you sure you are not planning to do something with her?"

"Don't talk rubbish."

"If you did, nobody in London would know."

"Look, look—"

"I know you're not interested in her like that, but what still puzzles me is what these women see in you."

Okeoma laughed and Ugwu was relieved. He did not want Miss Adebayo—or any woman—coming in to intrude and disrupt their lives. Some evenings, when the visitors left early, he would sit on the floor of the living room and listen to Master talk. Master mostly talked about things Ugwu did not understand, as if the brandy made him forget that Ugwu was not one of his visitors. But it didn't matter. All Ugwu needed was the deep voice, the melody of the English-inflected Igbo, the glint of the thick eyeglasses.

He had been with Master for four months when Master told him, "A special woman is coming for the weekend. Very special. You make sure the house is clean. I'll order the food from the staff club."

"But, sah, I can cook," Ugwu said, with a sad premonition.

"She's just come back from London, my good man, and she likes her rice a certain way. Fried rice, I think. I'm not sure you could make something suitable." Master turned to walk away.

"I can make that, sah," Ugwu said quickly, although he had no idea what fried rice was. "Let me make the rice, and you get the chicken from the staff club."

"Artful negotiation," Master said in English. "All right, then. You make the rice."

"Yes, sah," Ugwu said. Later, he cleaned the rooms and scrubbed the toilet carefully, as he always did, but Master looked at them and said they were not clean enough and went out and bought another jar of Vim powder and asked, sharply, why Ugwu didn't clean the spaces between the tiles. Ugwu cleaned them again. He scrubbed until sweat crawled down the sides of his face, until his arm ached. And on Saturday, he bristled as he cooked. Master had never complained about his work before. It was this woman's fault, this woman that Master considered too special even for him to cook for. Just come back from London, indeed.

When the doorbell rang, he muttered a curse under his breath about her stomach swelling from eating faeces. He heard Master's raised voice, excited and childlike, followed by a long silence and he imagined their hug, and her ugly body pressed to Master's. Then he heard her voice. He stood still. He had always thought that Master's English could not be compared to anybody's, not Professor Ezeka, whose English one could hardly hear, or Okeoma, who spoke English as if he were speaking Igbo, with the same cadences and pauses, or Patel, whose English was a faded lilt. Not even the white man Professor Lehman, with his words forced out through his nose, sounded as dignified as Master. Master's English was music, but what Ugwu was hearing now, from this woman, was magic. Here was a superior tongue, a luminous language, the kind of English he heard on Master's radio, rolling out with clipped precision. It reminded him of slicing a yam with a newly sharpened knife, the easy perfection in every slice.

"Ugwu!" Master called. "Bring Coke!"

Ugwu walked out to the living room. She smelt of coconuts. He greeted her, his "Good afternoon" a mumble, his eyes on the floor.

"*Kedu?*" she asked.

"I'm well, mah." He still did not look at her. As he uncorked the bottle, she laughed at something Master said. Ugwu was about to pour the cold Coke into her glass when she touched his hand and said, "*Rapuba*, don't worry about that."

Her hand was lightly moist. "Yes, mah."

"Your master has told me how well you take care of him, Ugwu," she said. Her Igbo words were softer than her English, and he was disappointed at how easily they came out. He wished she would stumble in her Igbo; he had not expected English that perfect to sit beside equally perfect Igbo.

"Yes, mah," he mumbled. His eyes were still focused on the floor.

"What have you cooked us, my good man?" Master asked, as if he did not know. He sounded annoyingly jaunty.

"I serve now, sah," Ugwu said, in English, and then wished he had said *I am serving now*, because it sounded better, because it would impress her more. As he set the table, he kept from glancing at the living room, although he could hear her laughter and Master's voice, with its irritating new timbre.

He finally looked at her as she and Master sat down at the table. Her oval face was smooth like an egg, the lush colour of rain-drenched earth, and her eyes were large and slanted and she looked like she was not supposed to be walking and talking like everyone else; she should be in a glass case like the one in Master's study, where people could admire her curvy, fleshy body, where she would be preserved untainted. Her hair was long; each of the plaits that hung down to her neck ended in a soft fuzz. She smiled easily; her teeth were the same bright white of her eyes. He did not know how long he stood staring at her until Master said, "Ugwu usually does a lot better than this. He makes a fantastic stew."

"It's quite tasteless, which is better than bad-tasting, of course," she said, and smiled at Master before turning to Ugwu. "I'll show you how to cook rice properly, Ugwu, without using so much oil."

"Yes, mah," Ugwu said. He had invented what he imagined was fried rice, frying the rice in groundnut oil, and had half-hoped it would send them both to the toilet in a hurry. Now, though, he wanted to cook a perfect meal, a savoury *jollof* rice or his special stew with *arigbe*, to show her how well he could cook. He delayed washing up so that the running water would not drown out her voice. When he served them tea, he took his time rearranging the biscuits on the saucer so that he could linger and listen to her, until Master said, "That's quite all right, my good man." Her name was Olanna. But Master said it only once; he mostly called her *nkem*, my own. They talked about the quarrel between the Sardauna and the premier of the Western Region, and then Master said something about waiting until she moved to Nsukka and how it was only a few weeks away after all. Ugwu held his breath to make sure he had heard clearly. Master was laughing now, saying, "But we will live here together, *nkem*, and you can keep the Elias Avenue flat as well."

She would move to Nsukka. She would live in this house. Ugwu walked away from the door and stared at the pot on the stove. His life would change. He would learn to cook fried rice and he would have to use less oil and he would take orders from her. He felt sad, and yet his sadness was incomplete; he felt expectant, too, an excitement he did not entirely understand.

That evening, he was washing Master's linen in the backyard, near the lemon tree, when he looked up from the basin of soapy water and saw her standing by the back door, watching him. At first, he was sure it was his imagination, because the people he thought the most about often appeared to him in visions. He had imaginary conversations with

Anulika all the time, and, right after he touched himself at night, Nnesinachi would appear briefly with a mysterious smile on her face. But Olanna was really at the door. She was walking across the yard towards him. She had only a wrapper tied around her chest, and as she walked, he imagined that she was a yellow cashew, shapely and ripe.

"Mah? You want anything?" he asked. He knew that if he reached out and touched her face, it would feel like butter, the kind Master unwrapped from a paper packet and spread on his bread.

"Let me help you with that." She pointed at the bedsheet he was rinsing, and slowly he took the dripping sheet out. She held one end and moved back. "Turn yours that way," she said.

He twisted his end of the sheet to his right while she twisted to her right, and they watched as the water was squeezed out. The sheet was slippery.

"Thank, mah," he said.

She smiled. Her smile made him feel taller. "Oh, look, those paw-paws are almost ripe. *Lotekwa*, don't forget to pluck them."

There was something polished about her voice, about her; she was like the stone that lay right below a gushing spring, rubbed smooth by years and years of sparkling water, and looking at her was similar to finding that stone, knowing that there were so few like it. He watched her walk back indoors.

He did not want to share the job of caring for Master with anyone, did not want to disrupt the balance of his life with Master, and yet it was suddenly unbearable to think of not seeing her again. Later, after dinner, he tiptoed to Master's bedroom and rested his ear on the door. She was moaning loudly, sounds that seemed so unlike her, so uncontrolled and stirring and throaty. He stood there for a long time, until the moans stopped, and then he went back to his room.

III Thinking, Talking and Writing About Literature

1 Textual Cognition

Make an introductory presentation on the following terms related to this literary work.

1) anti-growing up
2) war trauma

❷ Textual Reading

Search for evidence in the text and answer the following questions.

1) How do you understand Master's statement: "There are two answers to the things they will teach you about our land: the real answer and the answer you give in school to pass. You must read books and learn both answers. I will give you books, excellent books."

2) Why is Ugwu "the soul character" threading through the novel?

3) Odenigbo says "Education is a priority" for resisting "exploitation". How do you understand the significance of education in the context of postcolonism?

4) What features of the text—diction, images of characters, content, figurative language, etc. seem indicated as appropriate for the genre of Bildungsroman?

❸ Critical Reading

Discuss in groups the following questions to further explore this literary work.

1) Nigeria-Biafra Civil War is the historical and political background of *Half of the Yellow Sun*. What do you think is the function of this social background?

2) What are the relations between personal growth and national rebuilding in this book?

3) In 2019, Adichie attended Shanghai Book Fair and delivered a public lecture. The title of the speech is "Power of the Story". She claims that the story telling in large degree depends on power. How do you understand the relations between story telling and power?

4) Adichie refuses to tell the "single story" because she knows well that single story is "dangerous". How do you understand this statement?

❹ Writing About Literature

Read the following critical excerpt and then write an essay.

> Donnelly, Michael. "The Bildungsroman and Biafran Sovereignty in Chimamanda Ngozi Adichie's *Half of a Yellow Sun*." *Law & Literature* 30.2 (2018): 245–266.

Half of a Yellow Sun retells the story of the Nigerian Civil War from the vantage point of a small Igbo family: Professor Odenigbo, a lecturer and anticolonial revolutionary, his wife Olanna, and her sister Kainene. Rounding out the family is Ugwu, Odenigbo's houseboy and confidant, and Richard Churchill, a British expatriate who becomes romantically involved with Kainene and remains in Biafra during the war. While they begin the novel comfortably in affluence, the family becomes mired in the geopolitics of Biafran advocacy and suffer both its ideological setbacks and personal losses. As a member of Biafra's intelligentsia, Odenigbo works for the ministry, but his passion for the cause increasingly deflates in the face of the persistent failures that lead to feelings of helplessness. During the war, Odenigbo, Olanna, their baby, and Ugwu find themselves living in a rundown neighborhood where food is dangerously scarce and death by starvation an everyday occurrence. Kainene and Richard are better off because Kainene gets involved with the trafficking of supplies across borders and Richard becomes the token "white man" supporting Biafra. After three years of living precariously, the war ends, but not before Ugwu is drafted into the army, where he is involved in the killing and raping of civilians. Kainene goes missing at the novel's conclusion after traveling into Nigerian-occupied territory to secure the transfer of provisions. She is never found, and, like many others, is presumed dead.

Essay Writing

Read the above selection and write an essay on *Half of a Yellow Sun* from the perspective of coming of age with no less than 500 words.

IV Further Activity

Scan the QR code and watch a video clip "Chimamanda Adichie: The Danger of a Single Story".

Lecture 23
Chigozie Obioma

🔖 Profile of the Writer

Chigozie Obioma
(1986–)

 Chigozie Obioma was born in 1986 in Akure, Nigeria. His short stories have appeared in the *Virginia Quarterly Review* and *New Madrid*. He was a fall 2012 OMIFellow at Ledig House, New York. Obioma has lived in Nigeria, Cyprus, and Turkey, and currently resides in the United States, where he has completed an MFA increative writing at the University of Michigan. *The Fishermen* (2015) is his first novel which won the inaugural FT/Oppenheimer Funds Award for Fiction, the NAACP Image Award for Debut Author, and the Art Seidenbaum Award for First Fiction (*Los Angeles Times* Book Prizes); and was a finalist for The Booker Prize 2015, as well as for several other literary prizes in the U.S. and U.K. Obioma was named one of Foreign Policy's 100 Leading Global Thinkers of 2015. His work has been translated into more than 25 languages and adapted for the stage. He is an assistant professor of literature and creative writing at the University of Nebraska-Lincoln. His second book *An Orchestra of Minorities* is short-listed for The Booker Prize.

Lecture 23
Chigozie Obioma

I. Preview Questions

1. Obioma is described as "the heir to Chinua Achebe". How do you understand this honor?

2. Chigozie Obioma once put, "There is a lot to share with the world about the Igbo culture". What do you know about the Igbo culture?

II. Literary Reading: *The Fishermen* (Chapter 1)

We were fishermen:

My brothers and I became fishermen in January of 1996 after our father moved out of Akure, a town in the west of Nigeria, where we had lived together all our lives. His employer, the Central Bank of Nigeria, had transferred him to a branch of the bank in Yola—a town in the north that was a camel distance of more than one thousand kilometres away—in the first week of November of the previous year. I remember the night Father returned home with his transfer letter; it was on a Friday. From that Friday through that Saturday, Father and Mother held whispering consultations like shrine priests. By Sunday morning, Mother emerged a different being. She'd acquired the gait of a wet mouse, averting her eyes as she went about the house. She did not go to church that day, but stayed home and washed and ironed a stack of Father's clothes, wearing an impenetrable gloom on her face. Neither of them said a word to my brothers and me, and we did not ask. My brothers—Ikenna, Boja, Obembe—and I had come to understand that when the two ventricles of our home—our father and our mother—held silence as the ventricles of the heart retain blood, we could flood the house if we poked them. So, at times like these, we avoided the television in the eight-columned shelf in our sitting room. We sat in our rooms, studying or feigning to study, anxious but not asking questions. While there, we stuck out our antennae to gather whatever we could of the situation.

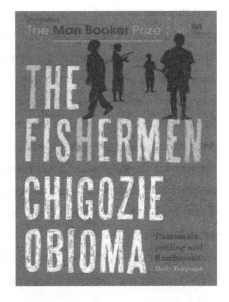

By nightfall on Sunday, crumbs of information began to fall from Mother's soliloquy like tots of

feathers from a richly-plumed bird: "What kind of job takes a man away from bringing up his growing sons? Even if I were born with seven hands, how would I be able to care for these children alone?"

Although these feverish questions were directed to no one in particular, they were certainly intended for Father's ears. He was seated alone on a lounge chair in the sitting room, his face veiled with a copy of his favourite newspaper, *The Guardian*, half reading and half listening to Mother. And although he heard everything she said, Father always turned deaf ears to words not directly addressed to him, the kind he often referred to as "cowardly words". He would simply read on, sometimes breaking off to loudly rebuke or applaud something he'd seen in the newspaper—"If there is any justice in this world, Abacha should soon be mourned by his witch of a wife." "Wow, Fela is a god! Good gracious!" "Reuben Abati should be sacked!"—anything just to create the impression that Mother's lamentations were futile; whimpers to which no one was paying attention.

Before we slept that night, Ikenna, who was nearly fifteen and on whom we relied for the interpretation of most things, had suggested Father was being transferred. Boja, a year his junior, who would have felt unwise if he didn't appear to have any idea about the situation, had said it must be that Father was travelling abroad to a "Western world" just as we often feared he someday would. Obembe who, at eleven, was two years my senior, did not have an opinion. Me neither. But we did not have to wait much longer.

The answer came the following morning when Father suddenly appeared in the room I shared with Obembe. He was dressed in a brown T-shirt. He placed his spectacles on the table, a gesture requesting our attention. "I will start living in Yola from today onwards, and I don't want you boys to give your mother any troubles." His face contorted when he said this, the way it did whenever he wanted to drive the hounds of fear into us. He spoke slowly, his voice deeper and louder, every word tacked nine-inches deep into the beams of our minds. So that, if we went ahead and disobeyed, he would make us conjure the exact moment he gave us the instruction in its complete detail with the simple phrase "I told you."

"I will call her regularly, and if I hear any bad news"—he struck his forefinger aloft to fortify his words—"I mean, any funny acts at all, I'll give you the Guerdon for them."

He'd said the word "Guerdon"—a word with which he emphasized a warning or highlighted the retribution for a wrong act—with so much vigour that veins bulged at both sides of his face. This word, once pronounced, often completed the message. He brought out two twenty-naira notes from the breast pocket of his coat and dropped them on our study table.

"For both of you," he said, and left the room.

Obembe and I were still sitting in our bed trying to make sense of all that when we heard Mother speaking to him outside the house in a voice so loud it seemed he was already far away.

"Eme, remember you have growing boys back here," she'd said. "I'm telling you, oh."

She was still speaking when Father started his Peugeot 504. At the sound of it, Obembe and I hurried from our room, but Father was already driving out of the gate. He was gone.

Whenever I think of our story, how that morning would mark the last time we'd live together, all of us, as the family we'd always been, I begin—even these two decades later—to wish he hadn't left, that he had never received that transfer letter. Before that letter came, everything was in place: Father went to work every morning and Mother, who ran a fresh food store in the open market, tended to my five siblings and me who, like the children of most families in Akure, went to school. Everything followed its natural course. We gave little thought to past events. Time meant nothing back then. The days came with clouds hanging in the sky filled with cupfuls of dust in the dry seasons, and the sun lasting into the night. It was as if a hand drew hazy pictures in the sky during the rainy seasons, when rain fell in deluges pulsating with spasms of thunderstorms for six uninterrupted months. Because things followed this known and structured pattern, no day was worthy of remembrance. All that mattered was the present and the foreseeable future. Glimpses of it mostly came like a locomotive train treading tracks of hope, with black coal in its heart and a loud elephantine toot. Sometimes these glimpses came through dreams or flights of fanciful thoughts that whispered in your head—*I will be a pilot, or the president of Nigeria, rich man, own helicopters*—for the future was what we made of it. It was a blank canvas on which anything could be imagined. But Father's move to Yola changed the equation of things: time and seasons and the past began to matter, and we started to yearn and crave for it even more than the present and the future.

He began to live in Yola from that morning. The green table telephone, which had been used mainly for receiving calls from Mr. Bayo, Father's childhood friend who lived in Canada, became the only way we reached him. Mother waited restlessly for his calls and marked the days he phoned on the calendar in her room. Whenever Father missed a day in the schedule, and Mother had exhausted her patience waiting, usually long into midnight, she would unfasten the knot at the hem of her *wrappa*, bring out the crumpled paper on which she'd scribbled his phone number, and dial endlessly until he answered. If we were still awake, we'd throng around her to hear Father's voice, urging her to pressure him to take us with him to the new city. But Father persistently refused. Yola, he reiterated, was a volatile city with a history of frequent large-scale violence especially against people of our tribe—the Igbo. We continued to push him until the bloody sectarian riots of March 1996 erupted. When finally Father got on the phone, he recounted—with the sound of sporadic shooting audible in the background—how he narrowly escaped death when rioters attacked his district and how an entire family was butchered in their house across the street from his. "Little children killed like fowls!" he'd said, placing a weighty emphasis on the phrase "little children" in such a way that no sane person could have dared mention moving to him again, and that was it.

Father made it a tradition to visit every other weekend, in his Peugeot 504 saloon, dusty, exhausted from the fifteen-hour drive. We looked forward to those Saturdays when his car honked at the gate, and we rushed to open it, all of us anxious to see what snack or gift he had brought for us this time. Then, as we slowly became accustomed to seeing him every few weeks or so, things changed. His mammoth frame that commandeered decorum and calm, gradually shrunk into the size of a pea. His established routine of composure, obedience, study, and compulsory siesta—long a pattern of our daily existence—gradually lost its grip. A veil spooled over his all-seeing eyes, which we believed were capable of noticing even the slightest wrong thing we did in secret. At the beginning of the third month, his long arm that often wielded the whip, the instrument of caution, snapped like a tired tree branch. Then we broke free.

We shelved our books and set out to explore the sacred world outside the one we were used to. We ventured to the municipality football pitch where most of the boys of the street played football every afternoon. But these boys were a pack of wolves; they did not welcome us. Although we did not know any of them except for one, Kayode, who lived a few blocks from us, these boys knew our family and us down to the names of our parents, and they constantly taunted us and flogged us daily with verbal whips. Despite Ikenna's stunning dribbling skills, and Obembe's goalkeeping wonders, they branded us "amateurs". They frequently joked, too, that our father, "Mr. Agwu", was a rich man who worked in the Central Bank of Nigeria, and that we were privileged kids. They adopted a curious moniker for Father: Baba Onile, after the principal character of a popular Yoruba soap who had six wives and twenty-one children. Hence, the name was intended to mock Father whose desire to have many children had become a legend in our district. It was also the Yoruba name for the Praying Mantis, a green ugly skeletal insect. We could not stand for these insults. Ikenna, seeing that we were outnumbered and would not have won a fight against the boys, begged them repeatedly in the custom of Christian children to refrain from insulting our parents who had done nothing wrong to them. Yet they continued, until one evening when Ikenna, maddened at the mention of the moniker, head-butted a boy. In one quick flash, the boy kicked Ikenna in the stomach and closed in on him. For a brief moment, their feet drew an imperfect gyre around the sand-covered pitch as they swirled together. But in the end, the boy threw Ikenna and poured a handful of dirt on his face. The rest of the kids cheered and lifted the boy up, their voices melding into a chorus of victory complete with boos and *uuh uuhs*. We went home that evening feeling beaten, and never returned there.

After this fight, we got tired of going outdoors. At my suggestion, we begged Mother to convince Father to release the console game set to play *Mortal Kombat*, which he seized and hid somewhere the previous year after Boja—who was known for his usual first position in his class—came home with 24th scribbled in red ink on his report card and the warning *likely to repeat*. Ikenna did not fare any better; his was sixteenth out of forty and it came with a personal letter to Father from his teacher, Mrs. Bukky. Father read out the letter in such a fit of anger that the only words I heard were "Gracious me! Gracious me!" which he repeated like a refrain. He would confiscate the games and forever cut off the moments that often sent us swirling with excitement, screaming and howling when the invisible commentator in the game ordered, "Finish him", and the conquering sprite would inflict serious blows on the vanquished sprite by either kicking it up to the sky or by slicing it into a grotesque explosion of bones and blood. The screen would then go abuzz with "fatality" inscribed in strobe letters of flame. Once, Obembe—in the midst of relieving himself—ran out of the toilet just to be there so he could join in and cry "That is fatal!" in an American accent that mimicked the console's voice-over. Mother would punish him later when she discovered he'd unknowingly dropped excreta on the rug.

Frustrated, we tried yet again to find a physical activity to fill up our after-school hours now that we were free from Father's strict regulations. So, we gathered neighbourhood friends to play football at the clearing behind our compound. We brought Kayode, the only boy we'd known among the pack of wolves we played with at the municipality football pitch. He had an androgynous face and a permanent gentle smile. Igbafe, our neighbour, and his cousin, Tobi—a half-deaf boy who strained your vocal chords only to ask *Jo, kini o nso?*—Please, what did you say?—also joined us. Tobi had large ears that did not appear to be part of his body. He was hardly offended—perhaps because he couldn't hear sometimes, for we often whispered it—when we called him *Eleti Ehoro*—One With a Hare's Ears. We'd run up the length and breadth of this pitch, dressed in cheap football jerseys and T-shirts on which we'd printed our football nicknames. We played as if unhinged, frequently volleying the balls into neighbouring houses, and embarking on botched attempts to retrieve them. Many times, we arrived at some of the places just in time to witness the neighbours puncturing the balls, paying no heed to our pleas to give them back because the ball had either hit someone or destroyed something. Once, the ball flew over a neighbour's fence and hit a crippled man on the head and knocked him off his chair. At another time, the ball shattered a glass window.

Every time they destroyed a ball, we contributed money and bought a new one except for Kayode, who, having come from the town's sprawling population of the acutely poor, could not afford even a kobo. He often dressed in worn-out, torn shorts, and lived with his aged parents, the spiritual heads of the small Christ Apostolic Church, in an unfinished two-storeyed building just down the bend of the road to our school. Because he couldn't contribute, he prayed for each ball, asking God to help us keep this one for much longer by preventing it from crossing the clearing.

One day, we bought a new fine white ball with the logo of the Atlanta 1996 Olympic Games. After Kayode prayed, we set out to play, but barely an hour into the game, Boja struck a kick that landed in a fenced compound owned by a medical doctor. The ball smashed one of the windows of the lush house with a din, sending two pigeons asleep on the roof to a frantic flight. We waited at some distance so we could have sufficient space to flee should someone come out in pursuit. After a long while, Ikenna and Boja started for the house while Kayode knelt and prayed for God's intervention. When the emissaries reached the compound, the doctor, as if already waiting for them, gave chase, sending us all running ankle-to-head to escape. We knew, once we got home that evening, panting and perspiring, that we'd had it with football.

We became fishermen when Ikenna came home from school the following week bursting with the novel idea. It was at the end of January because I remember that Boja's fourteenth birthday, which was on January 18th, 1996, had been celebrated that weekend with the home-baked cake and soft drinks that replaced dinner. His birthdays marked the "age-mate month", a period of one month in which he temporarily locked age with Ikenna, who was born on February 10th, one year before him. Ikenna's classmate, Solomon, had told him about the pleasures of fishing. Ikenna described how Solomon had called the sport a thrilling experience that was also rewarding since he could sell some of the fish and earn a bit of income. Ikenna was even more intrigued because the idea had awakened the possibility of resurrecting Yoyodon, the fish. The aquarium, which once sat beside the television, had housed a preternaturally beautiful Symphysodon fish that was a colony of colours—brown, violet, purple and even pale green. Father called the fish Yoyodon after Obembe came up with a similar sounding word while trying to pronounce Symphysodon: the name of the fish's specie. Father took the aquarium away after Ikenna and Boja, on a compassionate quest to free the fish from its "dirty water", removed and replaced it with clean drinking water. They would return later to notice the fish could no longer rise from among the row of glistening pebbles and corals.

Once Solomon told Ikenna about fishing, our brother vowed he would capture a new

Yoyodon. He went with Boja to Solomon's house the next day and returned raving about *this* fish and *that* fish. They bought two hooked fishing lines from somewhere Solomon had showed them. Ikenna set them on the table in their room and explained how they were used. The hooked fishing lines were long wooden staffs with a threadlike rope attached to the tip of the staff. The ropes carried iron hooks on their ends, and it was on these hooks, Ikenna said, that baits—earthworms, cockroaches, food crumbs, whatever—were attached to lure the fish and trap them. From the following day onwards, for a whole week, they rushed off every day after school and trekked the long tortuous path to the Omi-Ala River at the end of our district to fish, passing through a clearing behind our compound that stank in the rainy season and served as a home for a clan of swine. They went in the company of Solomon and other boys of the street, and returned with cans filled with fish. At first, they did not allow Obembe and me to go with them although our interests were piqued when we saw the small, coloured fish they caught. Then one day, Ikenna said to Obembe and me: "Follow us, and we will make you fishermen!"—and we followed.

We began going to the river every day after school in the company of other children of the street in a procession led by Solomon, Ikenna and Boja. These three often concealed hooked fishing lines in rags or old *wrappas*. The rest of us—Kayode, Igbafe, Tobi, Obembe and I—carried things that ranged from rucksacks with fishing clothes in them to nylon bags containing earthworms and dead roaches we used as baits, and empty beverage cans in which we kept the fish and tadpoles we caught. Together we trod to the river, wading through bushy tracks that were populated with schools of prickly dead nettles that flogged our bare legs and left white welts on our skin. The flogging the nettles inflicted on us matched the strange botanical name for the predominant grass in the area, *esan*, the Yoruba word for retribution or vengeance. We'd walk this trail single file and once we'd passed these grasses, we'd rush off to the river like madmen. The older ones among us, Solomon, Ikenna and Boja, would change into their dirty fishing clothes. They would then stand close to the river, and hold their lines up above the water so the baited hooks would disappear down into it. But although they fished like men of yore who'd known the river from its cradle, they mostly only harvested a few palm-sized smelts, or some brown cods that were much more difficult to catch, and, rarely, some tilapias. The rest of us just scooped tadpoles with beverage cans. I loved the tadpoles, their slick bodies, exaggerated heads and how they appeared nearly shapeless as if they were the miniature version of whales. So I would watch with awe as they hung suspended below the water and my fingers would blacken from rubbing off the grey glop that glossed their skins. Sometimes we picked up coral shells or empty shells of long dead arthropods. We caught rounded snails the shape of primal whorls, the teeth of some beast—which we came to believe belonged to a bygone era because Boja argued vehemently that it was that of a dinosaur and took it home with him—pieces of the moulted skin of a cobra shed just by the bank of the river, and anything of interest we could find.

Only once did we catch a fish that was big enough to sell, and I often think of that day. Solomon had pulled this humongous fish that was bigger than anything we'd ever seen in Omi-Ala. Then Ikenna and Solomon went off to the nearby food market, and returned to the river after a little more than half an hour with fifteen naira. My brothers and I went home with the six naira that was our share of the sale, our joy boundless. We began to fish more in earnest from then on, staying awake long into the nights to discuss the experience.

Our fishing was carried out with great zeal, as though a faithful audience gathered daily by the bank of the river to watch and cheer us. We did not mind the smell of the bracken waters, the winged insects that gathered in blobs around the banks every evening and the nauseating sight of algae and leaves that formed the shape of a map of troubled nations at the far end of the river bank where varicose trees dipped into the waters. We went every single day with corroding tins, dead insects, melting worms, dressed mostly in rags and old clothing. For we derived great joy from this fishing, despite the difficulties and meagre returns.

When I look back today, as I find myself doing more often now that I have sons of my own, I realize that it was during one of these trips to the river that our lives and our world changed. For it was here that time began to matter, at that river where we became fishermen.

Ⅲ Thinking, Talking and Writing About Literature

❶ Textual Cognition

Make an introductory presentation on the following terms related to this literary work.
1) magic realism
2) parable

❷ Textual Reading

Search for evidence in the text and answer the following questions.
1) The images of Father and Mother are vividly depicted in the opening page of the story. Could you figure out some key words that reflect the different natures of Father and Mother?

Make an analysis of different personalities of the parents.

2) "Whenever I think of our story, how that morning would mark the last time we'd live together, all of us, as the family we'd always been, I begin—even these two decades later—to wish he hadn't left, that he had never received that transfer letter." This passage shows that there were two first-person narrative perspectives, one is that of childhood, the other is adulthood. These are in fact the typical double narrative perspectives in the coming up stories. What are the functions of these unique narrative perspectives?

3) How do you understand Father's statement: "Yola was a volatile city with a history of frequent large-scale violence especially against people of our tribe—the Igbo"? And in what way does this statement reflect the complex relations between personal growth and national fate?

 Critical Reading

Discuss in groups the following questions to further explore this literary work.

1) *The Fisherman* is an essential novel about Africa, seen through the prism of one family's destiny. How do you understand this critical statement?

2) *The Fisherman* centers on the growth of four brothers instead of one, which is different from the central feature of Western Bildungsroman. In what way does this distinction reflect the different point of view of individual and community in the contexts of Western culture and African culture?

 Writing About Literature

Read the following critical excerpt and then write an essay.

> Kite, Lorien. "Chigozie Obioma—Emerging Voices 2015 Fiction Winner." *Financial Times*, October 6, 2015.

Few debut novels generated more excitement this year than Chigozie Obioma's *The Fishermen*. Published to critical acclaim on both sides of the Atlantic, the winner of the inaugural Emerging Voices prize for African and Middle Eastern fiction has also reached the later stages of four other literary awards, Britain's Man Booker shortlist included, and even prompted *The New York Times* to hail its 28-year-old Nigerian author as the heir to Chinua Achebe.

When I meet him on the fringes of the Edinburgh International Book Festival in August, the softly spoken Obioma plays down comparisons between *The Fishermen* and Achebe's *Things Fall Apart*. "The truth is this: I see myself first as an Igbo man," he says, referring to the Nigerian ethnic group. "Achebe was the first who really attempted to tell our story to the world, and it is nearly impossible not to have been influenced by that."

...

The Fishermen is the story of four brothers who, taking advantage of their disciplinarian father's absence, defy his warnings and fish in the Omi-Ala, a once-sacred river now shunned as a place of danger and pollution. They encounter a madman, Abulu, and learn of his prophecy that the eldest, Ikenna, will die at the hands of one of the others. The idea planted, trust breaks down and the boys are pulled inexorably apart.

Obioma explains how the novel was inspired by a telephone conversation with his father in 2009. Living abroad and nostalgic for home, he was told of the increasing closeness of his elder brothers, who had been bitter rivals for a period during adolescence. "I started thinking about what could have happened if they had continued on that path," he says. "So I decided to tell a story about a family whose unity is destroyed by an external force."

Nowhere is the mythic quality of *The Fishermen* felt more than in its signature device: the vivid images, often drawn from the natural world, through which its narrator recalls his childhood. "Father was an eagle," runs one. "The mighty bird that planted his nest high above the rest of his peers, hovering and watching over his young eagles, the way a king guards his throne."

...

Obioma will inevitably be considered alongside other talented Nigerian novelists to have emerged since the success of Chimamanda Ngozi Adichie's *Purple Hibiscus* in 2003—Helon Habila, A. Igoni Barrett, Teju Cole and Chinelo Okparanta to name a few—but, as he emphasises, he is a writer who has pursued a singular course.

Essay Writing

Read the above selection and write an essay on the relations between autobiographical elements and fictional elements in creative writings with no less than 500 words.

IV Further Activity

Scan the QR code and read the text "Chigozie Obioma: The WD Interview".